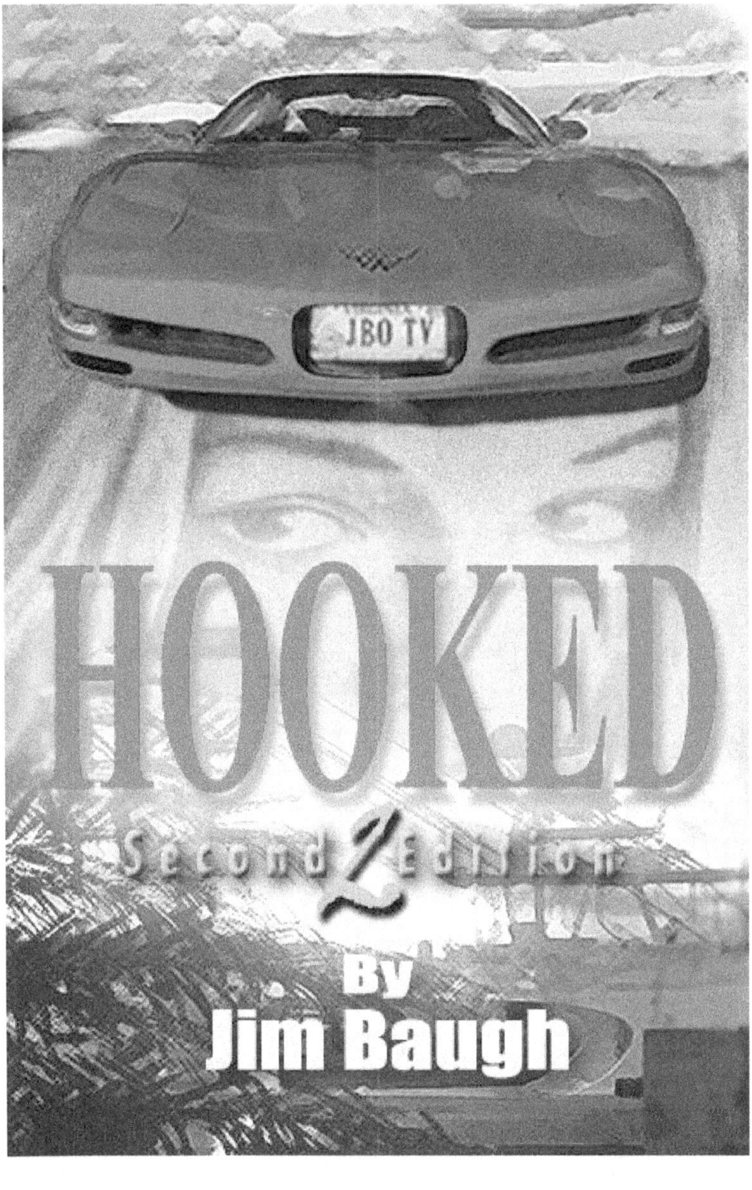

HOOKED

Second 2 Edition

By
Jim Baugh

Solstice Publishing
www.solsticepublishing.com

Jim Baugh ©2011, 2014
Second Edition V3 2014
ISBN: 978-0615501093

***

This book is dedicated to Ben and Casey Baugh
*May this book give you a better understanding of your
father's life,
Amen.*

HOOKED

"An uproarious novel based *(and not so loosely)* on his life. *"Hooked"* relates the adventures and misadventures that occur during the filming of an outdoors show, as well as in online computer dating.
~ *Jay Stafford, Richmond Times Dispatch*

"For anyone who's ever watched a favorite outdoors show and wondered what it would be like to seek one's fortune fishing or hunting, *Hooked* is a revelation. The life is everything one dreams – only crazier. Jim Baugh's account of the boat world – and of the men and women attracted to it – reads like a guidebook to a parallel universe. I was immediately hooked by his adventures and misadventures."
~ *Author Joe Jackson, 5 time Pulitzer Prize Nominee*

"*Hooked,"* is a humorous look at his life and some of the interesting events in it. From his childhood growing up in Gloucester, to married life, producing an outdoors television show, divorce, travels and middle-aged Internet dating, Baugh has either done it or seen it. His funny and often risqué stories are the kind of tales many can relate to. The book explores the solemn drama of dealing with divorce, death and mental illness. And despite some of the content, it's also a book about faith."
~ *Lee Tolliver, Virginia Pilot Newspaper*

Preface

I was on the second floor of the Hilton Hotel sitting in the swimming pool overlooking the Chesapeake Bay, sipping on a fresh cocktail. DC Nympho had just freshened our drinks and we were laughing our butts off at the hilarity of dating in our Mid-Life. We had both met each other on-line through a dating site and once we started swapping stories about how crazy it all was, I started to get an idea.

My idea was to create a TV game show called, *Meet My Match Game.* This would be a comedy game show similar to the old dating game with a little bit of *Hollywood Squares* and *Let's Make A Deal* thrown in.

"Which one would you like…Door number one the rich Doctor…Door number two the wealthy Architect, or…Door number three the Plastic Surgeon? Remember Ma'am, one of them is a hoax and you COULD end up with a goat and a rickshaw. Choose wisely."

We laughed for a long time about this in the swimming pool. The more I thought about it, the more I began to think it would make a great screenplay or memoir. I thought about this for years and then considered the fact that a lot of our behind the scenes Jim Baugh Outdoors TV stories were equally, if not more humorous. Maybe write a screenplay that would combine the two?

The characters I knew growing up as a young boy on the docks in Gloucester Virginia were amazing and hilarious people. Most of these people have all passed away, and I always wanted their legacy to live on. Only in my mind did they live, and it is not like they were around so that I could feature them on my TV Show.

So for a few more years I thought about how to combine these ideas. How could I combine these elements?

Like a flash it came to me. Just tell the story from the beginning so it would all make sense. For the most part write an autobiographical story that would incorporate all of these elements.

Though this may be a simple idea, it took me years to figure out.

Once I had everything in my mind and a brief outline, I was ready to write. But it was not long before I encountered major difficulties. I realized that my concentration writing the screenplay was more focused on the direction and scene setting than the actual story.

I called an old high school friend of mine who was a successful playwright for 30 years in New York City and ask him for his advice. I said, "Dave, I am trying to write this screenplay and I keep getting stuck. As an editor and producer my mind wants to keep setting up the shots, scene blocking and directing as opposed to writing... any suggestions?"

Dave told me that it did not matter if it was a screenplay or a book. The bottom line was to just to get it down on paper. I told Dave that I had published regular monthly columns for over 20 years, and maybe just writing in book form would be more similar to what I was used to. He said... "Do IT!"

I wrote the book in 12 days.

It would have been finished sooner but I was also editing and producing Jim Baugh Outdoors TV. Afterwards it did take longer to edit and polish the story.

This was a great experience for me to write and at times it was incredibly difficult to do. Many times I would have to leave the computer because emotionally I was a wreck from what I was writing. When you compact your life into 28 chapters it makes you face some things it takes a lifetime to deal with, and in only a matter of pages I got overwhelmed. Some of it was hard...Very hard.

On the other side, I have not laughed as much in my life. This book is based on true events and some of this stuff is so crazy and hilarious, no one could ever make this kind of stuff up.

Truth is always stranger than fiction.
Enjoy and God Bless!

Jim Baugh

"HOOKED"
Second Edition

Written by
Jim Baugh

The two brothers holding a string of brim and bass caught at a nearby pond, a favorite fishing spot the Judge often took his boys fishing. Standing to the left Perry, and to the right, little Jimmy Baugh circa 1965.

Chapter 1
Eastbound

"There comes a time in every rightly constructed boy's life that he has a raging desire to go somewhere and dig for hidden treasure."

~Mark Twain

One empty plastic milk jug on the kitchen table, a bottle of grape juice, pineapple juice, ginger ale, orange juice, five lemons and a fifth of Gin all sitting on the counter. This is what would soon be mixed together in a flourish of activity that ended at rest in a Styrofoam iced chilled cooler. Back in the late 60's, my Uncle Ed's "Recipe," also known as "Purple Passion" by some, is what the Judge liked to travel with on his way to…. "The Rivah."

"Jimmy! Perry! Are y'all ready to go? Come on! Get out here and get in the car!" My dad's voice was rather pronounced and large. Booming may be a good way to describe it…. the voice of authority. Both a mental health judge and an attorney, my dad had a way of making you listen to him with respect and dignity.

Anaheim Nathaniel Baugh, nicknamed "Nate" also known as… "The Judge". Son of Emanuel Dawson Baugh, also a southern Judge, liked nothing better than to throw us boys in the car and haul ass down interstate 64 eastbound to spend each weekend of our young lives on our boat in the York River.

Heading out of Charlottesville towards the Interstate I was tucked away in the back seat with a bag of Cheetoes in one hand and a root beer in the other. I was one happy kid. Nothing brought me as much joy as going to the Rivah with Dad. On the way out we would pass this huge building with a big sign that said, *Belleview*. This is where I would sometimes visit my mother.

A 23 foot wooden Owens may not be considered a yacht by today's standards, however to a six-year-old boy it

11

was the only boat in the world! York River Yacht Haven in those days was a paradise for us kids. Along with a cast of characters that would make the "Rat Pack" look tame. Boats, Booze and Booty is what captains on the dock were all about.

"A" dock is where we kept our boat and that pier was the one with always the most action. There was also B dock, C dock, D dock E dock, and then there were also the covered boat sheds. It seemed like on Fridays and Saturdays the entire marina swarmed to "A" dock and the crabs on those pilings were monsters!

At the end of "A" dock was a T-pier that was only about 50 yards away from the inlet and beach. Us kids would get a running start and jump off the pier and swim to the nearby beach. There waiting was always a bunch of our buddies in tin boats and Boston Whalers. Jay Jack, Bruce, Duck, and Skipper all had Whalers with 50 horsepower's that were the biggest outboards available at that time. These kids ruled Sarah's Creek. Those guys with the Whalers were the coolest kids on the water.

Starting around age five my life was lived in sullen suburbia during the week, and weekends at a crab catcher's paradise the York River and Sara's Creek. That is about all I did once Dad pulled into the parking lot on Fridays at the Marina was to swim and catch crabs. We had plenty of buddies our age to hang around with, running down the docks screaming, "Look at the size of this one!"

Meanwhile the Judge and his buddies were sipping on what was left of their tasty ice chilled tall toddies and cooking up grilled mammoth steaks above the plank wood docks. Fresh Backfin Chesapeake Bay blue crab meat, thick steak and salad are usually all we ate on the weekends. It was a wonderful cheerful exciting life and one I desperately did not want to go away.

My brother and I made a good team on our little tin boat. We had painted the hull red and the boat leaked like a sieve. I had taken one of the Judge's empty milk jug containers and cut it in half to use as a bailer. We did not have anything fancy like bilge pumps in those days. I would yell,

"Hey Perry! Let's jump in the boat! You grab the tiller killer and I will start bailing!" Off we went, venturing relentlessly in our leaky wet red tin boat with our monstrous 1966, 9.5 two stroke outboard having more fun than a barrel of monkeys.

My brother and I always kept some straw grass in the boat. Back in the day those engines cooling system affectionately known as pissers, were always getting clogged. We would use a strand to keep the exhaust lines free of debris and also stuffed the straw in the drippy rivets of the tin hull.

As a child one Christmas in Charlottesville my brother Perry and I had opened all our presents under the tree and were happy as two clams and a stick of butter, when my dad asked, "Did y'all boys look outside the window?"

Pulling back the shades in our little brick ranch there was a colossal, gorgeous, gleaming green Glastron 16-foot ski boat! I ran outside in amazement and simply just could not believe my eyes, never forgetting the first thing I asked my dad.

"Dad, love it, but…where is the engine?"

The Judge said, "Oh don't worry, that little 9.5 will push it until we get a bigger one."

Dad was quite the horse trader. He had legally represented someone who couldn't pay his fee, but did own a used 50 horsepower outboard. So, after putting around slowly with that 9.5 for a month or so we finally got the 50 installed and began to run up and down the river like a Mexican border patrol. After our weekends at the marina I hated the fact that we would have to go back to school on Mondays.

I did a lot of growing up on the docks of Sara's Creek.

It was on "A" dock, the first pier by the parking lot where I received my first passionate kiss. This is something that a young boy never forgets. I guess back then cougars were around like they are today because this 15 year-old blond hottie was in the steamy spirit of things and decided to lay one on me at the T-pier.

I will never forget that I thought it was the most disgusting awful thing that had ever happened to me and was not even sure what it was. Bewildered is really how I felt. After she left and walked back to her boat I figured it was her tongue that had made that racket. My buddy Jay Jack ran up to me and said,

"Did she kiss you? WOW! COOL MAN!"

I answered, "I don't really know what it was."

Later I realized it was my first kiss. I just thought I better stick to catching crabs for a while because this was a little over my head. It's obvious that eventually I grew to later change my mind of course, but at that time all I wanted was to catch fish, swim, go crabbing, eat pizza, play on boats, and see what The Crew was up to.

This turned out to be a large part of my lifetime goal.

Growing up on "The Rivah" on the weekends was always an event. Not a traditional lifestyle by any stretch of the means. The Judge and his boat cronies were always into practical jokes. I remember when our local mechanic Fred Farris grabbed his tow truck and we all followed him to our buddy Manny Cheeter's place on route 14. Manny was a real character that was in the masonry buiz and lived with his wife in a trailer on the property. Fred pulled up to their trailer with his tow truck lights flashing and all of our vehicles behind him. Fred knocked on the trailer door and Manny's wife answered. Fred asked confidently,

"Can Manny come out and play?"

Mrs. Cheeter said, "No! You drunks take your cars and get the hell outa here and leave my Manny alone!"

Fred pointed a finger at his tow truck and voiced loudly,

"If you don't let him out…. I am gonna hook your trailer up and tow your ass outa here, NOW! Let Manny out too play!"

The door slammed. What happened next?

Well Fred Farris did start to hook up his tow truck to Manny's trailer. It was all a joke and in fun. Sure enough it was only a minute before Manny came out and we all went over to Manny's boat, the Judge and the boys were ready to party now. The trailer was left alone unscathed and still attached to its' plumbing. The smoke coming out of Mrs. Cheeter's head must have smelled awful.

Funny things can happen on the water. When we got back to the marina Manny was excited about showing all of us what new device he recently installed on his rather nice boat. After the Judge and the boys brought all their hooch on board, Manny preceded to tell us about the brand new electric toilet that just came out and had never been used. It had a macerator grinder in the base of the head which would chew up just about anything. Manny was so excited he stood by the boat bar and mixed a tall drink, when all of the sudden we all heard this…..

BRRRRRRRRRRRRRRRRWWWWWWWWWAAA AAAA.

BBBBBRRRRRRWWWWWWWWWWWWWWW WWWWWWWWWWWWAAAA. Then some sort of swirling sounds.

The door to the head opened up in front of us there stood my Uncle Ed, the greatest partier of them all! The smell of what was killed, sacrificed, or whatever it was in the head was unreal. We all gagged. Manny screamed,

"What the hell are you doin!"

Uncle Ed said, "Manny I love your new toilet but…… do you have a plunger?"

Manny in a VERY loud voice said, "You shit in my brand new toilet before I even got to sit on it… AND you have already plugged it up? Damn YOU!"

Uncle Ed then walked over and mixed a drink and we all started laughing hysterically. To this day it was the worst smell I have ever experianced on a boat, including forgotten dead fish and squid bait.

My Uncle Ed was one heck of a character and besides my dad was my favorite person on earth. Yes, Ed was the life of every party and everyone including myself could not wait until he walked into a room, stepped on a boat, or just caught him walking on the dock.

Uncle Ed was very funny, a big partier, and also my dad's best friend and legal associate. Ed was also a juvenile Judge in Charlottesville. They worked hard during the week providing the best they could for their families and then partied like rock stars on the weekends, but with boats instead of buses.

Not all of the crew at the marina was married. Some of the guys were single like Ricky Johnson. Rick was good friends with the Judge, Uncle Ed, Toddy Grog, Johnny Major, Manny, Percy Parker, Travis Tully, and Doc Ravage, otherwise known as…….

"The Crew."

"The Crew" was made up of all professional men who worked hard Monday through Friday and opened the release valve on the weekends. At the Marina you would never know who was going to be there at any time and there were always new people showing up.

Ricky was a little younger than the rest of the boys in The Crew and had a slew of women on his boat non-stop. I could not imagine how this guy could get so many women and so easily. It just seemed like magic. It was only later in years until I understood how he did it.

When I was a teenager I asked my dad about it. He explained to me their secret. Remember the Judge and The Crew may have been the weekend warriors when it came to having fun but they were also highly intelligent gifted lawyers, doctors, and judges that got to where they were because they were smart, talented and determined.

They were also keen enough to know there is more than one way to skin a cat.

So when it came time that some of the boys wanted some female companionship for the weekend, they did not go out on dates, hang out in bars, or go to class reunions to see who is still single. Now remember this is way back in the day before internet dating sites. This was a time back before computers, before cell phones, and color TV's were only just coming on the market. It was the late 60's.

These guys were too smart for their own good. What they would do is put an ad in the newspaper for women who like to spend some time on boats, and then hold interviews at the office on Wednesdays for the upcoming weekend. Hey, what can I say. It worked big time. Ricky and the few other boys that were single never were without women for the weekends.

I remember back running swiftly up and down the docks on a Friday when I saw one woman check into Percy's boat. Then when I was catching crabs off his pilings on Saturday the woman had changed. It was someone else. Then on Sunday when he was leaving the marina, he was again with a different lady. The boys had figured out the newspaper trick and used it successfully and regularly.

Percy was what I called, "The Sinatra" of the group. Percy looked a bit like Frank Sinatra and acted a lot like him. Blue-eyed, very suave, debonair, funny, very intelligent, retired with money and the ladies just loved him to death. Some 40 years later Percy would pass away quietly in his sleep and yes, with a lovely lady by his side and a smile on his face.

Being just a little kid in the 60's, none of the womanizing at the marina mattered much to me. I was too young to appreciate what dating was all about anyway. If it was not a boat, a crab, foosball table or a pizza, I was not that interested.

For some reason I just understood the humor of it all and mostly really appreciated how much fun everyone seemed to be having at the docks. It was very contagious and joyous. We kids glorified aluminum boats, outboard motors, fishing, clamming, crabbing, and were having more fun than James Bond at a Playboy rally.

For me being a young boy I had it all. But it was all at the marina. We had an awesome swimming pool, a breakfast diner, a separate restaurant for dinner plus a nightclub with live music all on the water! There was even a ship's store and of course hundreds of boats that also had many parents with kids that were all looking for something to do. Well, we did it all and it mostly consisted of running around in Boston Whalers and tin boats with screaming two stroke outboards that barely left a wake. My brother and I were always motoring off in our little boats to find our own treasures and adventures on the York River.

I would find later in life that the treasure I was always in search for was my youth.

Being a huge music fan I loved going into the marina's nightclub on the weekends with my dad. Back then as long as you were with your parent, it was okay to be in the nightclub. Heck we river rats used to even sit at the bar and drink bitter Shirley Temples until they would run out of Cherry Juice.

The funny thing is I thought this lifestyle was normal. Growing up on the water with all the amenities and good healthy fun things to do for us kids was just something that everyone did. The thought of living a boring, dull, stay at home lifestyle scared me to death! My biggest fear is that one day it all would be gone.

No more marina, no more dock life, no more river rat buddies, nothing. The more the Judge talked about building a house on the Rappahannock River the more I feared my dock life would soon vanish. It was scary. Just thinking that the Judge would move the boat somewhere else or even worse, build a house and not be at any marina would really make me disturbed and depressed. I was just a kid and what ever would happen was not much I could do about it anyway. I just learned to glorify and relish every day I had on the docks, and I did it in abundance.

When the fog rolls in off the river the true test of a thick fog is whether or not you can see your hand in front of your face. That is a thick fog. I saw such a fog for myself once when the Judge helped a friend move his boat from the upper Bay down to the York River on what would be a rather scary overnight trip.

I was too young to go on this excursion with my dad. He did not want me going on a break-in overnight cruise at my age so I stayed back on the dock with some of the kids and moms. My dad's party was to arrive somewhere around 8pm, which turned into 9 pm, 10, 11, 12, and then 1 in the morning. I was incredibly scared and totally distraught. The feeling overwhelmed me that the Judge was lost at sea, drowned on a sunken vessel sitting on the bottom of the Chesapeake Bay. I could not stop crying. I felt like a total wimp and was mostly worried that I would never see my favorite person again, my father the Judge.

We called the Coast Guard to start a search. There was no radio contact with the boat at all. Things were not looking good. The next day morning came and still no Dad. At this time things started to get quite scary for everybody and the people at the marina were going nuts. Just the thought of the Judge, Uncle Ed and two others succumbing to the waters of the Chesapeake had everyone in an emotional turmoil....especially me.

The fog was not lifting which made things worse for everyone. Keep in mind in those days there was no GPS, Loran, Radar, or Epirb's, and most of the boats rarely had life rafts back then, only life jackets. VHF radios were fixed and there were not even handhelds. I was at the point where hope was diminishing and truly felt that I had lost my father.

Within the hour the fog parted at the inlet and there was just one boat. It was dad and The Crew. The boat was slowly, very slowly inching its way back to the marina. Once we got them secured to the dock the Judge was a little surprised at how worried everyone was. Well, they were like a day late and not even the Coast Guard could find them. Dad sat us down, mixed a cocktail and began to tell us the story which to this day I am not sure I believe.

The Judge started explaining, "Well we sort of ...... in the fog...... in the boat.......ran over a house. We knocked off one of the shafts and one prop and had to crawl our way back in the fog."

I said, "How do you run over a house in your boat Dad?"

Never did I get a real good answer except there were ruins of some house in some part of the Chesapeake Bay, and they ran over it. Looking back on it the incident probably was a good thing. The lost prop and shaft in turn made them cruise at near idle speed, which made for a safer running speed in what was the thickest fog I have ever seen in my life.

So what we thought was the worst thing possible actually ended up to be a blessing. This is a lesson I would continue to learn throughout my life. The Judge never talked much about that trip afterwards. I think he felt bad he had made so many people extremely worried. Things happen on the water, it is just a part of boating. This would not be the first or last scare I would have throughout my lifetime of living and working around the water.

Once the fog lifted that day everyone was in pretty good spirits, meaning The Crew had the liquid sprits running by mid-day, the pool was open, and thick steaks were once again beginning to char on "A" dock.

Life is good again.

The Judge did not have an exclusive on running aground in the Bay or anywhere else. My brother Perry and I were pretty fearless when it came to running our outboards. Perry really got into racing the boats and creeking where no ten year old has gone before.

The definition of creeking is maneuvering your boat in such shallow water until usually, you run aground. Perry and I got to be experts at this and with a 9.9 tiller motor on our straw plugged tin boat, we could just go about anywhere—except FINLEY!

Finley was a danger area located at the back of Sara's Creek. The danger was not in running aground but getting shot by some red neck waterman. My dad warned me that if we went back there and motored too close to a dock, we could get shot. I was raised with stories about people who ventured back into Finley and never ventured back out. Evidently some of the stories had been true. Finley is not a place you want to be stranded in either by car or boat. These are people who are mostly old time watermen whose families date back to the days this country was settled...and I think they still live in the same house!

Finley is a place that always reminded me of that scene in the film *Deliverance*. You know....the pig. Nuff said.

Fortunately the Judge and The Crew knew some folks back in Finley and sort of had clearance, however not us kids. We were to stay far away from the back of Sara's creek, and we did.

......As far as anyone knows.

The marina was the center of our universe and at the center was the swimming pool, and by the swimming pool was the largest most beautiful distinct Magnolia Tree one will ever see. This tree was a monument to the marina and cars would circle around and around the parking lot just to see this tree.

On Sunday mornings the local minister would come to the marina and hold church service right under the Magnolia before giving his first service down the street. This to me was awesome and certainly was my idea of going to church. He would bring a few folks from the choir and start the "Magnolia" service right under the tree with some of the most beautiful hymns you ever heard.

As the choir sang people would be coming out of their boats in robes, shorts, and even just underwear sometimes. Usually half the people had bloody marys or screwdrivers in hand singing merrily along with the choir. Voices would sing high and low...

"When we've been here ten thousand years, bright shining as the sun. We've no less days to sing God's praise, Than when we've first begun."

The parking lot would soon be overfilled with people while the minister gave his elated sermon under the Magnolia Tree. Some of us were so inspired that we even went to his church service afterwards. Even as a young boy this made a huge impression on me.

I thought this is how the Lord would have done it. Go to the people who need it the most and preach in nature without any regard to status, denominations, race, or outside influence. Just give the message in the way the Lord wants it to be given. Even some 45 years later my memories of those Sunday services under the old Magnolia tree are some of the most memorable in my lifetime. This would be the beginning of my life long faith that would eventually pull me out of some rather difficult times.

Fishing trips were always a highlight and the filets cooked back at the dock were what I lived for. I enjoyed catching fish but I loved cooking them and eating them more. My early love for cooking was mostly due to hanging out with my Uncle Ed.

Ed loved to cook stuff up on the dock or his galley. I learned some interesting recipes from my uncle like fresh "Buzzard Meat Surprise". Ed would put me in charge of trying to make bluefish cakes which I did, and he was going to fix the meat. Ed's definition of "buzzard meat" was any meat that was on super sale or sometimes given away at the end of the meat counter. He never really knew what it was so he affectionately called it,

"Buzzard meat".

On this day Ed had Johnny Major helped him with his dish, buzzard meat and gravy in a pot roast bag. They put this meat in a plastic bag with a bunch of vegetables and made a gravy bath. After about an hour and many cocktails, Ed checked the Buzzard roast only to find the bag had melted all over the meat and it smelled and tasted AWEFULL!

But I had an idea. I had made these bluefish cakes that were really good, then I put the gravy from the buzzard meat onto the bluefish cakes and VOILA! Perfection! Best darn thing we ever tasted. The buzzard meat was so bad no one could eat it. So on the way out to the trash we threw it out in the woods and left it for the buzzards. It did become true buzzard meat after all.

As a young boy cooking on the docks with the fresh fish and blue crabs we caught was something that would stick with me for a lifetime. When The Crew cooked steaks there was never any such thing as purchasing a packaged steak like you would today.

All steaks were immense, cut fresh locally from the butcher and usually around two inches thick. Since the butcher liked to party with The Crew often times he would just meet us all at the dock with stacks of white butcher paper filled with the thickest juiciest steaks you ever saw. The food was usually so good, we did not go out much except for one thing............PIZZA!

My love for pizza is not only because I worshiped the pie, it is also probably somewhat psychological. The memories of getting in the car leaving the marina to go to Mimi's Pizza and Foosball Palace stick in my mind like glue. Order up! The Crew would order several pies while us kids tore into the foosball tables. At such a young age I had a real knack for the foose. I would beat everybody back home and was considered one of the best young players in Charlottesville. However playing in Gloucester meant that us kids at the pizza joint would be playing the kids from, you guessed it.... FINLEY!

These rednecks were the BEST players I ever saw. You could not even see the spin, their hands were so fast it was all just a blur. Whenever I played those guys all I heard was PING PING PING PING!!!!

I was not bothered by it more like in awe. I mostly wondered if those guys not having any teeth had anything to do with them being such great foosball players. After getting my butt kicked by the local Finley kids it was time for the saucy pizza chow served up by Mimi herself.

Nick's was another popular place that The Crew would venture to. Nick's Seafood in Yorktown was a place the Judge would go to by boat, tie up at the Warf Restaurant, and go have dinner. You have never had lobster until you have had it from Nick's. Actually back in the late sixties Nick's was known all over the United States as one of the legendary restaurants on the east coast. Everyone knew about it. Elegant stone Greek statues everywhere, fountains, and décor of the mid 50's is what set the scene.

Food was awesome, but Nick's is sadly all gone now. When they auctioned off items from the restaurant, the Judge proudly bought one of their menus.

Like my early childhood things were starting to move on, fade, and soon vanish. This was my biggest fear. I did not want to let go of the lifestyle I was accustomed to and loved as a young boy running around the docks catching crabs.

The dock life.

Sometimes a good fishing trip could cure anyone's blues, and that is what it was time for. Uncle Ed had this great idea to take his boat down to Virginia Beach at Rudee Inlet and fish for our favorite, bluefish. The Judge, Ed, Johnny, myself and about three others all ventured out into what was one of the roughest seas we have ever been in. Water was coming over the fly bridge and none of us could see anything.

What we did see was 18-pound bluefish being steadily pulled in over the stern of Ed's sport fisherman. We just nailed these fish and since we loved to eat them we kept them all. When it was all said and done we had around 700 pounds of bluefish in the boat. It was time to head in. Unfortunately the swells at the inlet were way too high to be able to just run in. These waves were eight to ten feet tall, a very serious sea condition that made even the locals wait it out to ride the right wave.

Uncle Ed was anxiously impatient and just decided to run through the swells but the waves were faster than the boat. I was a little kid looking off the back of the stern straight to the sky and all I could see was this 10 foot wave getting ready to combat and engulf us. It did. As the wave came under the boat it turned the 36-foot sport fisherman on its' side exposing both shafts and props clean out of the water spinning with resonating screeching sounds of cavitation. The engines roared as the RPM increased with propulsion that was waterless. The boat was taking on water instantly and bluefish were swimming in the vee berth. The port prop fortunately got a brief bite of the sea and the boat started to roll over to the port side, filled with water and swamped.

Captain Ed rapidly spun the boat around and headed back to sea. The first wave threw the bow up so high a lot of the water in the boat went through and over the stern, along with everything else. Once stable, about 500 yards off the inlet and a lot of water pumped out, Uncle Ed tried it again. This time again, he did not wait for the right wave and just plunged forward. Mistake!

Now I was on the fly bridge with my lifejacket on and was ready to swim to shore. I felt comfortable with this plan, because there were not a lot of other options. The next gigantic wave approached the stern, turning the boat on its' side again, pushing the sport fisherman toward the rock jetties. I said,

"Dad, no problem.... I am swimming the rest of the way!"

I prepared to just step in the water, because it was sinking on its side and the water was parallel to the fly bridge. I'd rather swim than stay on a sinking boat with the bluefish.

The Judge grabbed me with his arm pulled me to the center of the fly bridge and instructed me to not move. I sort of thought this was a BAD idea but he was the Judge, so I listened.

Just before we were to hit the rocks on the jetty one of the props bit the water, causing the boat to right itself again. Now Ed was not going to head back to sea, we were full force pointing this swamped boat to the bottom of the inlet and praying the pumps would catch up before we sank.

Those Sundays by the Magnolia tree must have paid off, because by the grace of God we made it to the dock.

Even after we were tied up for quite some time the pumps were still running. I was in a state of shock. Someone had called the ambulance when they saw the boat broached in the inlet and paramedics were waiting for us at the fish cleaning station. They checked all of us out and everyone was accounted for.

I sure wish the hell they had Xanex back then.

I asked to be able to go clean the bluefish to help calm me down. I was allowed to; after all we did have 700 pounds of fish to clean. It was two hours later when Uncle Ed came over with a big cocktail in hand. He asked me how was I doing and I told him that I have not been able to feel my knees since I got off the boat. I was so scared and stunned. I could not really feel anything around my legs and it was cold, very cold.

Uncle Ed looked at me and said,

"Let me see your filet knife, Jimmy".

He then started going through the trash bags of bluefish heads from my fish cleaning. He said,

"Look, take the knife and go right behind the cheek, cut back and down to the eyeball and you will have a bluefish cheek Filet. Deeeeelicious!"

I said, "WOW that was pretty cool Uncle Ed!"

So I started cleaning the rest of the bluefish and also cutting out the cheek meat. This was Ed's way of helping me get my mind off what had happened and to calm down. It worked.

Remember, The Crew could drink alcohol after all this happened however my youth did not allow me that privilege. There was some damage to the boat and it had to remain at the dock for a while so we called a friend to take us back to Yorktown. I was not ready for another boat ride anyway.

Back at the Marina in Gloucester the first thing I did was to go to the bathroom. It had been a wild trip and I drank enough coke on the way back to fill Dad's empty gallon milk jug/purple passion container. I went off by myself to the restroom and did not realize until this day that I suffered from claustrophobia.

The marina had changed locks on the bathroom door and I did not have the code. I was able to open the door just fine, but when it closed it was like solitary confinement.

After taking a 5-minute leak, the door would not open. Claustrophobia can be a strange thing. All of the sudden everything started to feel smaller and very confined. In a matter of minutes, I felt like I was inside a small box that was starting to crush my head in.

I panicked. I was screaming for help however there was no one around to listen. I was praying that there must be SOMEONE else in this world besides me that surely has to open this door and use the bathroom!

But no, the door would not be opened for any reason.

Like a flash I realized that the metal ashtray would make for a perfect propelling object to bust through the window near the ceiling in the bathroom. It worked.

SMASH!!!!

A million pieces of glass shattered everywhere and then I started screaming at the top of my lungs. The dock master flew into the bathroom with a look on his face like I will never forget. He was panicked as well. I am sure he thought someone was being murdered or something because I was screaming at the top of my voice. I sprinted out of the door then stood still. I could breathe now.

My dad was standing there with one hell of a puzzled look on his face. My tears were gone and I was fine like nothing had happened at all. The second I was outside everything was perfect. The only thing the judge could think to appropriately say was,

"Sorry, Dock Master."

Everyone at the marina was always in a party mode. In the morning, it was bloody marys, mid day was beer and purple passion, afternoon and evenings was scotch, vodka, or bourbon. This was the late 60's and boaters just flat out partied all the time, at least the boaters I knew.

Looking back at my early childhood it is easy to see now why people would use the weekend on their boats as a huge release.

I mean really, back then, time and distance traveled in a car or boat was measured by a six-pack, a case, or a gallon jug. This was before M.A.D.D. and none of The Crew ever got a DUI or had any accidents.

To this day I am not sure why, but the guys never got in any real trouble. At worst one of The Crew would get drunk and fall down on someone's boat. That's about it. All of the good times on the weekends, all of the practical jokes, all the drinking, crab catching, fish catching, motor boating, womanizing, all of it was a fantastic time. It was reality, but a reality that would only last a couple of days a week.

There was a reason everyone tried to have such a good time, because what was back home in Charlottesville was nothing to smile about. It was always that way. Never really knew what to expect when I was at home.

The screams could be heard emanating out of our small brink rancher on Larribee Lane for at least three blocks. What at one time, would be considered possession of an evil entity, now is usually called severe mental illness. The windows would rattle and actually vibrate when my mother would bellow the most horrendous, deafening screech known on this earth.

The house filled with red lights flashing and people in medic uniforms were busting at the door. Four grown men trying to hold down my mother as she thrashed violently on the floor and then seemed to elevate in the air. The straps were not enough to hold her down. My ears were ringing from the noise of a resonant operatic scream and the sounds of the squealing sirens from the ambulance.

The ambulatory stretcher seemed to fill the entire living room. She was not going easy. In Mom's eyes, there were paratroopers that had dropped down from the ceiling and had guns pulled on her ready to fire. There was also a train on a track that was going through the house and we were all getting ready to be run over.

In a delusional mental paranoid schizophrenic state, she probably thought the medics trying to strap her in the stretcher were the army of paratroopers trying to get her. Thus making the delusion a reality in her mind, and the harder the straps were pulled the louder the screams.

A small crowed began to form outside the house. These were the inquisitive neighbors trying to see what was happening. I remember the red strobe lights going round and round on their faces with jaws dropped to the ground.

No one has heard a sound like my mother's thundering screams. Mom was an opera singer that was once offered a position with The Metropolitan Opera in New York City. She was that talented. Everyone around knew what a voice she had.

When she soloed in church you could hear her voice from outside the building when she sang. Never have I heard such a voice, ever.

Once the medics had her ambulatory and the back doors of the ambulance were shut, I could still hear her voice screaming in full operatic horror as I stood inside the house with the front door closed.

She was that loud. The red lights began to fade, as the ambulance sped off into the darkness. Left inside the house, were my brother Perry, my dad, and I. It would remain that way for quite a while.

Mom had gone into such a paranoid delusional state, that it took 13 shock treatments once at the hospital just to calm her down. Her psychotic state was total hysteria and paranoia beyond comprehension.

The paratroopers had followed her to the hospital and stood guard in her room. That is what she saw, in her eyes.

My mother was diagnosed as a full throttle paranoid schizophrenic. She had been delusional to the point where she was burning down the kitchen, to try to kill the invaders dropping down from the ceiling. All she could see was walls covered in blood and she was franticly trying to escape the intruders.

Not exactly a safe place to raise young kids. This was my father's dilemma. He had no choice but to admit Mom and get her the best treatment she could get.

This happened when I was very young and my mother started to have mental illness with the birth of my brother Perry. That is what started her imbalance. Then once I was born, well let's just say that tipped the scales. Yes, my birth is what caused my mother to go totally mental. There was nothing I could do.

Sometimes, I guess things can go sour just by being born.

I never really knew my mom. Her mental illness started before I was birthed. All I knew was the crazy woman who saw things burned down the kitchen, and screamed like a demon that drank holy water. It is very sad to have a mother that you never really have known.

All I knew is what my dad told me about her before she got sick. The Judge would sit me down and show me pictures of my mom when she was a bit younger. The most beautiful woman you ever saw with a voice that only God could have created. A real beauty with more talent than one person should ever be allowed to have. Dad spoke very highly of my mother and made us realize that it was not her fault she got sick.

It was no one's fault.

My mother's family, just about all of them was unbelievably gifted and talented in music and the arts. While Mom was the opera singer, her brother was about the best bluegrass player in the state of Virginia. All of her sisters were very talented singers and musicians.

Talent just ran in their family. It was nothing for me to visit my mom and there were five guitars in the back room being ripped to shreds by the fastest, most talented fingers ever. When my uncle would play bluegrass his hands just looked like a blur. Even my brother could just look at a guitar and it would start to play.

Although I never really knew my mother before she got sick, I owe a lot to her. Whatever creative and musical talent I possess I got from my mother's side of the family. It shows too, I started playing piano and organ when I was around eight years old and have not stopped since, I later degreed in music at 24 years old.

There is something very surreal about a mental institution. When I was a young kid visiting Mom at the crazy ward, was about the strangest thing I ever encountered. I actually lived *One Flew Over the Cuckoo's Nest*. No kidding, most everybody at the institution was zombied out, some of the strangest creepy people I ever saw.

My mother was not really too coherent when she was in the institution. She was drugged up pretty good. The mental health industry has come a long way since then and a lot of people live normal lives with the current medications that are available today. However in the sixties, there was not a lot more than shock treatments and a few meds that did sort of zombiefy the patient.

This was my life. Going to elementary school, visiting Mom at the mental institution, and catching crabs on the weekends. Little did I know that soon my time at home in Charlottesville would be even getting worse.

My dad was in a hard situation. His wife was confined to a mental ward, he had a law practice that he

32

was building and required a lot of his time, and he had two kids that were coming home from school every day at three o'clock. This meant that he would have to find sitters to cover us boys, until he got home from work.

I don't know how many people we went through. At one point it felt like one a week. It was not like we were bad kids or anything, we just hated these old ladies that dad found to watch us. It was horrible. They smelled too. All I wanted was a mother that was not crazy and to get these old ladies out of my house.

Simple, right? No... I didn't get my wish.

I really only had one parent. My dad was both mother and father. He did the best he could and was the best dad a son could have. Unfortunately he could not do it all, something had to give. The Judge knew that there would have to be some sort of replacement "Mother" that could help with the kids. Time had passed and my dad divorced. He had to.

My brother and I would continue to visit Mom in the institutions, which I hated. I never wanted to go. My mother was always out of it and the entire situation just gave me the total creeps. This is why I never really enjoyed visiting my mother, just all of it was too weird for me and I was just a young kid anyway.

As the many years would soon pass my mother would continue to be in and out of institutions. However, with the advancement in new medications, she eventually did better and got a job at the power company. She retired some 20 years later. As she aged her mental illness worsened and she also had a stroke. She is permanently in a medical retirement home and is watched closely. She is being well taken care of.

My mother was a strong willed person, with great talent who overcame her illness enough to lead a productive life. I may not have ever known my mom before she got sick, however there is no way I could have been more proud of her.

The thing is, as bad as it is when you're a kid, to have to watch your mother in a straight jacket being hauled off to the mental ward. There are things worse, as I would soon find out.

The Judge got remarried. Now the hell really starts.

Chapter 2

It Foams at the Mouth

"I cannot think of any need in childhood as strong as the need for a father's protection".

~Sigmund Freud

Probably the one thing I mastered as a youngster was something called diversions. Since things were not all that happy at home, I would do things to divert my attention in positive, fun ways. Magic and music soon became my salvation. At a very early age, close up magic was something that totally fascinated me, and playing the piano was as natural as breathing.

My love of cards started when I would visit my grandma and grandpa in Horanceville Virginia. Grandma also known as Naner Baugh was the sweetest lady I ever met in my life. She had the temperament of an angel. Dad used to take us there to visit and sometimes stay for a week at a time.

Grandpa was an old southern hanging moss judge that had a passion for hunting. He used to take my brother and me, with our 4-10 shotguns, dove and deer hunting all the time. I was never much into it at all. Hunting meant I had to get out of a warm bed, put on some funny looking orange vest and go stand by a tree in the cold, somewhere in the woods. Then, hurry up and wait and hope a deer passes you by.

Hunters used to put deer piss on them to attract deer. All this I thought, was a bit much. Hunting was just never my thing. I'd much rather stay back at the house and play in the kitchen, watch TV and most of all, build model ships. That is what I did most of the time at the grandparents' was put together model ships, planes and cars.

I would sometimes build three models at a time. Truth is that I pretty much sucked at building model toys and they always looked pretty terrible when I was finished. There was just something about putting together those little plastic model boats that I loved. Unfortunately, I would make a huge mess. One time, I had so much glue all over the back porch the dog got stuck to the floor.

I was so bad at building those model boats they would always sink when I put them in the tub. I would shout at Naner,

"Grandma come look at my model war ship in the tub."

"Jimmy, it looks all right, but it is sinking."

"No Naner….. It's a Navy Submersible!"

I always thought to myself, why would I want to stand in the woods or a cornfield, shooting things when I could be at the house building model ships or even better…… back at docks catching crabs, fishing, and seeing what The Crew was up to. Now THAT is fun! Not hunting with deer piss, it bored me to death.

Naner Baugh seemed to be the epicenter of Horanceville. Everyone knew and loved her except when she drove her car. I don't think she ever went over 15 mph anywhere but everyone knew her and just let her drive as slow as she wanted.

Her card parties are where I started my fascination with slight-of-hand. She used to have bridge parties and the house was full of these old ladies playing cards. They would sit there all day, drinking their toddies and playing cards. They loved it and I was fascinated by the fact that they could entertain themselves so well, with just a deck of Bicycles.

So I had the idea to see if I could make up some magic tricks and entertain the ladies during their card games. I would then buy books on magic, and really started practicing a lot. I came up with a few simple, but convincing tricks and the ladies at the bridge game just loved it. They had a ball.

I would much rather entertain, performing magic at the old lady's bridge game, than stand in the cold woods pouring deer pee on me.

Grandpa and I never got close. He was a highly respected man in his hometown of Horanceville and sat on the judge's bench longer than anyone else in the State of Virginia. He was a proud man whose second son was a lawyer and judge, and his first son was a successful doctor in Kingston. Grandpa was also known as one of the best shots in town. The man knew how to hunt and it was a great passion of his.

Judge Emanuel Baugh would go into a cornfield with his shotgun and 12 shells. He would come out with no shells and 12 birds. One shot for each bird. The Judge was a great shot that rarely missed a target. He was always the first one to return from the field. Everyone else would be out there shooting away blasting at anything that moved. Grandpa was pretty much done in a couple of hours and then he would walk back to the car and put away his gun.

Grandpa had a tradition that never changed. In the front seat of his car, there was a white Styrofoam cooler full of ice and one bottle of bourbon. After he got his 12 birds he would properly stow his hunting rifle. Grandpa then would fix a small bourbon on the rocks and stand by his car in the field enjoying his toddy. His friends would then later join him after their hunt and they would talk about how many shells they fired off that day. Grandpa was usually 12 for 12 and the first one back at the car.

Judge Baugh also enjoyed a toddy at dinner and he did not speak much. However when he spoke you had better listen, because whatever Judge Emanuel had to say was the most important words ever spoken. At least that is how he acted. Mostly true too, Grandpa was a very smart man, who was respected tremendously by everyone.

When Judge Emanuel Baugh died of cancer, he was at home in Horanceville and I was there when he passed. Throat cancer is a terrible thing and Emanuel was almost too proud to die. He hated being sick and felt it was beneath him. Grandpa did have a sense of humor. At his request, he was buried in his red pajamas with a bottle of bourbon under his pillow in the casket.

Here we were at the funeral home with an open casket. The most respected judge in Horanceville, laying at rest in his red jammies and a bottle of booze. I remember it like it was yesterday. My father was very upset at the loss of his father. It made me think of what would happen if I lost my dad, and that fear was too much to bear. I remember it was at that time I started to pray everyday for the health and happiness of my dad. Those prayers continued until his death on his 80th birthday. Another answered blessing from the Magnolia Tree.

Naner Baugh did not do well after my grandfather passed. She was inseparable with the Judge and the two of them completed one person. She just was lost. After a few years Naner Baugh would pass, without a doubt the finest and sweetest lady to have ever graced this earth. I am absolutely sure of this. If I ever get to heaven Naner Baugh will be standing there at the gates, with a bowl of her homemade vanilla ice cream and a big spoon. "Have some Jimmy."

Back in Charlottesville things did not get any better. After my fathers divorce we would continue to visit our mother in the mental institutions. In time Dad would start to date a little. Watching your father date when you're only 10 years old is an interesting thing to do. I was too young to know what was really going on. I don't know for sure the first time I met what would soon be my stepmother, or as I affectionately call her…

"THE BITCH FROM HELL!!!!"

The earliest memory I have of this person was going to her apartment and visiting with my dad. She had this wimpy ass dog called an east highland black terrier named "Boris". The most worthless spoiled dog I ever saw. Could not stand this pup and I am a person who LOVES dogs. The dog just had an attitude, like you were not worthy to be in its' presence. A bit like its' owner I might add.

Dad was sitting on the sofa with this woman, looking like he just found a permanent babysitter.

...Yeah, right. Here is a good reference. Let's get a baby sitter from the remake of the night of the living dead, directed by Joan Crawford. ... Sure, that will be great.... NOT!

This woman who was sitting next to the Judge is a name I will never forget for the rest of my life.

Carrie Regan.

She would in the future reign in a new title, given by me as the "Bitch from Hell".

From what unearthly demonic, poisoned shallow grave my father drug this possessed ugly beast from, I will never know. Someone must have sacrificed a goat in a gone wrong satanic ritual somewhere in the neighborhood, and then this thing showed up.

Oh brother, at that time none of us knew what was going to hit us. It is like Germany before Hitler arrived. Who knew? I mean, really, this woman should have been shipped out years ago to terrorize whoever deserved it, and certainly was not me. Like an innocent bystander being run over by a Mac truck. Or the day the UFO finally drops down out of the sky and lands on you guessed it, my head! Ouch... This is going to hurt, and boy it did.

Now, you have to understand that Carrie had a dual personality. To someone who did not know her she would come off being the nicest person in the world; extremely well mannered and gracious. Once the door was closed she could turn into a possessed, enraged, angry, vile beast that would make Mommy Dearest look like one of Santa's Elves.

I would think at any minute, Carrie would pee on the floor, spit pea soup, do a 360 degree head turn, and speak in foreign languages while levitating off the bed. I often wondered if under her hair there was a 666.

I guess my judge of character was not all that bad because even when I first was around her, I always felt like she was putting on airs. A real fake and I did not really buy into what she was selling. However my brother and I both were very nice and respectful toward her at all times.

So we were all at her place, when the Judge told us that they were getting married and that we would have a new mother. Well, I already could not stand the dog that shit all over the place but figured that if this makes Dad happy then I am 100% for it.

Of course the first thing the new wife wants is to move out of our house. In her genius, she only moved across the street. Literally, we moved three houses down across the street. I thought, gee this is stupid! If you're going to move then move dammit!"

Hell, I could see my old house from the bedroom window of my new house. What is up with that? But what does an 11 year old have to say about real estate ventures anyway? This was the parents' call. All I really cared about anyway was magic tricks playing the piano and trying to get the life back I had at the docks. Where the hell is the marina? Where is my Magnolia Tree? Not here!

Carrie did some things that I did not understand, like buying furniture and putting it in the living room. Not just furniture but furniture we were not allowed to sit in. I remember she said,

"You are not allowed to sit in these chairs, but we are going to have your portraits done and hang them over the chairs."

I thought to myself, Why not just let us sit in the chairs and skip the portraits?

That made sense to me, but the portraits came anyway and guests would come to the house and Carrie would show them into the room to look at the chairs and see our portraits hanging over them. I was so embarrassed by this. I would hide in the downstairs room and practice piano. I would play non-stop for hours and even days. Music and magic were the only two things that brought me happiness in Charlottesville at that time.

The only remaining photograph of the one time we were allowed to sit on the den sofa. The photo is old and blurry but you get the idea.

Carrie also had a thing about insisting that I ate things that would make me sick to my stomach. The number one thing was broccoli cooked for hours in the oven, until it turned into some sort of green slime that looked like pond scum.

Now I was reasonable as a child. I told her I would gladly eat many vegetables and really liked raw broccoli, just that when it is cooked that way it turns my stomach. "Please don't make me eat that! Please!!"

Well, no such luck. Carrie made sure that she made that broccoli at least three times per week. She would not let me leave the table until I ate it, but I could not because just the smell made me gag. Many times she would make me eat it and I would either throw up at the table or run to the bathroom.

What was done with my leftovers? You guessed it, what was left on my plate would be the only thing sitting on my plate for the next meal...... cold too. I could not believe it.

Other than the insane treatment at the dinner table and the chairs we could not sit in or the dog that was a pain in the ass and continued to shit everywhere, I thought she was ok. She was a fake but nothing really much else to complain about. But that changed soon. Her behavior patterns got really weird and she would transform herself into some sort of female B movie monster with hives that spit, foamed at the mouth and beat us like Holmes on Ali.

For no apparent reason except for the fact that she had some type of severe personality disorder, she would seriously become another person. One minute she is selling Avon acting like Princess Di, the next minute the Exorcist. This is what she would do:

When there was no one around, she would start to get this expression of just pure possession and evil. Her face would actually break out in hives and she would start ranting and screaming running around the house. She would just start yelling and for what I did not know.

I would be home by myself after school and she would get hives on her face from screaming and yelling so much. Then she would start to foam at the mouth just like a wild rabid hyena. Never saw anything like it and she would do this for several hours then fly up to her room and lock herself in. She would not come out for days. No sound no movement, nothing. At times she would stay in her room for over a week.

42

I remember talking to my dad a lot about this and asking him what did my brother or I do to get her so upset. He just never had an answer but he knew that he had made a huge mistake in marrying this crazy woman. He also knew that she had some mental issues that were not going to be corrected. He was stuck. He married Carrie because she put on a good front, and he desperately needed some help with the kids. The Judge thought he was doing the right thing.

As time went on her patterns got extremely predictable. She would blow up over nothing running around the house screaming and throwing dishes, all the while hitting my brother and myself with as many left and right hand jabs as she could swing.

Many times she would pack her bags and say she was leaving and then would lock herself in the bedroom and not come out for days.

I used to get very upset by this and felt very sorry for her. Every time I would ask if there is something I could do. I would bring her food to her room only to see that she would not even come out to eat. Nothing…. She would lock herself in and that was it. Days later, she would emerge and be nice again for a while and then repeat the exact same thing over and over.

One time when she was screaming and packing her bags to leave again, she ran out of the house and threw her bags in her car. Carrie then smoked her tires in reverse out of the driveway pulling around to the front of the house with the engine roaring. Next, she flew out of the car while it was running and ran upstairs in the house and locked herself in the room. It is there she would stay for the next week.

The car was still running outside with her suitcase in the trunk.

Right then the Judge pulled up in his car and asked what I was doing. I told him what had happened and he said to go cut off the car and bring him the keys. He walked inside and tried to talk to her but she would not come out of the room. This went on for years.

Carrie had family and going to see them really was a wicked experience. First up, we had to travel to the mountains. Now we were really getting far away from that place that I love and missed… the marina. I wanted to be catching crabs listening to music and drinking Shirley Temples. Instead I am in Harrisonburg watching the bitch's brother growl and drool spit all over his food at the dining room table.

"Rudy" was no buddy; a very tragic situation. Rudy was Carrie's brother who very sadly had an accident while in the military. He suffered massive brain damage and lost most of his motor skills. Confined to a wheelchair, he could not walk nor even talk. He just growled. I felt sorry for the man I really did. But he seemed to have this attitude. He would throw fits screaming, and for no reason at all…sort of like his sister.

Sometimes, I thought the only difference between "Rudy" and the "Bitch" was the wheelchair. At the dinner table the drool would be horrible. They would put bibs all over him and food and spit would just fall out of his mouth all over the table.

I remember going there for Thanksgiving. We are all supposed to be having a nice dinner with this "Rudy" who was throwing up at the table spitting on himself, and growling at the top of his lungs until his face turned beat red. This is how I spent Thanksgiving. The Pilgrims even would have left this dinner table.

"Get me the hell back to "A" Dock!!"

The upshot of it was this: Carrie's mother kept the money that the Army was paying for Rudy's care. He should have been properly cared for in a home with experienced staff and with people who are trained to deal with these types of injuries, not Grandma. Carrie's mother

44

kept the money and when she died it was passed to her and her brother. Carrie's other brother Damien was one hell of a nice fellow and was the only one in the entire family that seemed to be a decent human being. I always felt sorry for Rudy. He was confined to a wheelchair. Taken care of by his mother and he just never seemed happy about that. Certainly and understandably he was not happy about his condition either.

He was an angry pissed off brain damaged invalid who could not stand this world or anyone in it, including himself

Yeah, those trips to Harrisonburg were fun all right. After leaving "Rudy" and heading back to Charlottesville I had a lot to look forward to.

More screaming, yelling, foaming at the mouth, smoking tires, dog shit, pond scum broccoli, and chairs I was not allowed to sit in.

Many times during my teens, living with Carrie I would think about the old Magnolia Tree. In my faith, I always asked that in the future if I ever got married and had kids that they would never be subject to such abuse.

"Please Lord if I ever have a family may it be a peaceful and normal one. Something I never had…I have paid my dues!"

Those prayers were eventually answered with a resounding, "YES!!" The greatest gift I ever got.

Chapter 3

Magic Dick and a Woody

"The greatest escape I ever made was when I left Appleton, Wisconsin".

~Harry Houdini

This is the main reason I did so well at magic, music, comedy and entertaining. That was becoming the only fun I knew. I had to create it and hopefully one day return to the reign of *Master Crab Catcher* on "A" dock. The marina…the life I so missed with every breath I took.

As time went on both my piano and close up magic skills were developing at quite a high rate. Fortunately I had inherited a lot of my mother's musical talent, which in later years would prove to be very useful. My slight-of-hand was really getting pretty good and I ended up working at Busch Gardens in the Magic Shop. I preformed close up magic and also sold tricks in the store. It got so popular the store manager put me in charge of ordering all the magic tricks and even had me do shows in the street. At 16 years of age I was making money performing magic and having a ball. One thing is for sure, it beat staying at home with the Bitch from Hell!

I met a lot of people that first year at the park and hung out with some of the folks in the entertainment department. I found out that the entertainers in that department got paid a LOT more money than I did at the Magic Shop. I thought for the next year I would audition for the entertainment department as the official street magician. It was time for me to move on anyway because I was starting to get into a little trouble at the Magic Shop.

We had gotten a new manager assigned to the shop named Dick, who we all could not stand. The guy was just a real pill. No fun at all and he also was quite the fem.

Whenever he answered the phone at the shop he would pick up the phone in a soft voice and say, "Magic...Dick". We all would laugh our ass off every time he answered the phone. My friend Jerry was a very good artist and worked as cashier. He had the great idea to draw Dick's face on a Styrofoam head and put it in the display case with the other Halloween masks. I put a price tag on it as well and a nametag that just said "Dick". I would yell across the shop at Jerry and say,

"Hey man, put this Dick face in your case."

Sure enough, within five minutes we now had a "Dick Head" in the display case.

We all got a good laugh and started to ask customers if they saw our new "Dick Head". It did not take long before the big cheese saw this and immediately called me into his office upstairs for a conference. He was very upset at me and I figured I lost my job.

I remember telling him how awful I thought this new manager was, and that he really was a "Dick". I apologized for all the Dick Head references and told him Jerry had nothing to do with it. I took all the credit or blame. The big cheese only said one thing. He encouraged me to audition for the entertainment department and the next thing he did was to fire the "Dick". That was the end of the Magic Shop for me.

The next summer I auditioned for the street magician position and won the job. I was like making $400 bucks a week salary performing six shows a day thinking I had the world by the balls, and I did. There was a great hotel at the park that had both a bar and restaurant there. I auditioned for them to entertain at nights for $100 bucks and a room. They bought it. So I did six shows a day as a street magician and then entertained in the bar at the hotel at nights. Plus a FREE room!! I was on a roll. I did this for about six years.

The great thing about the gig at the hotel was that is where all the stars stayed when they would perform concerts. So next thing you know I am hanging out doing close up magic for Michael McDonald and the Doobie Brothers, Marie Osmond, just about anybody that came through got to see some slight of hand from Jim Baugh.

It was great and really helped to launch my career as a close up magician. The money was getting really good and I met thousands of people having a blast, and staying away as much as I could from the Physco Bitch from Hell!

One summer, while I was performing, the park management approached me. They wanted me to not only continue the magic shows but also host the *Great American High Dive* Show. Well, the pay then would be doubled and I loved this. I got paid to do the six magic shows a day, four high dive shows, and also paid to entertain in the bar at the hotel during the evenings. I was young, had the energy, and most of all this type of experience was going to be a godsend in my later career.

I was already a professional performing close up magician doing my own thing when I heard of this guy named Woody Sanders. I met Woody when I was around 17 years old. I was told that Woody was a retired professional close up magician and was considered one of the best card and coin guys in the country. Since I learned that Woody lived in Richmond, maybe I ought to hook up and see if this guy was any good. I was not a cocky kid. However, I was a professional close up guy making good money and doing pretty well. I was not expecting much out of this Woody fellow at all and almost did not make the effort to meet him.

Woody Sanders changed my life. There was close up magic before Woody then there was close up magic after Woody. I would never be the same performer after I met Mr. Sanders. This guy was not just good. He was great and unmatched by anyone I have ever seen even to this day.

The guy was a natural who had a talent and a brain that did nothing but ooze slight of hand. Woody was retired however, to my benefit he did teach and coach close up magic. I signed up on the spot.

"PLEASE WOODY I BOW TO YOU, JUST TEACH ME THAT DAMN TRICK!"

I studied hard under Woody for several years and got to know other close up artists through him. I would never have gotten to where I did in magic had it not been for this man. I ended up entertaining in Atlantic City and even opening up my own close up magic bar next to the Tobacco Company in Richmond. All because of the advances in slight of hand that Woody taught me.

He was quite the character. This was a small man who drove a Corvette and wore a hairpiece. He was single and just an average looking fellow. However his demeanor was that of Sean Connery overlooking the baccarat table. Woody was a very serious womanizer. He liked them up to three at a time and at the same time. Booze, booty, and slight of hand, that is what the man lived and breathed.

Woody was so good at close up magic he could walk into ANY bar or restaurant and walk out with two women on his side. He used his skills to pick up women all the time constantly with success. He loved it, and it worked for him. Women would fall for his clever wit and massive dexterity with his hands and fingers. He also would change up his routines and make them a little more "blue" to entice the ladies.

I have never seen a guy that was so successful at picking up girls in my life, without having to put ads in the newspaper. He would pull out the cards and coins and then they were hooked. It really was just like magic.

As a performer and entertainer I realized what Woody was doing and decided I would not have any part of it. I had no interest in running around picking up women using close up magic as the enticement. I looked at everything he taught and applied it professionally. That was a very smart move because it worked.

There were only two times that I can remember that I used magic as a way to meet and date women. All I can say, is it did work and it was very easy..... Too easy. Twice was it for me because it was not long before I would meet my wife and get married anyway.

In learning the art of close up magic I realized that you had to be three to five steps ahead of the audience all the time.

When I would walk up to a table to perform, the trick was already done. I was prepared to do anything that comes up and improvise tricks as well. The entire time I always had to be ahead of the audience. This was fantastic mental training for my later years as an editor and producer.

Woody became a life long friend and I stayed in touch with him often. He had bought a little motor scooter to cruise around his neighborhood with and it was on that scooter he died. A car hit him and Woody died immediately. I lost a good friend and the world lost one of the best card and coin guys ever. When I traveled entertaining doing shows up and down the East Coast I would always ask other close up guys,

"Have you ever seen anyone that had hands like Woody?" The answer was always no. He was the best.

Talk about an incredible waste, the James Bond of Close up Magicians left this world because of a motor scooter accident.

I get sick every time I think about it.
RIP Woody Sanders.

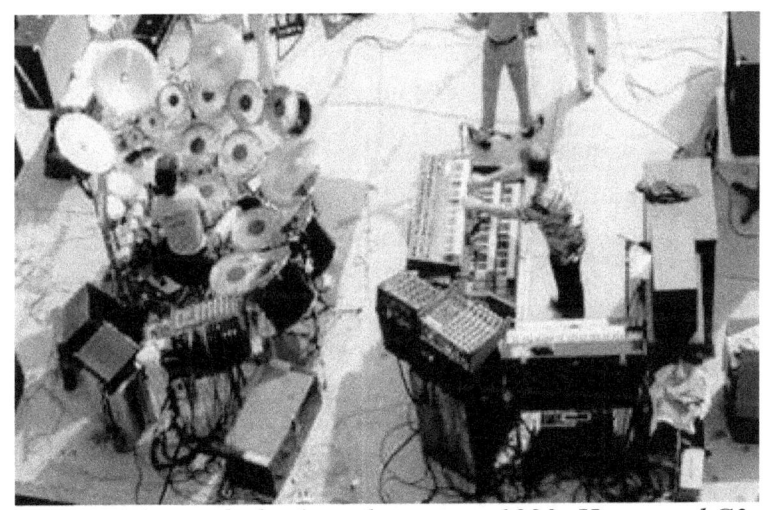

Jim Baugh's multi keyboard rig circa 1980: Hammond C3,
147 Leslie with reverb cabinet, Prophet 5 Synthesizer,
Moog Taurus Pedals, Farfisa Organ and Elka Piano.
Picture was taken during a concert at a Virginia University
circa 1980.

Chapter 4

Progresso

"A painter paints pictures on canvas. But musicians paint their pictures on silence".

~Leopold Stokowski

By the time I was 18 the den in our house downstairs was beginning to get a little crowded. I had been a huge Rick Wakeman and Keith Emerson fan since I was a kid and started mounting keyboards on top of one another. I had a Hammond Organ and a Farfisa as well as an electric Elka piano. I also had an acoustic piano and everything was set up in our now overly crowded downstairs den.

I would practice for hours on end and would play anything off the *Fragile* album. At high school there was always a grand piano in the auditorium and some teacher was regularly kicking me off the piano. I would skip class and be in the auditorium practicing a jazz riff I heard Keith Emerson play. The problem was the piano back home barely worked. Lots of the keys stuck and it could not hold a tuning. It was something I would bang on and develop my dexterity, but I really took advantage of any piano I could find to practice on. High school was a fairly easy place for me to develop my music skills. After football practice I would sneak in the auditorium and play the stage piano for several hours' right up until the janitor would throw me out.

One day a very pretty sweet girl who was one grade under me sat in and listened while I was working on some compositions I had written. She was a singer and was in the drama department. She never paid any attention to me until she heard me play that day. Later that week my classmate told me that this girl had a crush on me and was wondering if I was interested. Of course!

Her name was Rita Everly and we got along great. She could sing beautifully and really had a lot of talent. I dated her for a while during my last year in high school, then her family moved away and I would not see nor hear from her ever again.

I always wondered what happened to Rita, because I did really like her back then. Over 30 years later I found out some rather disturbing news. Rita had joined the Samtha Cult out in Oregon State and was the common law wife of an opera singer/talent coach who was accused of raping their students. They both had their kids taken away from them by protective services and charges were filed. Samtha was approached to testify about a confession that Rita made about the sexual abuse they were doing to some students. Evidently the Judge threw the case out because by bringing in Samtha to testify would be a complete circus. Samtha was a bizarre cult where their leader was claiming he was channeling a 40,000-year-old warrior princess. One can understand why the judge would not allow this case in his court.

So innocently I wondered what ever happened to my old high school girlfriend and guess what I found out. She joined the Samtha Cult, so much for that old girlfriend.

It became my mission to find places I could practice piano. One Sunday I was in a local church and realized they had a huge grand piano by the pulpit. This sucker I had to play. I used to drive my car to the church during the week, sneak in and play that grand for hours. Right after school my compass was always set for that church. It was the best sounding piano I had heard and the action was great. I figured everyday I practiced there that it was a gift, because I was not supposed to be there. I was not even a member of the church, just a high school kid looking for some good keys to play.

The name of the church was Dove Avenue Baptist Church and the preacher's name was Gander Warner.

Gander was a popular televangelist and operated a really great and huge Baptist church.

I had been getting away with playing in that sanctuary for well over a year probably knocking that darn piano out of tune every time I played it. One day I was just on a roll and playing some improvisations based around Tarkus by Emerson Lake and Palmer. It was some really wild music. Gander came walking down the isle with his music director and both their jaws were dropped to the floor. I don't think they had heard music like that before…. certainly not in their church. So I quickly started playing my blues jazz version of Amazing Grace.

"Tis Grace that brought me safe thus far, and Grace will lead me home."

They stood for like five minutes before I finally stopped playing and there was silence for maybe 30 seconds. Both of them were just staring at me. Gander said,

"Who are you!"

…..I said, "My name is Jimmy Baugh."

"Are you a member of this church?"

"…No sir. But I am Christian and fond of Magnolia Trees."

"Who in God's name gave you permission to play our piano?" I said,

"… Good Reverend I am not aware that God has given anyone a name yet to give me permission to play your fine piano…. Sir."

At that time I started to get up and leave and that's when they told me to please never play their piano again. The good reverend was very nice to me yet quite firm. I respected this preacher and had watched him on TV for years. Now he was staring me down kicking me off his $50,000 church piano.

Respectfully I never played THAT one again.

Funny thing happened when I was walking out of the church. Down this long hallway there were all these rooms where they would hold classes at the church. In each room guess what they had… A PIANO! I was like a hog in slop. I played every piano in every room and continued to go back to the church and practice on those class pianos. I guess no one cared at that point. I figured I was true to my word. I never played again the one in the sanctuary, but sure did bang the hell out of those class pianos.

I remember finding it odd that everywhere I went I was getting kicked off of some piano. Figured people should encourage music, not discourage it. Regardless by the time I was 19 I had the reputation of being one of the best keyboard players around anywhere. People even wanted me to teach. So I did. I actually was getting paid to perform close up magic and tutor piano students. Music and magic is what my life was about back then and all I really wanted to do was play in a progressive rock band.

After high school it was time for college and college meant to me these things: Snow skiing, chasing skirt, playing in a rock band, and making money performing close up magic. I was able to do these things because I was getting a degree in music and since I was already an accomplished player, school would be a breeze. It really was….that is once I got in.

I did not have good grades at all in school, because I never studied. Never! Getting into college was not going to be because of my scholastic abilities. I actually auditioned in order to get into Virginia Commonwealth University Music School. My appointment for the audition was with the school's most accomplished classical pianist, Dr. London Balue.

The good Dr. had me into his study, where there sat a baby grand. He said, laughing,

"Jim, your grades suck. Did you ever study at all?"

I answered, "Not really."

He then started to look through some Rachmaninoff and simply said,

"Jim, why don't you just play me something you like?"

So, I was fine with that. I started off with some improv's of *Wakeman's Six Wives of King Henry the Eighth*, then segued into a little jazz and then moved into some very progressive original compositions that I was working on.

Hell, I was just glad to be sitting down playing piano. Here is a guy that is actually asking me to play and not kicking me off.

I played for maybe 15 minutes and I will never forget the look on his face. It was just a blank stare. No emotion, just sitting there with these very harsh looks at me. I really was not sure what he was thinking. Now, I knew this guy was a top classical pianist and was a highly respected musician. Heck the guy was a professor in music and I am sitting there playing for the man on HIS piano.

I thought that was pretty cool.

He did finally speak and he mentioned that my type of dexterity was fairly rare. So I thought that was a good thing. Then he put up a chart of some classical, it was a Rachmaninoff piece. The Dr. said,

"Play it."

I could not. It was impossible, because I did not sight read music. I could tell him what the notes were, however could not sight-read them. He took the sheet music down and said,

"I am admitting you to our music school based on technical ability alone."

To be honest, that is how I got through college, just playing the piano. Other musicians were much more intelligent musically than I was. The jazz guys were tremendous sight-readers and were just top-flight musicians. Their problem was basic understanding and performance on a keyboard.

You see in music school, the piano was something that all musicians had to have basic skills on. The horn guys just hated the keyboard and kind of hated me because all I had to do was walk in once a week, tear up the keyboard, walk out and go snow skiing chasing skirt. That was all I did in college. Unfortunately, I may have been the only person to get an "F" in Choir.

My mother may have been an opera singer but I could not sing a lick. I did not enjoy singing at all and skipped most of the choir classes. Finally the instructor just gave me an "F" for not showing up. I did not like the guy. He was a voice dude that was having sex with half the women in the class … a real player. I did not like him or his choir class. It did not matter much. As long as I could play piano real well I was going to get my music degree, and I did.

Hanging around music school you meet a lot of musicians. I wanted to put together a band that would play all original music and would be very progressive in nature. I met a guitar player named Garry Wood who had the same musical interest as I. Garry then ran into a fellow named Brek Bonner who was a Santana clone musically. Brek had played with a bass player named Trent Tarron, who was a Chris Squire clone. My kind of guys!

Brek and Trent called their little group "Progresso". I pulled these guys together and discussed us forming a group with all original compositions. I was not that thrilled naming the group after chicken soup. But "Progresso" to the guys meant progressive rock music. So I agreed to keep the name. We would start off writing music that was in the vein of Yes, Emerson Lake and Palmer, Genesis, etc. Everyone agreed to give it a try. So we formed the band and all moved into a band house that the drummer owned.

We would practice everyday for a couple of years. I found the music exciting and very progressive. These tunes

57

held my interest greatly. All the guys in the band were pretty cool and we all got along fairly well.

The design of the band was try and achieve something similar to what the rock band Boston had done. Just cut a killer progressive demo tape and away you go. That was the idea that most everyone shared, except me. I really thought we should be out performing and gaining as large an audience as we could. I had some success in getting these guys out of the house to play, but not that much. All they wanted was to cut the reel and not be a touring band.

One concert I booked us at was none other than my own college, Virginia Commonwealth University's Shafer Court stage. Back then this was a popular place that bands always played on Friday nights.

Well…. We thought we were the Beatles.

The crowd went nuts and we had three encores. Remember, this was a big art and music community so something like "Progresso" went over big. I was signing autographs and had ladies coming up to the stage after the show, actually wanting my phone number. It was a huge ego boost and was confirmation that our music was going to be big. For the moment, we were ROCK STARS! YEPPEEE!

I learned a lot about marketing by playing in the band. The most important thing I learned was to know your audience. Two weeks later I booked us at the University of Richmond. Now, I was setting up my racks of keyboards on stage and noticed that everyone is wearing Alligator Shirts. You remember the colored shirts with the little Alligators on them. I did not think this was a good sign. Everyone looked preppy and a fear came over me that these folks might not be into our progressive hard edge contemporary, heavy keyboard compositions with screaming lead guitars.

We fired off our first song and I remember I was very happy with how we played. We were kicking ass! At the end of our rather long intro, we came to the end of our first tune and you could hear the small drip of water in the bathroom two rooms down. 1000 people in a room full of beer and all we hear was a faint voice that said,

"Play Huey Lewis"............ "Duran Duran!" And then...

"Y'all Guys SUCK!"

We were in some serious trouble. Only into our second song and we are getting booed off the stage. There was a beer that was thrown at us and eventually we just apologized. Then we packed up and returned the money that we were paid. Next... We got outta there as fast as we could before those Alligator shirts started to bite us. While we were leaving, someone brought in a boom box that was blaring preppy Alligator music.

So one day, we are the next Beatles... The next day dog shit.

Welcome to the music business.

We all met and the guys thought that the band would alter the music to more of a three-chord guitar sound. This bored the hell out of me and just was not interested in it. Here I was holding one note for 24 measures while the guitars were playing the same three cords. There was no way I was hauling around my Hammond C-3 Organ 147 Leslie Cabinet and Profit 5 Synthesizer PLUS my ass just to play a *Flock of Seagulls*. Holding one sustained note for three minutes was not my idea of progressive keyboard playing. I had enough.

If we were not going to be playing really awesome progressive keyboard influenced music I would move on. Progresso would continue to champion chicken soup with original rock music and they bought out my share of the band. They continued to play in the band house for another year and then they disbanded, never to play as a group again.

All of the musicians were really a great bunch of guys. The drummer has remained a friend for the past 25 years. The rest of the guys moved on, married, and still play music in some capacity, a bunch of very talented musicians, regardless.

"Progresso"…a taste of the good life!

Chapter 5

Jimdini's, Pregnancy, and Soft 86

"When I think about those nights in Montreal, I get the sweetest thoughts of you and me"

~Gino Vannelli

Canada can be quite cold in January. Back in High School and College, the Ski East area of Quebec is where my ski buddies and I traveled to a lot. If I was not playing music or performing close up magic, I usually was snow skiing. Quebec Canada, is where I met my fantastic future wife of 25 years,

...Helen.

A tall very attractive brunette who was also skiing with her friends on the same bus trip our group was on. She was getting her masters in nursing and really enjoyed snow skiing.

On this trip, we started to ski together around the slopes and hung out at the lodge after our long day on the mountain.

The next day our busses loaded us up on a wintertime adventure to "The City of Mary"

...Montreal.

Helen and I were so taken with this beautiful clean snow-white city, we could hardly believe it. Canada's cultural capital of Montreal would be for evermore our favorite Canadian destination.

We walked around town and even caught a show at a theater. It was amazing! The art and architecture that surrounded us was totally magnificent. We saw the historic Notre-Dame Basilica and shopped at Bonsecours Market. For over 100 years this was Montreal's major public market and we were in awe of its history and beauty.

The both of us were mere college students in our youth. Snow skiing in the Ski East areas of Quebec Canada and hanging out in one of the greatest cities in the world… Montreal. We really were having a lovely, wonderful, romantic, experience and enjoying every minute of it.

After several more days of very enthusiastic icy down hill snow skiing, it was time for the wrap up skiing party back at the Grandbian Hotel in Quebec. The band was great but I was very tired from a week worth of skiing.

We were both whipped.

Helen and I chatted some about our ski adventures and before I knew it, I was ready to collapse. I suggested we just go up to the room and have a nightcap. When we got to the room there were several of my ski buddies hanging around, which was fine.

Quickly Helen and I both fell asleep right there on top of the covers, only to awake to a fury of…PACKING! The bus is LEAVING! Back to Richmond!!

The bus ride back from Quebec Canada was a long one maybe around 21 hours. Helen and I just cozied up together for the entire trip. It was very special. A very unique experience that was real, authentic, and very human.

We were falling in love and did not even really know it yet.

That is what made it so special.

When we returned to Richmond I remember so clearly asking my buddy and ski bum Skip Beatty, if I should get her phone number before everyone left. I saw Helen in the car leaving and Skip said,

"Jim, why not! What can it hurt?"

I took Skip's advice and ran over and got her number. Little did I know then, that she was soon to be my wife and the future mother of my two children.

It was always easy being around Helen. We were more like brother and sister. She just was easy going as hell. One of her best qualities was that she was a very even-tempered person with no emotional swings at all. Helen was just an extremely balanced, beautiful and intelligent lady. Everyone got along with her just fine. She was never the "life" of the party but did enjoy a good time. Helen was always interested in doing things in the outdoors. Dating through college was quite fun and Hellen and I went snow skiing all the time. We were always traveling looking for some nice slopes.

After we both graduated we just sort of, well, lack of a better phrase, did not know what to do. College is over and I was now 24 years old. There was no pressure at all to get married and neither one of us talked about it. I just did not know what else to do. It just seemed the time was right to get married. Helen was a great gal who was easy as heck to get along with and I loved her.

...So I asked and she said yes.

We got married near my dad's house on the Rappahannock River in an old historic church. The reception was held on the water back at the house. The Judge had since divorced the Bitch From Hell and was living mostly at the river house he had built. Dad also was then dating the sweetest lady named Cynthia. Finally Pops was with a woman with no mental illness or personality disorders. In fact she was a gift from God.

She was one of the most wonderful gracious and intelligent ladies in the world. It was with Cynthia he would find his happiness. She was a great lady. It seemed to me that the old Magnolia tree was starting to show some grace to the Judge. It was about time!

I remember we catered our wedding reception ourselves. We had the idea for everyone to bring "A covered dish" and we would provide the bar, bushels of steamed Chesapeake Bay Blue Crabs and fresh roasted Rappahannock oysters on the half shell. The open bar was well used of course and everything was served up waterside. My friend who worked at Bowery Organ Studios performed the music. Nell was quite the keyboard player and loved to play dance music with Caribbean rhythms.

I met Nell during a brief job stint I had selling Bowery Organs in the Legency Square Shopping Mall. Nell was the number one salesman and everybody loved the guy. The other salesperson was a beautiful African American woman named LuTina.

LuTina believe it or not, was a prostitute that used the organ store as a cover and a place to find Johns. She was really a character for sure. All I did was sit around and play the pianos and organs and watch LuTina pick up Johns.

The other thing we did at the organ store was drink. We used to all frequently get loaded on a gin mixture and go to lunch at Chinese restaurants and drink zombies. Then we would return and crank up the organs full blast and party like hell. I never sold many organs working there. But hey! This was another place I could play a great piano for free and not worry about getting kicked off.

At the wedding, Nell was a big hit and the people there thought the reception was fantastic. We had beer, booze, crabs, oysters, smoked salmon, and a dude playing Caribbean dance music on a portable Bowery Organ, drinking rum. What fun! And it was!

After the wedding, Helen and I honeymooned on the Eastern Shore for a week during the Pony Penning. This event began with the early settlers of the Eastern Shore of Virginia, who used both Chincoteague and Assateague Islands as grazing grounds for the ponies. Watching the animals swim from one island to the next is a huge tradition that is close to the hearts of thousands of Virginians.

To see the ponies swim, it is an early call. Helen and I were out at the break of dawn, watching the horses swim vigorously as the sun rose behind them. Once the Ponies are all hearded up on land then the auction begins. This all- day auction event was a big crowed pleaser and lots of vendors were selling everything from fresh soft-shell crabs to oyster and clam fritters. We loved it.

The hotel we stayed in was this little place across the street from the Oyster Museum. I thought, an Oyster Museum? Just what kind of place are we staying at anyway? We had one fantastic honeymoon that was rich in tradition, history, and fantastic scenery on Virginia's Atlantic coast. Believe it or not our entire honeymoon cost about $500 bucks.

Times sure have changed. Once back from our honeymoon we decided instead of renting we would build our first house together in Chesterfield. Within 30 days the three bedroom cape cod was built and within a month, Helen was pregnant with our first child whom we named *Ben Baugh*.

Now, things were changing just a little fast for me. One minute I am snow skiing in Canada, playing in rock bands, performing close up magic and the next minute, I am married with a house and a child on the way. I remember thinking that I have really gotten far away from "A" Dock. A place I never intended or wanted to leave.

It was time for me to grow up and get a real job. We both needed steady incomes to raise the family and my only income was performing magic tricks.

Well, my idea of a real job was to open up my own close up magic bar in downtown Richmond Virginia. I had the idea from a place in Washington, DC called *Brookfarm Inn of Magic*. Brookfarm was a dinner theater that featured close up magic in the bar area and a full comedy magic show in the main dining hall.

Steve Spill and Bob Sheets were the main acts and they were fantastic. These two were a true comedy pair that the audience just loved. No one else could get 15 minutes of laughter from an audience by using one roll of toilet paper and a catcher's mitt.

I became friends with Steve when he saw me perform at a close up magic convention. I was doing some of the card manipulations that Woody had taught me and Steve loved them. He used to invite me up to DC for the weekend to work on magic and hang out at the close up bar. I met a lot of great and popular close up guys there including John Kennedy, inventor of the floating dollar bill and man other world famous close up illusions.

My idea was to open up something similar to the close up magic bar section at Brookfarm, however do it in Richmond Virginia. I was house magician at the *2001 Supper Club* and pitched the idea there. However, it did not fly. Then I came across the old comedy club next to the *Tobacco Company* in Shockoe Slip. The location was under *Mat's British Pub* and they were looking for someone to fill the old comedy club space. That someone turned out to be me.

I opened up *Jimdini's Close Up Magic Bar* and immediately began to book the close up magic talent and all other street type entertainment I could find. Woody Sanders back then was a regular and I was honored to have him perform.

I would book a lot of street performing acts that I worked with at Busch Gardens. Jugglers were a popular act to book in my club. People always loved comedy-juggling acts. One night I booked this guy who juggled a live ferret, a cat, and a crawfish. I told him he was juggling the F.C.C.

The only money that I made was whatever cover charge I collected at the door. All the food and beverage sales went to the owner upstairs. This took some kahoonas, I had no upfront money and the only dollar I saw was the people who would come to the club and watch us perform. That was it. I would show up to work at 5 pm and get home at 5 am.

Sunday through Tuesday hardly anyone showed up at the door. Wednesday through Saturday it would be hit or miss. Sometimes we would have a line out the door other times only a few people. It was very hard to predict if at the end of the night, I would have any money to take home.

This was a time when my wife was pregnant with our first child and she was a nurse during the day, and I was at *Jimdini's* all night. This close up magic bar career obviously was not going to last.

Fortunately we had a flood some nine months after we opened and *Jimdini's*, for the most part, destroyed the interior of our little magic bar. I decided it was a gift from the Magnolia Tree. There was no way I could continue this path.

I remember thinking clearly that I had done what I wanted to do for a long time, open up a close up magic bar. Not a lot of people have done this, because it is a fairly specialized type of entertainment. I did it, was glad I did, and glad it was over. It was one of those things that had I not done in life, I would have regretted it. However the restaurant nightclub business was not to be for me and I was happy about that.

I did a mix of jobs at that point. The one where I made the most money was selling car stereos. This was back in the day when car stereo equipment was on the rise and cell phones had just barley come into the market. Our store was the first store to have a cell phone available to sell. I was an Alpine cell phone and the sticker price was over $3000.00 and there was not even cell service available yet. Wow have things changed! This is no joke; I could sell car audio equipment like no one else. It was as easy as selling heaters to an Eskimo or diesel to a truck driver. The money was good back then too.

What I did was to take what I learned from trying to sell Bowery Organs and applied it to selling car stereos and it worked. We would have "Spiff" sheets that were a list of products that if we sold it, we would get extra money called a "Spiff". We also had qualifying points in sales, in order to qualify for the spiffs at the end of the week.

Once I got in there and started selling, they had to change the entire Spiff program because I oversold everything including the qualifiers. For example a guy would come into the store with cash in hand, ready to buy his set of speakers. By the time I got through with him, he left the store with an amplifier that was on the spiff sheet. If it was not on the Spiff sheet, I was not going to sell it.

This became a bit of a joke to the owners and manager, because I would design complete systems based on what money I would make. I figured if they did not want me to sell a certain product, it would not be on the Spiff sheet.

I may not have sold many organs back at the Bowery Organ store but the sales techniques I learned from the regional manager there proved to be quite valuable. What I learned was that in sales, you need to be several steps ahead of the customer mentally and be prepared to overcome any objection. In a way this was very similar to how I would entertain with close up magic. All of this was a fantastic training ground for what would turn out to be a fairly long television career.

Never will I forget the owner of the stereo store. He loved the fact that I oversold the spiff sheet. His name was Dean Yemen and he was also a real character. Dean only drove Jaguars and had four Labrador Retrievers he carried with him everywhere he went.

Four Labs and a Jag, Dean was a happy camper. He was a very hands-on owner and manager who took no shit off anyone… especially his employees. One day I was ordered to clean the men's bathroom because the sales floor had gotten rather slow with no real customer traffic. I took it as a challenge to show them what cleaning a toilet meant. Never before had that bathroom been as clean.

The manager showed the other sales associates my work and told everyone that when it was their turn to clean the bathroom… it had to look like this. Interesting thing was they never asked me to clean the toilet again. I got the feeling that the owners would push me and other employees sometimes in a negative way just to see what response they would get.

One day after work, Dean brought down a bottle of booze to the showroom floor and mixed a cocktail. He said,

"Jim how in the hell do you sell so much off the Spiff sheet? No one else turns sales around like that." I said,

"It is all what I learned from the sales manager back at the organ store. He taught me to overcome any objection relating to the product." Dean said,

"Give me an example JB."

"Ok Dean, a guy walks into our stereo store with cash in hand to buy the speakers he desperately wants and I ask him,

'Hi there, I see you got your money for those speakers! Why don't we go over to the display and listen to them one more time before you buy! They are some GREAT speakers, dude!'

Then, I would walk the guy over to our working display and play them through the same amp I knew he had in his car. The speakers he wanted to purchase were also on working display and so I fired up the CD player. MUSIC! Rock and Roll! Sounds good right?

Next, I would switch amps while the music was playing and,

………… WWWOOOOOOWWWW!! The music was twice as loud, more clear, and lots more bass. The customer would then say,

"Wow Jim, what did you do?"

I said, "Oh I just switched the amps on the display board using these same speakers you wanted to buy. You see the trick is to start at the heart of the system first… the amp. This one is the best made."

"Really!?!?"

The customer would look at me a little confused.

"I did not know that." I said,

"Oh, let me check… Guess what? That amp is on sale for our one-day sale. With the money you save on the amp, you can put down a deposit on the speakers for layaway for next month." He said,

"Let's do it!! I sure am glad I bumped into you today Jim. Write me up for that amp now!"

You see, the amp was on the Spiff sheet. The speakers were not. The speakers WOULD be on the sheet for the next month, so I would get the Spiff commission on that as well 30 days later.

Dean laughed and just said, "Keep it up Jim. Good work!"

I sometimes got a little carried away and would get customers so wound up and confused they would leave the store with what I sold them and not know what they had wanted. This would happen sometimes and they would later return some items. What did I care? I had a baby on the way and was trying to sell everything I could to make every penny I could.

Selling car stereos is where I learned to be respectful to everyone no matter how they treat you. Keep my mouth shut and make as much money as I can. I did not care about being humiliated at times by over-stressed managers as long as my check cleared. That became key for me, just getting paid. My wife Helen was not getting any smaller, and soon Ben Baugh would be arriving.

In time the commissions continued to decrease and I was not interested in making car audio a career, so I left the store. I remember Dean telling me very nicely this:

"Jim if you EVER need a job for any reason just come back here. I will put you back to work the second you walk in the door."

I actually felt a certain comfort in that and I did take him up on his offer once more a couple years later when times got tight economically. Back then those were the days you could walk into a store talk to the manager and be working that afternoon. Try that in today's world. You have to take a drug test, physiological test, five interviews and then wait for two months for a call that says maybe they will hire you part time for minimum wage on the overnight shift.

Boy things have changed.

Not having a clue what to do next. I don't even remember how I got the idea about selling radio advertising. Here I was a musician, magician that sold car stereos. Somehow, I got the idea of selling radio ads. At the time it seemed like an actual professional sales job and I had to do something. The wonderful wife was getting bigger everyday.

Interviewing with several radio stations in Richmond was not a fun task because I hated the music they played. Eventually, I interviewed with a station called *Soft 86*, which was a station that played elevator music. They also had a jazz show on Sunday nights that I did like. The general manager for some reason gave me the opportunity to sell for them starting on a draw based on commissions.

My territory was the Tri-City area that was bringing in zero revenue for the station. My job was to establish the area and bring in all new revenue to *Soft 86*.

When you are selling radio or TV, you meet a LOT of people and are making new contacts everyday. I had some success in selling radio however there just were no new accounts that were big money coming through my territory. The Tri-City area I always felt, was a bit

71

depressed. To get any sales out of this area, I thought was a pretty good accomplishment.

The sales manager at the station always wanted more sales. This was the nature of ad sales. I sold for two years there, met a boatload of people and established a territory that had not been there before. I believed this road was going to be ending soon because there was just no more growth in sales to be had.

The water had all been squeezed out of this turnip and there just simply was not any more additional business coming. What I did not know was that *Soft 86* would lead me to the job that soon would become what helped launch Jim Baugh Outdoors TV. It was time to bail from the radio station. Move on, and try to find something else… But first!

Driving to the hospital was an experience I will never forget. My mind had more endorphins pumping through it than Arnold Schwartzinager pumping iron in competition. Never in my life until this point had I been so excited.

It is a good thing that pregnancy lasts as long as it does to help prepare everyone. I knew it was coming but when it is time, hell I just could not believe it! Here I was a magician, car stereo salesman and past radio sales associate getting ready to help deliver my first child. Just nuts! Man, I had better find a job fast and my butt is a LOOONG way from "A" dock now.

The Dr. that delivered Ben Baugh was a real comedian and I of course had a rather large sense of humor as well. The entire time Helen was in delivery we were cracking the worst jokes you ever heard. It was relentless. Just one baby joke after another. I think Helen will never forget when I said,

"Hey Doctor! I'll take some onions with that placenta!"

Helen was a real baby factory.... that is once she got the epidural. She did a great job and when Ben Baugh was at rest in Helen's arms I then cut the umbilical cord. The boy was here and Helen had pulled through fine. For that moment the single most excited time in my life, and would only be repeated one other time later with the birth of my beautiful daughter Casey.

Helen and I got home from the hospital with Ben Baugh in this little tiny baby cradle that simply was a cradle with a handle on it. You could just park it and sit Ben wherever and he was safe in his little cradle. We walked into our new house that was recently built and sat Ben and his cradle down on the floor in the living room. Helen and I looked around the room with no furniture because we had no money. We had nothing in the house except one mattress on the floor in the back bedroom. We did not even have enough money to finish the upstairs bedroom.

Here we were both looking down at Ben, this newborn baby sitting on the floor of this empty house. Helen and I started laughing because we had NO idea what to do. Not a clue. It was funny and very scary at the same time. All of the sudden we were responsible for...

This thing on our floor called *Baby Ben Baugh!* Wow, I had better find my new job fast!

Jim Baugh with guest Robert Goulet circa 1988 on Talk TV cable television, "The Jim Baugh Show" just prior to Jim producing the Fishing Virginia Television Series.

Chapter 6

Talk TV and The Hook and Line

"I fish better with a lit cigar, some people fish better with talent."

~Nick Lyons

I had met a lot of people during my time selling radio and met the general manager of Talk TV through a mutual friend. The word on the street was that Talk TV was looking for a new general manager to produce the nightly live call in talk shows and bring in new business. This I thought was an ideal position for me and actually would pay me a salary, something I desperately needed at that time.

Meeting with the owner of Talk TV was quite an experience and one I will never forget. His name was Ned Virel and this man was the quintessential salesman who was a big believer in Talk TV. I respected Ned a lot and he was the kind of guy you just liked. Ned was very sure of himself and of Talk TV. He felt that there was not a client that could not truly benefit in big ways from his cable network. His was right in many ways.

Talk TV was a local feed from three cable stations that produced its own live television programming. It was sort of like talk radio but on TV. For example, we would produce a car stereo show where the representatives of the store would come on air and answer questions live about various products and installations. It really was a good idea and worked very well for certain types of business. Ned and his wife offered me the GM position and I went to work immediately. Thank you Ned! Baby Ben thanks you too!

Stress was a big factor for me with this job. The reason is I would work all day selling various shows, then the on air live broadcast would start at 7pm and I would have to manage that as well. Everything was live so being on your toes was a must even after working all day.

I also hosted my own live entertainment show on Talk TV called the *Jim Baugh Show*. Since my background was in magic and entertainment I thought I could make a buck or two selling airtime within this local live show. Surprised is how I felt many times when I would actually get some rather large stars to appear on my little cable show. It felt like *Wayne's World* but with a coat and tie instead of tee shirts.

One of my contacts that I had met selling radio was the manager at The Mosque, which was where a lot of the big name concerts and plays were held. So I sort of had an inside connection as to who was approachable and who was not, star wise.

Believe it or not I had a lot of celebrities on this little show, including Robert Goulet, James "Scotty" Doohan, Paula Poundstone, and Emo Phillips. I always had musical guests such as Page Wilson and loads of magicians and comedians. It was a good time on live TV and gave me a LOT of experience in front of a camera.

Not all of the airtime slots were sold during the evening and the station had a policy of only airing live programming. So what we did with unsold airtime was to do a show called *Marketplace*. This is where a guest and I would sit behind a table in front of two microphones and ask viewers live on air if they have anything they would like to sell. It was a live TV classifieds show that actually had a big audience.

Before I started at Talk TV Ned had shown me tapes of the Marketplace filler show and it really looked pretty boring. Ned asked if I could do anything to liven it up and of course, I had plenty of ideas!

Usually I would ask one of my best childhood friends Bobby Thoms, to come fill in and sit with me on the Marketplace show. Bob had a lot of experience as a stand up comic and I never had a shortage of jokes. The Marketplace filler show became a vehicle for the *Jim and Bob Comedy Hour*. Everything was improvised and we did some really crazy stuff.

Once I learned what a "Key" was in television, (like the local weatherman with the map behind him) I had the great idea to have some interesting footage rolling behind Bob and me while we were doing our live Marketplace show. My favorite was footage of seagulls flying behind us during a nice sunset scene. Then one of the stagehands would drop what looked like bird pooh down from the ceiling above us. It was sort of a 3D bird shit effect that really made the phones light up.

"Bob! Did you see that bird shit on you?" And it went downhill from there.

Our craziness got me in a bit of trouble. Someone called in and I made a 'gay' joke reference about someone I knew. This guy then sued me for a million dollars. It was a farce, but not funny at the time. My father the Judge was really pissed at me and my wife was furious. Everyone was mad as hell at me and my attorney asked to see the tape of the show where I made this reference.

We were in my attorney's office and the attorney and my dad put in the tape of the Marketplace. Again, the Judge was very upset that I had gotten in this trouble and the lawyer said it could cost me a ton of money to get out of this... money I did not have. I sat there in the conference room scared to death at what I was about to look at. The Judge had the most serious skrouling look on his face I ever saw. The tape went in and started to play.

Within minutes both Dad and my lawyer were laughing their asses off. They could not stop laughing and said it was one of the funniest things they ever saw and did not feel at all this would ever go to court. I had said on air that it was only a joke and Bob and I were clearly doing a comedy show.

I settled out of court for less than the cost of court and attorney fees and that was the last time I would ever make an inappropriate reference on television again. When I delivered the check to the other attorney who was trying to prosecute me, I asked him why would he take on a case that obviously was frivolous and would never make it to trial.

He said, "I owed his parents a favor, so I sued you."

For me it was an important lesson and a good one to learn before I went any further in my television career.

Because I was missing my 'Life on the Docks' early childhood, fishing shows became something that I lived for. I would watch them all and then go to the video store and rent every fishing tape I could find. In some way this was relaxing to me and also gave me the idea to produce a live call in fishing talk show on Talk TV.

I hit the streets in an effort to find a good host for the show and a sponsor as well. First up, was to get the sponsor and luckily came across Lester Marine in Petersburg. I had called on them back when I sold radio and was hoping the manager Moe Dudley would like my idea. Moe did like what he heard and next, was to hire the hosts of the live fishing show. We found a brother and sister named Mark and Melanie Lure that seemed to be a good choice.

I did not know the local bass-fishing scene at all back then. Mark and Melanie were a fishing team that seemed to have some recognition in the area. They seemed like a good pair to host, so I hired them.

Little did I know that there was some controversy about the two cheating in some bass tournament. The upshot was these two were going to really get the airwaves going with LOTS of calls, and they sure did.

Probably the most successful show we aired was the *Hook and Line Fishing Show* and it usually was a riot to watch. Many times they would bring in coolers filled with live bass and show them on the air. The problem was they were often too drunk and could not hold on to the fish. Yes, drinking on the set was common practice in the studio back then. At least on this show those coffee cups were not full of java that's for sure.

One time, Mark was trying to feature a fishing lure. But he could not hold it up, the bait kept falling out of his hands because he was so loaded. We would go in for a close up on a spinner bait then… BAM! It would disappear out of camera view because he had dropped it again.

"Wide shot, go to wide shot…..Cut to commercial now!"

We all had hoped that he was not going to try and hold up his four-pound small mouth that was in his fresh water filled cooler. This was live TV and anything could happen. We did not even have a delay on the broadcast. Whatever happened spilled out into the airwaves in real time.

It did not take long before Mark went to grab the fish. That lasted about three seconds because the fish jumped out of the cooler and Mark desperately tried to catch the fish flapping on the studio floor.

Remember this guy was drunk off his ass. He could hardly stand up much less hold up a bait or handle a live slimy thrashing fish. In the process of trying to catch the fish on the set, Mark in his drunken state knocks over the *Hook and Line* TV set and it goes crashing down.

"Station break! Station break! Cut to commercial! Somebody pick that flapping fish up off the floor and pour Mark back up in his chair!"

This actually happened on a fairly regular basis and we could not control them at all. In a way it was good, because the viewers would tune in just to see what these two folks were going to do next. It made for some funny and a little controversial live television.

Before long the station was sold and I was to be replaced by the new management team. Talk TV went on for a few more years and then closed its doors.

My first thought when the station was sold was to produce a fishing show. The *Hook and Line* had been so popular, I just imagined that producing a broadcast version to feature Virginia locations would be a great idea. So I gave myself 90 days to come up with enough sponsors to produce a show concept called *Fishing Virginia.* This would be Virginia's first commercial production for television that featured Virginia guides, captains, and area fishing locations and travel destinations.

Fishing Virginia would soon become a syndicated TV hit state wide.

Chapter 7

Time for Two

"If one feels the need of something grand, something infinite, something that makes one feel aware of God, one need not go far to find it. I think that I see something deeper, more infinite, more eternal than the ocean in the expression of the eyes of a little baby when it wakes in the morning and coos or laughs because it sees the sun shining on its cradle".

~Vincent van Gogh

The same time my stint at Talk TV was ending, Helen was about to give birth to our second child. A beautiful little angel we named Casey Lee Baugh. This would be my second and last child. Both Ben and Casey would later appear on our outdoor television show for the next 20 years.

Things are not always easy, like naming our daughter. Helen and I could not agree on a name. This may have been our only real argument in 25 years.

I LOVED the name Casey and wanted the name Lee in her name after her grandmother, Naner Lee. Helen had a close friend named Casey and did not want to name her daughter Casey also, so she was never in favor of it. Pretty much, I thought that idea was lame because Helen's friend Casey Farlow was an awesome and beautiful lady.

Soon, Casey was born, and she was born with no name.

During birth, I believe I did more than the doctor. After all I had been down this road once before and I was ready. At this exciting time I did cut the cord again for my second child and then went to work on Helen for the name. Finally, I won. She agreed to the name Casey and she was glad she did.

No other name would have captured her sweetness… She was a Casey!

Casey screamed for six months every night until Helen would hold and feed her. My baby daughter did settle down after six months however it sure made for a lot of sleepless nights. She was worth it of course.

Both of my kids had very funny personalities even at a young age. When Casey was just a toddler, she was in the back seat with Ben and we were going through a McDonalds to get them a couple of Happy Meals. Back then Ben lived off of fish sticks and chicken nuggets. That is all the kid ate. On this trip in the drive through, Ben and Casey both ordered the chicken nuggets and we pulled out of McDonalds, flying down the road trying to get back home.

A small, little, sad voice said in the back seat, "Dad… I got cheeseburger."

I said, "Awe Sweeeeeetheart, it will be ok. Try it, you will love it! Baby, I can't turn around now. We need to get home. It is getting late."

"Daddy… no toy in box."

Once again, "Awwwwwwwwe, Baby, I am sorry. We will get you a nice toy later and you can share Ben's Happy Meal Toy."

Casey then said in the saddest and quaking little disturbed voice,

"Dad…. This is not a very Happy Meal."

Helen and I laughed for about an hour. Casey fell asleep quickly and did eat some of her cheeseburger.

Kids grow very, very, very fast.

Now when Ben was a teenager he just loved the practical joke. When he was in high school Ben had the bright idea at Halloween to dress up like a tampon. He would knock on the neighbor's door and say,

"Trick or Treat."

"……What are you boy?"

82

"I am a Tampon."

".....You're kidding; well here is some candy kid."

"Thanks, see ya next month!"

I got in trouble for this one.

Helen was mad at me when I got home and she said, "Ben is in big trouble and we are getting complaint calls from all over the neighborhood! I want YOU to do something about it. What are you going to do Jim!?!"

I was worried. I figured my perfect boy has finally gone down the dark path of drugs or alcohol and that this is only the beginning. I was getting stressed. I asked Helen, "Ok. What has he gotten into?"

Helen said loudly, "He dressed up as a tampon, asking for candy then telling them...See ya next month!"

When I saw Ben I told him that was not appropriate, but funny as hell. Helen never quite saw the humor in that one. I think it was a guy thing.

I was very lucky that both my kids were pretty much as close to perfect children as you could get. Always, I wanted four kids but with two awesome children and the amount of time it took to raise them and try to run a business, we decided not to have any more and just concentrate on the two.

It was a wise decision.

A little bit of a compromise would soon occur. Instead of not having more children we did have Tina Turner. The new addition to the family and our soon to be TV show mascot, was one awesomely hyper chocolate lab we named *Tina Turner Baugh*. I took Ben and Casey to pick Tina out of a litter when she was just a newborn pup. We made a great selection. Tina was an awesome dog and has traveled all across the country. Best dog in the world.

At times I would get in trouble with the neighbors over Tina. Helen would get upset about Tina's love for the newspaper. Tina was a fantastic and very smart retriever. In the mornings, I would open the front door and say,

83

"Tina... Go fetch the paper!"

Off she would run and by the time I poured my first cup of hot coffee, Tina would come running into the kitchen and drop the paper by my feet.

In time, it turns out, that Helen was getting phone calls from the neighbors,

"Your damn dog is stealing my paper!"

Tina was getting a little bored just going to our driveway, so she was venturing out further. At the time, I did not believe it.

A couple weeks later, Tina fetched the paper and brought it to me, dropping it in my lap.

It was the *New York Times*.

That is when I knew Tina was having a little too much fun. I looked at Tina and said, "I don't think you ran to New York. Take it back. Let's go!"

Tina would walk out the front door return the paper and on the way back pick up our paper in the driveway. What a dog!

Once, I was asked in an interview, what was the best accomplishment I have ever had in my life. Without any hesitation I answered, "Ben and Casey of course, well, and Tina. How can I ever do better than that!"

The old Magnolia Tree had given me the peace and assurance of two healthy children and a sound, stable wife and mother. I had gotten what I had asked for. My kids were never going to live through the trauma like I did during early childhood. The only sound my children would hear around their home was the sound of peace and Tina chasing squirrels.

My kids would continue to grow and prosper. Casey received her bachelor's degree and Ben received his Masters in geology spending a lot of time in the Pacific North West and eventually Denver. I could not have been more proud of them.

Back then with the growing family, it was time to get very busy producing Fishing Virginia. Now I had two kids, a wife, and Tina Turner the New York Times fetching Lab. The pressure was on.

Filming location on the spillway of Fairy Stone State Park in Virginia circa 1993

Chapter 8

Lights, Camera, Action!

"Mickey Mouse popped out of my mind onto a drawing pad 20 years ago on a train ride from Manhattan to Hollywood at a time when business fortunes of my brother Roy and myself were at lowest ebb and disaster seemed right around the corner."

~Walt Disney

There was a lot to do in setting up a new TV show for broadcast. One of which is negotiating airtime with a TV station. This was not my favorite thing to do by any stretch of the means. I had many calls and appointments with sales managers regarding the cost of airtime slots to broadcast, contracts, etc. Airtime for a new show was going to be expensive and we were just starting out. Fortunately my good friend Moe Dudley at Lester Marine had signed on to be our first sponsor for the show.

When I met with the sales manager for one particular affiliate, I felt very comfortable with our meeting. She was a close friend with the national sales manager at *Soft 86* radio, whom I knew very well. During the meeting she told me she had to know the content and advertisers before she could even discuss broadcasting the show. She said that she would have to make sure there was no conflict with her station or on-air advertisers.

I did not like at all the fact that I was going to have to let the cat out of the bag and tell her my idea, in fear that she or anyone could steal it before I had a chance to produce the show. Well, in fear that I did not have any other choice, I proceeded to tell her what I was up to and she said that was fine.

The TV biz, as I found out early in the game is a real snake business. You can't trust anybody. Moe at Lester

Marine and I were becoming good friends and he was kind enough to call me one day.

"Jim, I am sitting here in my office and I just got a phone call from Channel 3, wondering if I would be interested in sponsoring their new fishing show."

I said, "You have got to be kiddin' me! This is a joke, right?" The sales manager at Channel 3 was already trying to steal my idea and potential sponsor, produce the fishing show in house and cut me out of what I was trying to produce.

I had this idea to really set up the TV station.... And I did! I suggested to Moe to go ahead and set up the meeting with the station, and let me sit in on the meeting. We would just tell them I was with BASS and was acting as an advisor to my old friend, Moe. They bought it and I was in the meeting.

The station had sent a salesman to Moe's office and there I was, having a cup of coffee just dying to hear the bullshit that was going to come flying out of this guy's mouth. He proceeded to sell Moe on this fishing show that the station ITSELF was producing. Moe asks.

"What was the name of the show?"

"..........We don't have the information yet, regarding the name."

Then I ask, "Where is the show going to be filmed and who is going to edit and produce it?"

"..........We don't have the information yet, however I can tell you it is going to be produced in house by Channel 3."

I did not really need to hear anymore and Moe was done with the guy, so we sent him on his way. To this day, that salesman never knew who I was, nor that the meeting was a set up.

The station had tried to steal the *Fishing Virginia* TV show right from under me, without thinking about it twice. I never complained or spoke to the station manager again. I just never did business with her and soon contracted with the Fox affiliate in Richmond who was their competitor. Funny thing, this station manager at Channel 3 later was hired by Talk TV to manage it… just before Talk TV fired everyone and closed its doors for good. There is justice after all.

Many production meetings later, with many film companies, we finally had an agreement with Sark Teleproductions to sub-contract them and their equipment in order to produce our show. The Judge set me up as a corporation and called it *Jim Baugh Productions, Inc.*

I was now self-employed with a new family at home, trying to produce *Fishing Virginia* and was in charge of the production, broadcast, and the sponsors. I started off wearing a lot of hats, only to find out by the time it was all said and done, I would wear many, many more hats.

One thing we needed was a show host. We wanted someone who was a local fisherman who could relate to our viewing audience and appear authentic. We wanted someone who could also help us book guides on the show. My role as producer was to handle all aspects of the program. Not once did I ever consider hosting the show during this time.

To aid in the format, I did appear in the producer's note segment at the end of the show where I would feature cooking or travel tips. In our search for a show host we came across a fisherman named Gill Fisch. We met with Gill, liked the fellow and thought he would do a good job. A retired policeman who was not really that good in front of the camera, but he was a respected fisherman, who came off as a 'Real' angler. Gill was easy to work with and being host of the show of course, helped his guide buiz and bait company which was fine with us.

Gill Fisch was good friends with lots of popular B.A.S.S. fisherman. Some of the more famous B.A.S.S anglers would appear on Fishing Virginia which was also good for the show. Unfortunately, the show was driven by advertisement and after the first season, we no longer could afford to pay Gill, we had to make cuts.

The Judge and I had to make a decision either to end the show or continue on with me as the host. That was very hard to decide because I had no interest in hosting the show... None! Producing it was fine with me and I wanted nothing else to do with any additional on-air segments where I would appear.

The Judge sat me down and gave me some good advice. He said,

"Jim you will never go anywhere in this TV Business unless you build your name. That is where your success and value will lie."

It was hard advice to listen to because I did not want to do it. Realizing that I did not have any choice, I decided I would take a stab at hosting the show. My fear was that I was not a professional fisherman. I was just a young television producer, that could play piano, crack jokes, and do magic tricks.

What did I know about hosting a fishing show?
...Nothing.

Since my only choice was to either host the show or go back to selling radio advertisement or car stereos, I chose to reluctantly get in front of the camera. We also changed the name of the show to, *Jim Baugh Outdoors TV*. Changing the name also made it easier to syndicate outside of the state of Virginia, because as we soon found out neighboring Carolina stations were not going to broadcast a show named *Fishing Virginia*.

So, two things happened. I was now hosting the show, *Fishing Virginia* was gone and *Jim Baugh Outdoors TV* was what the show would be called. The Judge was right. Self-promotion was the only way I was going to make it in this business and no one else was going to do it for me.

Since the first time I hosted the show, I did not want to come off like I was a professional fisherman. Mostly I thought it would be best to just carry the show and feature other captains and guides. Put the spotlight on them and let me keep the show moving and entertaining. This also kept the program honest. I was not trying to sell myself as something that I was not.

This format worked well and our ratings soared. It is a format that I kept for the entire life of the show, over 25 years. Because of my background in television and entertainment, it was easy for me to crack a joke on air and keep everything alive and fresh. It just worked. Also, everyone else on TV was trying to sell some bass lure available at Wal-Mart, while I was just putting on an entertaining and informative program. *Jim Baugh Outdoors* was a rather soft sell when it came to sponsors' product, but that kept it more real and enjoyable to watch, which meant better ratings.

When the Judge and I told Gill Fisch that we could no longer afford to pay a host, we asked him if he ever wanted to donate his time and do a show, he was always welcome. We paid him in full and there just was no money left. No new sponsors were coming on board. Hell, this was just wrapping up our first season. Gill seemed very polite during the meeting and we were all fine with it. He seemed to understand what was happening and I thought he actually was very professional.

Later that year at a trade show I found out that Gill had been bad-mouthing the Judge and me, saying some pretty horrible things. To this day I never understood why and could not believe it at first. Gill Fisch would never appear on any of our productions again, which was unfortunate because I always liked the guy.

Filming with a production company on our tight budget, meant that we needed to film two shows per day.

Most of what we were filming those early years was freshwater shows which made it easy to stage release shots.

We would go to an area and film catching bass, crappie, walleye, and get whatever we could get, live on camera and often times for photo reasons have to stage the release of the fish. This was good, because we could get clear and close up film of the fish being released in the water. Promoting catch and release especially in freshwater was always important to us. We were filming on usually two boats and position and lighting would change constantly. It was next to impossible to get everything in one take and have it look right. Half the time once a fish was caught, the boat would have drifted with the tide and the fish was now in the shade.

"Cut, reposition the boats and lets get back in the sunlight."

I used to yell that all the time. When you're in the shade and the video scene is high contrast, it is next to impossible to see the fish. Full sunlight is what we needed to film and we did not always have it.

Things were always a bit hectic, trying to get the right shots and get enough film in for two shows in one day. I had to shoot this way until we could afford to purchase our own equipment and spend more time in the field.

There were those days on some lakes with full sun, where we would be anchored up just catching crappie, one right after another. I used to thank God for those days because it almost made filming seem easy. Most of the time, it was a bear to get the footage and back then we had to carry a lot of heavy and expensive production gear to get the quality we wanted.

For the most part in our early production, we were on the clock all the time. A very beautiful lake called, *Lake Moo Maw* in Virginia, was a place that I thought would make for a fantastic show. The problem was it was far away from Richmond and just getting there and back was going to kill a lot of the day. There was no budget for hotel rooms and additional travel expense, so I had to do a lot of research to see if we could even pull this off.

There was a great little tackle shop located before you got to the lake. I had talked on the phone with them at great length, about working with fisherman up there to get us on fish fast. We could not afford to waste all our time and money and get a 'No Show'. Always, we would have to get something shot that could be produced and aired.

The lady on the phone told me that if it would help, they had this pet bass in their aquarium and that we could use it and photograph it. I started laughing on the phone and then realized that it may be a good idea, in case we get busted with no fish, I would have to film something even if it just was B roll of a fish swimming around.

So sure enough, this is what we did. We pulled up to the tackle shop with our bass boat and filled the livewell with water. Next up we went inside and got this fantastic bass out of the aquarium and put it in our livewell on the boat. This was not something we thought we would use, but had it as a back up for B roll just in case.

When we got to the lake, I told our guide I had this fish as a back up to shoot some B roll in case we got skunked all day. I explained we may do an interview with him and while talking we could edit in some footage of this fish swimming around some sunken trees or something. He thought that was fine. No Problem.

The fishing SUCKED! We caught nothing on camera except some very small bass that were not going to make an entire show at all. So by the end of the day, I took the fish out of the livewell and put a safety line on him. Let him swim around some trees and put the fish in different settings. The bass seemed to be happy as hell, being back in the lake and we got some useful B roll that we could use for instructional purposes during an interview.

I put the pet fish back in the boat and left the lake. We stopped by the tackle shop and returned the bass to its aquarium and thanked the folks so much for letting us take pictures of their pet fish. The fact is, we could have just filmed the fish in the aquarium, but having the fish around some trees underwater looked much better. We all thought it was rather funny and actually the show turned out pretty good. The scenery was just so awesome up there.

Filming two shows in a day was not at all the most optimum way to produce the show, but it did give us our start. I soon realized that getting our own studio and field equipment was a must. The problem was the expense. $30,000 for a camera, $40,000 for an editing deck and that was only the beginning. We needed several decks, switchers, effects, monitors and the list went on and on. These were the days way before computer non linear inexpensive editing solutions.

One day, we were at a company called Southwest and we had just purchased our Beta SP Camera from them. $30,000 bucks was a lot for a camera, I thought. The excitement of having our own camera and we could actually film by ourselves, without another production company was just an awesome feeling. We could now have the ability to take all the time in the field we wanted and it made a big difference in the quality of our show. This also allowed us to produce for other companies that generated for us some extra revenue.

The excitement of owning our new camera did not last long because when I got back to our office I went to plug it in, there was no cord. Thinking to myself, "Why did he not put the cord in here for the camera? It is a new camera maybe he just forgot?" The phone call went like this.

"Hey John, Jim here, how's it going?"
"….Fine, JB."

"Look, I think you forgot to put the power cord in here with the camera, I can't find it at all."

"….Oh, you want to plug it into the wall?"

"AHHHHH, Yes, is that a problem?"

"….Well Jim I sold you the battery pack for the camera, but if you want to plug it into the wall, you will have to purchase an adaptor called an *AC 500*."

"You're kidding! I spent $30,000 on a camera and now I have to spend another $20 bucks on a cord just to plug it in the wall?"

"….No Jim, that is not correct. The AC 500 is around $600 bucks."

Now I was pissed. This guy is not talking to some TV station with huge budgets. We were a small, very small family operation that did not have discretionary funds lying around. We came up with the money for the adaptor and thus began my love hate relationship with professional video gear. During these early years, professional video equipment was the biggest rip off in the history of rip offs. Thank the Lord that computers would eventually come down the pike and revolutionize the industry.

Once we had purchased the video equipment we needed, the time we took in producing the show lengthened quite a bit. Eventually, most shows we produced we would film up to a year in advance and take a week to edit. Since I was doing all the production and was not on the clock, we could take the time we wanted to produce the kind of show we always strived for.

The uproarious cast of characters I met along the show's journey was something to behold.

Although a blurry picture, this is the only photo we have left remaining of the official "Raft Shack" somewhere last seen floating (somewhat), in Tennessee.

Chapter 9

Tennessee Tim

"If you own a home with wheels on it and several cars without, you just might be a redneck."

~Jeff Foxworthy

Traveling, making appearances at boat and fishing shows was something we did often and it helped get our name out there. What I enjoyed most was it gave us the chance to talk to the people who watch our program. Trade shows also gave me the opportunity to meet other outdoor TV producers. The fans of *Jim Baugh Outdoors TV* always amazed me, people just really got into it and everyone wanted to talk with me about the show and of course suggest topics, which I appreciated.

I looked at making public appearances as an opportunity to get free advice on our program from the people who know best, our audience. During the many years of traveling to various public appearances I can honestly say that I never had a negative experience with any fan, which always kind of surprised me. The Judge and I were very careful to review our shows before they aired and made sure not only were they good, but nothing would be said or done that potentially could offend someone.

There were several occasions when my dad would have me re-edit a show, because he thought something might come back on us. As an editor, I always took the advice of the Judge and also our viewers. Usually without question if a viewer of our show made a comment to me, I acted on it no matter how small the suggestion was.

There is one interesting thing that started to happen as we continued to air the show and make public appearances. *Jim Baugh Outdoors TV* had a unique look due to the style of editing and footage we used from various places like Belize. A lot of viewers did not think our program was produced locally in Virginia. The really funny thing was because of all the exposure through TV and print that the name "Jim Baugh" was getting, many times people would be talking to me and not know it was Jim Baugh.

This would go on for years and I usually would not know how to break it to them that the Jim Baugh they were talking about was the guy standing in front of them. Usually toward the end of a conversion I would introduce myself and the person would say, "Oh, YOU'RE JIM BAUGH?" I would laugh and the fan would laugh along with me. It never was a problem and when it did happen, and I tried to handle it graciously…. Except for this one time.

I was hauling our showboat behind our old black Suburban coming back from my dad's river house. We had been trying to film some rockfish for a future episode. I pulled into a fast food joint and of course, with the truck and boat I had to park way in the back because it took up so much room. I got out of the truck and was really whipped out from filming. This nice man comes up and approaches me and says,

"Hi there! Say, how long have you been driving for *Jim Baugh Outdoors*?"

Without hesitation I decided I was going to have some fun with this, just this one time. I answered,

"Oh it has been years now."

"Wow!" he said.

Then he started asking me a lot of questions about where we were filming and if I knew where Jim was at that time. I replied,

"Well you see, we keep Jim up in the airplane most of the time. We will have several crews throughout the country, radio into him and let him know where to land based on where the fish are biting."

"You're kidding!" he said.

"No, really it is the most efficient way to produce the show. This way, as soon as Jim arrives he is on the fish immediately. Then he will get back in the plane and wait for the next call."

The man just had this blank stare and said,

"I always wondered how these guys would always catch fish because I don't catch fish every time I wet a line."

I replied, "The key is the airplane. One time we actually had to parachute Jim down in the ocean on a marlin trip offshore, it made for a great show."

I thanked him for asking about our program, grabbed my burger and left. I never let on that I was kidding him the entire time. This is something I only did once but figured the rumor mill would be quite hilarious on this one.

One of my favorite videotapes that I would rent from other outdoor TV personalities was of a guy named Tim Runnards. Tim was a guide in Tennessee who at the time had over 18 rockfish catches over 50 pounds. He also had a local / regional fishing show and I always wanted to meet this character.

Tim weighed in at about 340 pounds and wore a white brimmed Key West hat, Hawaiian shirt and white Bermuda shorts. His white beard and mustache were always perfectly trimmed and he really looked like something out of an Earnest Hemingway novel on steroids.

Savannah, Georgia was the location of this one particular boat and fishing show in which I would be appearing and as luck would have it, Tim Runnards was attending the same show. I walked up and here was this larger than life character with a booming heavy eastern

Tennessee accent sitting in front of his display of huge rockfish.

"Howdy Jim, shuuur is a nice to a be meetin' ya. How ya doin?"

Tim and I became friends the second he opened his mouth. I just knew this was a guy I was going to have a good time hanging out with. I was only talking with him a few minutes before I already started calling him Tennessee Tim.

Talking with Tim he told me the only reason he came to this show was because he and his buddy wanted to get away from their wives and go to the all you can eat seafood buffet at Captain George's. The boat show was just an excuse to get there. So my cameraman and I hooked up with them for dinner and proceeded to eat more snow crab legs than they could bring out. We stayed there and ate for three hours.

It was very refreshing to talk TV buiz with someone else who had a fishing show. Years earlier I met Jerry McKinnis at the AFTMA show, but he was respectfully too busy to give me any real time. Nice fellow though and I had been a big fan of the *Fishin Hole TV Show* for years. But here now I could sit down and really talk to someone who was for the most part in the same position that I was. We were both syndicating our shows and always looking for sponsors and new ways to market our programs. Tennessee Tim was very easy to talk to and we both got along great and had fun exchanging TV war stories. We really became good friends.

The more I talked to Tim, the more I appreciated his common sense attitude to business. Looking at the guy and listening to him talk, one would not figure Tim to be a super keen guy who had a knack for advertising his show. But he did. Tim told me this story that I will never forget.

"Jim, a... let me tell ya how I promoted my show nationally on the Bassmasters."

100

I said, "Now I know you did not have the budget for that. What is the deal?"

Tim said, "Well ya know dat ole entrance to da big coliseum where all dem basser boats enter da stadium for de tourney?"

I said, "Sure Tim, what about it?"

He said, "Well whaaat Izz fixen to do and den done did, waaas to have a sign made that read, 'TIM RUNNARDS TV SHOW WELCOMES THE BASSMASTERS CLASSIC'. I hung it over dat der entrance of the building where everyone der entered."

I said, "Were you nuts? Certainly of course, they must have taken it down?"

Tim said, "Y sure day did! But it was up dher fur four days fore they ever dun figured it out!"

"It was seen on ESPN, all da' local news, had one feller call me from Cali-Forn-I-A and said ....Tim, Loved your sign for your show, saw it on the Bassmasters!"

They asked Tennessee Tim who gave him permission to hang up his welcome sign and he told them no one ever gave him permission. It was just a nice gesture from one TV show to another. I laughed my ass off. What balls!

Tim and his crew really played the TV fishing show celebrity card. They would travel down to Mexico and send in first his cameraman and grip several days before Tim would arrive. They then proceeded to hang out in the bars and talk up Tim big time and ask permission, you guessed it, to put up more signs.

"Tim Runnards TV Show Welcomes Mexico," would be hung up in the bar area for days before Tim would arrive. Once Tim got there all the Mexicans treated him like he was Elvis. Free drinks, free food, senoritas, free fishing and accommodations all provided for the popular celebrity. Tennessee Tim did this for years. The guy got more mileage out of signage than anyone else I knew. I just loved Tennessee Tim.

Tim mentioned to me that he had this houseboat that he had fully renovated and wanted us to come down and shoot a show on striper fishing. He said we could stay and hang out on the his new houseboat, and as Tim would say, "Frolic".

"Frolicking" meant a lot of drinking, cooking, partying, and fishing. That always sounded good to me. Tim said he had plenty of room on his renovated houseboat and we would not need a hotel. I was fine with that and thought it sounded like fun.

I set aside some time to go down to Tennessee to do a shoot with Tim. On the way I picked up my brother in-law Bill Harman to go with me and help with the camera. We were both just looking forward to getting away and having some fun. Bill and I arrived somewhere in Eastern Tennessee at the lake where Tim had his houseboat. We met up with Tim and followed him the rest of the way in.

Arriving at a dirt driveway with nothing but woods around, we drove down the dirt road until we got to a clearing and we all got out of our cars. Tim said, "What da ya dink Jim. She's a bute, isn't she?"

I looked at Tim and said, "What are you talking about Tim?"

He pointed down the bank and floating just off the water was a 10 by 10 raft shack that had a combination of Christmas lights and lit strands of plastic swans, all powered by a boat battery sitting at the bottom of the shack. I said, "Tim, what the hell is that?"

Tim said, "Dat's B my refurb ishet house boat. Chu b likin it!"

We started laughing in a nice way then asked Tim to give us the tour.

We walked on board to look inside. There was one inflatable pool toy sitting in the middle of this very small dark floating room. Tim said that was where we would sleep. Bill and I figured we needed to start drinking fast because this was going to be an uncomfortable night's sleep for sure. Tim showed us the filet station outside the raft shack that was simply a cooler and a bucket. He would filet the stripers on the cooler and use the bucket to get lake water to clean the fish. All kidding aside, it did work and the fish we cooked up tasted great.

I think Tim and I had a little different perspective of what a houseboat was. His renovation meant that he bought a pool toy at Wal Mart and stuck it inside the shack. The additional renovation included his new marine head. He cut the weeds down around this huge oak tree that was leaning next to his raft shack. This was his new so called marine head also known as an outhouse. The john was an oak tree, where Tim had graciously cut away the poison ivy around the base. A stick in the ground is what held up the toilet paper. This set the stage for one interesting and fun experience with Tennessee Tim on his home lake of Old Apple.

When you fish with Tim it is an early call. There was really nowhere to sleep on the raft shack and I chose to sleep in my truck. Getting up early is easy when you sleep in your Suburban. We were on the water at 4am. Tim tied his bass boat up to the raft shack. We took off at 60 mph in the pitch dark and Tim then started looking for fresh bait. It did not take many casts before he had enough to fill his cooler. The fishwell consisted yet again, of a Styrofoam cooler with some lake water in it. I ask Tim why not a protected live well so we could keep the bait longer. Tim said,

"Jim by da time deese baits start to a b ah dieyn and R a floatin, we will of done limited out on stripers and eating Turkey omelets at dat der diner up da street. Ain't nooo need to keep da bait past dat ya figure .....u recon so?"

Fishing did not take long. Within one hour we limited out on stripers and caught some nice rainbow trout. It was a fantastic catch and made for a great show. There was one other boat there that was a friend of Tim's who did not have as much luck catching bait or fish. They motored over to Tim's boat and we gave them a bunch of fresh bait. These fishermen only floated away maybe thirty feet from us and started fishing. They had no luck whatsoever. Meanwhile we continued to catch and release more stripers and rainbow trout.

After we left the fishing hole to go out to breakfast I ask Tennessee Tim what was the secret. Why did we catch all the fish while the other boat did nothing even though they were using our bait? Tim smiled and said that all rigs were the same and there was no difference at all in the presentation except one thing. Tim whispered,

"My bass boat be a Reddun."

"I don't understand Tim So what if you boat is the same color as your neck?"

"Well Jim, dat boat got der a whiate hull, and dem stripers arr liiiiiiite sensitive. So much so they be a feedin under my boat and done strayed away from datun!"

All I can say is that I saw it for myself. Tennessee Tim's boat always caught the fish. And to the fish's eyes, his dark red boat was a lot harder to see than the other boats white hull.

Breakfast with Tim was a real adventure. They made all of us a special turkey, sausage, squirrel and cheese omelet that was really good. After a huge meal it was only around 8 in the morning, remember we started at 4am. I did not really know what we were going to do the rest of the day, so I asked Tim,

"Hey man what's on the agenda for the rest of the day?"

He answered with one word…. "Frolickin."

Now I was ready to experience frolickin on the lake with my buddy Captain Tennessee Tim. We started out by buying some crab legs that we were going to steam up for dinner, along with some fresh fried rockfish that we had caught only a few hours before. This was going to be a VERY good dinner!

The drinking started early, like around 10am at the raft shack. Let's see if I can remember, Bloody Mary's, moonshine, a case of beer, and a lot of rum. In our ultimate wisdom, Tim decided to do some Fly By's. I was not sure what a fly by was but soon found out it meant Tim hauling ass in his Bass boat at 70 mph, within about 20 feet of the raft shack. I think he saw *Top Gun* way too many times.

We were lucky no one got killed. At the time, we were laughing pretty hard. It was the last Fly By I ever saw. The good Lord was looking after me once again.

After the Fly Bys there was a lot more frolickin to be had back at the raft shack. After a few more cocktails I began to search out the cooking locations for the big cook out of crabs and fried rockfish. Hollered over to Tim,

"Tennessee Tim… Hey… going to need a boiling pot for the crab legs and a cast iron skillet for the fried rockfish." Tim bounced out of the inside of the raft shack with the Wally Mart pool toy around his waist and shouted,

"Gotter all Jim! Gotter all!"

So I filet the fish and got out the crab legs. I was ready to get these pans going. Tim brought out two flat cast iron griddles and I said,

"Tim, what the hell are those?" He said,

"Dar fur yur a cookin if ya be a fixen to."

Once I stopped laughing I realized he was serious. How the hell am I going to boil or even steam crab legs with a flat skillet, much less deep fry fish in a pan that had no sides? Needless to say, I had enough rum in me to start improvising very fast. Between the bucket, cooler, trash can lid and two flat skillets, I somehow made it work. Of course there was no table. We just grabbed the food once cooked and threw the shells overboard for the catfish. In a way it was like camping out on an island.

After Tim's big day it was time for his bath. When Tennessee Tim yelled out,

"Time fur a scrubeeeeee do!"

I thought to myself, the head, john or also called bathroom was the oak tree, the bed was a blow up pool toy from Wally Mart, so now what in the world was the bath tub going to be?

KaaaaaaaaSplllllaaaaaassssssssssssssshhhhhhh!!!

340 pounds of fish smelling moonshine soaked crab claw flesh goes cannon balling into the lake. The submarine wave rocks the raft shack to pieces. I walked over to the edge of the raft shack and Tim asked me to pass his Tupperware. I handed him a Tupperware container that was sitting by a plastic parrot of which he carefully proceeded to open.

There lies Tennessee Tim's bar of soap, razor blade, and washcloth. He started to scrub himself down swimming in the lake with great furbish. Soon a huge soap scum line started to spread out around Tim's body similar to the fallout of a nuclear bomb. This was only the first wave of the soap scum blast. Before we knew it, the cove was covered with little soap bubbles floating on top of the water. Captain Tim was a happy camper with his fresh lake water bath.

After one more night sleeping in the truck, Bill and I were ready to head back to his house in Roanoke. We were sober and very, very tired. Bill suggested we pull off for a country steak and egg breakfast and it was delicious. Problem was, it really did us in. I barely could keep my eyes open for the drive home, but we did make it back without any incident. Thank the Lord.

I had Tennessee Tim up to fish with us several times in Hampton Virginia and we always had a fantastic time. Every time he would visit, we would go slaughter the crab legs at Captain Georges buffet. Tim is one of those characters that make being in the TV Business a real joy.

The last time Tennessee Tim came to film with me in Hampton I had a sign made and got permission from the hotel to hang it up for one day. The sign said, "Jim Baugh Outdoors TV Welcomes the Tennessee Tim Fishing Show."

Captain Tim would sit at the bar in his wide brimmed white hat and Hawaiian shirt, enjoying free drinks for his entire stay.

…. What a celebrity.

Chapter 10

Dam Control to Captain Tont

"Many men go fishing all of their lives without knowing that it is not fish they are after."

~Henry David Thoreau

Whenever I returned back home from filming a show it usually was a very busy week that followed. There was always a lot of time in the studio editing and preparing programs that included a lot of writing and music composition. All the while acting as a shuttle service for my two kids because Helen and I both agreed early on we would get our kids involved in a lot of activities. Whether it was church, school plays, sports, Boy Scouts, etc, we were always taking the kids somewhere and I usually happily did the cooking at dinnertime. So my time at home was very busy between parenting and trying to produce Jim Baugh Outdoors TV.

Fortunately when our kids were young, my in-law's bought a nice little condo at Smith Mountain Lake. This was just awesome because we had no money to speak of. Any money we had went to raising and paying for the kids. So getting away to the condo at Smith Mountain was a great break and enabled me to meet a lot of the fisherman who specialized in deep water striper fishing. There were plenty of characters on the lake that were all great fisherman, Captain Earl, Spike, Cathy, Rip and one young fellow named Captain Melvin Tont.

Melvin was a young buck who was one hell of a nice fellow who always insisted that the BIG stripers were in the lake below, called Leesville. You see, Smith Mountain Lake is a pump back lake that lets water out to create hydraulic power then pumps the water back from Leesville Lake below in order to keep the lake's water levels consistent. Whenever Smith Mountain Dam is either letting water out or pumping it back in, the current causes the stripers to feed like crazy. The trick is to know when and where the water will be moving, and be there when it does.

Now I knew nothing about fishing Leesville Lake. Captain Tont had been bugging me to go for a long time to catch some of these stripers he was on. So we planned the trip and away we went.

When we arrived at Leesville, Captain Tont was very sure of himself and his capabilities of catching us some monsters. I had the camera with me and figured this would be a great opportunity to get some hog stripers on film. I did notice that the lake was pretty low and we had to go off the ramp just to get the boat in the water. I try to make it a practice not to question a captain I'm with. This is just good manners and it is always good to have only one captain on board.

We took off flying through these very scenic winding river landscapes below Smith Mountain Dam. The view looking up at this huge green mountain and the valley surrounding us was terrific. Once we got near the dam Melvin slowed the boat down and said,

"Jim they are really pumping back into Smith Mountain Lake, this is going to be some awesome fishing. Fish should be turned on BIG TIME!"

I thought that sounded good! We put out our live bait. The anchor was holding securely and we were ready for the big bite.

It was only in about 15 minutes I noticed that the landscape was starting to change. There was more of it, and soon a lot more! I checked the anchor and it was holding, but things started to look different. All of the sudden an island started to appear in the river that was not there 15 minutes ago. Silent was the call for me. I didn't want to look stupid by asking Captain Tont a stupid question like,

"Hey Captain, what is that new island over there?" Looking at the banks, the water line was down around another 8 inches. Now I had to say something.

"Captain Tont. Have you fished this place before?"

Melvin answered, "Awe yes. Once."

Now I was starting to worry. We had made a long run up to the dam and the lake was running out of water fast, REAL FAST! I asked, "Hey Captain. Why don't you get on your radio and call the dam, and tell them we are down here and we don't want to walk home. Maybe just maybe, give us an idea of how long it will be before they stop pumping the water out?"

"Well Jim that is a pretty good idea." The next thing I hear is this.

"Captain Tont to Dam Control, Captain Tont to Dam Control."

Then, "This is Dam Control to Captain Tont."

I tell you this. I did not know if I was fishing or in a David Bowe video. Captain Melvin Tont then ask, "Dam Control can you look out your window and see us down here?"

"This is Dam Control. Yes we see you."

Captain says, "You know…. things are starting to get a little dry down here. Any chance you guys can stop pumping the water out and letting some back in?"

The voice on the radio says, "Dam Control, Sorry, this is an automated system and is controlled by a computer in Kansas."

Captain Tont said, "Jim, it does not sound like Dam Control has much dam control after all." The first words out of my mouth were these, as another four inches of water dropped down from the banks, "Let's get outta here, NOW!!"

We did. The good captain ran at wide-open throttle and we were passing all sorts of new real estate we had not seen on the way out. Things were really getting shallow.

There just was no way we were going to make it out of there because we now had been traveling in only a few feet of water and had a long way to go.

When we did reach where we launched the boat, the cove had no water. It was dry. The captain got as close as he could and ran to his truck, backed all the way down the dry part of the lakebed and I quickly attached the strap from the trailer to the boat. Both of us pulled on that darn strap until the boat was securely on the trailer.

Captain Tont already had her in four wheel drive and was driving as fast as he could through the muddy lake bed. I was rather panicked and was just glad we had gotten to this point. Trying to hold on in the truck and catch my breath Captain Tont said, "Hey Jim. Look at those shrubs over there that had been under water, bet there will be some good bass there when she fills back up!"

I said, "Captain, will you just get this dam rig to the road and quit worrying about bass fishing! I don't like lakes with no water in them!"

Once we got up to where the concrete was on the boat landing, there were some serious shakes and jolts getting up on the concrete. For sure, we thought we blew out a tire. Fortunately we made it out unscathed. It must have taken the captain a good while to clean off all the mud and dirt from his boat and trailer after hauling it through that riverbed.

Sometimes I can't get to a glass of rum fast enough. This was one of those days. We did laugh about the experience later, however that would be my first and last time ever fishing Leesville Lake.

There have been many times that not only do we not catch fish on a shoot, we are just happy to have water in the lake. Certainly this had been one of those trips.

Captain Melvin Tont later took up salt water fishing and we fished together in Hatteras North Carolina. When I saw him I gave him a present. A tide chart.

I told Captain Tont that knowing and understanding water levels is a good thing.

Chapter 11

How many of you can swim?

"There is no dilemma compared with that of the deep-sea diver who hears the message from the ship above, 'Come up at once. We are sinking.'"

~Robert Cooper

Smith Mountain Lake was a place we filmed for about 10 years. The place was gorgeous and our family had a place to stay there. The lake was a fairly dangerous lake due to its water depth, water temperature and underwater standing timbers.

It seemed like just about every year someone was getting killed on the lake usually due to people who just did not practice safe boating. I was always super careful on the lake and was cautious with my kids around the water wherever we were. Sure enough, if you're going to be on the water long enough something is going to happen. I already had enough scares being around the water and was not planning on any more. Unfortunately, that was not meant to be.

One of the fisherman on the lake who was a good friend of mine named Captain Rob Cleat asked me if I was interested in getting some striper footage on one of his guide trips. Sure, I was in big time. This was during late fall and the lake was turning over and getting very cold. Wintertime boating is when the word *hypothermia* always crosses my mind. Should something happen and you go in the drink your chance of survival is solely based on exposure and time. With water temperature around 40 degrees hypothermia can set in within minutes or even seconds.

The boat we were on was a 23-foot center console and we had five people on board. Back then I used our big

Beta SP camera that was half the cost as my first house. Powered by a big battery belt I was ready to shoot some great wintertime footage on the lake. The ride of course, was very cold. The captain slowed the boat as we reached the dam area and were sitting in 250 feet of water. This is a deep, very cold lake with standing timbers underwater coming within 10 to 20 feet from the surface. The lake was flooded with only about 100 feet of land cleared. Most everything else was left as is. This meant that not only were there trees underwater, but houses, cars, tractors, roads, bridges, all sorts of stuff.

When the boat came to a complete stop, Captain Rob put out all the lines and started drifting for live bait. In about five minutes a stream of water was coming out below his center console. I said, "Hey Captain, looks like you have a small leak in your livewell, we don't want to loose any bait."

The good captain lifted up the lid to the livewell and it was full of water. We both had a puzzled look on our faces and the stern was now only inches from being underwater.

"All lines in!! All lines in!! Lifejackets on!!"

Captain Rob started the engine. By that time the stern was at the water line and water was pouring in the boat. We were going down very quickly and our time before death of hypothermia was going to be short.

My first thought was to save the camera. There was a cooler on the boat that I could put it in. I could hang on to the cooler while swimming with a life jacket and save the camera. There was nothing I could do about the hypothermia. So I yelled out, "Everyone can swim, right?"

Shocked, just shocked. Three guys standing in water on a sinking boat and they all said, "Nope, never learned."

Not one of them could swim!

FUUUUUUUUUCCCCCCKKKKKKKK!! The Judge was going to KILL ME!! I would have to give up the cooler for the camera and give it to these idiots who never learned to swim. Hell, these were the first people I ever met that could not swim and there were THREE of them!!

Ok, I was going to have the camera at the bottom of the lake in 250 feet of water. I am screwed. Hopefully, I could swim out of this before hypothermia sets in, only to later hear the Judge cuss me out like a sailor on shore leave. I think I'd rather stay in the lake.

The boat was half way underwater and the engine was stuttering and I asked the captain,

"Captain Rob, if you keep it floored and don't stop, we may make it over to the other island, but you will have to run it and hit shore. Should you slow any time before that, we're going down under like a fast attack submarine."

The captain and I had the same plan. By the good Lord's guidance and a big Magnolia tree boom, we slammed the boat on the island at 15 mph before it could sink. The boat was damaged, but no cracks in the hull and the stern was still underwater.

Captain Rob dove down behind the boat to check the plug, it was gone. The lake had turned over and debris caught on the drain plug removing it from the hull. That is all that caused this entire ordeal. Five people could have died all because of a loose plug.

The captain of course had a spare, put it in, and then we started bailing and running the bilge. In about 30 minutes, we had the boat floating again and by now one of the passengers had just finished throwing up. They were in shock.

The captain and I inspected the boat and ran it to make sure everything was ok. When we got back to the island to pick up the three passengers one said, "I will be so glad to get our butts home!"

I said, "Nope…. we are going fishing, I did not go through all this and help to save your butts only to go home with no footage nor filets!"

We put them on board and went back to fishing. Like I said, if you spend enough time on the water, things are going to happen.

We caught fish and back on the docks, I showed the three passengers how to clean a striper. I bagged the filets and happily gave the fish to them to cook for dinner. I also gave them one of my favorite recipes.

Then I handed them the telephone number for the local YMCA and told them, before they go back on a boat, LEARN HOW TO SWIM!

Chapter12

Always bring something back from the sea

A bad day of fishing is better than a good day of work.

~Author Unknown

Many times viewers of *Jim Baugh Outdoors TV* would ask me, "How in the world do you guys always catch those fish and in less than 30 minutes?"

The fact is usually we don't. There are those fairly rare times when our production crew can go out and get enough footage for several episodes in 45 minutes on the other hand we can take up to a year to produce one show. Certainly, the key is in how the program is produced and edited. I always tried to give a factual representation of what we did on a trip because it just keeps everything real and honest. Not at all, do we catch fish every time we go out. Usually we will get enough footage for a small segment or sometimes a complete show. There are those shoots that take several attempts just to complete the story.

I remember one of my more memorable trips fishing off the Eastern Shore when we were fishing for rockfish. These fish can move up to twenty miles in a day and often times they won't even come into the Bay. The federal line for rockfish in the ocean is only three miles out so based on bait and water temperature the fish can easily stay offshore out of reach. This was one of those trips where the fish stayed offshore, and there was nothing we could do about it.

I had faith and told my crew we would catch and bring back something. Not to worry. We were not going to get busted or skunked. Four hours later I was beginning to wonder if it was such a good idea to have given such a pep talk. Whenever you are not catching fish, it is always the captain's fault. I never agreed with this philosophy, didn't matter because that is just the way it was. I hate being blamed for something that is not in my control.

Fishing legally in the Chesapeake Bay for rockfish can mean a lot of times not catching any fish. When the bait and water temps are right outside the three-mile line, you can't make the fish swim back into the Bay. It was the end of the day and yet I still had faith we were going to boat something.

One of the fishermen asked me if I thought the severe West wind we had the day prior had anything to do with the fish moving out to the ocean, and I replied, "You would have to ask the fish."

I don't think he thought it was too funny, so I told everyone to get to the back of the boat and reel them in ......we were going home.

I turned around at the helm and looked off my starboard side about three o' clock and could not believe my eyes. There, floating in the water was a swimming pool. Yes, a swimming pool! This was a first. I told the guys on board to get ready, because we are about to haul in our first and only catch of the day. These guys thought I was crazy. Sure enough, I spun the boat around and we all grabbed the swimming pool and hauled it in over the back of the boat. My cameraman asked me what in the world I was going to do with it. I told him I caught it, it was mine, and was taking it home. Evidently, the previous hard west wind we had the day before blew some child's swimming pool out of their back yard and landed in the ocean.

When we pulled the boat up to the dock and tied up back in Hampton, my buddy Mike hollered out from the dock,

"Hey Jim, wad ya catch?"

Next thing he saw was a swimming pool flying through the air and landing at the center of the dock. He said, "What the hell is this Jim?"

118

I said, "It is my catch for the day and I am damn proud of it!"

We left the swimming pool right there on the dock, filled it up with ice, then beer, wine, and a lot of bottles of rum and had a two day cook out on the dock. Yes, sometimes even we have to buy fish from the market. This was one of those times.

You really never know what you are going to catch and bring back from the sea.

When I was on the inland waterway with Captain Beau Katz we were doing a little fishing trip on board his 24 Parker. The fishing was pretty much non-existent. Beau was old-timer who loved to fish and hunt, he just hated to buy any meat from a store. If Captain Katz did not catch it or grow it in his garden, then he just as soon not eat. For snacks on board all he had and had lot of, was venison jerky. I must admit it was delicious.

Beau had several versions, mild, hot, and what he called, "Get the hell off my boat venison". This Jerky was so hot, he said for me to not even try it. I LOVE spicy food and insisted he let me try some. He just smiled revealing his three teeth and Captain Katz said, "Ger ahead."

Once I tasted it I screamed,

"Get me the hell off of this boat!"

Catching him off guard, the Captain had a big laugh. It was a good time fishing the only problem was once again, this looked like a skunk day. No fish. -It happens.

The Captain said we might see something on the way as we were going back in. Sure enough the captain stopped the boat ran down in the cabin and brought out his 12 gauge shotgun. I had no idea what in the world he was doing but did not like the idea of getting out a gun at all. What the hell was going on now? Don't tell me next someone is going to break out some deer piss!

Captain Beau ran up to the bow and fired off three rounds pointing down at the water, I had no idea what he was shooting at. Looking over the side of the boat I saw blood and a wild boar that was on its' side.

The captain had shot a wild hog swimming across the inland waterway. I was a little stunned by all this and before I knew it, he had this hog tied up and began to actually lift it with this small crane he had onboard. It looked like something you would see on *The Orca* in the movie *Jaws*, just was smaller but just as rusty.

Now shooting a wild pig and boarding it was not enough for this captain. He immediately gutted the pig and cleaned it right there on the boat. He said it was easier to do it on his boat, and he was right. All he did was take the water hose and leave it running as he gutted the pig. Everything went overboard and the sea gulls were going nuts. As he cleaned and cut the pig into quarters etc, he would throw the meat in the iced fish cooler. The cuts of meat did look good and they were very well iced down. It didn't take the captain long at all to clean the boat. You would have never known there was a wild boar slaughtered on the back of his vessel.

We then made it to the dock and tied up at this old country marina that had plenty of wooden boards that were all curved upwards. One of Captain Kats' fishing cronies came up to the dock and asked how our catch was.

Beau said, "Great, big poundage, one of the best hauls we ever had!"

He then lifted up the lid to the cooler that was facing the helm and threw out of the cooler on to the dock a pork shoulder. Then he threw a pork butt and then a rack of ribs. He yelled out, "Surf - 0, Turf –1."

The next day we all enjoyed fresh hickory smoked pork BBQ along the banks of the Inland Waterway.

When you head out on a fishing trip, you never really know what you will bring back.

120

Sometimes it's a pool, sometimes it's a pig.

*Veteran Cameraman Wayne Baker to the Left, Jim Baugh
to the Right. Photo taken offshore filming the Suzuki
Marine West Palm Beach King Tournament 2007*

Chapter 13

Who is this Hippie

"Good morning! What we have in mind is breakfast in bed for 400,000".

~Wavy Gravy at Woodstock

Time on the road filming Jim Baugh Outdoors always meant meeting a cast of characters that were full of color and life. Many experiences were quite extreme and believe it or not, I did enjoy coming back home to the rather normal family life I was blessed with.

Both my kids and wife were the best and I could have never asked for a better life, with the exception for all the yard work. Actually, that is what would eventually lead to our divorce. Other than that, I was a happy camper for the most part and always fully understood how blessed I was with my kids. The neighbors would tell me horror stories about raising their kids. I would always look stunned, like, how in the hell did their kids get so screwed up?

Many times people would come up to me and say, "Jim, your kids are great! Don't they ever get in trouble?"

I don't think Helen and I ever let our kids have enough time too get in trouble. Heck, we got them involved in everything. The old phrase, *idle hands are the work of the Devil* is something I always believed in.

My life in Richmond at home was full of normalcy, which I always prayed for. I made a deal with God when Ben was born and asked him for this.

"Dear Lord, since for some reason you put me through shit with two mothers when I was young, please grant me a normal happy family life for me and my kids."

The good Lord answered that prayer in a huge way. I felt I always owed him for that. The Magnolia Tree spoke loud when it came to the blessings of raising my kids.

At my office and studio, I was always wearing the hats of five different jobs, so I was too busy to do much else. The crazy and exciting times happened on the road, and that is where I wanted them to stay. Home was for raising the kids and trying to keep everything running. That took 100% of my time.

Cameramen were generally freelancers and I needed another cameraman in the pool of people I was traveling with. I called an associate and ask if he knew anyone and he suggested a fellow named Wayne Baker. I called in Wayne for an interview at my office and was a little surprised when he walked in the door.

Enter.......... Wayne Baker.

Here standing before me was something that looked like it crawled out of the mud at Woodstock. Wayne had very long red hair that came down past his shoulders, a belly bigger than mine, and a huge red beard that really looked like Santa Claus. He wore ragged clothes, sandals, and had thin John Lennon style glasses. My first thought was this, I run into enough characters on the road; I don't need to travel with one too!

Meeting and talking with Wayne I quickly realized this guy had a lot going on. He had masters in art and had his own photography company. Reviewing a lot of his pictures, immediately I knew that Wayne looking through my camera lens was going to be a good thing. He also made clear that he takes direction very well. Whatever I tell him to shoot he is going to shoot it without question. This is a bit of a problem with a lot of video photographers. They want to shoot what they want, with disregard to what the producer wants.

I edit the show; I know what shots I need and I HATE to waste tape because I'm the one that pays for it.

Also, it's a waste of my time to cipher through a lot of useless B roll that I don't need just to get what I wanted to use in the show in the first place.

Wayne understood this because he was a poor photographer like me. We did not waste anything, tapes, batteries, nothing. I got editing and filming down so well and exact that I could shoot on one 30-minute tape enough footage for a 30-minute show, which was really about 19 minutes of new program material. Wayne and I saw eye to eye and he was an easy going fellow who could make me laugh. So, Wayne was going to be my full time camera guy for quite some time. This was the beginning of a life long friendship that I would truly cherish every day.

Now one thing about Wayne and myself together, we really did do a lot of partying. We did not go anywhere without a stocked bar and I mean nowhere. Wayne loved his vodka and I liked my rum. Together we could be quite a handful, especially when we were on the road. I had strict rules while we were on the road, there would be no drinking and driving, and total sobriety while we were working. However, once off the clock that was a different story.

I was such an ass. I would not let Wayne even mix a cocktail until all equipment was unloaded and batteries charged. We traveled with a lot of expensive gear that was paid for by my poor wallet. I took very careful care of our cameras and gear.

After a long day of filming and all gear secured Wayne would ask, "Is there anything else, any more bats to be charged?"

I would do an inventory of everything and realize that maybe one bat is missing. Wayne would run out to the truck find it and get it on charge in a flash. Once all was accounted for and prepped for the next day's shoot, we would look at each other briefly and say, OFF THE CLOCK! We tore into those cocktails like seagulls on bread. 90% of the time once we were back at our accommodations, we never went anywhere. Just stayed, drank, told war stories and had dinner where we were staying.

Jim Baugh Outdoors TV Studio was in Richmond and Wayne lived in a trailer in Ashland. I had outlined an upcoming shoot and wanted to review all the shoot locations with him before we left, so I headed over to his trailer for a meeting.

Wayne Baker I found out had lots of friends. Lots! This was the first time I went to his trailer and it looked like it should have been condemned from the outside. Inside, it looked like a condemned Mexican restaurant. Wayne for years worked as a photographer in Phoenix Arizona and loved the southwestern décor. His kitchen table was a wooden booth that came from a Mexican joint and he had lit jalapeno pepper lights strung up all over the place. This no doubt, was Party Central. The trailer was pretty cozy after all and the walls were filled with Wayne's excellent art and photography. The place should have been donated to some museum. It truly was something to see.

"Come on in Jim! Have a cocktail! These are my friends Anna Hooter, Jewly Jewels, Ralph, Slick Montgomery and Betty Humpter."

I said hello to everybody then made my way to the candle lit bar next to the sink and mixed a tall one. I had a feeling I was not going to get the work done I came to do.

Wayne said, "Hey buddy, we just ordered three pizzas from Dominick's and I will be breaking out a bottle of tequila. Stay for a while"…How could I refuse?

Within about 20 minutes the pizza delivery boy shows up and knocks on the door. Wayne opens the door and says, "Thank ya buddy and keep the change." I could see through the door this guy's car was running, head lights on, and looked like 50 pizzas stacked up in the back seat.

Wayne looks at this kid and says, "You are working hard dude, look a little thirsty. Ya wanna come in for a drink, take a break?"

The pizza guy looked a little puzzled and said, "Yeah, man, that's very nice of you, I could take five."

By this time my rather strong cocktail was taking effect and we were all talking and laughing, having a ball in Wayne's should-be-condemned Mexican trailer. For that night that was the last thing I really remember.

Waking up the next morning on the floor I saw a couple of the girls passed out in the kitchen drooped over in the booth. Ralph was nowhere to be seen. I heard some snoring and I turned around to look back in the trailer to see Wayne passed out on his bed with his cowboy hat on, shirt off, and an upside down Dominick's Pizza Box spread out over his stomach. The cocktail glass by his bed was empty except for a little melted ice. His plastic parrot light was on in the artificial palm tree leaning against the headboard.

Walking back to the front of the trailer on the sofa was the conked out Dominick's Pizza Delivery guy. I opened the door and outside was his car still running, door open, and now 50 cold pizzas in the back seat.

Everyone then woke up and Wayne apologized to the delivery guy for getting him so drunk that he passed out and didn't make any other deliveries.

The Pizza guy said, "You know, I'm sure I'm fired after this…….. What are y'all doing for breakfast?"

Wayne said, "Looks like pizza to me dude!"

The Dominick's delivery guy thought that was a good idea and started hauling in stacks of cold pizza to the trailer that soon became breakfast. Afterwards, he left probably to find a new job and wondering how he ever got so stoned drunk at Wayne's. We waved goodbye to him as he got back into his car, which was still running from the previous night.

That was the last time we ever saw the Dominick's Pizza delivery boy.

Before I left I asked Wayne if I could use his bathroom. He said sure and showed me the way. When done, Wayne asked if I saw the nude bust in the bathroom. It was sitting there right by the vanity. Wayne began to explain the trouble he got into with the *Bust Head*.
"Ya see Jim, I was sort a like, dating these two women and I did not really tell them I was seeing somebody else. This one chic had the nicest set of breasts I ever saw and I asked her if I could do a sculpture of the pair."

It turns out this girl also was an art major and she thought a sculpture of her big breast was a good idea. So Wayne Baker proceeded to make this sculpture out of papier-mâché that really looked incredible. He showed the bust to the woman and she loved it and wanted him to display it in his trailer. So he put it in the bathroom at first, in the corner by the towel rack.

The next day, Wayne had prepared a candle lit bath for his other girlfriend, complete with champagne. They both sank into the tub in the darkened bathroom and then had a very romantic candle lit bath. All was good and Wayne was just happy as a clam, until these words were screamed out of the tub.

"Who the hell tits are those!"

Wayne looked at her and said, "UUUGGGHHH."

Her next words were, "Damn you Wayne Baker, I know those aren't my tits you motha faulkeer!" Then she steamed out of the trailer in only her towel.

I asked him why did he not take the bust down after she left and he said, "Because the woman who posed for the bust is coming over tonight for a tub party."

He later told me that she did come over that night sit in the tub and told Wayne how sweet it was to have her bust on the vanity. She then made love to him and they continued to date for another couple of years.

128

Wayne sold the soon to be condemned Mexican trailer and moved to Virginia Beach where we would continue to film together for years.

Jim Baugh holding a nice Rockfish catch while filming on location in the Chesapeake Bay just west of the Eastern Shore of Virginia.

Chapter 14

Chocolate Anyone?

"All you need is love. But a little chocolate now and then doesn't hurt."

~ Charles M. Schulz

We produced in cooperation with Virginia Tourism some 30 plus programs that featured different locations in Virginia. *Jim Baugh Outdoors* would film the various locations and show why the area would be good place to visit, fish, and all of this would help increase Virginia Tourism efforts. It was a very successful program and we did this for a span of about 10 years. All of these programs broadcast nationally as a part of our TV series. Through this association with Virginia Tourism is how we eventually ended up with our home base of operations on the water in Hampton Virginia.

One of our programs we contracted was a show that was to feature the Eastern Shore. Wayne and I both were very excited about this and the Eastern Shore was special to me, because that is where I spent my honeymoon many years earlier.

The tourism folks always put a positive spin on whatever area we would be featuring. They often times would book Wayne and me into some rather nice five star accommodations. This was nice of course, however what the tourism folks did not understand is that we would travel up to 250 miles in a day and have over 30 location shoots all in about a 14 hour period. I always over booked our days simply because we had so much material we needed to shoot. At the end of a production day the last thing Wayne and I wanted was some haute taughty fancy hotel. Hell no, all we were going to do once the gear was packed for the night was to have some cocktails and go to sleep.

Well on the Eastern Shore they booked *Jim Baugh Outdoors* into our first and probably last fancy bed and breakfast. Although the Brickstone Bed and Breakfast was a beautiful place and was run exceptionally well, it just is not our sort of thing. Don't get me wrong, the owners treated us fantastic and were wonderful people but it is a little like letting a hound dog on your fine furniture. It just does not work. This place reminded me a little of my youth, lots of chairs I was not allowed to sit it.

At the end of the day Wayne and I were totally exhausted and was not the time to worry if we were being too loud, if our camera gear was going to scratch the walls, or if we had to be at breakfast or dinner at a certain time. I liked staying in places that if we spilled a drink, it was not really going to matter that much. This was our prerequisite for the accommodations we liked, a working ice machine and pre stained carpet.

The other thing about this particular B & B is that it couldn't get cool enough. The hot summer sun was baking that old house and the temp inside on the second floor where we stayed was WAY too warm. 90+ degrees. This meant for a sweaty nights sleep.

The other thing about the B & B is that they were always sticking little things all over the place like little bars of soap that I thought were small coffee creamers. It took me three days to figure out why the coffee tasted like detergent.

One morning I sat on the little sewing kit that was placed on a chair. That one hurt like hell.
Guess that was another chair I was not supposed to sit on.

The liquid soap and mouthwash containers in the bathroom were identical and the same color. I guess I cussed too much because I did end up washing my mouth out with soap.

132

The second night I stayed in that hot room it was a very restless nights sleep. I was all over the place in that darn hot bed trying to get some cool air. I may have only slept three hours and had a full day of shooting ahead.

As soon as I stepped out of bed Wayne opened the door to check the batteries and my back was to him. He could not stop laughing. I turned around to face him and he was in tears.

I said, "Ok Wayne what the heck is so funny? Hell I just got out of bed."

He said, "Hold on a minute. Turn around and I will show you." I thought to myself, what the hell is he talking about?

Once I turned around he put one hand on my left shoulder and took his right hand and started peeling what was left of this little chocolate mint bar they had put on the fucking pillow the night before. I could actually hear it peeling off my back.

Wayne laughing in hysterics said, "Jim you idiot, didn't you see this before you went to bed?"

"Hell no damit! Get out of my room, I need to shower! We got a big day ahead and you are fucking with me about this dam chocolate mint that is splattered all over my back."

After getting cleaned up we went down stairs to have breakfast with the owners. I was careful to select the right chairs to sit in. They were extremely polite, talkative and wanted to know everything about the TV Buiz. They were very sweet and I told them what a wonderful job they had done restoring such a fine home. They appreciated that and waved us goodbye as we left to film all day.

When we returned that evening for dinner, Wayne and I mixed a couple of big cocktails and went down for supper. There sat the husband and wife with absolute blank faces on them. We tried to talk to them and they would not say a word. This went on for ten minutes and I figured we had done something they did not like. Scratch the walls, sit in a wrong chair, something, I could not figure it out. All of the sudden it came to me..... these guys do the laundry themselves!

"It's chocolate It's chocolate! I yelled out very loud at the table again. "It was chocolate!!"

They both looked at me with the biggest surprised faces you ever saw. He said, "Thank God! I thought you had a serious problem or something. I never saw such a mess in those sheets before. We were wondering if you had some sort of disorder or something."

I said, "No sir, the only problem I have is that your B & B is 100 degrees and you put chocolates in your guest's beds. Please don't do that anymore and I will leave you clean sheets and a big tip!"

They were really good sports and chuckled about it for a long time. We became friends and would send people to their B & B often.

Wayne and I had a full schedule filming the Eastern Shore and that included producing a piece for the show on Tangier Island. When I was a young boy my dad would take my brother and me to Tangier by boat and we always enjoyed this little Island. There are no cars only bikes and golf carts. In the early days there was just one restaurant that was open and served everything family style. *Crockett's* was legendary to the island and everyone on the Chesapeake Bay knew about this place.

I had the idea to get some aerial photography of the island. This would be achieved by contracting a local pilot with a Sesna 147 airplane. This particular plane had a small hole in the bottom of the floor that I could stick my camera lens through to get some good shots.

We got in the plane, took off, and noticed the pilot was a very accommodating fellow. He said anything we need just ask. So once we got over the island I told the pilot that the air was a bit bumpy and I could not get the shot.

He said, "No problem Jim, we will lower the revs some."

Soon I was able to get about 20 seconds of smooth footage without any bumps, but not enough, I was not satisfied. I asked the pilot, "Hey bud, I think maybe if we slow down just a bit more, we may get it."

He said, "No problem Jim, taking her down some more."

The plane really started to get into a bumpy ride. It just was not working so I asked again, "Maybe a little slower, I only need a few more shots and I will have it."

The pilot agreed and slowed down the plane again. All of the sudden....... BeeepBeeepBeeepBeeep! I ask the pilot what was that? He answered, "Jim that is the stall alarm. It is going off."

I said, "Stall? What is that? You got a bathroom in this small plane?"

He answered, "No, but you wanted the plane to go so slow that we are stalling in mid air."

Not knowing much about airplanes, I asked, "What does that mean?"

"It means were are gonna crash if we don't speed up!"

I yelled at the pilot, "Dammit man! Don't listen to me! I don't know a fucking thing about flying an airplane, just photography! Fly the damn plane and don't listen to a word I say!"

We were very low to the ground. He gave the plane a full throttle and we pulled out of it. As I was looking to see if I wet my pants, I wondered if he had just been screwing with me. You know, having some fun with the TV boys, scaring the shit out of them flying over the Chesapeake Bay. I never found out because I kept my mouth shut for the rest of the trip.

Hell, my day started off washing my mouth out with liquid soap then peeling melted chocolate mints of my back while trying to convince some B&B owner that I was not incontinent. Next, I was in an airplane with a pilot who had a sick sense of humor. Figured I would try to keep a low profile for the rest of the shoot.

Back to the B&B, wrap up the day and try to recoup. The temperature in my room was 83 degrees and the fan was broken. It was time for a tall glass of rum and a bath.

I looked over at my newly made bed with fresh linens and hot puffy throw pillows. There were two new chocolate mints on the top of each pillow and a new miniature sewing kit sitting on the bed side chair.

Oh boy........., here we go again.

Chapter 15

Danderun State Park

"Always do sober what you said you'd do drunk. That will teach you to keep your mouth shut."

~Ernest Hemingway

Heading out to the western part of the state of Virginia was our next location shoot, Danderun State Park. As usual Wayne and I loaded up our entire gear and full bar to shoot yet another tourism feature for our show.

In my pre-production interviews with the people who work at the park, they said that they would like to welcome us when we got there with a nice outdoor cocktail party. Now this was sounding like a place that old Wayne and I would fit right in.

When we arrived, all I can say is that the place was just beautiful. Gorgeous mountains and cliffs and a wonderful whitewater river than ran right through the park. The restaurant at the park overlooked the mountains and a whitewater river below. I just could not believe how pretty the place was and it was the first time I had ever stepped foot in the area.

After Wayne and I unloaded everything into our room, I looked at my cell phone and there was no cell service. Oh well, I could live without that. Then I looked around and asked Wayne if he knew where the thermostat was because it was hotter than hell. Even in the mountains this August was hot as blue blazes. Wayne called down to the guest services and asked them how to adjust the air temperature.

The lady said, "Open a window."

There was no air conditioning. I got on the phone and asked if any of the rooms had air and the answer was no. When I then asked why these recently renovated rooms that were so nice had no air conditioning she replied, "We don't need air conditioning up here in the mountains."

Really? Boy could have fooled me. To me, 100 degrees is 100 degrees whether you're in the mountains or at the beach. According to my math, it is the same temperature.

Who cares, Wayne and I would suffer through it. Shooting all day in 100 degree heat only to come back and haul all our equipment in a 100 degree room without air-conditioning or a fan. Life was good though because we got this cocktail party that we are going to and is being held just for us! Oh Boy!

It was my idea to sit back before we go, and have a big toddy. After all it had been a long trip and we were going to a cocktail party. This was going to be fun! After a big tall one or two, we walked out of the sauna/room and walked down to this covered area where there must have been 50 people all waiting to greet us.

It was so sweet. There were all sorts of little finger foods and a lot of people who worked at the park. Some local politicians were there and some members of the local press as well. As soon as I got there I was doing some interviews which were fine, and being introduced to everyone.

Once the little hoopla settled down, the park ranger asked,

"Jim and Wayne y'all ready for a cocktail?"

Boy those words sure sounded GOOD!

"Yes Mam we are parched and ready for a stiff one. I even brought my own double insulated tumbler."

She said, "Grape or Cherry." I looked at Wayne, he looked at me and we both looked back at the ranger and said, "Excuse me, ...what?"

"Grape or Cherry."

Then I sort of mumbled a few words that to me did not make sense, and I was the one talking.

138

"Ummm, I think I like cherries better but only if they don't have those little seeds in them but grapes are good too as long as the skin is not to thick. A little fruit would be nice before dinner, that's fine."

She said, "You don't understand. Would you like to drink Grape or Cherry."

I replied, "That is very nice of you, but I try to not mix my drinks with either, because of the calories in juice. I will just take some diet tonic water with some rum, that's all."

Once again she said, "You don't understand. This is all we have here is juice, no alcohol."

"What? I was told this was a cocktail party held for us. Am I missing something?"

She said, "Yes. Alcohol. We don't believe in it or serve it. Now what kind of juice would you like?"

Respectfully, I said, "None. Thank you. I am trying to cut down."

Both Wayne and I started to get this sort of weird feeling about this place. No air conditioner, no cell service, no alcohol, what was going to be next? ....Dinner!

We went to the lodge with our tourism representative from the area to have a nice dinner and review our shooting schedule. I thought it was interesting they had the Freon on high in the restaurant but installed no air conditioning in the rooms.

The waitress came over and asked what we would like to drink and Wayne said after that cocktail party, he would like just a glass of wine, merlot please. The tourism lady leaned over and said,

"Wayne... this is a clean place."

I nodded my head. Wayne looked around and said, "Yes it is a clean place, looks good. Can you make my glass a double?"

Our tourism lady leaned over again and said, "No Wayne, this is a clean place."

Wayne once again said, "Darn tootin'! They really do keep it nice in here."

Even I did not get what she was talking about. What she explained to us was that *clean* meant no alcohol whatsoever, not even wine or hard cider. Ok that is fine. Now we are staying in the mountains in a dry place, no air conditioning, no fan, and it is 100 degrees. The shoot has not even started yet. Thankfully, we were good boy scouts and brought the bar. Unfortunately, that would not last long. I thought what in the world is going to be next on this trip?

I go back to the room first, to mix a cocktail while Wayne finds a pay phone and makes a call. Five minutes later, he runs in the door screaming,

"Turn on the TV, turn on the TV!" I said, "What channel?"

Wayne yelled, "It doesn't matter just turn it on now!"

The TV warms up. This took a while with this old black and white. My cocktail was in hand, just wondering what the hell I am going to see and low and behold, there it was.

O.J. Simpson being chased in his Bronco by 100 police cars just flying down the highway.

"What the hell is this Wayne?"

"Jim, it looks like O.J. may have just killed his wife and some guy, not sure, but it looks like they are trying to stop him for questioning. I am sure O.J. is innocent, got to be."

Well, this became the joke of the shoot. The entire O.J. drama unfolding before our eyes, as we are running around the mountains in a dry county trying to find interesting things to film. When we had traveled some 50 miles away from the county going to some location that was of some tourist importance, the tourist rep looked at me in the car and pointed to this red barn over by the road and said, "That's a dirty place."

I said, "You mean that may be a place like a country restaurant that sells a glass of wine?"

She said, "Exactly!"

Ok, now I of course treated all these people with great respect and we did film a beautiful show there. However after three days of filming there, no kidding, I was ready to get the hell out. All this *clean* and *dirty* talk was enough to make me puke, and I was sober!

On the way out leaving the park I noticed for the first time this little store that sold gas up on the hill. For some reason I had not seen it before. It was kind of tucked away in the mountain. To be honest I had seen so many mountains, I really did not know where I was half the time. I told Wayne let's just run across the street get some gas and a snack for the road. The store was close, which meant I could get out of this place soon.

Wayne was filling up the truck and I was inside talking to the guy behind the counter, nice fellow.

"Hey man, I love your store and we have really enjoyed visiting this area for the first time. This place has some pretty mountains and the river is fantastic."

Cashier said, "Glad you liked it and hope it will be a good show, thanks for coming."

I looked at him and said, "You know, we travel a lot of places and very rarely run into a dry county like this. I really respect these people for holding their ground and staying true to what they believe. I really do admire that. Good folks here."

The guy looked right at me and said, "What the hell are you talking about, Jim? This is not a dry county! The liquor store is two streets down to the right next to the bar and steak house."

Without thinking these words came out of my mouth, "Those bastards!! We been outa rum for two days now! You mean to tell me......."

Then I shut up, paid for the gas, and left. The cashier was laughing; he thought it was hilarious that we had been hood winked like that.

We got back in the truck, heading home, never to return to Dunderun State Park.

Chapter 16

Everything must change, nothing stays the same

*"A lawyer is never entirely comfortable with a friendly divorce,
anymore than a good mortician wants to finish his job and then have
the patient sit up on the table."*

~Jean Kerr

It may be one of my favorite Quincy Jones songs but there
is a lot of truth to it.

   *"The young become the old, and mysteries do
unfold."*

   I never thought my kids would grow as fast as they
did. During the time I was raising them that was my entire
world. Simply trying to run the business of the show, and
then being a full time dad and taxi service that required
more time than in a 24 hour day. We put everything into
our kids and then one day, when you really are not prepared
for it, they are gone.

   There is no slope for it either. For years you do
nothing but do everything that entails raising children,
then…poof, those youngens are gone and off to college. I
was not prepared for the empty nest syndrome. Let me tell
you it does exist, and last for a while.

   It probably was a combination of a lot of things
during my early 40's that eventually led to my separation
and divorce from one of the greatest ladies in the world,
Helen. Why did I do this? Here was a great lady and
mother of my two kids, good looking girl who had a great
career and was a very good person. I really thought I was
crazy for even thinking of separating from a woman I never
even had an argument with nor raised my voice with for
around 25 years.

   So why then bring up separation?

For me it was the hardest decision I ever made and I guess it was the right thing to do. Not sure I will ever know for sure. Here is the thing that my family and friends I hope will understand. Raising a family was the best thing I ever did and will do, however it was a detour of what I ultimately wanted and that was to live back on the water. Be that little kid on the dock again. I loved that life so much. Now that my kids for the most part were grown and gone, I could not see myself pushing a lawn mower in suburbia for the remainder of my later years. It just was not me.

My lovely wife, Helen was fine with it and I talked to her once about the future and she was happy to stay right there in that awesome big house in Suburbia, giving me honey do lists and continuing to watch me do yard work which I hated. For me, this would be a jail sentence. But who can blame my wife? She had a great house, great career, and great family, why not just stay there? Helen did nothing wrong in her desire to stay and live in Suburbia. Heck, it is the American Dream.....Just not my dream.

One day no one was in the house and I looked down the hallway from the studio and like a tidal wave came over me. I asked myself a question to either be happy here in suburbia doing yard work, or get out and start a new life on the water somewhere. I will never know if I made the 100% right decision. I decided to talk to my wife about a trial separation to find out if that is what would or would not be best for the future.

She was upset, so was I when we talked. I mean Helen was and is a great lady. I still was thinking I lost my mind even for bringing this whole thing up. I figured if it turned out that we would stay separated it would be hard for the present time, but in the long run be better off for everybody. I was a good husband however if I ended up stuck in suburbia, I was afraid I would loose it and start to treat her in a negative way. I did not want that at all. She was too good a lady. It was a serious gamble I made, often times seriously wondering if I ever should have even brought up separating at all.

To my surprise after a week or so Helen talked to me and said that she too thought that in the long run it would be best. Although everything was fine now, we did want different things in our futures and we were both calm, reasonable people. So I suggested since I was traveling a fair amount, that we would not say anything to the kids yet. Casey, I think only had a year left in high school and Ben was in college. I wanted to wait until Casey was off in college before we told them that we were amicably separating. Helen agreed.

This did not last long. My wife came to me and said it would be better for her if we went ahead and told the kids. Be honest about it and move on. Now, I did not agree with this at all. Had I thought it would go down this path I doubt I would have brought it up. I think I would have waited another year or so then bring it up if I still felt the same way.

Here is the thing. This was all my initial idea anyway and felt horrible about it. I respected Helen so much that if that is what she felt she wanted to do then I would have to respect that, and I did.

OH BOY! I am a piece of dog shit!

Telling my daughter and watching her cry to this day is the hardest thing I have ever done. I wanted to be strong, but failed. After about 1/2 hour, I went to the bathroom and cried my eyes out for hours. I could not deal with what I had done, I hurt my daughter and son and I will never get over that.

Casey soon realized that her life would not change really at all, and that her mom and I loved each other, we just thought this would be best in the long run. She did understand and agreed, but still hurt like hell.

Ben was upset but he was older and had a feeling something was up. He was not happy but in very short time, everyone realized that the kids' lives would not really change. We kept the house until Casey was half way through college and I saw Casey about as much as I did when I was living there. Both my kids were adults now and leading their own successful lives. Ben and Casey both are still very close to both their mother and father and show great respect to us.

In hind sight had I known I had to tell my kids we were separating, I would not have brought it up until they were both grown and out of college. It did not work out that way. The Lord has plans for things to happen in their own time. I put my faith in him and trust there is a good reason for all things.

To be honest, I thought the good Lord had already answered my prayers. The Magnolia Tree was shining bright!

20 years ago when Ben was born, I prayed for a calm and happy family life for my kids. For them to not have to go threw what I went through as a kid dealing with mothers that suffered from mental illness and personality disorders. My prayers had been answered in a very great way. Ben and Casey had an awesome childhood in a home without yelling or screaming. They were raised in a loving place without any craziness and both my kids turned out wonderful.

The world is a better place because they are in it. The great thing about my relationship with Helen is that it really has not changed much since we were happily married. Helen was always family and I sort of felt like she was my sister in some way. Helen and I communicated maybe even more about things after we were separated than we did while we were married. It really was and is a great relationship.

146

Even when we both started dating again, we always would tell stories about how crazy things were and would give each other advice all the time. One thing for sure is that it is a valuable thing to have an ex-wife who loves you and only wants the best for you. I don't think I would ever re-marry unless Helen approved of the girl. That may sound strange to some people, but I trust her judgment. Just like my dad the Judge, they just are not wrong that often. I trust and listen to what the few family members I have left have to say.

As time went on Helen proved correct many times by her advice on some women I would be dating. Some she was in favor of and thought I should maybe marry, others she was brutally honest and told me to run for the hills and don't ever look back. She was usually right.

It is a very great thing to be able to communicate like this with your ex-wife. Personally, I never liked the name ex- wife. Helen is not an x anything. There should be a nicer more pleasant name for people who separate and divorce in a pleasant way and still remain family.

It may sound very hard to believe for a lot of people who have gone through horrible violent divorces to look at my situation and actually believe it. But the fact is there are those of us out there that as a couple for 25. 30. 40 + years, eventually want different things out of life. It does not mean you don't love each other, it just means you grow apart in some ways. That is all. Sometimes it happens in couples, sometimes not.

Whether or not ultimately I made the right decision, is a tough call. What helped me in the end to figure it out were a few things. Realizing my kids have grown to be fantastic people and both college degreed. Helen has done exceptionally well in her career and now a PHD with a ton of friends and people who love her to death. I have followed the path that I thought would be best and never looked back on doing yard work in suburbia.

Probably one of the biggest signs that let me know that maybe in the long run our decision was just.....

Helen is living in a giant house happily in the state of Maine under four feet of snow.

I am living in a condo on the water on the Chesapeake Bay.

Chances are we did want different things after all, at least longitudinally and we are both happy and talk every week.

Chapter 17

Back on the docks, living my youth big time.

All that is good in man lies in youthful feeling and mature thought"

~Joseph Joubert

Jim Baugh Outdoors had been producing a lot of
programming featuring the state of Virginia for years and
we desperately wanted a salt-water home base of
operations. We had featured Hampton Virginia several
times and I approached the city about making Hampton our
home for *Jim Baugh Outdoors TV*.

The location was perfect. Hampton is located in the
lower Bay area with easy access to the tidal rivers, the
Chesapeake, and the Atlantic Ocean. We made the deal
with the city for us to promote Hampton in our show and
feature many of the tourist attractions in the area. I still had
the house in Richmond, so I didn't want to purchase more
real estate until we sold the house.

This gave me the idea to purchase a boat and live on
it right on the water in Downtown Hampton. We would
also have our showboat tied up right next to our 36-foot
Trojan live-aboard in the marina right downtown. This was
a good idea and was a cheap way to live and work in the
area while we shot the show.

The best way I could describe the Downtown
Hampton Waterfront in those days was that it was the Key
West of the Mid Atlantic. I had never seen anything quite
like this. Not even when I was a kid running around
catching crabs on "A" dock. Quite frankly I was blown
away.

Picture this; I am living on a 36 foot Trojan boat
docked only about 60 feet from the Radisson Hotel. There
was an outdoor patio restaurant on the waterfront called
Oyster Alley and of course a bar and restaurant inside the

hotel. The hotel gave us boaters full access to the amenities including the swimming pool, work out room, everything. They had bands set up on a stage by the outside bar and had music during the week.

During the weekend on a Saturday night the docks were jammed packed with people, so many sometimes you could hardly walk down the pier. Everyone was always partying having a ball and grilling out on their boats consuming plenty of cocktails. I didn't even have to get off my boat. Sitting on the fly bridge we could clearly see the bands which were only about 100 feet away.

Just down the walkway from the hotel was Mill Point Park. The park had a big stage that featured tons of music acts and various festivals. Friday nights would kick off with jazz concerts. I was there for every performance with my rum and tonic in hand.

As if this is not good enough get this. Walk one block off the marina hotel and there lies the Saturday night Block Party. Hampton would close down several blocks and bring in the city stage and feature bands and beer trucks. Not just any bands… we are talking groups like Blue Oyster Cult, Molly Hatchet and hundreds of others.

The streets were all lined with the local bars, pubs and restaurants that also had live entertainment performing inside and out on the decks. It was nothing for me to go listen to six or seven bands in one night and never even pay a cover charge. The streets were packed and the downtown waterfront was the place to be. Remember, this would be just for an average weekend. If there were a festival going on like Bay Days there would be 300,000 people jamming downtown, partying like rock stars. Groups like Charlie Daniels, Fabulous Thunderbirds and Bruce Hornsby would be headlining plus all the other music acts as well.

I had never seen a festival atmosphere like this and I was living in the middle of it on a 36 foot boat with my 28 foot Pursuit showboat tied up adjacent. For me all that was fine. But being a music major, I mostly enjoyed all the music acts. Hampton was a town that embraced artists and even had blues bars dedicated to regional and national blues groups. Just fantastic!

I had free concerts all over the place that did not cost me a dime. I drank on the docks and my boat for free and everyone in the world wanted to stop by and party on my boat.

For sure, this was much more than I even experienced on "A" dock as a kid. Again, I remember the old saying, *Be careful what you ask for, you might just get it.* I got it all right, and in spades! Yes I will not lie... I loved it!

Advancements in computers made it so that I could edit on lap top computers. This enabled me to set up an edit suite and playback system on the boat that I lived on. We would go out on our showboat and get some filming done come back and dock the Pursuit, jump on the 36 Trojan and start editing. This was a great and very productive way to produce Jim Baugh Outdoors TV.

I don't know of any other producer out there that produced their show this way. Our show was filmed and edited on boats right on the water in Downtown Hampton. Once I finished editing a show I would jump off the boat, ride my bike four blocks away to the post office and mail the tape to our national syndicator. On the way back from the Post Office I peddled two blocks away to the liquor store to get rum for the evening then would stop by the grocery store and fill up my bike saddlebags with groceries. Everywhere I went downtown I traveled by either boat or bicycle. I had this down big time. The great thing was there was no time wasted. I worked lived and played, all on a 1974, 36-foot Trojan Tri-Cabin docked on the Downtown Hampton Waterway.

Fishing, boating, sailing, being on the water was an everyday experience. I lived and slept on one boat and

fished out of the other. The showboat was large enough
where I could weekend on it. So for my time off, I would
sometimes just take the boat out for the weekend and tour
the lower Chesapeake Bay.

Staying at different marinas was always fun and I
only stayed at places that had lots of amenities, pools,
restaurants, pubs, etc. It was always a good time. I would
take the boat over to Portsmouth and anchor out in front of
the concert pavilion. When groups like the Doobie Brothers
would come and play, I would not buy a ticket. I would
anchor up in front of the pavilion light the on-board grill,
fire up some steaks, have a cocktail and enjoy the show.
What is not to LOVE! Michael McDonald and Steely Dan
were playing one night and there I was, sitting out on the
anchored showboat in the marlin tower sipping on some
rum watching the stars in the sky. I loved this.

All of my dock buddies knew that I lived and
worked editing our TV shows right there on the boat. So I
was there most the time. Usually I would be sitting on the
boat, editing the show and sure enough…. here Jonah Top
Knot would come blazing through the fly bridge door.
Jonah was a sailor and pirate who lived to sail and spent the
previous three years living and sailing in the Florida Keys.
Jonah had sailed up to Hampton to do a high paying
welding job in the shipyard for about 13 months. I never
knew what Jonah's last name really was, but it didn't
matter. This captain loved to take me sailing and I would
jump at the chance every time he offered. Jonah would
teach me from what a grommet was, to how to tend bar
while the boat is heeling in a heavy Sea. Sailing with Jonah
was always a memorable mid week treat.

Sundays I really looked forward to. Here was my
regular Sunday Schedule.

First, we would cook up a breakfast on the docks
with a few bloody marys. Afterwards a quick dip in the
swimming pool and hot tub at the hotel, a little work out,

then board our showboat and cruise out in the Chesapeake over to Salt Ponds Marina. Beautiful white sandy beaches surround the inlet at Salt Ponds. Low-lying shrubs and salty marsh grass covered the area and also hid some of the nude bathers. This is one of the more popular nude beaches on the Bay and I have seen some incredible sights there especially on a full moon.

The water and marsh area behind Salt Ponds was teaming with sea life and was a great place that we would catch fiddler crabs for tog fishing. This place is also a kayaker's heaven with tons of little channels crawling back through the sea marshes.

Once docked at Salt Ponds we would walk up to the Tiki Bar where there was a Caribbean band playing. There was a swimming pool with a volleyball net and a first class Tiki Bar with every tacky light imaginable strung up all over the place. The pool was great because it was located right next to the bar and they had a gas grill cooking up seafood schishkabobs.

We would have cocktails in the pool while the band was playing and eat fresh grilled scallops all while swimming in the pool. I had a lot of friends at Salt Ponds and it was a different setting than Downtown Hampton. Salt Ponds is one of the prettier places you will ever see on the Chesapeake Bay.

When we were done at Salt Ponds I would motor back to my slip in downtown Hampton and head over to the deck at Marker 20 for the Sunday afternoon David Carter Concert. Dave was a popular musician who did a lot of Jimmy Buffet tunes and some good originals as well. Dave was quite the entertainer and put on a good Sunday afternoon show that lasted until late in the evening.

Dinner on the Deck at Marker 20 usually meant the steamed crustation platter for two with a bucket of iced Cerveza's. After dinner we all would head back to the boats light up a cigar on the fly bridge and watch the sunset.

That was how I would wrap up my weekends…I never touched a lawn mower again.

During the week I would stay busy shooting and editing the show on the boats. Wednesdays was always boater's night at the bar in the hotel. They would have drink specials for us boaters and put out appetizers. That was always a good time and often we would get a little out of hand. But we knew the owner of the hotel, he liked us and I was a good friend with his son. For some reason the hotel embraced the boaters. We were probably good for business because we did spend a ton of money in there as a group. It was only one night a week and people downtown knew that if you went to the bar at the hotel on a Wednesday you were going to get your fill of the boaters. It was just the way it was. We owned that bar on Wednesday nights.

It is very exciting to be living on a boat at the marina. There was always something going on and always something to do. Boats require a lot of maintenance and we were always working on them. We would all help each other out with whatever boat projects were being done. For a while I lived and breathed Boater's World. Living on a boat that was really the only place I shopped. I would even buy my clothes at the store, great place. Sorry it is no longer, I always will miss Boater's World.

There was always activity at the marina, always. I was a part of a large boating community that was not just of downtown Hampton but all the boaters that would come and visit. The public piers were actually attached to our private marina, so we always were being introduced to transient boaters. This place was just a boater's paradise for sure.

The public piers pretty much ran the gamut of the clientele that would come dock their boats. Anything from multimillion-dollar yachts to 20-foot sailboats is what would tie up to the transient slips. I would also meet a lot of snowbirds traveling down to the Florida Keys for the winter. These boaters were always fun to talk with who were usually older retired couples that just had a passion for boating.

There are those boaters who are sort of on the other end of the stick. These are people who live aboard 23-foot sailboats that are sort of homeless. They really have no money at all and just float around at sea because it doesn't cost anything to live. I did not think these people existed, sort of like Waterworld but on the Chesapeake Bay.

One day I was on the boat and the Dock Master stopped by and asked,

"Jim have you met Stan yet? He is the live aboard on that little 23-foot sailboat at the piers. The guy is sort of out of it. No food, no money, sort of a crazy dude."

I talked to a couple of friends at the marina and suggested we make some food and take it over to him. I had never met this guy but figured he would appreciate a hot meal. I made up a lot of homemade spicy jambalaya grabbed a buddy and went over to see this fellow.

We walked over and knocked on the door and all we heard was, "Cooooooooome on in mate!"

We opened up the door to the little sailboat and here was this very thin crazed looking guy who looked like he had been lost at sea for years. He had charcoal on his face and there was no hair on his left arm. He was wearing a ragged tee shirt with the right shoulder cut out. The center of the shirt had one printed word on it. *BEER*. That was it. His name was Stan and I think he may have been around 30 years old.

"Hi Stan my name is Jim, welcome to Hampton. I had a lot of left over food here and was wondering if you would like some."

He said, "Dam Skippy!"

Stan then took what looked like a fork that had been burned up in a fire and started diving into that food like a

155

starving dog on a steak biscuit. I don't know the last time he ate, but I could figure the last time he drank. He was stoned drunk and had this charcoal looking paste all over his face and body. Looking around the boat the entire top of the ceiling had been burned and the some of the fiberglass had hundreds of little black bubbles in it.

I asked, "Say Stan, what happened here man, looks like some sort of fire or something?"

He said, "Oh…. I put that out days ago."

I said, "Well, what happened?"

Stan replied, "It was really cold and I didn't have any heat when I was anchored out, so I started a little fire here in the corner of the boat and it got sorta out of hand. I tried to put it out with my bottle of 151 rum and it seemed to make it much worse. Good thing I had already drank most of it."

I said, "Yeah, that's a good thing Stan."

Stan finished his grub and we left to go back to our boats. After that meal, he was going to be passed out soon enough.

The next day I was riding my bike down past the marina and I saw Stan sitting over on the bench, with about five of the regular homeless people who regularly reside in downtown Hampton. These are the homeless that we often take food to and we would see them almost daily during the summer. During the winter, these guys would make their way down south to Florida and bum down there. They were homeless snowbirds.

Stan and the homeless crew had a couple of brown bags with some sort of spirits and these guys were raising hell having a ball. I waved as I rode by on my bike and was just hoping Stan was not going to get the idea of bringing everyone down to the docks and visit me on my boat. I get in enough trouble all by myself and did not need these guys' help.

I got to the boat and walking down the docks behind me is Stan, five homeless dudes and two brown bags.

Oh hell. Here we go.

I go down into my cabin, mix a drink and pray these guys are not coming to invade my boat. I had just stocked the bar and did not want it emptied, like pulling a plug in a tub. An hour fortunately passes and no Stan or crew. Then I hear what sounds like about five police cars right outside my boat.

I run out of the cabin and head up to the hotel to see what's up. Here is Stan and the five homeless dudes being escorted out of the hotel down to the public piers. I said to one of the officers, "Excuse me is there any problem with Stan and the homeless guys?"

He said, "Sir, do you know these people? Are they guests of yours?"

I said, "No sir, officer. Stan is staying at the public piers in a charcoal sailboat. The other guys are sail boaters without boats so they live on the public bench over behind Pirate P.D. Cooper's wooden pirate boat… Any problems? What did these guys do?"

Officer said, "Only hotel guests and boaters are allowed up to the hotel pool and some of the guest were complaining about these five homeless guys skinny-dipping in the pool in broad daylight."

Evidently the only thing they were wearing was two wet brown paper bags.

I could not believe that Stan did this. Sure it was funny but come on. Really, taking five homeless dudes and two brown bags full of ripple swimming nude in the middle of the day in a five star hotel, that of course… they had no business being in?

It probably would not have been so bad if there was not the regional Baptist Woman's Ministers Conference going on at the hotel. The local ladies Red Hat Society was dining on the third floor and that did not help matters either. The new hotel manager Mrs. Ratchet, saw no humor in the mid day nude swim from Stan and the boys. She was the one that called the cops. The timing was not that good for old Stan and our homeless friends.

Stan was not going to be staying around long. He was already causing trouble at the hotel and at the public piers. I felt sorry for him and continued to bring him some food, up until he got kicked out of the marina.

The story on Stan was that he was a young fellow who had his share of trouble with drugs and alcohol. He came from a wealthy prominent family who couldn't do anything with him. So instead of taking him in, they bought him a small sailboat and told him he could live on that anywhere he wanted. So Stan would travel around the Chesapeake Bay just anchoring out and only really checking into marinas to have his parents wire him some money once in a while.

When Stan would get his family funding he would move on to his next location, The Florida Keys. He said if he was going to be homeless on a sailboat, it might as well be in Key West. That was the last I saw of Charcoal Stan.

Before he left he thanked me again for all the food I had brought him. I could really tell that it had been a long time since anyone had showed him some grace.

There are people who live like this. I have met several others similar over the years. You just meet all kinds living on the water from all walks of life. Help the ones you can, spread some grace and move on.

Jim Baugh Outdoors TV live aboard and camera boat 1974 Trojan Tri Cabin. This picture was taken when JBOTV purchased and surveyed the boat in Myrtle Beach South Carolina winter of 1998.

One of the White Marlin caught, filmed and released on Jim Baugh Outdoors TV.

Chapter 18

King of the Sea

"If you would not be forgotten, as soon as you are dead and rotten, either write things worth reading, or do things worth the writing."

~Benjamin Franklin

One of our favorite locations to film and also vacation was Hatteras Village on the Outer Banks of North Carolina. My days in Hatteras go way back to when I was only 19 years old, surf fishing and hauling in big bluefish out of the surf. Summertime was a great time on the point but most of our fishing was done during the fall and winter. Cruising on the beach in our four wheel drives with a cooler loaded up with ice and bait looking for seagulls diving was always a blast. I spent so much time in Hatteras I almost considered it my second home.

Hatteras Village had a beautiful hotel right on the water and our show had a promotional consideration agreement with the property. They let us stay there in exchange for mentions on our TV show. The Village was sort of at the end of the world and the place was never jammed packed with people, that is the way I liked it.

A lot of tourists coming to the Outer Banks like to stay in a poplar area called Duck. This a nice place to stay during the off-season. Not my kind of place during the peak tourist times. There are maybe 50,000 people packed in houses in a relatively small area with one two-lane road a few restaurants and a grocery store. Pretty place but the northern Outer Banks I always felt was for the tourist trade. Lots of crowds and beaches were jam packed as well. This is great for the vacationing family tourist.

Three families will pitch in together on some monstrous house and cook in a lot. For me this usually meant too many people and too many dishes. It's ok for a couple of days but for a week stay I will take the Village any day. Traveling along the Outer Banks I would never even light up a cigar until I cruised past Oregon Inlet.

Hatteras Village was where it was at for me. The Village was my kind of place. This was a real fishing village that lived and breathed boats, clamming, fishing and boat building. Because of my love for Hatteras we have produced many programs featuring this quaint ocean side respite.

Everyone in the Village loved to fish and party. This place had a real community feel to it. Brown bagging was allowed in most restaurants so we would just pack up the bar and go out to eat.

During our early years of producing the show I got so carried away with offshore fishing we began to get some criticism. Some fans thought we were doing too much offshore fishing and wanted more inshore and inland programs. I thought this criticism was warranted and we took the time necessary to review our programming. What I did was to try our best to divide all of our locations into thirds. A third offshore, a third Bay and tidal rivers, and a third inland would be a nice programming balance to try and achieve. This was a reasonable idea and did help equal out the fishing segments of our show. During this span was a time when we started considering also featuring more cooking segments. Whenever we would air one of our cooking features the phones would light up like a Christmas tree.

Since we now were going to produce maybe one to three offshore shows a year, I decided to try and make a huge impact with the programs we produced in the Gulf Stream. My first thought was to produce a fantastic show on white marlin fishing. We had filmed some marlin before but never quite got the shots we wanted so a marlin show was on the top of the list.

I was going to put every piece of production knowledge I had into this show and make it the best. Fortunately, I had several contacts in the fishing industry that knew a lot about white marlin fishing. I called them and went to work on pre production. I had the guest lined up for the show and four charters on 24-hour call. When the bite was on, we would be filming within 24 hours. Everybody was set and scheduled.

I thought that for this next shoot it was worth writing a brand new exciting and symphonic soundtrack. I went into the studio and started writing a music score just for the fish catching sequence that we would soon be filming. I locked myself in the studio and three weeks later I came out for a breather. This piece of music was draining for me because I used all 48 tracks of Midi and was also using our automated 24-channel mixer, plus four synthesizer modules. It was a dynamic progressive rock orchestral piece that had a lot of synthesizer leads and expansive orchestration.

I would picture in my mind a marlin flying through the air crashing into the ocean. Then I would play on the keyboard music inspired by this marlin vision. Next I would be thinking about the shots I would need to get in order to match the vision in my head. The soundtrack turned out awesome and I continued to use this piece of music throughout the show for years. Once I had the piece finished, I mastered it and saved it off to a digital audio tape machine. I had the music complet now and all I needed now was to film the offshore marlin footage.

A week later I get the call. "Bite is on!" I gather my crew and headed to Hatteras. Driving down south we cross over the Bonner Bridge heading to Pea Island and I can see the ocean. Even on top of the Bridge, the wind was gusting so fierce there was a coating of sand on the windshield.

"Hey Wayne, what are those gigantic things out there rolling around?"

"…Ahhhhhh, looks like waves to me dude."

It was rough. In my excitement about finishing the soundtrack and getting the call to shoot the marlin I neglected to ask how the weather was. Usually the captain is not going to call unless the sea is fishable.

We made it down to Hatteras Village met with the captain on the boat and discussed tomorrow's trip.

"So Captain the bite is on big time?"

"…We are going to get some fantastic footage Jim."

"Any thoughts on the sea conditions?"

"…She is a 55 custom Carolina sport fish. She can handle it."

The boat may be able to handle it, but not sure Wayne and I could. The seas were 10 feet and climbing. Before we left the boat I set up several stations around the fly bridge and along the gunnels of the boat. These stations would have safety lines attached to the boat and then tied to whoever was running the camera. I would also have an emergency line hooked to the camera secured to the cameraman.

I put on the waterproof housing over the equipment and fitted Wayne and I with life jackets. The reason for the life jacket was not in fear of the boat sinking. Rather one of us would go over because we would be hanging off the side of the boat with a camera in a 10 to 15 foot sea.

I have been on a shoot before where it was so rough on a 90-foot head boat one of the fishermen was thrown over the side. Taking safety precautions is always a good idea especially in the seas we would be facing.

Wayne and I were finished prepping the equipment and left to go have dinner with my national fishing line representative and sponsor. His name was Trick Stillman and this guy knew everything about offshore fishing he was one hell of a nice guy that just lived for every chance to go marlin fishing. Trick was going to be fishing with us and testing out some new fishing line. I had told Trick about the

164

really dramatic and exciting music score I had written for this marlin footage that we hopefully were going to get and we all felt we were going to have a good day.

None of us were too thrilled about the sea conditions and I explained how Wayne and I would be filming this particular shoot. Because of the rough seas everyone had to have signals for what to do and when. With the big diesel engines roaring and 12-foot seas crashing around you, screaming out direction does not help much. So I showed Trick several hand signals that would get us threw what was going to be one knee-numbing day at offshore.

Dinner was delicious. Whenever I go offshore I always eat light, nothing fried or too greasy. Wayne had the steamed clams but unfortunately the clams decided they wanted to get back to sea in about six hours.

Wayne woke up feeling horrible, bent over and could hardly move. He could barely open his eyes and I thought this was a bad case of food poisoning. Wayne said he thought that was all it was and wanted to try and go through with the shoot. I helped Wayne down to the boat and we were all in the salon for a meeting. When we are filming the Captain is always in charge of the boat and the fishing, it is my job to let them know what to expect out of us TV guys. What I told them was this,

"Captain, it looks like we are in for a rough ride even in a 55 sport fish."

He said, "Yes, everyone will be wearing instant inflatable lifejackets and all persons need to be on their toes, eyes wide open."

I said, "Folks, here is the deal. Wayne is here but we think he is suffering from food poisoning and I am planning on him not being able to film. We will see how he feels as the day goes on. So I am going to plan on doing most of the filming myself. One or two times I will pass off the camera to one of you mates in order to get myself on film."

I then proceeded to show one of the mates how to hold the camera and that he would be on a safety line. I would only need to do this once or twice for about five minutes each and everything else I would shoot.

Wayne was going downhill fast. I had never seen food poisoning like this. His head was in the toilet and he was very sick. At this time we were just turning out of the sound approaching the inlet. Unfortunately we would later find out after this shoot, Wayne was not suffering from food poisoning but diverticulitis. He would later be hospitalized where he almost died. He was extremely sick and we did not realize it at the time.

There is no sound like 14 foot waves crashing in the inlet at 5 in the morning. Hatteras Inlet is an extremely dangerous inlet and the sea was roaring with a thick salty mist immediately covering the entire boat. This 55 sport fish was one awesome boat however it was already being bounced around like a cat top. It was dark and sea foam was filling the cockpit. The captain charged eastwardly as I went down below to ready our production gear.

The conditions were so rough I used about all of our emergency straps and bungee cords just to secure everything down below. In seas like this you don't want anything flying around that can damage the boat or injure someone.

It was during this time sitting on the floor in the salon that I started to get my game plan for how I was going to shoot this. I already had the shots in my head based on the music I had written for this particular offshore trip. First up I figured Wayne was out. I tied him up in the bathroom with a safety line so he wouldn't fall and he could keep the toilet right in front of his face for easy projectile vomiting. All the safety lines I had rigged on the boat were set up and ready.

The captain sent a message down from up top and asks if I wanted to turn around because the seas were getting worse, however he thought the bite would be worth it if we stayed.

Because we had a very sick person on board I ask Wayne if he thought he could make it the rest of the day. He said if he could just stay on the sofa for us to continue heading out to sea. So that is what we did. If Wayne had asked to go back I would have cancelled the trip. Wayne was being a tough sport and hung in there. He knew that if we caught a marlin in these weather conditions the footage was going to be some of the best ever filmed. He turned out to be right.

Due to the rough seas we were only doing about 10 knots heading out. It took us almost two hours to get to our blue water fishing grounds. Finally we reached the area where the captain thought we would have a shot at a nice white marlin.

I walked out of the salon and told Trick that I wanted him to reel in the marlin once hooked up. I was going to be filming from different locations on the boat. Trick was all excited and was ready for the big bite.

The mate got all lines out and Trick was sitting strapped in THE chair. I had started walking up the deck towards the mid-ship holding on to the gunnel rails and soon reached the safety line I had previously rigged. The powerful cresting seas were somewhere between 10 and 15 feet high. I thought we were nuts for trying to film this however things were planned out and other than Wayne being so sick, everything was going okay. Once the safety line was attached to the camera and me, I powered everything up and looked through the lenses and just was in awe of what I saw.

I was in an elevated camera position mid-ship looking back down toward the back deck with 15-foot waves rolling out from under the stern. Sea foam was flying through the air like snow. I hit the record button because the footage was dramatic and I wanted to check camera levels. Tape was rolling and I felt safe hanging off the side of the boat filming. Looking through the viewfinder I saw the rod slam down horizontal and could hear the bait alarm squealing. I slowly tilted up the camera off the stern and in the picture was a white marlin piercing threw the top of a 15-foot wave clearing the air by five feet. The airborne thrashing marlin was now twenty feet above the trough of the wave. WOW!! What a sight and caught live on camera!

Watching the marlin begin to crash down back into the sea in my mind the very first beat of the soundtrack was getting ready to fire off. The first two notes of this music were 48 tracks of guitars, synths, and an orchestra all firing off 300 voices at the same time with enough musical force to knock down a wall. When that marlin hit the water it was in perfect sync with the soundtrack in my mind. What I had planned many weeks ago was now playing real time in the ocean with a 15-foot sea and a white marlin that was half fish and half airplane. I never saw a fish jump like this.

This marlin to me was king of the sea.

Next the 55 sports fish fell off a top of a huge wave and was then down in the trough. This monster wave rolled under us and then off the stern. As it passed about 20 yards away the panicked marlin jumped through the top of the wave dancing in an acrobatic way throwing its bill trying to free itself. The footage was unreal and tape was rolling.

After about 15 minutes of filming I repositioned three other times to continue to get the shots I wanted. Trick was in awe of this fish and with the excitement of the sea conditions made everyone's hair stand on end.

Off the northeast port side the dark skies plummeted down to the tips of the waves and there merged a wide waterspout. The ocean and cloudy sky above was now connected and the white marlin was racing through the tops of the waves like a bat out of hell. The captain pointed the boat southwest to divert from the waterspout. Unfortunately the spout did not help the sea conditions any.

The captain had the second mate haul in the outriggers fearing that they were getting too close to the crest of the waves. After the outriggers were secured, I attempted to get the mate to hold the camera and I was going to try and get an interview with Trick while he was fighting the fish. This did not work. In these conditions it was not wise to turn over this piece of camera gear to anyone. I called up on the intercom to the captain from below and told him that I was going to be doing some things with the camera in the back, and not to be concerned. I would have a safety line on me the entire time. This was an opportunity to get some once in a lifetime footage and I was going to get it.

The captain replied on the intercom, "Jim, that is fine, but be careful and also pass this on to the crew below. I have been on the VHF and there is a charter boat from the northern fleet that is beginning to take on water. The Coast Guard has been notified and we are now heading in that direction in case they need assistance. We are on standby. If I flash the floodlights three times that means lines in immediately. Try to get that fish in ASAP."

I replied, "Okay Captain. We will keep an eye on the floods. By the way, your bilge lights keep coming on down here on the circuit breaker panel."

Captain says, "That's fine Jim. We have a staged bilge system and that is just the service pump. No problem."

I said, "Captain, all three bilge lights are on. Do you have three service pumps?"

The captain flew downstairs waved me aside and opened the flooded engine compartment. The raw water intake to the engine had come loose and the boat was flooding with water.

He quickly secured the hose by re-clamping the seacock with two clamps. Then the captain hit the switch to the mother of all bilge pumps. This thing could have raised the Titanic. After the water was pumped out the captain flew back up the ladder to the fly bridge just in time for the port side canvas to rip off. This let a lot of spray into the fly bridge, however was not going to stop the captain from fishing.

I repositioned myself on the stern and tied a line on me to a secured cleat. Then I lay on the floor on the back deck with the camera pointing upwards. The sea would slide me around the back deck, which would enable me to get some incredible angle shots of reeling in the white marlin. This camera angle was also an interesting perspective of the massive waves that seemed to engulf us. This worked for about 15 minutes before my safety line broke and decided it was time to get shots from the fly bridge. This is where I would film the remaining of the marlin sequence.

The marlin was jumping directly behind the stern which is always a dangerous situation. People get stabbed and sometimes even pulled over when the fish gets this close. It was only two weeks prior when a mate fishing offshore Hatteras was pulled over by a marlin. He got caught up twisted in the line the marlin dove and pulled the mate overboard. He was never seen again. These things do happen and did not want it happening to us.

I told the captain that I had 20 minutes of footage and most all of it was usable. The seas were building more and I told him to do a quick release of the fish and we would be done.

The mate released the marlin unharmed and as the last roller moved beneath our boat, the freed marlin spiked through a wave and gave us one last frantic poetic dance. The marlin fell back crashing against the sea in a trough. Then his bill fenced across the waves for a moment while

170

quickly submerging beneath a vast enraged sea blanketed by rain.

That was the last we saw of that magnificent fish.

We pointed the boat northwest and headed in. The other boat in the northern fleet that was taking on water was escorted in by the Coast Guard and returned safely.

The inlet at Hatters is one of the most dangerous in the world. There is a reason why they call this area the graveyard of the Mid-Atlantic. Even in the 55 sports fish we cavitated the port prop as we made the south turn in the inlet. We hit a wave broadside and threw the boat on its side like it was a 12 foot puffer sailboat. My knees would continue to stay blue until we were steady in the sound.

We were finally out of the Atlantic.

The Magnolia Tree had blessed us once more.

Back at the dock Wayne was still passed out. I figured it was a combination of food poisoning and seasickness. By the time the boat was cleaned up the day was shot. We would stay one more night in Hatteras Village before heading back.

The captain asks me if we wanted to stop by his favorite local bar for some fresh bluefin tuna. He had caught this fish and wanted the bar to cook it up and celebrate the day's shoot and safe return. We took Wayne to the room where he continued to rest and hopefully get better. I went down the street to meet the captain at the Sandbar for drinks and fresh Tuna. I also brought my camera to show him some of the footage.

We ordered several drinks because it had been an extremely rough day out at sea. I explained to the captain the soundtrack I had written for this marlin shoot and just how awesome the footage was going to work with the music I had written. I was VERY excited about editing this show, more so than any other show I had produced so far. The captain was very gracious and he knew that the footage we got was fairly rare for those days. I knew I was sitting on film that once edited was going to drive our viewers nuts with excitement. We would be the talk of the town for years.

…. At least that is what I thought.

The next day we got up and Wayne was still in horrible shape and this is when I began to think something might be seriously wrong with him. In my buiz people get seasick and eat bad food on the road all the time. It happens frequently but this now seemed to be something much more.

On the road traveling north on the outerbanks the waves were still crashing the shoreline. I thought to myself I was so grateful the marlin gave us such a good show then was set free to live its life in the ocean.

The anticipation of editing this show was killing me.

Worrying about Wayne I called his girlfriend and told her about his illness. I explained that we thought it was food poisoning and seasickness; however now I was thinking it could be something else. I told her, "I am bringing him to you and want you to keep a close eye on him. I am worried that something is going on but I don't know what."

She appreciated it and said she would take care of him and keep a watchful eye.

I drove Wayne to his girlfriends and his condition worsened. He could hardly get out of the truck. Things were not looking good. She said to put him on the sofa and she would watch him and see how he does. She said there was a medical center close to her house and she would take him there if necessary.

She said for me to go home get some rest and if there were any change she would call me.

I got a call at 8 pm that night from her saying that Wayne was taken in an ambulance and was in the hospital. She had left him on the sofa and he was awake but not feeling well. She took a shower and when she came out Wayne was passed out and could not be wakened. He was breathing, but she said he had gotten very white and would not wake. She called her nursing friend and then an ambulance.

I rushed to the hospital to see Wayne and was worried to death. After several tests the doctors had found out Wayne had a severe case of diverticulitis and could have easily died. They rushed him to surgery where he remained in the hospital for a month. He was going to survive this however he would continue to have complications for the next year.

My good friend Wayne lost 70 pounds during this ordeal and I was extremely happy that he had lived through it. All of us were grateful that he survived and none of us thought it was Wayne's time to go.

The Magnolia Tree had blossomed once more.

Wayne's illness distracted me greatly and I was not able to edit the marlin show for about two months. Once I had my head clear I was ready to concentrate on editing. I had a very dramatic original soundtrack, high impact exciting marlin footage that together was going to make the best fishing episode on TV. I was excited.

I locked myself into the studio and began to edit this show. The footage was so thrilling that the entire story about filming this offshore excursion was going to take up about 15 minutes of edited program material which was about enough to almost make an entire show. For 15 hours I edited that footage syncing it up to every beat of the soundtrack I had produced. Once done I then would preview it and look for places that I could add sound effects, tweak the audio, balance the video and just polish this feature segment until it was perfect.

I left the editing alone for two days. I wanted to be able to take a fresh look at the segment before I finished. I fired up the studio cranked everything up and sat in front of my main studio television monitor with an Alesis audio reference monitor to my left, and one to the right. I was sitting dead center of the stereo field.

I hit enter on my editor and sat back to watch this marlin feature I had edited.

"OH WOW.........THIS IS GOOOOD SHIT!"

The music, the marlin jumping out of 15-foot seas, the dark sky, I just knew that it was going to blow everyone's socks right off. I was so proud of what we had accomplished. The footage and the soundtrack together worked better than anything else I ever seen on any outdoor program. This was going to be big...I thought.

There was one little problem though. I did not have enough footage to finish the show, so I needed a filler segment to complete the program. The previous Thanksgiving we shot a little segment in my back yard overlooking the lake about how to deep fry a turkey. It was a simple little piece that was one take with me just talking about the deep fryer and a few tips on how best to deep fry turkeys.

The good thing was that the little cooking segment was only about three minutes and fit perfectly at the end of the marlin episode. By including the deep fried turkey cooking segment the marlin show would be completed and ready for air. I could have this feature airing on national TV in one month. Okay...turkey segment is in. I wanted this show to air ASAP because I was so excited about how it turned out.

One of the magazines I wrote for needed a column for the next issue, so I wrote all about this marlin program and also sent a press release promoting this show everyway I could.

In my glory and excitement I was ready to change my name to Ahab, Quint, or Ernest.

A month later the marlin show airs in National syndication. I remember watching it live on air and just so happy with how it turned out.

I was a little put off that I had to put a turkey segment at the end of such dramatic footage, but other than that this show was killer.

I was so happy sitting there watching it having several cocktails and when the show ended I was done and ready for bed.

I accomplished producing the best saltwater feature I had ever done and better than anything I had ever seen on TV at that time. I was ready for the accolades.

I slept in late the next day. Once up and coffee in me I thought I would go to the studio and check to see if I got any email or phone calls about the marlin program that aired the night before.

When I walked in the studio the light was flashing on my answering machine and it said it had 15 messages. I did not check them yet. Turning on my office computer I was thinking I might have a few emails regarding the marlin feature.

Once logged on to my email account her it comes. Over 100 emails about the marlin show. I thought, "Man I must have been right about that footage, the best!" I quickly reviewed all the emails.

Three emails talked about the great marlin fishing…that was it!

98+ emails all ask for more information on how to cook a turkey.

"WHAAATT DA HELL!"

I could not believe what I was reading.

"Hey Jim, what kind of oil did you use?"

"Jim do you ever get the oil too hot and have it blow over the pot?"

"Jim, can you inject the turkey and fry it as well?"

"How long did you say you cook it for?"

"Does the bird have to be fresh?"

"Jim, how big of a turkey can you put in that pot?"

"Can you re-use the oil?"

"Jim, can you do this during the winter?"

"What was the name of the company that makes your fryer?"

"Jim, will you come over and deep fry a turkey for me?"

You get the idea. Even years later people would come up to me and ask me about deep-frying birds. Never about the marlin footage we almost died trying to get.

This made me realize that viewers are incredibly interested in our cooking segments. This of course made a big change in how we produce our program. From then on most every show would have a cooking segment and I would also start writing cooking columns in various magazines. Eventually I would also have a "Galley Blog" site that was featured on our Jim Baugh Outdoors main web page and a cooking DVD.

I thought about it for a long time why we never got the response I thought we would from that incredible marlin show. For years I would ask viewers if they ever saw that episode and lots of times I would get a, "Yeah man, really cool! Especially that deep fried turkey at the end!"

I asked to this one fellow, "So you liked the turkey better than the marlin?"

He replied, "The marlin was great, but it was like a video version of a Hemingway novel. It was really cool, but not something I think I would ever get to do."

I said, "So you may not often get the chance to hook up on a white marlin in a 15 foot sea, but you can enjoy frying a turkey in your backyard any day of the week?"

He said, "That's right! But we really did enjoy that great marlin you caught. Hey… By the way…what kind of oil did you say you use when fry that thing?"

For me this was like a light bulb that went off in my head. Produce outdoor television segments that feature a lot of things that people can relate to in their daily lives. For fishing, that would mean not a lot of offshore angling, more like bottom fishing in the Bay, surf fishing, tidal fishing, etc. This would be a good strategy that still would allow us to do big offshore features, just not as many as we had done in the past. Overall this would provide a better balance for our type of program and it showed in the ratings.

The truth is this.

Never in my wildest dreams would I of thought an 80-pound thrashing white marlin would get upstaged by a backyard 10-pound fried turkey.

Who knew?

………..And the show goes on.

One of Pirate P.D. Cooper's piratical art drawings.

Chapter 19

The Pirates are Coming the Pirates are coming!

"The Crew was restless I gave um Rum. All was calm"

~Edward Teach, AKA Blackbeard.

Without knowing it at first I was living on a boat where only 100 yards away is where the head of Blackbeard the pirate was posted on a stick in the Hampton River. To say the least Hampton was home to a large pirate crew who loved to shanty, raid, and pillage.... all in fun of course. These are many of the historical re-enactors that you will see at the annual Hampton Blackbeard and Pirate Festival of which I was living right in the middle.

The Pirates were all a bunch of fun colorful people who prided themselves to be the best and most entertaining partiers around. I was one of the few outsiders that, sort of would be let into the crew. I had no interest in dressing up like a pirate singing shanty songs, but I sure did enjoy it while other people did.

Many of the pirates and I became friends, however there was one in particular that I became close friends with. His name was Pirate P.D. Cooper. He was considered the greatest pirate of them all. Everyone knew of Pirate P.D. Cooper and his pirate antics were stuff of legends. Heck, whenever I would take P.D. fishing he would show up with a double bottom dropper rig for an ear ring.

P.D. Cooper lived on an old crooked wooden boat and on the bow was a real human skeleton that he pirated from the local hospital. P.D. was once admitted for a knife wound where he saw this skeleton and later creatively retrieved it.

"Bones" was stationed on the bow leaning aside a burnt treasure chest with beads flowing from every corner of that old wooden box. There were wood plaques plastered all over the outside of the boat and many pirate lights hung off the stern. One petrified dead rodent was kept near the steps just to keep people away from his floating, molding, wooden encased castle. With the amount of guns, gunpowder, swords and knives just on the fly bridge, the good captain did not want strangers on board.

P.D. was a master craftsman and fabricator who was very talented at tig welding. He also LOVED guns and motorcycles. P.D. received an engineering degree from M.I.T. and he had a great idea to create a unique helm station out of his Harley motorcycle that was recently retired. P.D. rigged the motorcycle helm station with gears that would control the boat and his bar at the same time. He really wanted to patent his creation however I explained to him that I seriously thought this was a one off. Not something that would be mass-produced. The contraption he created out of his Harley did work very well though.

It is the only helm station I ever saw that was a Knucklehead Harley with a hidden nine-millimeter that also served drinks. Very unique to say the least, no one had ever seen a helm station like this.

The pirate boat he lived on was called the *Pierce Deere*. He made a wooden carving of two mermaids making love with pierced belly buttons that was proudly displayed on the Stern of his boat. Pirate Cooper did not pay for this wooden pirate ship…. it was a sunken boat that was donated to him. P.D. Cooper was a shipbuilder, fabricator, and scuba diver by trade and had no problem floating the boat and then restoring it. This pirate really did build his ship from the waterline up all with his own two damp rum stained pirate hands.

I never knew for sure where Pirate Cooper got all his money from, but he sure did have plenty. P.D thought nothing of walking into a bar and picking up the tab for the entire bar! One night we tied the boat up to a waterside bar and he dropped $1500 bucks in one hour. He did not talk about it much but evidently P.D. had some rather successful military patents in the marine industry relating to ships that made him a ton of money.

What is the rum of choice on this boat? *Bilge Water Rum.*

This was Pirate P.D. Coopers own homemade swill he made in his bilge. P.D actually had a working still in the bilge of his creaky wooden boat that produced some of the strongest Rum I have ever had. The proof was so high he used it to also clean his diesel engines. He fabricated this still from a marine air-conditioning compressor so from a quick glance one would never know that there was a working still on board.

This pirate had a long ponytail down past the back of his shoulders. P.D. would have small chains and pirate ornaments stuck throughout his long facial beard. Depending on the season he would sometimes have Christmas ornaments or Halloween candy attached to his long furry beard. His beard ended in a ponytail attached to his nipple with a cock ring.

This pirate was also a well-respected tattoo and piercing artist. One time he pierced a women's navel right on my boat with nothing but a needle, cork, and a bottle of *Bilge Water Rum.*

His talents also included being a male dancer at the Crystal Cock Nightclub and an absolute artisan with anything wood. He hated fiberglass boats and would only have a wooden boat. It was the pirate in him I guess.

Pirate P.D. would navigate up from South Carolina and dock his boat most weekends at the marina. I was docked maybe 30 boats away. Saturday nights were the big cookouts on our dock and P.D. Cooper and I just simply ruled the docks. We would set up two or three grills on Saturday nights and invite everybody down. All we did was just cook and party for hours listening to the live bands at the marina.

Because we were on the docks and the docks were private, we could drink and do anything we wanted because we were not on public property. The public property was only one foot away where the hotel and bands were. As long as we were down on the dock there would be no police, no public intoxication, nothing. Everyone left us alone. Fact is we did not do anything except have cocktails, cook, and enjoy the music. There was never any trouble. Everyone was just out to enjoy the evening.

There were always a lot of women on the docks especially around P.D Coopers' pirate boat. The captain had a way with the ladies and he was always walking around the docks only wearing black tap shorts with no shirt exposing his pierced nipple ring and oiled pecks. P.D. worked out a lot and had to stay physically fit because of his diving work. A lot of the women had a one-word nickname for Pirate Cooper. …. "Buff". This guy could've kicked Blackbeard's ass.

I think the most trouble I got in on the docks is when I decided to cook a whole lot of chicken wings on the grill. I thought this was a good idea but did notice that everyone at the Oyster Alley outside grill was chocking on a thick cloud of smoke. The band had to stop playing all because my chicken wings were smoking out everyone including the hotel. I had never seen so much smoke and was glad no one called the fire department. I apologized and just cooked steaks from then on.

During the summer season the only slow or "off" day was Tuesdays. This didn't last long. Pirate Cooper decided he would talk to the Crystal Cock Nightclub about making Tuesday's a special entertainment day at the bar. Pirate Cooper had the idea of getting our friend Pirate Wilson, who was a guitar player and singer that played pure bread American mongrel music, to entertain while the male dancers did their show. This was Cajun zydeco music with a mix of country and bluegrass. A rather strange mix

182

of music for a strip club but the manager said he would give it a shot. Business on Tuesdays things were dead anyway so he did not have anything really to lose.

P. D. Cooper said that he would do it and they would only work for tips, as long as they put in a taco bar. That's right… a taco bar in a strip club. P.D. really did have a funny sense of humor. Pirate Cooper also requested some of the male dancers to sport their wares out by the street to attract the ladies. He felt that if the other business like the coffee shop could send a guy out in a coffee cup costume to draw attention to their business, the Crystal Cock should do the same….. But with a G string. The owner agreed with restrictions of course.

P.D. Cooper had a knack for good ideas that made him money. For two months every Tuesday that darn club was packed to the gills with woman. They spent a ton of money and the word got out fast that this was the fun place to go. Even the office crowd would show up and have a ball. Every woman in the area single or married seemed to be there at the Crystal Cock for the male dancers, Cajun zydeco music, and of course, the taco bar.

P.D. would make over $1000 in tip money every Tuesday and that was just the lunch crowd. Eventually there were enough complaints about the dancers out by the streets that they had to stop. P.D Coopers new pirate girlfriend did not want him dancing any more. It was a good idea while it lasted.

Back to the docks.

I spent most of my time living on the boat, filming, editing and producing the show, hanging out with the fun and crazy pirates, listening to a lot of music and drinking plenty of Bilge Water Rum. Life was good.

Now the totally psycho, nuts'o, bizzar'o, insane, uproarious, berserk, deranged, exhilarating and exhausting lunatic world of dating during my mid-life would begin….

Sometimes I wish I'd just stayed married pushing a lawnmower and raking leaves.

"Bubba Hunter" was only missing two things, teeth and an education. Bubba's highest achievement was his police record.

Chapter 20

Dating in the Mid Life...OUCH! WHAT A STING!

The Black Widow

"It's better to be healthy alone than sick with someone else."

~Dr. Phil

I was only around 19 years old when I met my wife Helen. We dated for around five years and then married for over another 20 years. As an adult normalcy was all I knew in a relationship with a woman. I came from a marriage without drama and certainly did not expect any drama on the dating front. Boy was I wrong there.

Also being with one person for as long as I did, how can I say this, well I sort of felt like a 42 year old virgin. I mean I had NO experience in the dating world and the first thing that popped up I was going to be on it. BIG mistake! I had been married all of my adult life. I was ripe for the picking. And BOY did I get picked.

I guess my time was not enough at the old Magnolia Tree. I should have prayed more I guess. Even so I did not think I deserved what I was about to go through with this woman. On the positive note at least it was going to be an education I would never forget, an education on the PhD level. Sometimes I really wish I was a quicker study.

Without a doubt when I first met Tracey that was it for me. Ignorance is bliss. A Jewish beautiful blue-eyed brunette with a nice figure and perfect shining white teeth captured me at first glance. This North Carolina southern belle I fell head and shoulders for. Sometimes I wonder if I was more in love with the idea of her, rather than the actual person. Tracey at the time was working in the Tobacco industry and her family had been Tobacco farmers for generations.

I was not divorced yet and neither was she. We were both separated and it was ok to date, so we did. I fell in love real fast and I did see several warning signs early in the relationship. Things like she did not want me to be around my friends, tried to isolate me, and she had issues with just about everyone in her family.

That was just the beginning. The tip of a very deep and razor sharp large iceberg that would take me on a Titanic like journey. A trip that I wish had never left the dock.

Tracey's soon-to-be ex-husband's name was Bubba Hunter. Bubba was a huge red neck that beat Tracey up regularly and had spent jail time for spousal abuse as well as drug possession. Tracy's kids also were constantly in trouble. They were in and out of juvenile dentition, thrown out of public high school, thrown out of military school, thrown out of Boys School, even thrown out of private boarding schools where the worst of the worst kids go.

One of her kids said there was no school he could not get kicked out of and he proved it. He got kicked out of one of the most expensive boarding schools by tossing a brick threw the window of the headmasters office, with an attached lit cherry bomb. He stood there in the grass and waited there for officials to come get him and kick him out.

They did.

This kid had a history with explosives. When he was a child blowing up mailboxes with homemade pipe bombs was what he did for weekend enjoyment. Other heinous activities included drowning litters of kittens by putting them in cages and tossing them in the local river. He hated cats and other animals as well. A real sicko of a kid for sure that looked like he was going to turn out like his red neck father who was more than just a cat killer.

Tracey had other troubling issues including her first ex-husband J.T. Delmus. J.T. was suing her for back child support and had her charged with grand theft because

187

Tracey claimed one of his cars was hers and she took it. Tracey also had a young daughter only three years old that screamed constantly and for some reason tried to break every dish in her house.

I should have run like a safari leopard the second I met her but instead I threw caution to the wind and allowed myself to fall in love with her and all the worn and torn baggage that came with it.

She had so much baggage she should have had a retractable handle coming out of her ass and rubber wheels instead of feet.

When I introduced Tracey to the Judge within two minutes, he took me aside and said,

"You know she is crazy don't you? Send her back to the far hills of North Carolina."

These were the words coming from an experienced mental health judge. I know I should have run right then. But I did not. I had fallen in love with her. She had a southern charm that really entranced me. From the beginning she knew how much I cared for her and that…she took advantage of many times.

What I went through in the first three months of dating this woman I would not wish on anyone. We were only together a little over a three months and she sent me an email saying she was pregnant. Now realize, I had a vasectomy and could not have any more kids so obviously she was sleeping with someone else.

The guy who she was divorcing who would beat her up all the time….Bubba…. well, she slept with him during the first few months we were dating and got pregnant. Much later I found out she was also sleeping with her first ex-husband J.T. Delmus. This was her effort to get her child support reduced and keep the car. What a gal.

Ok… That is the end of this relationship for me. Good thing it ended early… I wish.

I was sure she was going to keep this child for many reasons. One, she had always wanted another daughter and this could have been her chance.

But…she was with me and the thought of her sleeping with anyone else while I was seeing her gave me the creeps and also made me mad as hell. Instead of being combative with her, I did my best to show some grace. Personally, grace is not always an easy thing to muster up and it was a part of my personality I was trying to improve. I was looking for direction from the old Magnolia Tree. Then I had an idea come to me.

I did something to show some grace and that I understood her situation. I gave her several hundred dollars, both for her young daughter and what would also be her newborn baby. I asked her to take the money and set up education accounts for both kids. That would be my gift and a way of letting her know that I had been serious about her. I wished her happiness with her abusive, drug possessed, alcoholic red neck Bubba, and the new baby. That was all I could do.

She appreciated my gift and left to go back to her small country double wide home in North Carolina. That was the last I expected to hear from her. I had heard from one of her friends who told me that Tracey had told her family that she was excited about the new baby and was looking forward to it. Tracey was going to go back to a life with wife beating Bubba and even have another baby with him. I was out of her mind and a thing of the past. This was a good thing for me because Tracey was trouble with a capital T!

Too bad I had allowed myself to fall in love with her.

I would never hear from her again… that's what I thought at the time.

I got an email stating that Bubba came to her stoned drunk and beat her up again while pregnant. Tracey then said that she was not going to bring another child into this world with him as a father. She had changed her mind and asked me if I would go with her to get an abortion.

Can you say…drama!

After some consideration I respectfully said yes, I would go with her. I knew this would be a difficult thing for her to go through by herself. Having an abortion is a very serious issue, not something I took lightly at all. I felt very sorry for her, cared for her a lot, and was trying to show compassion and grace.

I met her at the medical building in Raleigh. We had a very strange moment. I just told her I was sorry for what she was going through and did my best to support her. Within an hour she was under and had the procedure.

Afterwards, she went back to her double wide in North Carolina. I went back to the boat not knowing what to think. A week passed, she called and said she still loved me and wanted to see me. Now remember this is a woman who was in a relationship with me and goes off and gets pregnant by Bubba. Then she gets an abortion and now she said I was the only man for her in the world? She wants to come back to Jim?

Sure… I am a HUGE idiot….Dumb ass is written on my forehead….. Meet me Friday! Oh Boy!

I was docked at Waterside Marina and Tracey came down to the boat and we held each other for hours. I loved the woman, even after what we had just been through. She left to go back home, I mixed a drink on the boat and was trying to sort things out. I didn't hear from her for a week.

Several more days had passed and I finally got a text message on my phone.

Tracey was in Raleigh North Carolina, at the hospital and was near death. The pregnancy was ectopic; they did not get the fetus during the abortion. It later ruptured. Tracey was bleeding to death and was rushed to the hospital. Neither Bubba nor her family knew she had an abortion. All she told them was that the pregnancy was ectopic. She would barely survive, not sure I would.

Because Tracey allowed Bubba to be at the hospital I could not be there for her. She kept me out of it because she did not want a scene where Bubba could easily blow up and cause a lot of trouble. I didn't understand this too well at the time because I didn't quite understand how bad Bubba really was. I could not figure out why Tracey would allow him to always be around her. Why would she do this and act this way?

Well in time, I would find out what a horrible lunatic this Bubba redneck was and he had the reputation and police record to back it up. Her ex was a steel worker by trade and was a violent wife beating asshole…and that is when he was sober. When he was drunk or on drugs he was a real handful that no one could control. Some women who are abused by their partner have a pattern of going back to the person who beats them up. I would find later this to be the case with Tracey.

What was I doing with a girl who would marry a guy like that anyway? I asked myself that question a million times.

So the woman I loved and cared for immensely got pregnant by the redneck, had an abortion that did not work, almost died from the ectopic pregnancy, and is now lying in the hospital where I couldn't see nor talk to her because of wife beating Bubba. All of this in the first few of months we were dating.

What the FUCK did I get myself into!

She got out of the hospital weeks later and was still in rough shape. She really had been in some serious health trouble. I met her later at a Mexican restaurant, this was the first time I had seen her in a while. It was a nice meeting. She somehow convinced me it was over between her and Bubba. It was an easy sell. For one, I was an inexperienced idiot in the dating world. And two, I wanted to hear the words she was saying. Tracey knew what to say and how to push my buttons. I was an easy mark and a fast sell. I was so stupid.

So that summer we had about ninety good days together, after the hell of the first three months of dating. I fell in love with her more and we did a lot of trips together on the water and spent a lot of time on the boat cruising the Inland Waterway. I would always be so excited to see her just walk down the dock. I loved the woman to death and could not imagine a life without her. Why I felt this way at times even puzzled me.

During that summer I took the boat down to Hatteras where Tracey and I would spend some great times together. She was far away from the hills of North Carolina and all of her issues seemed to be behind her. We would stay on the boat in Hatteras and go clamming in the sound filling up bucket after bucket of clams. Then we would have a clam roast on the docks with all the charter boats once they got back in from their day's catch. The charter guys would have a ton of fish and before you knew it, we were all cooking fresh clams grilling tuna and dolphin and enjoying the westwardly sunset over the Pamlico Sound.

The next day Tracey had the great idea of doing a little skinny dipping and clamming out in the sound behind the inlet. This seemed like a good idea to me so we loaded up our rented skiff with buckets, coolers of beer and wine and of course, suntan lotion.

We found one awesome spot in the sound that had only about five inches of water and it looked like a lot of sand and grass underwater. I threw out the anchor and Tracey threw off her clothes and jumped in, but it was only five inches of water. She was a gorgeous woman and I thought this was going to be one fantastic clamming trip, and it was.

I will never look at clamming the same way again!

We filled up the buckets of clams then made passionate love on the skiff. This was very romantic and exciting for both of us and we were enjoying ourselves immensely, until something reminded us that this was a wooden skiff…not fiberglass.

I immediately had Tracey turn around and throw her ass up to my face so I could try to get out the splinter. It was a little sucker and I was having a hard time getting it out. I was using my fish pliers to try and retrieve the splinter, while I took my right hand and picked up my beer. At that exact moment,

"HOOOOOOONK HOOOOOOOOONK"

I turned around and there only forty yards away in the channel was the Ocracoke Ferry heading back to Hatteras with 100 people all waving at us and taking pictures. Yeah, I was quite embarrassed. Oh well, we were in Hatteras. It is all good on the water.

Tracey put her clothes back on and we enjoyed the afternoon cooking fresh seafood on the docks.

Each night Tracey and I would retire to the boat for a nightcap and a good night's rest.

These were three fantastic romantic, fun months that we would spend together.

They also would forever be our last.

The holidays can just be a bitch when you're dating someone. Thanksgiving came around and I was to go to North Carolina to meet her family and spend the holiday there. I would meet her parents whom I respected greatly as well as all her four brothers. I remember clearly everyone always looking at me with this inquisitive expression like, "Does this nice guy have any clue what he is doing?"

That is how they made me feel. I didn't care. I only wanted to be with Tracey and if that meant I got looked at weird, then so be it.

Tracey blew up over Thanksgiving and I cannot for the life of me remember what it was about. It didn't take anything to set her off. I did stay the weekend and it was the first time I felt the eggshell walk. I felt like I had to do anything to make her happy again. This is all she would do for the rest of our relationship together and nothing would make her satisfied. I would be so upset at the thought of losing her, I would do anything. She played this card like an ace. Doc Holiday never played cards so well.

I noticed that after Thanksgiving I would not see her again until Christmas. There always were excuses as to why I could not go down there nor could she come up to the boat. I am glad I enjoyed the summer because that was the last time we would enjoy time together again. Very sad.

Over Christmas we were together but she was still keeping to herself … there was no intimacy…. nothing really. Then it would only be a couple of times I would see her between then and Valentines Day I think she was just holding out for her Valentine's gift. Then I would not see her for over three months. I would call and write but little response. This is from a woman that I maybe wanted to marry? I loved her very much and just could not understand why she would be shutting us off. I called it, *distancing*.

After Valentines she sat me down in the hotel lobby at the Hilton. She would not meet me on the boat. She sat me down and I had no idea what she was going to say.

"Jim… until you sell your house in Richmond where your daughter is finishing high school, I will have nothing to do with you."

"What? UHH, wait a minute. What did you just say?"

She repeated it and it became clear to me that she had her salary cut in half the week prior and she thought that if I sold the house somehow I would bail her out.

I said clearly, "I will not sell my house until my daughter graduates from high school and I don't appreciate you even suggesting this. It is not going to happen."

194

Tracey left. It would be a while before I saw her again.

I finally was able to go see her in the spring and I walked up to where she was sitting on a bench by her house. Her young daughter was swinging on a swing set. I walked up to her and she was in a catatonic state eyes gleaming ahead, looking at nothing, no response at all. I said,

"Tracey, Tracey, are you ok, dahlin?"

Nothing, just a blank stare with no emotion and she was totally withdrawn. I slowly sat down beside her and just sat there. She gradually stood up and walked over to her daughter and touched her hand, then walked to her double wide.

Now, I have seen mental illness before and I know what it looks like. Her behaviors were starting to make a little more sense now and I figured something was possibly wrong with her. But I am not a psychiatrist, so what was I going to do? Tracey got to her house and I pulled up my truck to unload some plants I was going to put in her garden area. I asked her where to put them and she just pointed to the ground and walked inside.

Now I got a divorce partially because of yard work, and here I am planting plants in Tracey's yard trying to make points. I was really trying but also wondering what the hell was going on.

Next, an old beat up pick up truck is flying up the driveway with a gun rack full of shotguns mounted on the rear window. There were three rusted oil barrels, a busted spring mattress, a banged up wet cat cage and deer antlers sticking out of the truck bed. This truck was also sporting a small confederate flag, hanging off the radio antenna and two bulls balls dangling down from the rubber fish head-capped trailer hitch. The bumper sticker simply said, "Buckshot Powered". It is none other than Bubba Hunter, who stood about six and a half feet tall and weighed about

195

320 pounds. The guy's flying towards me packing a pistol and got in my face.

"If you don't B ah leavin heare and stay way from Tracey, you B grettin it the rest of yoh life. I knowz wheres your chilldn live, you bettaaa go po-tect them!"

It was everything too not haul off and knock this red neck's head clean off. Of course the idiot that throws the first punch gets the lawsuit. Fortunately Tracey came out of the house and said she had called the police and sure enough they were already at the foot of the driveway. Tracy had restraining orders on him several times and the local authorities knew this guy well. Bubba had a long history of spousal abuse.

Bubba beat up his first wife so bad she was hospitalized and had to spend a week in recovery. He had totally rearranged her face. Why this redneck was not in jail is beyond me.

Just for grins I yelled out to the police officer, "I smelled marijuana on him, better check his truck!" The officer opened the truck door and three empty beer cans rolled onto the gravel. They searched the truck and did find a small bag of pot then they put the handcuffs on him. I never smelled anything but just took a chance the idiot was toting some drugs.

Gee, what a lovely way to spend a Sunday afternoon. I would rather have had my wisdom teeth pulled and toenails yanked. I could not believe I had allowed myself to get into this situation.

Tracey never spoke to me nor acknowledged my leaving that day. She was too busy talking to hand cuffed Bubba and the police officers.

While I was driving back I called Tracey and she said Bubba was taken away by the police and that she was fine.

I ask her, "Tracey, this guy is unstable and dangerous. You have had restraining orders on him before.

What are you going to do now before someone gets hurt or even worse, killed?"

She said, "Jim, I have custody of my daughter and I will not allow Bubba anywhere on my property again. I will put up no trespassing signs and contact the local sheriff's office that he is not allowed anywhere near my property. Whenever he visits our daughter I will meet him somewhere in a public place that the Sheriff's office suggests. That is how I will handle it Jim."

I replied, "That sounds like the right thing to do and should work. I have known divorced couples who work that way with their ex-spouses all the time. It should not be a problem and you are handling it well."

I was still upset about what had happened but felt some relief that Tracey was getting a handle on things...WRONG!

Two days passed and guess who is inside her house?

Bubba Hunter.

He was there all day trying to win her back and convince her that she cannot live without him. He stayed for dinner and then according to Tracey, does some chores around her house. I was really beginning to think Tracy had some serious mental issues. Nothing she did made sense at all. I also was beginning to think I was a little nuts for getting involved with this entire situation.

One minute she is calling the police on Bubba, the next minute she's serving him mashed potatoes and gravy.

I was trying to figure this out.

I called one of her family members and was explaining how she was behaving and if her family ever considered getting her some psychological help. The reply was that they tried to for years and she would never get it. She would explode at the notion of the idea that anything was ever wrong with her.

One other time I spoke to a family member for advice on how to help her and all her relative said was, "When you are dealing with Tracey, expect the worst."

That was good advice and I found it out to be true. I also realized that Tracey had known about Bubba's past before she married him. She knew he abused women, had a bad police record and married him regardless. This really made me begin to wonder what I was ever doing with this girl. None of it made any sense to me. I was slowly learning.

Now get this…. another month passed and I get a call, "Jim, I love you. I am ready to totally commit to you and I want you to take me to Italy to celebrate. You see, they are having the Papal Coronation ceremony for the new Pope and I would like you to take me."

"……..Ahhh, What?"

"Jim, I want you to take me to Italy to see the new Pope."

Yeah, right. Off to see the Pope. Who's Catholic around here? She is Jewish and I am Methodist. I could not figure this out at all, so we met for lunch.

We met and this is what she wanted. I was just so glad to see her I did not care. She had me by a string and she knew how to pull it. I checked out with the travel agent about Italy…. no luck. This thing was booked for years. So I thought a nice trip to Nassau would be nice. I hadn't vacationed for a long time and was due. So I told her of my idea, it did not go over to well.

She did not want Nassau. She wanted the Pope and she was not even Catholic. I never understood that one. The reason and logic totally eluded me, probably because there was none.

We did get on the plane and spend one lackluster week in Nassau. I loved the place and thought this would be a great opportunity for Tracey and me to be together and show each other how much we loved each other…. Wrong again!

Not only did she really hardly talk to me on the trip, there was not anything else going on either. What a waste! I could have just taken one of my boat buddies and really had a ball partying in the Bahamas. The place was beautiful but Tracey was off in another time and place. Probably wondering what Bubba, Delmus, and whatever other red neck guys she was manipulating were up to. I was an idiot.

Once we got off the airplane I did not see her again for three more months. She always had some sort of excuse. One day I had business in the area where she lived. I drove down there, did my buiz and came back to the boat. Next thing I get this call.

"Jim, were you in our area today?"

"Yes, I dropped off some stuff to a client and then came back, ….why?"

"My ex-husband Bubba had someone tell him they saw your truck around here."

"Yeah, so what?"

Tracey said, "Listen, until I tell you otherwise don't ever come to this area again, unless you have cleared it with me first."

"What? Why would you care if your ex sees my car… and aren't we supposed to be in a committed relationship anyway?"

Click. The phone hangs up. I was so stupid I did not seriously consider the fact that she was probably sleeping with her ex again. That is why she didn't want me around anywhere near the area. I never had proof at that time but that is what it was beginning to look like.

Now, I did not know what to do. Everyone I knew said that I should have gotten out of this relationship the day I got in it. Before I would call it quits for good I would seek the advice of someone I did not know, a professional counselor that hopefully could help me sort this out.

So here goes Jim the idiot, looking in the phone book to go talk to someone I don't know, to give me advice about a girl he has never met. I did. Blindly, find a counselor who was willing to listen to me.

So I go in this counselors office and the first thing I tell him is, that if he thinks I am crazy please tell me because I am in one crazy situation and no sane guy would put up with this crap.

He laughed and said, "Jim, start at the beginning, and don't leave out any detail."

For 45 minutes I did not stop talking. I told this guy everything that happened in great detail for the entire relationship. When I was done he started to laugh.

I asked, "Are you laughing because you think I am a nut?"

He said, "No I am laughing because almost the exact same thing happened to me and I luckily got out of it with a divorce."

The counselor reassured me that I was not crazy however, since I did come out of a normal 25-year relationship I could easily fall for manipulation. He pulled out a book of personality disorders and he said, "Look, I can not diagnose a person I have never met. However from the things you describe it sounds like a classic case of Narcissistic Borderline Personality Disorder, with maybe a mix of Depression."

I said, "So you are telling me to run for the hills and never look back?"

He replied, "I can't tell you that as a professional but Jim you seem like a real nice fellow and I am sure you will figure out the answer." He said this as he was pointing west to the hills.

I laughed.

Even after this I still hung in there. What an idiot.

This may be hard for people to understand, why someone falls for the kind of manipulation that is evident with a person like Tracey. I will try to explain.

People who have or may have borderline personality disorder can be very convincing to their partners. What they do is build you up, all the while trying to isolate you from your family and friends. Once they can successfully isolate you then they go to work on manipulating your every moment. The borderline has to feel in total control over their partner and wants no outside influences around like family or friends. The reason for isolation is a simple one. They don't want anyone to advise you of the danger that you may be falling into. Remember what my father said when he first met Tracey, and in only two minutes?

"Jim she is crazy, you know that don't you?"

Of course Tracey did not want me around people at all she wanted me tucked away in the country if possible, where her manipulations could go unseen, and I would not have other people to advise me of anything else.

This is similar the way that cults work. Remember my old high school girlfriend Rita Everly who got taken in by those cults in Oregon State? And how did they do that? They isolated her and then began to brain wash her. That is how cults work.

"Don't ever get near your family and friends, they are bad, you must follow me!"

Sound familiar? These are the words the likes of Jim Jones, David Koresh, Charles Manson, etc.

This is how Tracy acted. Of course, it was a serious red flag for sure but I was being manipulated and she was very good at it. She was a master at making me feel that my only goal in life was to make her happy and do what she said, but she could never be happy. That is the manipulation and paradox.

You are always on edge trying to please when all they are really doing is controlling you to get what they want. In this case she wanted money. She wanted to control someone to the point that they would pay for her way. She did not want to work. She wanted to stay at home and be treated like Queen Bee.

Tracey's attempts at isolation were so strong, even close to a year after being with her she would never meet my kids. One day I took out a calendar and gave her a date when my kids and their friends would be on the boat, THREE MONTHS IN ADVANCE! I would remind her of the day and when that day came, I even called her in the morning to make sure she would be there.

"Sure I will be there, no problem Jim."

She never showed. This is when I realized she wanted nothing to do with my kids, family, or friends. All she ever tried to do was to isolate me. Fortunately in the long run, it did not work.

So I fell for a lot of the manipulation and she played me like a grand piano. It was an education I would get, but have to pay for dearly.

The other serious issue with people that may have borderline personality disorder is that they have a massive fear of abandonment.

When someone has a fear of abandonment there is no normal relationship, because the borderline will fear that you have abandoned them over and over and for no reason. The reaction of the borderline will be that they shut you off, will not talk to you and cut you out of their lives constantly, because they are in fear that their partner will abandon them. When in reality no one abandons anyone. It is just a part of the disorder that they can't control. By pushing their partner away, they create the abandonment of which they try to avoid. It's a paradox. A paradox you can't win and there is no cure for.

The other sad news is that people who do have borderline personality disorder are among the hardest to treat in therapy, because they are in denial and insist that there is nothing wrong with them. Often if they do get treatment it doesn't last long because the borderline alienates everyone as a part of their control mechanism.

So they run out on their therapist and refuse treatment. People with this disorder also are subject to a high rate of suicide. Out of all the mental and personality disorders borderlines are among the worst. I, like a world champion idiot allowed myself to fall in love with one.

HOWEVER their allure is strong. You will never meet anyone as charming as a borderline personality disorder. That is the lure that gets you in. It reminds me a lot of the black widow spider that lures its mate into the web and makes awesome love to him. Then when the male walks away the female spider attacks, kills him, and wraps him up in a cocoon only to... Eat Later!

That describes Tracey to a tee.

So here we go with my continuing...Getting sucked in by the Black Widow.

Tracey told me she would not see me until September. This is when her family was going on vacation. That was the next time I would see her. Before we left she wanted to meet me at her double wide in North Carolina to help pack things. I did.

When I got there I noticed that her home had been remodeled, walls knocked out, hardwood floors put in and everything. I said, "Wow, Tracey this is quite something. Who in the world did all this work? Who was the contractor?"

And the Black Widow speaks, "Oh, Bubba owed me favor, so he did all of it."

I just felt the piercing sting of the Black Window's fangs.

Now I understood why I was not allowed in her area. Bubba was there everyday probably living there and sleeping with her, some sort of trade deal I guess. I could not believe how foolish I was. And now I was leaving to go on vacation with her and her family?

I was SUCH a doofball… Idiot…. Stupid… Brain dead…ignorant fool!!

That was me. But I finally was starting to get a little smarter. Soon I would be out of this.

After the uneventful vacation week this was the last I saw of Tracey for a very long time. Another two months would pass and I had not even had intimacy with this woman for a year and we were supposed to be in a serious committed relationship. Gee, I began to think just how wonderful marriage would be with her. I began to see why she had already been divorced three times. I was not going to be the fourth victim.

When I called her on the phone on one Wednesday and I told her that if she was not going to at least start acting like a girlfriend we were done. She said nope, nothing is going to be different.

I said clearly. "We are done."

That was on a Wednesday. By Saturday I was in Washington DC meeting a new woman that would help me get this Tracey nut job case off of my mind.

For the next year I would occasionally hear from Tracey by text or e-mail. Turns out she did go back to Bubba and even moved in with him. I guess some people just can't get enough spousal abuse.

She had been playing him and me the entire time we were together. She now was back living with Bubba and then trying to get back together with me at the same time. I could not believe it.

It is very difficult for me to understand why a woman would keep going back to a guy that beats them up, does not pay child support, and treats them like total cow shit. Tracey reminded me of those people I would see on those crazy trash talk TV shows. The ones where the girls would bring out their boyfriends who beat them up consistently and the woman would keep going back for more abuse. It is just nuts and I never understood why these people would submit themselves to such violence over and over again.

White trailer trash and mental illness is what it really comes down to.

Without a doubt, Tracey could be the permanent poster child for the Jerry Springer Show.

A year passes and I remember like it was yesterday. Sitting at the Annapolis Boat Show while Tracey was once again texting me about maybe meeting the following week to talk. Then, no more text messages, no emails......nothing. I figured Bubba walked into the room.

The small commuter plane had been continuing to lose altitude and with the loss of its single engine glided right into the side of the Blue Ridge Mountains. The pilot and four passengers were killed on impact and within seconds flames would engulf the small cabin.

A car passing by whose driver happened to be a retired firefighter pulled out the fifth passenger immediately. The young teenager pulled from the plane was the only survivor. Tracey's son cat killing mailbox demolitionist Cletus, at 18 years old, the apple of her eye was in a fatal plane crash and died five days later in the burn ward. Tracey never left his side in the hospital, even when he passed she was holding his hand bedside.

I did not think Tracey was going to live through this. There was no way she could have accepted the loss of her son. This was not something she could manipulate… It was finality. I could be of no comfort to her because she was still back living with Bubba and he would be at the hospital and funeral. So, I could not be there to show her my sympathy at all. I did send a basket for her family and that was about all I could do.

It was six months later that I got a message from her telling me that she was leaving Bubba again. Tracy also explained that her mom had terminal cancer. I liked her parents and they were always very supportive of me. I felt that I should certainly pay my respects to her mom while I could.

Before arriving at the hospital I bought her mother some flowers to give to her. Due to her rapid decline I was only able to visit her for a few minutes to pay my respects. This was the last time I ever saw her mother again. She passed later that week.

After my brief visit Tracey took me down to the cafeteria and we sat and had a cup of coffee. I asked how she was and she explained to me that not that long ago she had tried to commit suicide with an overdose and was committed to an institution where she stayed for several months. She said she was later released and has been on psychiatric meds ever since.

Tracey then said she was soon moving to Plumersville, South Carolina to live in a trailer with her new boyfriend at the Buck Head trailer park. His name was Butch Beaver and she told me he worked in the sanitation industry. I said, "No Shit?"

Tracey then said she was considering getting into the medical field.

Could you imagine having Tracey as your physician?

I'd rather take up Scientology!

I wished her good luck and good fortune.

For the next several years I would hear from Tracey… She is still out there. From the occasional messages she would send me it sounded like her time in South Carolina living in the trailer did not last long. Bubba Hunter was stalking Tracey again and tried to break in their double wide. Bubba was packing a pistol and fired off two shots before the police came to haul him away again. No surprise that Butch soon afterwards moved on with his home on wheels and sent Tracey packing back to North Carolina.

The last message I got from her was a picture of her on a motorcycle sporting a wet tee shirt that said "What a Beautiful Ride."

I am not sure about the beautiful ride, but it did look like something had been rode hard and put up wet.

The biker sitting in front of her behind the windshield was wearing black leather biker pants and a leather zip out black Harley jacket. There seemed to be about twenty other Harleys around them.

Tracey's text message said, "Sturgis or bust."

For me, I was not interested in Sturgis or the bust. She could keep both.

I learned a lot from dating Tracey and being in that relationship proved to me just how stupid I could be. If I can give any advice if you see red flags in the beginning, don't stick around to try and fix them...... you will regret it.

Move on to calmer waters and stay there.

My father who was a mental health commitment judge for most of his career gave me this advice about someone who has Borderline Personality Disorder.

The Judge said, "Do you know how to tell if a Borderline is lying to you?"

"…….. Ah, no Dad, how do you tell?"

"Check to see if they are breathing."

In retrospect Tracey always seemed to have a tornado or maybe even a hurricane surrounding her all the time. Whether it was work, kids, ex-husbands, family, personal relationships, whatever turmoil, all avenues in her life were a tempest. These are now warning signs for me.

Anytime I would meet someone with these similarities… I move on. Good lesson to learn.

Believe it or not to this day I have no ill feelings towards Tracey at all. There were certain things that I really loved about her. She also gave me a new outlook on clamming, and have always wanted the best for her.

It truly saddens me to think that people with personality characteristics and/or disorder like hers may never find real happiness. Their personality disorder will prevent it from happening and that is unfortunate.

As far as how I look back on the events during our relationship, I don't really put the blame on her. She was the same person when I was with her as she was before I ever met her. She is the same person afterwards as well. She has never changed. She can't.

I look at it like this. If you stand on a railroad track and get run over by a train, you surely can't blame the train, but you can blame the idiot standing on the tracks. I was the idiot on the track.

Remember if you play with a Black Widow it can possibly kill you if you give it the chance. It's not the Black Widow's fault. It is what it is.

My advice, stay out of the widow's web and off the train tracks.

You will thank me.

NEVERMORE!

And the Raven, never flitting, still is sitting, still is sitting
On the pallid bust of Pallas just above my chamber door;
And his eyes have all the seeming of a demon's that is dreaming,
And the lamplight o'er him streaming throws his shadow on the floor;
And my soul from out that shadow that lies floating on the floor
Shall be lifted- nevermore!

~Edgar Allen Poe, The Raven

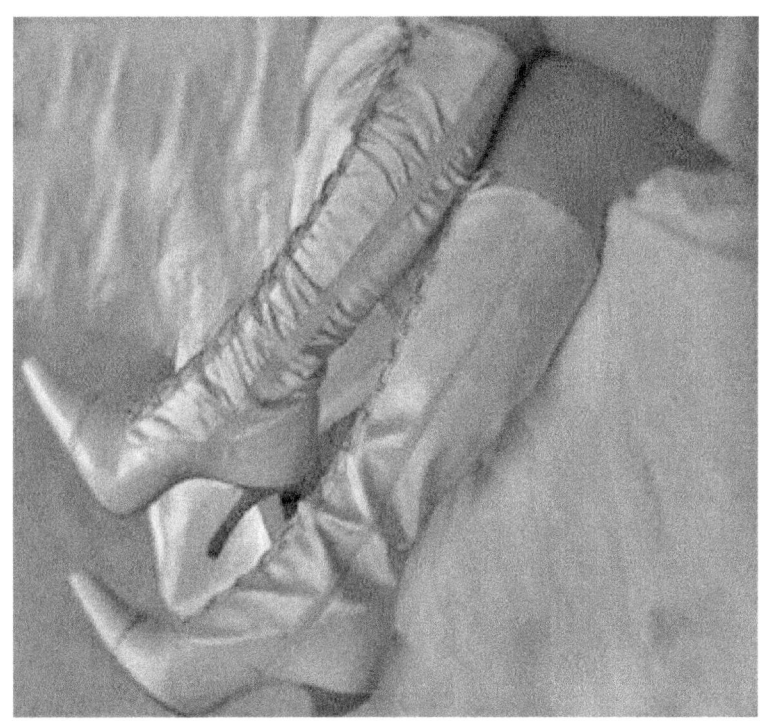

Every dog has his day...

Chapter 21
DC Nympho
The Cougar from Vancouver

"Picasso had his pink period and his blue period. I am in my blonde period right now."

~Hugh Hefner

I was single again from Tracey on a Wednesday and in Washington DC on Saturday with a new lady on a first date. What a ride I was in for. No amusement park could offer so many thrills, chills, and flat out fun. I was in for yet again a new education and I got my masters!

After my final spilt up with Tracey I went back to the boat and was upset and depressed as hell. I didn't even want a cocktail because I was so disturbed. Fortunately Captain Phil happened to stop by and I told him what I had been through. Phil had always told me to leave that crazy nut alone. He knew she was a psycho. I should have listened.

Phil said, "Jim, man I have been having a huge success with online dating. You would not believe all the women out there. Don't fret at all about Tracey. Get out there and find someone new and don't worry about it."

Sounded like good advice to me. I always thought that when you fall off the horse best thing to do is get back on. So I did take Phil's advice and check out the on line dating deal. It was cheap, easy, and something I could do right on my boat. Better than going out and hanging in bars. So I gave it a try.

Meetyourmatch.com

This is where I started to look and found out some things real fast. First off, it looked to be like catching fish out of an aquarium. Hell it could not be this easy. I tried to think about whom I wanted to search for. I wanted to find a woman that did not have ANY of the things that Tracey had. Things like insane red neck ex-husbands who lived down the street, wild young kids, etc. So here was the profile of the woman I was looking for.

Older: Between 48 - 55. This meant that their kids most likely would be gone.

Established: Successful career, someone who does not want or need me for money.

Zip Code: I wanted someone who was not going to be in the area that way if things don't work out, no "GUESS WHO'S HERE AT THE DOOR" surprises.

No ex's: With all the trouble I had with the red neck from hell, I tried to find women who were widowed.

This is true. I went through a period I only dated widowed women. They would have money, single, kids probably gone, and I certainly would not have any issues with the dead and buried husband. I thought this was a good idea.

I was wrong.

The first experience I had with a widowed woman was with this gorgeous elegant blond whom I met online. Her name was Craven Richard. I met her for coffee in Virginia Beach and had a very nice time. I noticed just how detailed and immaculate she was in her appearance. Just everything about her was perfect. A very pretty lady and this was of course, one of my first online dates. After our coffee she invited me to her house to have dinner later in the week. I thought that was a good idea and we would just do some simple steaks on the grill, nothing fancy.

When I arrived at her very big house she zealously greeted me at the door with a glass of champagne and WOW did she look fantastic! This was one hot very tall beautiful blonde that had to be 36-24-36. We stepped inside her house and it looked like a place you could manufacture microchips.

The reason was there was not a speck of dust anywhere. Everything was in the utmost perfect order. I had never seen a house that was so clean and orderly. It was unreal. She continued to give me a tour of the house and with each room it just got more spectacular. I don't know who did her cleaning but they were very good.

We got back downstairs to the kitchen and I started to make dinner. I noticed she was EXTREMELY nervous every time I touched a dish, pot, or pan, just anything. I really did not understand it so I took a break and walked over to the bar and mixed a drink.

She had these new bar stools that were still covered in plastic. I said, "Hey Craven, I love your new bar stools, where did you buy them. They look great!"

She said, "Oh, those aren't new. I have had them for three years. Would you like to see the dining room?"

My first thought was, Oh shit, not another one. More chairs I can't sit in! I can't get a break.

We walked through the kitchen and there were the dining room table and chairs all wrapped up in plastic.

I said, "Let me guess, this furniture is least three years old?"

She said, "No…. I have had these about eight years."

OK! This was some sort of weird compulsive disorder, another personality disorder that I was going to have no part of. No wonder she was so nervous when I was preparing food in the kitchen. I began to think, how would one have sex with this woman? The prophylactic would probably be a sterilized piece of plastic from her furniture.

No thanks.

I cooked dinner and left. I heard from her for years. I would get a text a couple of times a year from her just saying hello. By now I am sure the entire house is covered in plastic. Someplace E.T. would be proud to live in.

Moving on, back to online zip code dating and hopefully finding someone less compulsive.

In my continued search on the dating web site I found a lot of gorgeous women in the DC \ Fairfax area and lot of them fitting the profile I was looking for. Magnificent! I also liked the idea of dating women in DC, because it is a very professional area and my chance of running into another real red neck woman ......another Tracey, was probably pretty slim.

The other great thing about dating a woman in south DC was the traffic, yes the traffic. If your girlfriend was going to be pissed at you and come bitch you out..... Once they got in all that traffic they probably would figure it's not worth it, turn around and go back home. I mean who is going to sit in traffic for hours, just for a surprise visit or to bitch at you..... no one. I liked this idea and really honed in on women in the DC area zip codes. I had the profile down, I had the plan, now the only thing left to do was little searching on the dating site.

Ok back to the search. This time, jackpot! There were a lot of women that came up on the search. I looked at them all. There was one in particular that really caught my eye. There was this beautiful very sexy, tall, voluptuous Canadian girl with blonde hair and blue eyes that had a great body and the face of an angel.

Her profile stated that she loved surfing, boating and traveling. She worked in lower Northern Virginia and had a beach house on the Eastern Shore, one in Bermuda, a condo in DC and a main residence in Fredericksburg. Her profile also said she was originally from Vancouver Canada. She was a professional lady who loved to work hard and play hard. Sign me up!

I contacted her and she was interested. So I had a lunch date set up in Fairfax for this coming Saturday. Tracey was gone on Wednesday and I had new blond on Saturday. I liked this. Truth be told I was in misery from the end of Tracey. I had really loved that woman, even though she had drug me through the mud in every way. I just thought meeting someone new would be a healthy diversion. The diversion did not help as much as I thought it would at first, but it did help eventually.

We met at a very quaint Italian restaurant for an early lunch on Saturday. She was quite stunning looking, a really pretty, sensuous, tall blond with a gorgeous body and legs that never ended. She had pearly white teeth, nice skin, and I could tell when she first started talking that she was a very intelligent professional lady that had a good career.

She told me a lot of stories about growing up in Canada and how much she loved going back to visit her hometown. She was confident, sure of herself, and could just talk up a storm. She even spoke several languages. She did a great British accent when she wanted to. That was my favorite. She had degreed from the University of London and loved the United Kingdom. This lady truly had an aura of 1950's movie star.

The first real words out of my mouth were, "Now, let me get this straight. Both your kids are grown, gone and live in Canada?"

In a very sexy voice she said, "Yeeeeeeesssss."

Next, "Now, your ex-husband, is he around much? Live nearby?"

In an even sexier voice, "He has been gone for 25 years, lives somewhere in Fairbanks Alaska, I think. Not sure exactly, I have not seen nor talked to him for many years."

Boy I am getting some good answers here!

.... Kids are in Canada and the ex is in Alaska... My kind a gal!

This lady was older about 49 and looked 33. She managed three doctors' offices and made around $350,000 a year and all she wanted to do was to have a full time younger boyfriend that could keep up with her.

She wanted a partner to travel with and just have as much fun as humanly possible. She also told me she had

214

her pilot's license enjoyed skydiving and was taking up scuba. This gal would use the company commuter plane to fly herself to her weekend home in Bermuda. She really had a good setup.

Turns out her family owned the medical practice and all the kinfolk were loaded. I mean REALLY loaded. She said she just used her salary for travel money. She didn't have to work. The medical practice just gave her something to do during the week.

All of this sounded almost too good to be true but she was being totally honest. She knew who she was and what she wanted to do. I respected that.

I liked the fact that this gal earned a good living. Because after being with a woman who was more interested in getting something from me as opposed to just wanting me, I was more comfortable knowing that this new lady did not need me for money.

Our lunch went rather long and the restaurant asked us if we wanted to stay but they had to start setting up for dinner.

Well, this woman could talk. So we looked at each other and said, "Sure we will just stay here and have dinner later. Bring more wine please."

We sat there all day and just talked up a storm. It was in the afternoon when she told me that she had just gotten out of the hospital and recovering from plastic surgery. She had a face-lift, a tummy tuck, a boob job, and also lypoed her thighs some. She looked fabulous. Like I said, she looked about 33 years old.

She was a very pretty lady who decided she was going to keep her looks and have a little work done. I respected that. Truthfully I didn't even think about it much. Her body was so good and she was so attractive, what did I care? She had the money to do what she wanted. If I had the bucks, I would get a tummy tuck too!

One thing I could not get over was the voice this lady had. This girl was a real "Ten" and had the voice of a top porn star. It was very deep smooth and whispery. I don't think I have ever heard such a sultry voice.

If you wonder what her voice sounded like just imagine Marilyn Monroe times 2. That is a pretty good description of how breathy and sexy her voice was. She could also talk like a mile a minute if she wanted to. A very intelligent and complex lady and she was a lot to take in at first.

After sitting in the restaurant for eight hours, I was ready to head back to Hampton. It would be a three-hour trip without traffic. Before I left she asked me if I would like to stop by her studio nearby to see her sculpture she was working on. Besides her other talents the lady was an accomplished artist. She was very pleasant and I agreed I would stop by for a minute.

We arrived at her studio, inside it was immaculate and decorated to the tee. One of the nicest places I had seen. When she showed me the sculptures she was working on I could not believe it. It was incredible. She also had many sculptures and some paintings hanging around her gallery that I saw, just stunning. I was in awe that she did all this.

She walked out and she gave me a little kiss on the cheek and said good night. I thanked her for a wonderful day and appreciated her letting me see her art. She told me to call on the way back to make sure I got back all right.

This lady was good.

I did call on the way back and asked her if she wanted to get together again. She then invited me to her home the next weekend so I promised to make her a nice dinner. We had an offshore sea bass shoot scheduled that week and taking some fresh filets for the next date was a great idea.

Friday afternoon I decided on the menu that I was going to prepare for Saturday night; it was my famous three-pepper shrimp sauce over fresh fried sea bass. The recipe I learned from Bubby Vereen of the Sunny Side Seafood restaurant in Myrles Inlet South Carolina. We had featured Bubby on the show, and this just stuck out as one of my all-time favorite yummy dishes we have ever featured on TV. Later I would enter this dish in cooking competitions and in one contest it did win the most popular dish.

This recipe is not quick to make. It involves a lot of chopping and prep work before you ever start cooking. When I entered this entree in competition and working as fast as I could it still took over two hours to prepare. The other reason I thought this would be a good dish to make was because I did not know this woman. I only met her once, and having a supper that would require a lot of effort would be a good way to pass some time if the date did not go well.

I had the truck all packed and headed north for my date with the hottie tall blond. There were still some snow flurries and it had been a very cold week. I was looking forward to getting warmed up a little!

When I arrived at her door she greeted me kindly and was dressed very professional and conservative. The house was beautiful. She seemed glad to see me and had some cheese and crackers out and an open bar. I remember that our conversation was mostly about family and what our kids were up to. As we got to chatting away, I mentioned that the dinner I was going to make was going to be the best she ever had.

She said, "Oh, why don't you make it right now?"

I said, "Sure! We can enjoy some wine and listen to more Sinatra."

I started chopping away and she was telling me some stories about some of the things that were going on at the doctor's office. A couple of times I asked her to repeat what she said because she talked so fast I couldn't always catch all of it.

"I am sorry Jim, this happens a lot. My mouth has the ability to spit out a thousand words in a second. People are always telling me to slow down."

I began to wonder if this was a type of person that could really wear me down after a while. I am a rather laid back person for the most part and this I can already begin to see would wear me down just listening to her. This lady had excellent communication skills and was very intelligent. Also, she had a lot to say…always. Overall she was a bit hyper and exhausting but a great lady.

Without a doubt, I also figured that this blue-eyed blonde was the real deal. She just had her shit together and had no drama in her life at all. That began to perplex me. Why has this good-looking babe with no baggage and loads of money not already re-married? I asked her and she said she didn't know for sure. She did mention that she probably was just too much for most guys and she knew she was always wound up way too tight. The Energizer Bunny never had as much energy as she. She also had her own money and did not *need* a man.

So, I was trying to just put all the pieces together figuring out this lady and also chop a ton of vegetables for tonight's sea bass dish. After about an hour she looked at me with her conservative black business suit and tailored blouse and asked, "Jim, do mind if I go upstairs for a moment? I would like to finally get out of my work clothes. This has been a long day and the traffic coming home was ridiculous."

I said, 'Sure! I will be right here chopping up another five peppers and I know where the wine is."

I get to chopping vegetables big time. The music was enjoyable and the wine was delicious. Looking through the cupboards, trying to find enough containers to put all the veggies in I found an awesome knife. Surely she would not mind me using this one, and away I go again slicing and dicing the peppers, then onions, and then another tall glass of wine.

Before long the CD player had stopped and was ready for more music. I put in some Tony Bennett and cranked it up. Her CD collection mostly consisted of music the rat pack would sing. She was older than me and loved that era of music. I did as well, but was getting real close to having a jazz attack. Pat Metheny would soon follow.

I started rapidly peeling the shrimp and then realized that I am really ready to start frying the fish and get this dish finished. Where did the blonde go? Where did she say she was going? Something about changing her suit or maybe she said she had to go to the store? I was not sure at that time, because I had a lot of wine to drink. This had been a long week and already a very long day. By then I figured since I had now listened to two CD's, quite an amount of time had passed.

So I am in the kitchen frying the fish and cooking the sauce. This takes another 30 minutes and still no blonde. I opened up another bottle of wine and finished off the dish- everything was now ready to serve. I had bent down to look under the cabinets to see if I could find some serving dishes. Found Um!

I stood back up.

There? It? She? Someone…. was standing at the bottom of the stairs slowly approaching me.

At first I did not know who it was. I was in a strange place with a woman whom I only met once and now this other person is approaching me? She had very, very long shimmering blonde hair that looked just like Dolly Parton's and was wearing a full-length fur coat. She got to five feet in front of me and dropped her fur to the floor. I could not believe what I saw. I yelled,

"Who….. and what the hell is that!!"

She had turned into DC Nympho with a strap-on!

It was like Clark Kent running into a phone booth and turning into superman. In this case blond-e had turned into a raging sex goddess with an XXX large attitude.

All she was wearing was an S & M Bondage outfit made of leather straps with black fish net stockings, leather boots, and chains around her neck that attached to her nipple ring on her bulging inviting breast. The garter belt exposed all of her vagina and there were large round holes in the leather around her bust. Heavy make up adorned her face and provocatively wearing a brilliant blond wig with hair that came down near the top of her leather strapped naked ass.

I had never seen anything like it before in my life and was totally caught off guard. The first thing I did was the only thing I could think to do, and I did it in a BIG way.

I laughed my ass off and could not stop!

I laughed so hard I fell to the floor and turned beat red in the face. There was no way I could hold this back. This was the funniest situation I had ever been in. Tears were rolling down my face and actually started to gag a little because I was hysterical with laughter. I mean, come on, here I am just a host of a fishing travel show and before me is a medical business professional by day, and S & M porn star by night. What the hell have I gotten myself into now! Get me back to 'A' Dock….. PLEASE!

Once I stopped laughing she sadly said, "This was not the reaction I was expecting at all."

I apologized and explained to her that this old county boy needs a little warming up and the strap on would have to go. I said, "You look great and I really appreciate the outfit. Maybe that would be appropriate for later but for now can you put your fur on, sit down, and let's enjoy dinner?"

As she lifted her fish net stocking leg with patent leather boot on the counter she said, "What would you like to eat for dinner big boy?"

I said, "Looks like fast food and a happy meal!"

We had a great time and did enjoy a great dinner. She explained to me that she is a one-man gal and does not sleep around at all. She said that she is quite picky and singular about whom she dates and does not like the entire *Doctor* scene.

She was very clear that she would never date anybody through work or even anyone who was remotely connected to her business. She wanted someone fun and unattached but would commit to just her in a relationship.

I mentioned it was only our second date, but I thought it was going very well.

She also made clear that she was a one man nympho. As long as she was in a relationship she would do anything, *ANYTHING* to please her man in bed. She also said she loved to dress up in all sorts of outfits and pretend she is other beautiful aggressive women. Foreign women too! She spoke French, Spanish, and Italian and had the play outfits to match the language.

Her Spanish sex outfit consisted of maracas attached to her waist with leather straps. That was her *Spanish Thong*. And man could she play those things. Shake, rattle and roll!

I did not really understand this but she felt that by wearing different outfits and role-playing, her man would never get tired of her. I thought that was a pretty wild and in a way unique idea, but for me, could be a hell of a lot of fun to find out.

…And I did.

After dinner she walked me upstairs to her bedroom and wanted to show me something, it was her nighttime FUN wardrobe suite. This I could not believe. An entire room crammed full with lingerie and about 35 different wigs all neatly placed on several shelves. The dressing room had a closet the size of a large bathroom and was full exclusively with boots. I could not count how many boots she had and in every color you could think of.

This woman was SERIOUS about her playtime and she called them her play clothes. I commented that she must have spent a fortune on all this stuff. She said she stopped counting after the first year at forty grand. That was several years ago.

She then picked up a couple of spray cans with black tops that were sitting next to a black afro wig. The can said "Tayshaun Zau'shee Sex."

I said, "What in the world is this?" DC Nympho replied,

"I cover all fantasies baby. You want it with a hot black chick …you got it!"

The cans she ordered from France. They were similar to the spray-on suntan from a can however in this case; it was spray-on ethnic.

Well all this was new to me and I was about to get one hell of an education. I went up to her room Friday evening and I came out Sunday afternoon. It was one tired trip driving back to Hampton.

Now, I did figure pretty quick that this was a woman I was going to have a blast with, but not someone I could be with all the time. The main reason was she talked a mile a minute and she would wear me out. The good thing about intimacy with her is that she wasn't talking, that was a good thing. Other than that she hit all the marks. Compatibility in a relationship has to work in all areas for me, not just in the bedroom. But WOW! What a great time with one fascinating super hot long legged lady!

So I began to already plan how I could date this incredible girl. A few days at a time were all I would be able to handle. I would have to take a break from the mile a minute talking and recoup from her incredible bedroom antics. This is when I would get work done during the week. Lots of editing and recoup time from the weekends with the DC Nympho.

I would be sitting there on my boat editing video and guess what email I would receive? Loads of pictures of different outfits from the DC Nympho just ready for shipping. She would have me look at different outfits online and she would match them up with various wigs. She even would have me pick out a new name for her for our next weekend date. This was all pretty wild, but it was fun for a while.

DC Nympho LOVED to do 900 sex calls. She would call out of the blue in a different voice and just go at it. Sometimes I would be in a business meeting and get the call.

I would take it and listen for a while and say, "Yes, we need to get those batteries on charge for the weekend."

My client then said, "You got a big shoot coming up Jim?"

I said, "Yeah, I work all the time."

DC Nympho not only liked to dress up she also LOVED toys. I really had no idea what most of those things were. I asked her if some of them came with directions. With all the artillery she had I was not sure why she even needed a man. DC Nympho told me she shops the wholesale clubs just for batteries.

The thing was she just loved it all and I thought a lot of it was humorous. I was very thankful she had a sense of humor or I would have gotten slapped a lot. This is a good example of just how horny DC Nympho was.

One day I called her on the phone and asked what she was up to.

"Oh, I was really feeling in the mood and wanted a release so I grabbed my vibrator and started to play with my pussy."

I said, "Really? Oh, well I am sure you are enjoying yourself at home then."

She says, "No… not really, it's just not doing it, wait a minute…… ahhhh….. yes… yes.. YES!!!!! That is much better!!"

I ask, "What are you doing now?"

DC Nympho in a stern voice says, "That vibrator was just not doing it so I also stuck this new toy up my ass and now I am sky rocketing!"

I dropped my cell phone. Could not believe what I just heard. The image in my mind again started to make me cackle. Once again I was caught off guard on this one. Picking up the phone I said, "You mean to tell me that you are laying in the bed with one remote control vibrator in one hand that is attached to your pussey, and you have another remote control vibrator inserted in your ass?"

She replied, "No not at all, I have been walking around the house for 45 minutes. I found the bottom of the stairs to be the best position."

She was serious. To her, this was just a way to pass time in the afternoon, nothing to it. I on the other hand could not believe my ears she had shocked me again. The fact is DC Nympho just loved toys and never found one she didn't like.

I was surprised her house did not have a generator.

This began to give me some ideas on how I could really have some fun with this girl. It was time to show her off! All of my pirate buddies considered themselves to be the ultimate partiers and couldn't be challenged. I thought different.

Pirate P.D. Cooper had a planned party on his boat at the Jolly Oyster Marina in South Carolina. When the weather gets cooler in the Chesapeake Bay, P.D. always heads further south and he loved Charleston. This was during the winter and the marina was quite desolate and not much going on. Except whatever was going on in P. D. Cooper's boat.

I called the Nympho and told her of my idea to really freak out these pirates. I asked her to dress up like a world class $20,000.00 per hour French prostitute and let's go have some fun with the pirates. This was going to be good. DC Nympho was all over this idea and ordered a special outfit just for this occasion.

She suggested I stop by the toy store and see what I could find to kick the humor up a notch. Now remember, this was all just a practical joke. Here was the perfect opportunity to set up the pirates because none of them had met the DC Nympho yet. They didn't have a clue what was about to BUST in their door.

All I told them was that I was bringing a sweet new little lady from France that I started dating from church... that was it.

So for this joke I did stop by the toy store, again not knowing what half the stuff was. Looking around I saw these blow up dolls that for some reason I found humorous. They looked hilarious and the thought that someone could actually find these things attractive, made me chuckle even harder.

So I hauled up a package containing the blow up doll to the counter ready for the check out. There was this nice girl working the check out and I explained to her what we were going to do. She smiled and said they sell as much merchandise for jokes as they do for what they were intended for. I could see that.

While she was packing up the doll I noticed the glass jar full of small flashlights. I said, "Boy that is interesting, a bowl full of flashlights. That is something I would expect to see at an auto store check out not a sex shop."

She reached down into the jar and pulled out one of the flashlights, spun the top, and the flashlight lit up.

I said, "Looks good, they work but I don't need a flashlight."

She then took my hand and placed the flashlight on my arm and,

BBBBBBBBBRRRRRRRRRRRRRRBBBBBBBBBBRRRR!

It was a key chain flashlight vibrator. I said, "I will take five! These are going to be some hilarious party favors!"

So here we go. We fly down to Charleston in her plane and soon arrive at the dock. The DC Nympho was dressed to the hilt. She wore a total spandex outfit that looked like she was poured into every inch. There were two see through holes on each side of the outfit. The color was a brilliant bright red sequined spandex outfit, red patent leather boots, red fish net stockings, a red wig that came down past her shoulders, thick red lipstick, and a black and red checkerboard leather whip attached by her side with a black chain.

I was secretly toting the blow up doll and five key chain flashlight vibrators.

When we were walking down the dock at the Jolly Oyster Marina it was very cold, dark, and windy. This of course made the DC Nympho's nipples stick out like large erasers. I thought it would be a good idea to continue to keep the doll concealed and then blow it up in the downstairs back stateroom for a real surprise. Nice touch for this practical joke.

Arriving at the boat we knocked on the door and P.D. Cooper hollered, "Just come on down, Jim."

I sent DC Nympho down the hatch first, and then I followed. First thing she said in French was, "Bonjour tout le monde. Avez-vous comme mes vêtements."

Everyone's jaw was dropped. No one knew what to say, except one Pirate who understood French.

"We are fine, nice to meet you and yes, your outfit is spectacular."

226

I said, "Hi everyone let me introduce you to my new girlfriend. We just left a covered dish early supper at church and flew down from Fairfax… Great to see yall!"

One of the other female pirates grabbed me aside and said, "Jim that's bull shit. You know she is a prostitute?"

I said, "Well, not sure. I haven't gotten a bill yet."

I ran down below and left Nympho with the pirates to mingle while I got the blow up doll going. Once I had her fully inflated I opened the door back to the cabin and said, "Hey guys, I brought someone along for the threesome!"

Then, several of the pirate gals jumped down on the doll and making all sorts of gestures; they were being very silly.

Once they were done I said, "Laaaaaadies, I have a house warming gift for you". Placing these flashlights in each of their hands, they didn't know what to think.

"Ok girls, on the count of three all at once, turn the end of the flashlight."

1… 2… 3…

BBBBBBRBRBBBBBBBBBBBRRRRRRRRRBBBB RR!!

Guffaw! Huge belly laughs! They were screaming and yelling at the thought of a key chain flashlight vibrator. Before anyone really got the wrong idea, I made the announcement.

"Everyone, before you guys get thinking anything crazy, let me just say. Y'all have been had. This is all a joke. We planned this, even the prostitute costume. This is all a joke on our part to trump you Pirates."

The swashbucklers were very relieved. Hell, even one of Pirate P.D. Cooper's leftover New Year's ornaments fell out of his beard. They didn't know what to expect and thought I lost my mind bringing this prostitute down to the boat. I re-introduced DC Nympho to everyone and she started speaking English. We then all cooked up a nice dinner and enjoyed a pleasant evening. It was truly something when they first saw the DC Nympho and they were stunned beyond belief. We had trumped the pirates.

The funny thing is, this is how DC Nympho dressed for me all the time. She had many more outfits that were a LOT more revealing. But…I kept that to myself. None of the pirates ever knew who DC Nympho really was, her real name, what she did for a living or where she lived. All they knew was that she was a great gal with a good sense of humor.

P.D. Cooper creatively put the blow up doll to good use. He named it HOV for high occupancy vehicle. He would later put it in his truck for when the interstate traffic got too heavy.

For my birthday DC Nympho made a very nice suggestion. She wanted to fly us both out to California rent a Corvette and take in some Napa Valley wine tours. I had never been to California and always wanted to go. The problem was I could only take the Nympho in doses of several days due to her intensity. The thought of spending a week was not something I was quite sure I could do. So I reluctantly backed out.

I told her we should just do something local. She was so intense that after several days I would just need some downtime. She was such a nice lady and was so good to me I never had the heart to tell her that is how I felt. She really was a fine person and wished her energy level was a bit less, but that is not the type of person she was. She super excelled at everything she did and she did not have an off button. DC Nympho was always in high gear running full speed all the time. She also was a very generous and considerate person who was extremely talented artistically.

She was quite something.

One day I told her I had a dream about her wearing a yellow bikini.

Next time I visited her she opened the door wearing a tight yellow bikini with yellow pumps, a blonde Dolly Parton wig, while she was holding a yellow rose in her teeth and a yellow vibrator in her hand. That is how she greeted me at the door, quite unreal.

She of course, loved to have her picture taken and videos as well. These were fun to look at while back on the boat during the week. All in all she was a very entertaining lady that was a whole lot of fun. DC Nympho would produce up to four to five complete costume changes in one evening. When we traveled together on the weekends she packed four suitcases all loaded with play outfits. The people at the hotel thought I had three different women with me in one weekend.

One blond, one brunette, and one red head.

They were all one person. DC Nympho.........just having a good time with her costumes.

She had two cars one for work and one for play. Her play car was a red Lamborghini that she kept covered in her garage. One night she took me out to a nice inn for dinner and drove me in the sports car. Wow what a ride! We had some martinis at dinner and it did not sit well with her, unfortunately she got very sick and asked if I could drive home.

That car was amazing! I was not really too much into cars but this thing was unreal! When I got back to the boat after that weekend, my interest was peaked greatly about getting a car that would handle real well on the road and get decent gas mileage. There was no way I could afford a sports car like hers but did end up getting an old Corvette. I was driving up and back to Fairfax every week, driving to Richmond, and also down to the Florida Keys a lot, so a fast car with decent gas mileage helped me out. The Vette I bought cheap and restored it. We would enter it in car shows and I actually placed second in a couple of those Corvette events. It was a lot of fun and good promotion for our TV show.

Once, the Nympho drove down in her Lamborghini to the boat when I was docked in Virginia Beach. For the weekend I planned a trip that featured bars and restaurants that were only on the water. We started cruising in the Lamborghini in Yorktown and ended up in Virginia Beach. One fun way to spend a Saturday!

I kept hearing her say many times that she could never be satisfied… never get enough sex. She claimed that no man could ever wear her out. So one day in jest I made a bet. We would get together for three days and the last one that could get up and walk would win the contest. I thought this was amusing…she took it as a challenge so the bet was on.

There is no need to get into the details. All I can say is that by Sunday at 6pm I could get up and stand. She could not move, she was paralyzed in bed and could not speak. I had to let her dog out clean the kitchen, then pack. Before I left I checked on her and she was still out. I left a note on her table by the bed that said, "I WON".

Later that week she presented me with a gift that certainly was an original. It was a blue jewelry box and when I opened it there was a bronzed medal with an engraving that said, 2005 East Coast Busted Nympho Champion.

The medal was sitting on top of one of her thongs inside the box.

Once again DC Nympho had me laughing hysterically. I jokingly showed it to one of my married buddies and told him that now I was an award winning sex machine with a multiple award-winning Corvette. He smiled and said he hated me.

It was all in fun. This was a time when just prior, I truly went through a very rough depressing time with

Tracey. For now I was ready for all the fun I could get. In a weird way I felt I deserved it.

I had the boat in Georgia doing some filming and was there about a week. DC Nympho insisted she fly down to feature her latest online outfit and she said she was desperate for some fresh Georgia Shrimp. So here she comes.

The creativity DC Nympho put into some of her outfits was amazing and surprising. On this trip she put together a very unique costume package. This consisted of a Lava Lamp, a black light, glow in the dark make up, a glowing purple wig, neon spandex purple leggings and a one-piece leopard skin camisole. To top it off, she had glow in the dark purple contact lenses.

She had me hide in the vee berth while she decorated the salon and changed into her outfit. Well, when she told me to come out it was like some sort of 1960's acid trip that went horribly wrong. There were streamers hanging down from the ceiling along with inflatable breasts dangling just over my head. There was a black light and a purple lava lamp that made all of her glow in the dark outfit light up like the Vegas Strip.

The purple wig was the darndest thing I ever saw. When she approached me with the purple glow in the dark eyes it really freaked me out. Had she turned into a Klingon?

I could tell she put a lot of effort into this *themed* evening. I was not sure what the theme was. Something you would see in an adult version of Star Trek I guess. At the time I wish I did have beam-me-up technology.

I kindly told her how impressed I was with all she had done and then mixed a very stiff tall drink and hurriedly downed the entire glass. I figured I had better get in the mood fast.

We were in the middle of our activities in sort of an inverted position and my foot got caught between the bedding and the fiberglass wall of the forward vee berth. I had put enormous pressure on my ankle and I was about to pay the price.

Yes, I fractured my ankle playing with the DC Nympho.

I went to the hospital they took x-rays then put me in a cast and gave me crutches for six months. Have you ever tried to walk with crutches on a dock much less get on an aft cabin boat?

Now, I was an award winning sex machine on crutches hobbling down the dock carrying groceries dropping stuff all over the place. My loaf of bread would end up falling down on the dock, crushed by my crutch and the sour cream just rolled down into the water. Splash! The apples went rolling off as well.

It was a rough six months.

When I was in the Florida Keys filming she would fly down and I would drive up to meet her in Naples for a few days. Her office had some condos down there on the beaches that were very nice. I just loved the Gulf of Mexico. This was enjoyable of course but at the end of the day, a few days were still about as much time as I could take.

When she flew me to her home in Bermuda, it was a great trip and the first time I ever had sex in the ocean. The entire time I was thinking about sharks and wondering if this was really a good idea. Three days in Bermuda was wonderful but again, I felt like I had begun to have enough.

She eventually wanted more time and more of a commitment. She deserved it and she was an incredible gal in so many ways. However, there is a difference between loving someone and being in love. Unfortunately, during the time I dated DC Nympho I was still somewhat rebounding from the horrible past experiences with Tracey. However DC Nympho was a fun, stunning, highly intelligent beautiful woman who was incredibly talented, with a gigantic personality.

I dated her for two out of a three year period of time before she figured all I ever was going to give her was a few days at a stretch. She ended it to move on to someone who could give her more of a commitment and more time.

I did not blame her one bit.

The DC Nympho and I would remain friends, we never really had a cross word between us. Occasionally, I would get a brief pleasant email from her with pictures of her grandkids. She eventually started dating a millionaire surfer. They fly together all over the world and they both skydive as well. I was always happy she found a man that could keep up with her. More power to her, her boyfriend, and the Duracell Company.

One thing is for sure. These two have probably brought a whole new meaning to *Surf's Up*.

Go Get um girl! Take no prisoners!

Chapter 22

Double D Tip Jar

"Tipping isn't just for cows anymore"
~Pirate P.D. Cooper

After dating DC Nympho, I really was ready to take things slow and hopefully find a lady that would be compatible in all areas with me. This would take some time to find and after the whirlwind of the DC Nympho I was just fine concentrating on work and taking it easy for a while. That is what I thought would happen. I don't know why but whatever I think is going to happen, usually just the opposite occurs. I would never nickname myself, *Nostradamus Jim* because I cannot predict things worth a damn.

I would put on fishing tournaments in downtown Hampton for a number of years and also kick the event off with a huge Oyster Bash. We would close several blocks down and bring in beer trucks, bands, fire barrels, and a caterer that would have all the roasted oysters you could eat as well as a hickory smoked whole pig.

The fishermen would weigh in their fish on stage then I would announce the winners and give out the prize money. Once the last check was handed out.... 1 2 3 ROCK & ROLL! The band would fire off with their first set of tunes. This was a good time of course and was a popular tournament event in downtown Hampton for many years.

One of my responsibilities was to find vendors that would set up sponsor booths at the Oyster Bash and Tournament Weigh In. I had some success with this and would get various vendors that included local fishing and tackle shops, real estate agents, hot tub companies, and even a spa company that was doing free manicures to all the ladies at the party. This was a big hit and the manager of the Morning Wood Spa was this gorgeous little blond named Cherry. She only stood about five foot six inches and her breasts looked like they stood out four feet. They may be the biggest set I have ever seen on a thin woman in my life. She really was very beautiful and buckstrum.

I had talked to her on the phone to book them for the event but once I saw her, my interest was a bit more than just business. I said, "Cherry, first I got to ask you. Are those things real?"

She said, "Absolutely! They are the best that you will never see."

I laughed pretty hard. This girl was a hottie with a sense of humor and that to me was a winning combination.

After the tournament was over we were all packing up and she came over to thank me for asking her company to be a vendor. She asked me if I had ever had a real massage by a professional. I told her I had one in Nassau with my old girlfriend Tracey but since she had acted like such a bitch, I did not enjoy myself at all during the trip.

She said, "So you don't see her anymore. Single?"

I said, "Yes, I was dating the DC Nympho, but that is behind me now."

She goes, "DC what?"

I said, "It is a long story. Sometime if you want to come down to the boat I will fix you a cocktail and spin some yarn."

She said, "I'm not really doing anything right now."

Ok now here I go with Cherry, the hot blond manager of the Morning Wood Spa, off to the boat for cocktails. Not in my wildest dreams did I think that this would be happening tonight.

One moment I am weighing fish and eating oysters the next moment cuddling with Cherry, the boob-a-licious hottie thinking about Morning Wood.

We get down into my cabin on the boat and mix us a couple of strong toddies. This had already been a long day and I don't think either one of us was up for much. We sat down and started talking; I soon realized that this was just one really cool lady with a great sense of humor with the biggest rack I ever saw.

I asked her, "I like the name of your spa. How did you come up with the name, *Morning Wood*?"

She said, "It is what every woman wants."

After a big laugh we started to make out a little which was very sweet. I didn't ever expect what was going to happen next.

She leaned back and took off her blue v-neck shirt. Then she reached back behind her and un-attached her Mt. Everest size bra. The bra projected away from her breasts, because of the pressure from being cooped up and there stood, in perfect sync, the most beautiful boobs in the world. They did not move an inch, no droop, nothing, just perfect breast that looked like they were the top monthly centerfold out of some magazine.

I said, "They can't be real!"

She then proved to me that they were totally authentic. These were not medically manufactured. Sometimes the good Lord sends down the perfect set, and these were one of those sets.

All right, after about 20 minutes of almost total suffocation, I came up for air and grabbed her bra. Had I had a snorkel I could have stayed down longer. I told her I had never seen a bra this big and did not even know they came this large.

She said, "Jim, I have the most perfect spot for this bra."

Cherry spun around and placed it over top of the lampshade in my salon.

Hell, I was honored!

"You mean I get to keep it here on the boat and show everyone my new decoration?"

She said, "It's all yours Baby! Try and beat that!"

We laughed like crazy and had one more cocktail before I walked her to her car. She was a great gal and we remained friends for years. For some reason we never really dated, due to timing mostly. She was always going back and forth with her ex-husband and I had already had enough of that crap for one lifetime. But I liked her a lot and we have always been good friends.

The next day Pirate P.D. Cooper came down to the boat for a drink. First thing he said was, "Look at the size of those tits on the lampshade."

I told him about the boobalishous fun the night previous and did think the bra on the lampshade looked good, so I decided to just leave it there.

During the next month I had a bunch of people down on the boat and everyone commented how much they loved the big bra on the lampshade. I even had a couple of people come over from the public piers just to check it out.

In the next week, Captain Phil had some out-of-town guests he wanted me to meet. A couple of girls who were single and he figured he would make the introduction. Before I went over to his boat that night to meet these ladies I thought to myself, maybe I should take the bra down off the lampshade. Maybe this would give the wrong impression of me or maybe someone I wanted to date might find this offensive.

So I thought about it, and decided this:

There was no way I was taking that freaking bra off the lampshade.

If a woman were not going to see the humor in it, then she probably would not like me that much anyway. It would be like Jimmy Buffet dating a girl that does not like margaritas. So the bra stays on the lampshade… for now.

I went to Captain Phil's boat to meet these girls and here was this one very attractive brunette named Barbra-Elle. She was a professional career lady who was dressed very nicely and was recently divorced from a real-estate mogul.

After we chatted and had several cocktails she asked me, "So you live on a couple of boats here at the marina?"

I said, "I live on the 36-foot Trojan and film our show on the 28-foot express fisherman. They are tied up next to each other just down the dock."

She said, "I would love to see them."

Well here I went, walking Barbra-Elle to my boat and I was hoping she had a real good sense of humor. Now Barbra- Elle does have the word "Bra" in her name, maybe she won't mind my lampshade bra too badly. This was a real nice woman and I did not want to offend her.

We got to the boat and I helped her downstairs into the cabin. She looked at the galley and liked the bar set up. I immediately mixed her a drink and she turned to sit down and saw the big bra on the lampshade.

"AAHHHHH…... What the heck is that Jim?"

Ok, here we go. I said, "Well I met this attractive blond the other week and she wanted to show me how nice her breasts were, and then she told me to keep the bra."

Barbra-Elle says, "Hell Jim, I bet mine are twice as pretty as hers!"

She set down her drink, pulled off her top, unlatched her bra, and stuck those things in my face. I could NOT believe this! I am enjoying it a lot, but never thought this was a technique to get women to take their tops off.

Who would of thunk it? Not me!

Later I walked her back to Phil's boat then I headed back to go to bed. The next morning I woke up and there from the night before were now two nice bras hanging over my lampshade.

I walked over to Marker 20 for breakfast and sat at the bar. In front of me were these one-gallon empty olive jars with the word 'TIPS' written on them.

It hit me like a bolt of lighting. Like when Bugsy had the idea about Las Vegas, or Newton getting hit in the head with an apple. Here was something I had to get for the boat.

"Tip Jar!"

The bartender I knew well, and nicknamed him Kilometer.

I said, "Hey Kil, dude, can you give me a spare one of these jars? I have an idea for my boat."

I walked out of Marker 20 with the olive jar and rushed down to the boat. I took a permanent marker and wrote, TIPS, on the jar. Next I took the bras off of the lampshade and placed them in the new boat tip jar. To kick it up a bit I threw in some one-dollar bills, and also a thong that was left in the back drawer from Tracey.

That was the most action out of Tracey's thong I ever got.

I also put some loose change in the bottom of the jar and placed it prominently above the lampshade over the sofa.

From that day on anyone that would come on the boat had to leave something in the tip jar. The guys would leave jokingly, anything from a package of rubbers to one ounce bottles of booze. One night I served up so many cocktails, the guys put in two twenty's and a ten.

The ladies that would come on board just loved the tip jar. I would entertain them with music, food, beverages, and card tricks. People would contribute to the tip jar with money, bras, and panties. The tip jar filled up quickly and I had to even get an additional one. By the time the second one was filled, I could not believe what was in these things. The money was always great. Before I went to the liquor

239

store I would just reach in the tip jar and that would pay for the store run.

I briefly dated a lady named Deloris who had an older son around 23 years old who was living with his mom for a while. Deloris was a real sweetheart who I had several dinners with down on the boat and she too, had happily contributed to the tip jar. Deloris and I were cooking steaks one night and her son called and asked if he could head over and check out the boat. I thought sure…. love to meet the boy and we had plenty of steak.

Her son John shows up and we are down in the salon all having a cocktail, just talking up a storm for about 20 minutes. All of the sudden, John looks at the tip jar sitting close to him and gets this very blank stare.

There was silence for a moment and then John says, "Ahhhh, Jim? What in the world is this?"

I replied, "John, that is my tip jar and man you can contribute to it if you like. We of course are glad to take dollar bills and even loose change."

As he began to look through the jar, he had these panties in his hands and really started laughing hard, "Jim where did all these panties come from?"

I said, "Well, not everyone leaves money. The ladies can leave bras, thongs, whatever they feel they want to leave is fine with me."

John started to laugh so hard tears are coming out of his eyes. John thought this was the funniest thing he ever saw. All of the sudden he stopped, took a huge gasp, looked down at the underwear in his hand, and he turned beat red in the face. He then quickly stuffed the panties back in the jar, and did not utter a word.

John had recognized his mother's, lets say, …undergarment?

I quickly changed the conversation and suggested we move up to the fly bridge. After we all had a few more libations, I gave John some advice.

240

"When you live with your parent, don't do your laundry with your mother's."

The tip jars have always stayed with me, and they are sitting on my bar even now. It is always an interesting topic of conversation when people come over.

My grandfather was buried with his bottle of bourbon and red jammies. I think when it is my time; I would like to go with my tip jar lying beside me. Maybe at the funeral people will still contribute, one last time, before Jim's bar finally closes.

Here is a list of the current items that are in my tip jars. Items do change seasonally as people take what they want, and then re-contribute.

13 bras, 8 thongs, 5 panties, 3 fish net stockings, four surgical rubber gloves, one bottle of Tabasco, love jelly number six, 16 one dollar bills, 1 mini Chevas Regal bottle, 4 antacids, 2 aspirin, 2 hotel room keys, 1 wine opener, 1 blond pony tail wig, 2 sticks of gum, 3 small rubber ducks, 40 strands of pirate beads, 1 rubber glow in the dark cock ring, a pack of cocktail peanuts, tissues, 1 toothbrush, 1 mini flashlight, 2 silver bullet vibrators, three mice dice, 26 poker chips, 1 small rubber chicken, two Christmas ornaments, five Cuban cigars, and six dollars and seventy five cents in change.

And, a good time was had by all!

One of our many trips to the Miami International Boat Show. Circa 2007.

Chapter 23
Miami International Boat Show

"I'm just a simple guy swimming in a sea of sharks."

~Don Johnson

For many years I would look forward to holidays because after the New Year is here, that is when I would start to prepare my trips to head down to Miami for the Miami International Boat Show and the Florida Keys. I would always drive the trip and set some records getting down to Florida. I would make it from Hampton Virginia to Florida in less than six hours. The Vette was an awesome car to drive down to the Keys with and cruising with the top down to Key West, hell there was nothing like it.

Things worked out pretty cool at that time because I had a lot of friends in Florida. Moe had moved to Jacksonville and Wayne Baker bought a fantastic condo in West Palm Beach with his lovely wife Susan. My next-door neighbor Larry, would also stay in the Keys during February and March. Many of my fishing buddies guide on the Gulf Coast around the Naples area, which I really loved. So for the most part I had friends all over the state of Florida. This came in handy for shooting shows and just general information as to what is biting where.

The first trip down to Miami for the boat show I picked up Moe in Jacksonville and we blindly headed to Miami. We had no reservations anywhere and just thought we would get there and figure out a place to stay when we got there. No big deal. Once we arrived downtown we soon found out that everything was of course booked and there was simply no place to stay. Moe and I ended up driving the Corvette 70 blocks away and we found this average little strip hotel that said *Vacancy*. Pulling into the hotel I noticed that it was sitting waterfront on Biscayne Bay, had a small pool, palm trees everywhere, sort of a casual homey looking place. This by no means, was a five star hotel but was all we needed for a few days and the price was right…$70 per night.

We had to pay for the stay in advance and they only took cash. I thought this was strange but what did I care? Moe and I checked in and made our first cocktail. We walked in the hotel and found that there was a little rustic Caribbean jerk restaurant on the property. In minutes we were ordering up some grilled eats, pronto!

I loved to cook and had a few cocktails in me and before I knew it, I was back in the kitchen with the cook grilling up a storm. These were some very adventitious people for sure and they thought it was fun that a customer was back in the kitchen having a cooking party. We did cook up some tasty delights that I will never forget. Just awesome!

Sitting outside by Biscayne Bay enjoying our grilled dinner, we noticed a bunch of police surrounding the hotel. They stayed there for about a half hour and then everyone left.

Once back at the room I got a call from the lobby suggesting I move my Corvette across the street in the secured garage. I thought that was a pretty good idea and proceeded to take the Vette over to lock her up.

Walking back to the hotel a policeman was standing at the door and he stopped me.

"Excuse me sir."

I said, "Howdy officer, nice evening."

"Are you staying at this hotel?"

I replied, "Why, yes. We are here for the boat show and this is the closest place we could find. I liked the name of the hotel too, *Friendlys.*"

The officer smiled and said, "Be sure to lock your doors to the hotel when you leave, tourists get stuff stolen all the time, have a nice night."

I thought that was nice of the officer and went on up to the room and met Moe. We continued to have several cocktails and then fell asleep.

We both were awakened by what sounded like a herd of buffalo running outside of the room, then what sounded like three gunshots being fired. Moe said it maybe was just a car backfiring and for us to get back to sleep.

I got up and went to use the bathroom and saw a bunch of flashlights outside our window. By the time I got out of the bathroom, whatever or whoever was there was gone now.

In about an hour two guys were yelling a couple of doors down, awakening us again. Next we heard a bunch of cuss words, and then a door slammed. Finally things settled down and we slept the rest of the night.

The next morning there were 10 police cars outside and they were questioning the guy behind the counter. We walked past got in the Vette and headed to the boat show.

This was before I had my GPS in the car and Moe and I only had an idea of where the Convention Center was. We ended up south of the boat show at the bottom end of Miami.

I told Moe, "Hey man, instead of us wasting a bunch of time looking for the place, I will just run into the Sheraton and ask them. They will know."

I walked up to the hotel and asked the doorman, "Hey man, where is the Boat Show, can you point us in the right direction?"

He looked at me and uttered something, but it was not English.

So I run inside and asked the guy by the elevator, "Hey man, where is the Boat Show? Can you point us in the direction?"

He looked at me and uttered something, but it was not English.

Now I go to the front desk and again, "Hey man, where is the Boat Show? Can you point us in the direction?"

He looked at me and uttered something, but it was not English.

I go outside to the Corvette and there is a delivery guy walking up to the hotel. Surely, this guy can help us.

"Hey man, where is the Boat Show? Can you point us in the direction?"

He looked at me and uttered something, but it was not English.

Now, I get in the Vette and Moe says, "Which way?"

I just said, 'Ahhhhhhh, dammit Moe, drive up to the next hotel and let me try there.' We pull up to another very nice hotel that was by the beach. There again was a doorman.

"Hey man, where is the Boat Show? Can you point us in the direction?"

He looked at me and uttered something, but it was not English.

I walk inside and step up to the counter.

"Hey man, where is the Boat Show? Can you point us in the direction?"

He looked at me and uttered something, but it was not English.

OK!! Now I go out to the car, jump in looked at Moe and said, "There is not a fucking person in Miami that speaks English!"

He laughed and we tore out of there in the Corvette and were cruising around south Miami. Crockett and Tubbs had nothing on us!

We were smoking in the Corvette. I mean we were REALLY smoking. I said, "Moe do you think that burning oil smell and that smoke coming out of the hood has anything to do with each other?"

We pulled over popped the hood, and my Corvette was on fire.

All in the world I wanted to do was to get to the show and film our engine sponsor, and here I am on the side of the road in downtown Miami, with my car on fire and no one speaks English! Moe grabbed some bottled water, doused the flame and started to figure out what was going on. The C4 Corvettes ran very hot; it was a part of their design. We waited and let the engine cool and Moe felt if we did not push the engine hard, we should be all right.

So now I am driving off at 30mph trying to find the Convention Center. Finally! We get there, park and walk into the show.

WOW! The greatest boat show on earth! I had never seen anything like it. The show was so big it took me an hour just to find our engine sponsor. Once at the booth we all hooked up and started filming different engine products.

My sponsor representative that signs our contract and check for advertising was talking to me and laughing about our experience that morning. All these dudes were from California and every one of them owned Corvettes. One guy on break went out and checked my engine. He said I had some leaking seals and if I did not push it hard we would get back okay. Just keep it under 80 and check the oil often.

They were curious as to where we were staying. I told them we could not get anything close by and we had to travel out 70 blocks.

He said, "70 blocks? Uuummmm that would put you out around……" I interrupted him, "Yes… *Friendly's Hotel*. That is where we are staying."

He could not stop laughing. He said, "You mean the *Crack Head Motel*?"

"….What?"

He said, "Jim you idiot, you are staying at Crack Head Central. That is the major distribution point for drugs in Miami and gets raided almost nightly!"

I said, "Ooohhhh, now I get it. That is why the police were everywhere and we were always being wakened up by gunshots."

All I can say is that it was the only hotel that had a vacancy and actually was a pretty cool place, with exception of the drugs of course. We figured we better get out of there as soon as we get back. Check out a day early and head down to Marathon and Key West.

We did check out and headed south out of Miami, then met up with my friend Larry in Marathon Key. We had a great time fishing and cooking. After a few days in Marathon we went down to Key West to film a show and partied like hell all along Duval Street.

The fishing out of Key West was great. We went out with one of the guides who also worked with our marine sponsor and ventured out for some excellent yellow tail action. The water was crystal blue at the Western Sambo Reef and it seemed like you could see underwater forever. We drifted live bait offshore off our stern and immediately started to catch nice yellow tail for hours. We filled the coolers with fish and shot some great footage for the show. We headed back to the Hurricane Hole Marina and then readied ourselves for some time in the Keys. We started out by ordering some local fare dockside the Hurricane Hole. First up Moe ordered some conk steaks that were delicious then we split a Lobster Enchalau entrée made with fresh local lobsters.

I loved Wyland's Gallery in Key West and was fortunate to meet Wyland and I also bought one of his paintings. Wyland and I had a close mutual friend who worked at the Cousteu Society. I really loved Key West and after my experience down in the Keys, I made it my mission to one day live down there somewhere in south Florida. Naples is really where I had my eye on. I had produced shows down there with Captain Earl and just loved the area, very beautiful.

When I returned to Hampton I had my Corvette checked out and the news was not good. My mechanic that I knew well and trusted suggested I trade it in and get the C5. I took his advice and found a mag red C5 with only 12 thousand miles on it. This was the prettiest Vette I ever saw and it had a lot more room in it than my C4. I got a very good deal and bought it on the spot.

I loved driving that car and it really helped me out to get to where I was going. It was fast, safe, and economical. If I drove the speed limit I would get close to 30 miles per gallon. Not bad at all. The car just handled so well, I always felt very safe in it. I very much was looking forward to our next trip down to the Florida Keys in this sucker!

My next Miami trip the following year for the International Boat Show I discussed with Moe the idea of staying right by the convention center and bypass the Crack Head Hotel. He agreed and I began to look at places to stay. Remember that we are just a poor fishing show and don't have the budget of multi-million dollar boat companies. When I found that the cheapest place we could stay was $400 bucks per night, I was not happy at all.

I talked to Moe and we figured if we split the cost, we could stay two nights costing us a total off $400 each. We did not like, it but figured this would be the most expensive of all our accommodations and they did have parking for the Corvette. So we booked it.

I flew south in the Vette and picked up Moe in Jacksonville Florida. Then cruised down to Miami in the Mag red C5, totally awesome ride! We get to the hotel and register; the car was still parked out front. We go upstairs and check into a real dumpy room that didn't even have cable TV and the heater sucked. Not too happy, but oh well, it was a short stay anyway.

Moe said, "Jim lets go park the Vette and I will help you put the cover on it." Good idea.

I walked downstairs and asked the guy behind the desk, "Where is the garage?" He said, "Garage? Parking is in the front."

I replied, "Front? Front of what?"

He said, "The hotel."

I said, "I only see those four spaces with four cars in them."

He said, "That is right, we are full."

"What? You mean to tell me that is all you have? You said on the phone you had parking for my Corvette dammit!!"

He answered, "We do, but as you can see all four spaces are taken."

I looked at him and said, "Dude! That is not parking. Have you ever seen what a parking lot looks like?"

All the guy said was to head north and try to find a garage. We would now have to pay for parking, which really pissed me off considering we were paying $400 bucks a night for a freaking dump!

Moe and I get in the Vette and see the parking garage one block away. No big deal. We pull up, "Lot Full"

No problem, there is another garage down the street. "Lot Full."

Now 10 blocks away, "Lot Full."

20 blocks away, "Lot Full."

40 blocks away, "Lot Full."

No I am really getting freakin' pissed.

50 Blocks Away, "Lot Full."

We finally get to 70 blocks and find a parking lot that is going to charge us $20 bucks per day to keep the

Vette there. It was the only place we could find so we parked the car, got our ticket and walked to the street to now get a cab to dive us back 70 blocks to where our piece of shit $400 per night hotel is, with no freaking parking. A cab pulls up and Moe gets into the car, before I got in I looked up and.........

We were parked directly in front of the Crack Head Motel.

I said, "Moe look! It's the Crack Head and the vacancy sign is still on! We could have just stayed there and not gone through all this shit!" We wisely decided to shorten our stay in Miami, stay only one night, do the boat show and haul ass to the Florida Keys as fast as we could.

That was the plan and that is what we did.

Goodbye Miami!

Vrooooom Vrooooom!

Top center (photo taken on Duval Street Key West FL) and lower right Jim Baugh Outdoors C4 show corvette placing in the top two for restoration in C4 class Hampton Virginia Corvette Club Competition. This is the Vette that caught on fire in Miami. The lower left was our C5 Vette at the Corvettes at Carlisle show in Pennsylvania.

Chapter 24

I'll take that bet!

*"Humor has bailed me out of more tight situations than I can think of.
If you go with your instincts and keep your humor, creativity follows.
With luck, success comes, too."*

~Jimmy Buffet

Screaming out of Miami in the Corvette heading south to
Key Largo was a quick lively trip for us. This Vette didn't
have any problem with its seals and was one cruising
machine. We had the top down and tunes as loud as they
can be. We let up some big cigars and was soon passing
Key Largo, Islamorada, and then arriving down in
Marathon Key to hook up with my buddy Larry. Moe and I
had planned on fishing again with Larry and spending
maybe five days down there fishing, cooking, drinking, and
as Tennessee Tim would say, *frolicking*.

    We met Larry not at his house he was renting, but at
the local Conk & Romp bar that was across the street from
his rental. The bar was called the Conk & Romp because
they served fresh local seafood and had mud wrestling with
the wait staff on Saturday nights. If it is 3pm and you want
to find Larry, the Conk & Romp bar is the only place you
will find him.

    "Hi Larry. Awesome to see you man! We just drove
down from the Miami show."

    "Great Jim, did the Vette do alright?"

    "Absolutely! Best ride yet and really looking
forward to driving down to Key West after we do our
fishing."

    Larry Moe and I had several cocktails at the Conk
& Romp bar catching up on fishing stories…and then she
walks in.

I will never forget when I first saw this gorgeous woman. She was very tall with a dark complexion and had perfectly straight hair that fell half way down her back. The legs on this lady seemed to go on forever. She was the prettiest woman I had seen in a long time and the entire bar parted when she walked through the doorway.

She sat down on the other side of the bar and the waitress already had her cocktail poured and placed it in front of her. Once I caught my breath Larry looked at me and said these words:

"Jim, you can forget it. There is no way. Every guy in this bar and in Florida Keys has tried to get that thing and no one has succeeded. She is the best looking gal around and she is rich. Her family owns houses on just about every Key down here."

I thought, Good looking and rich. This sounds good to me!

Realizing I didn't have a chance in hell getting a date with this woman, I decided I would have some fun.

"Larry, I will make a bet with you. If I can get her number and a date with her, you pick up our cocktail tab."

Larry says, "JB, if you can get a date with that woman, not only will I pick up the tab but buy all of us dinner as well."

This sounded like a plan to me. I did ask one thing.

"Larry, do you by chance know her name?"

"It's Destiny."

All right, here I go; time to start planning my strategy. I first thought of close up magic tricks, then, nawww, she's an experienced tigress and would see right through that. Then I thought maybe the television show host line, nawww, she would not be impressed. So, I went into the slaughterhouse, getting ready to be slaughtered without any real game plan at all. The only thing I knew was that I was going to have to be buying the rest of the drinks for Larry and Moe. Oh well, at least I was in the Florida Keys.

I walked around the bar and looked back and Larry and Moe had the biggest smiles on their faces. Larry took his finger and made the slitting your throat gesture. They were enjoying the fact how badly I was going to crash and burn.

I get to her chair; no one was sitting around her, and here I go.

"Excuse me, Dahlin'. How are you doing this afternoon?"

She looked at me like I was just one more sheep that had been slaughtered on the slab, standing in that same spot. She did not look happy that I was there and all she said was, "Fine."

"My name is Jim and those are my friends, Larry and Moe. We just stopped in for a cool one."

She replies, "I recognize Larry he is here all the time, especially after 3."

I said, "Well I am just down here doing a little buiz and really did not know anyone in the area."

She goes, "I can see why."

I am crashing fast here. "What is your name and can I buy you a drink?"

"My name is Destiny and no thank you I already have one."

This is going nowhere fast, just like I expected. The next dumb thing I said was, "Are you staying for dinner?"

She said, and I will never forget, "…NOT if you're here."

Ok, good thing I had enough cash to buy my buddies' tab. I was stepping to walk away and in a very giving up voice I said, "You live around here right? Looking for some shrimp for Larry's dinner tonight. Where is a good spot?"

"…Well Jim, what are you making?"

"I am going to do a fresh Mango Salsa with a coconut shrimp, glazed with Grand Mariner and habanero bacon scallops grilled on the side."

"…So, you are a pretty good cook there Jim, are you?"

"Well, not to toot my own horn, but we do cooking segments on our TV show almost every episode. I have also produced a seafood cooking DVD and also regularly enter cooking competitions."

"… Mr. Jim! Well let me tell you! I am writing my own cookbook right now and I bet I can challenge you to any recipe. Sit down, let me buy YOU a drink and we will talk about it."

As I pushed out the stool to sit next to her, I saw Larry and Moe's faces get very serious and their eyes wide open.

Destiny and I talked and drank for about an hour having a blast. Finally, I said I really enjoyed meeting her and hope to see her again sometime.

"Jim, here is my number. Call me and I will fix you dinner. I am on my way to my other house in Boca Raton. Maybe on your way back, you can stop in and I will fix us up something special."

Okay, this was great. My first stop in Marathon Key and I pick up a rich good looking woman who is a gourmet cook and wants me over for dinner in Boca. At this point, I did not care if we caught fish or not. Jim is partying in the Keys and the boys are buying me dinner!

When I walked back to the guys, Larry said, "Jim, you are the only person I have ever heard of that has ever gotten a date with Destiny. She never dates anyone around here and believe me, everyone has tried."

I laughed and was happy they picked up the tab. We all had a good laugh and went out to find some shrimp.

Our stay in Marathon was fantastic! We did catch a lot of fish and filmed a great show. Every day I was there

Destiny would call me on the phone. We spoke like five times a day. I was very surprised by it all and excited to have met such a beautiful, entertaining, and engaging woman. She had a house in Boca Raton, Marathon, and Key West. WOW, who knows if I dated this girl and things worked out, I could be living in Key West sooner than I thought!

Moe and I loved driving the Vette down in the Keys. It must be the most awesome drive in the United States, Atlantic Ocean on the left, and Gulf Coast on the right. The view and ride was just too awesome. We hung out in Key West, and then made it back to Key Largo. Every day Destiny would call me and just chat away. She was really excited about getting together in Boca. I dropped Moe off with Larry on the way back so they could fish some more. Then Moe was going to fly back to Jacksonville.

The excruciating pain in my left toe was so bad I could hardly push the gas pedal in the Corvette. Eating a lot of shellfish and the consuming many cocktails, caused me to have a gout attack. Gout is the most painful of all arthritis and my foot was swelling the size of a football. I called Destiny on the phone and told her I still planned on coming, but I would be in a lot of pain and not real good company. She assured me that she would relieve any pain I had. Okay… Whatever. We will see.

I pull into Boca Raton in the Vette and arrive at her huge house on the beach. This place was fantastic and she even had a pool and a hot tub in the back. She greeted me at the door, dressed to kill. Damn this was one good-looking woman!

She gave me a huge hug and kiss and said, "Baby! Damn, am I glad to see you!"

Hell, I was happy. Destiny was one hottie and I was ready to get off my feet.

257

We were sitting down on the sofa, having a cocktail and she starts telling me how she felt this connection to me and how she always wanted to get re-married. She also explained to me that if I ever hurt her, her uncle Guido from Jersey would have me in a cement bag underwater. She was serious about her family having mafia ties and she herself had a bit of a Jersey accent.

As we kept talking the more I heard, the more my radar was coming up, and some thoughts I had included whether I should really be here in the first place. About that time, she pulls out a jewelry box and out comes an engagement ring. She for the most part, proposed to me right then. She said she wanted this ring to be ours and that I would make a great stepfather to her two sons.

Now, keep in mind I just met this woman for the second time and had not been in her house but for about an hour and already I am getting a marriage proposal. Something about all this just did not start to feel right at all.

Next I hear, "Honey, I hope you don't mind but I wanted to surprise you. I booked a flight to Key West where we are going to stay at my home for a few days, then I booked us in this B & B that is next to my favorite bar on the water. While we are down there, I will introduce you to my mother, father, and the rest of...*The Family*."

"And Jim, that little TV show you do? You don't have to worry about that. You'll never have to work again."

Now, I immediately thought of two scenarios right that second.

1) The life
   If I continue to stay here tonight this woman is going to make love to me, then haul me down to the keys and meet her family and party. All the sex, fun and money I wanted. Marry this woman, never have to work again, and live in houses all over the Florida Keys. To top it, off this woman is hot, with a perfect figure and breasts that just won't quit.

258

Yes... the dream has come true. That is what would happen if I made love with this woman tonight, and she is ready.

2) The reality

There was no way in hell I was going to be a kept man. I don't know this person from Adam and would have to date someone a very long time before even considering marriage. I did not want to live my life in fear of pissing her off and getting a visit from Uncle Guido. The Magnolia Tree was sending me a strong signal. You know when that little angel taps on your shoulder and says---RUN!!!!

THE DECISION

WAAAAASSS Door Number #2.

I made the decision to get the hell out of there. But how?

She has made flight and hotel reservations, made all these plans, how in the world could I get out of this? How can I NOT make love to her. She was already taking her clothes off on the sofa. What can I do? Someone help me please! Hello, where's "A" Dock?

Then I thought, Damn. I got the Gout! ....I will use that excuse.

My additional plan was to get so much booze in her, she would pass out. Once out I could grab my suitcase get in the Vette and head Northbound.

This was the only plan I could come up with and I got it into action fast. "Damn, Destiny, my foot hurts so much. It hurts even when you touch my shoulder."

"..... Oh Honey, I am sorry."

"It hurts like hell, more rum, more rum please and fix yourself a big one too."

"..... Ok, what else can I do????"

"Well, Destiny, I don't think I am going to be able to make love to you like I wanted. Nothing down there is going to work. The pain is radiating all the way up my

259

back. Maybe if I could lay down in your bed and prop my foot up that may help."

So we went to bed and fortunately she passed out in an hour. At 3 am. I got out of bed, grabbed my suitcase, got in my Corvette and headed northbound at 100 mph.

When she woke up, Jim would not be there, vanished into thin air….. gone. One hell of a magic trick.

My cell phone first started ringing at 5am. I had checked into a hotel and was trying to get some sleep. I woke around 10 am and there were 35 messages on my phone.

"Please, please come back. I will do anything for you, please turn around and come to me!"

I felt really bad about this, but I had no other choice. Destiny was a very strong willed person and she was not going to let me out of her house. She would of never taken a no for an answer. I would have been stuck. That is why I left, before anything could really get going.

By the end of the day she had called me 123 times, before I finally called and simply said, "Destiny, you are a beautiful woman, but I don't know you and I am not ready to marry someone I don't know. Why don't you just give us some time and take things slower."

She said, "I totally understand and sorry I pushed you so hard."

Well, she must have been on a mission to get married after I left her because she got married within the next six months and continued to call me and try to hook up. The reason…Unknown.

When I left Destiny's home in Boca and headed north for the hotel my plan after that was to meet up with my dad and stepmother at their condo in Daytona Beach. They usually stay there each year for a couple months at a time.

My foot was raging and I could not put any pressure on it at all. A gout attack feels like a thousand knives being stabbed in your foot. Extremely painful!

Seeing Dad and Cynthia was a welcome sight. They had already drunk a few cocktails and were anxious to hear about my trip to the Keys. When I told them my Destiny story they could not believe it.

My dad the Judge said, "Son, you left a hot, rich woman in Boca just to see us?"

He was laughing. They could not believe what I had gotten into down there. After a few hours we all went out for dinner. The thing was, by this time, we were loaded. We continued to drink at dinner and I had way too much, so had the Judge.

In our drunken state we walked out of the restaurant off the back deck where they were doing construction and we both fell off the deck onto the asphalt, three feet down.

Both Dad and I fell at the exact same time, he smashed his head and I fell and thought I broke my right ankle. Dad slowly got up… I could not. I had gout in one foot and the other foot was either broken or sprained very badly. It swelled up bigger than my left foot with gout.

This was the most agonizing pain I had ever been in and I truly could not walk. I stayed in Daytona three more days because I couldn't get out of the bed.

I was bored out of my mind and in severe pain. My state of mind was pretty bad and thought I would go nuts staying there any longer.

With a lot of help, I finally got back in the Corvette and slowly made it back to Hampton. On the way back several times I had to check into a hotel just to lie down and get off my feet. Checking into the hotels was interesting and now I knew what it felt like to be handicapped and not be able to walk.

This experience made me a lot more careful about drinking and doing anything. I also got a prescription for when I would get another gout attack.

This was an exhausting trip that included a little bit of everything from fishing in the Keys, to marriage proposals, to gout attacks and sprained ankles.

Getting back to the Chesapeake Bay was again a welcome sight. I was glad to be home on the boat.

A year later, Destiny called me on the phone, "Jim, dahlin, I am flying out and have a ticket waiting for you at the airport for New York City. I am taking some time off to go up there to shop and eat Italian. You're coming with me."

I said, "Ahhh good to hear from you but ahhhh, where is your husband?"

She says, "Oh, he just went in for heart surgery. He will be fine. I am leaving now."

I thanked her for the invitation, however did respectfully decline. She would call me again, when she got back and tell me all the restaurants she went to and said we will do it some other time.

I would stay in touch with Destiny by phone. However, I have never seen her again. I often wonder if I would have stayed and went with her to Key West how things probably would have turned out.

Being a kept man in the Florida Keys by a beautiful fun woman sometimes does not sound so bad. This was one of those decisions you make and at that time you know it is the right thing to do. However, looking back on it I always wonder.

Gee, wouldn't it be nice lying on a beach in Key West with my hottie wife getting my back rubbed drinking rum out of a coconut never worrying about working again?

Yeah…Sometimes I think about that. I really do.

Right up until Uncle Guido pops into my mind.

Jim Baugh with one of the best in the world, progressive rock, jazz percussionist and composer Bill Bruford. Picture was taken standing by the Trojan Tri Cabin after filming a JBOTV show. This was Bill's first fish he had ever caught in his life and enjoyed his trip thoroughly. Bill even wrote about this adventure in his book, "Bill Bruford the Autobiography".

Chapter 25

Roundabout

I will remember you
Your silhouette will charge the view
Of distant atmosphere Call it morning driving
Through the south Even in the valley

~Jon Anderson

Back on the boat and trying to recoup after a long trip in the Keys, I put in my favorite Yes DVD concert and cranked up the stereo full blast.

"In and around the lake, mountains come out of the sky and they stand there."

I just loved this fine group and had followed their musical career, ever since I was a little kid learning to play piano. Rick Wakeman was the keyboard player for YES and I learned a bunch of his tunes on piano. Even though he was the keyboardist, my favorite musician in the band and favorite musician period was and is drummer, Bill Bruford.

Bill Bruford was one of the few founders of the progressive rock era. Groups like Yes, Emerson Lake and Palmer, Genesis, King Crimson, U.K, these were groups that pioneered progressive rock. Bill Bruford played in all those bands, with the exception of Emerson Lake and Palmer and also played in a ton of other bands as well. His long-standing jazz band Earthworks gained him a lot of respect in the jazz community. Bill was known as a great odd time signature drummer. I just loved what this guy could do, playing around a 4/4 beat.

I was watching the DVD thinking now here is a guy I would love to meet. No chance in hell I could ever meet this English rock legend that had played in all my favorite bands. I live in America and have seen him in concert when he would tour here, but there was never a chance of meeting him backstage. Looking up his website I saw that he had come out with a new jazz CD and would be touring the states. With a rum and tonic in hand next thing I knew I was calling his record company in Los Angles California.

"Hi there, this is Jim Baugh of Jim Baugh Outdoors TV and would like to speak to Bill Bruford's agent."

…..Hold please.

"Hello?"

"Hi, my name is Jim Baugh of the Jim Baugh Outdoors TV show and we were wondering if Bill would like to appear on our TV show to promote his wonderful new jazz CD."

I hear, "Who the hell is Jim Baugh Outdoors?"

I replied, "Hey man, if you are on line just go to this website and check us out. We feature fishing, cooking, travel, and we do like to have on occasion, prominent famous English rock stars on our TV show."

He starts chuckling on the other end of the phone.

"Jim, this is pretty cool, I am watching your show right now on line. Tell ya what, I will talk to Bill and see if he has any interest at all." I thanked him for his time and taking my call and that was the last I thought I would hear from him.

Two days later I get a call, "Hey Jim talked to Bill. He would like to do it, but will not have time on his current tour. He said he was coming back in 10 months for vacation in the USA and bringing his son. If you could meet up with Bill then, he said he would do it."

Sure, right, ok, like this is ever going to happen. Hell, I just called the guy on a whim when I was having a drink on the boat, never even thought I would get this far. I hung up the phone and never thought about it again.

10 months pass.

I have a missed call on my cell phone. In voice mail and in this very heavy English accent I hear the following message.

"Hello James, this is Bill Bruford in the UK. Sorry I missed you chap, you can call me back at this tele num. We would like to appear on your tele show in the States. Cheerio, good fellow."

Flying out of the fly bridge I landed on the dock and sprinted up to the bar where my buddy Rudy was working. Rudy was a drummer in a local band and a big Yes fan. I said, "Dude listen to this!" I put on my speakerphone and replayed Bill's message.

Rudy screamed, "NOOOOO SHIT!"

I called Bill back on the phone and talked with him about his trip back over to the USA. He was going to fly over and spend some time in the Washington DC area with his son Alex. We were to pick Bill up at his hotel in our show Suburban and drive him to Hampton, provide his accommodations, and he would stay with us for a total of four days. WOW! I get to hang with Bill Bruford for four days and then drive him back to DC. This is going to be good!

Since I was going to have him in the car with me for over three hours, I thought this would be a good opportunity to set him up a little. I had some of the music that I had done on CD and loaded it up in the CD Changer.

I met Bill and his son, and they were the most courteous people you would ever have the pleasure of meeting. Bill was a real English gentleman that came from good English blood. We talked for hours in the car and it did not take long for me to realize, that Bill Bruford had a great sense of humor and was a very funny guy.

While some of my original music was playing. I asked him what he thought of the keyboards.

He said, "Sounds like a Keith Emerson clone."

I figured I would take that as a complement. He liked the idea that I was a music major and could relate to him in a musical conversation. I mean, we sat and talked about the implementation of midi drums and triggers for a

266

long time. Not the average conversation you would have with a fishing show host.

Bill loved the hotel and liked Hampton a lot. He said Hampton was a pretty waterfront town and loved all the activity with the concerts that were happening on the streets. We went into the blues bar, Goodfellas, and listened to some music. I knew the band and the drummer. When they met Bill, the guy went into shock. Many drummers all over the world idolize Bruford. It was a real treat to walk him around and introduce him to people. I think he thought it was fun.

Bill said, "You know, Jim, I played the Hampton Coliseum, but of course was not able to spend any time here. I really am enjoying this a lot, thank you."

After dinner we all ended up on my boat on the fly bridge, sitting around drinking wine and smoking cigars. Bill lit one up and was having a ball.

He said, "So Jim, this is your job. You go fishing; hang out listening to bands, smoke cigars and drink wine on the boat, right chap?"

I said, "Yes Bill, as much as we can get away with."

He really was enjoying himself.

We took Bill out on a charter for flounder and this was the first time Bill Bruford had ever been fishing in his life. I was really honored. He and his son were having a blast out on the charter and they were sort of acting like little kids, because all of this was so new to them. Fortunately, we hooked into a 23-inch flounder and Bill went nuts. This actually was a very special moment for Bill and his son, it was the first fish they had ever caught and they did it on our TV Show.

My son Ben Baugh was there to meet Bill Bruford and I will never forget when Ben asked Bill this question.

"Bill, I know you are a great jazz artist but don't you miss playing those huge rock concerts to 20, 000 people with Yes or Genesis? Is that not just the biggest thrill in the world?"

Bill replied. "Ben, your dad told me that you were in a school play once. Correct?"

"Yes, Bill."

"Now Ben, how many times did your play perform and did you enjoy it?"

"Oh, we only had to do it three times, but did enjoy doing it."

"Now Ben, imagine if you had to do that play, say, 3000 times, would you still enjoy it?"

Ben said, "Now I understand. And you want to play other music and grow, instead of staying stagnant just for the money."

Bill said, "Absolutely."

I asked a lot of questions to Bill about the music business and felt that it was a huge blessing to meet Bill and his son. It was a wonderful four days, with memories that will stay with me until the day I die.

I'll be the roundabout
The words will make you out 'n' out
You spend the day your way
Call it morning driving thru the sound and in and out the valley
Jon Anderson

Chapter 26

Travis Tully Looks Really Good

"Well Excccuuuuuuuse Me!"

~Steve Martin

The Judge had met me in Richmond Virginia and we were sitting in our favorite deli sandwich shop that we called *The Basement*. Dad was enjoying his Sailor Sandwich and I was getting chowing down on the *Downstairs* Sub with anchovies. The Basement was a legendary sandwich joint in the fan district that only sat around 20 people at most and they served the best New York style sandwiches I ever had.

My dad had been taking me there since I was a kid and we ate there a lot when I was attending VCU getting my music degree. After the Judge and I had about two beers our "A" dock buddy Doc Ravage came in and announced the awful, grave news. Our life time friend and one of the marina rat pack *The Crew* Travis Tully, was killed in a car accident. We were shocked and silent. Neither of us could believe what we just heard.

Travis Tully was a character who loved the marina life. He had plenty of money and enjoyed spending it on a lot of ladies, cars, boats, and booze. Travis owned about five restaurants and bars in Richmond and for about 10 years he owned the most popular nightspot in the West End. This was a sad day learning of his passing. The Judge also used to represent Tully in several legal matters and they also enjoyed fishing together most of their lives.

Funerals aren't something that most people enjoy going to and the Judge and I are no exception. We loved Travis Tully and certainly were going to pay or respects to him and the family. After all this was one of the marina rat pack and we had to give him a proper send off.

There was not even a parking space available at the funeral home. We had to park across the street where one of Travis's restaurants happened to be located. Once parked, we waited in line for what seemed like forever just to get in to pay our respects to our beloved Tully.

The room was jam packed with people and way in the front we could hardly see what looked like the open casket where Travis laid. Another hour would pass before we could even get close to the casket to pay our respects. This was a very somber moment for Dad and me, because it gave us a lot of time to reflect on the many memories we had with the famous Travis Tully. This guy had been like family to us and we hated the thought of another member of *The Crew* passing away.

Dad and I finally arrived at the casket and there he lay. Travis Tully never looked so good. Even in death, his soul gleamed out like a ray of sunshine. This man lived a full life and was loved by many, many, people.

I could not hold back my tears any longer. The Judge started to weep as well. We just loved our friend and did not want him to be gone.

"Dad this is the most depressing day I have had since I can remember. I can't believe he is gone."

"Son, I know. I have known Travis since we were in college and you grew up eating at his restaurants. We will miss him greatly son."

"Dad, don't you think it is a shame that he had to leave this earth in a car wreck?"

"Yes. Son, he was too good of a man to have been taken that way."

"But Dad, didn't you say he died from severe head injury?"

"Yes Jim. I really don't want to talk about it any more. Just say your prayers for Travis and let's go talk to the family."

"Sure Dad but got to tell ya, I have never seen old Tully look so good. It is like they shaved a few years off of him!"

"I know son it is amazing, when I go I want to come here and have them do my makeover. Maybe if we stay here long enough I will get my wish."

I started to look at the people patiently waiting behind us and there were just so many people! I did not see any of our "A" Dock people at all.

"Say Pops, do you recognize any of the people here?"

Dad looked up and around then shrugged his shoulders.

"Uumm, Dad. Let me ask you something. Did Travis always have that mole there behind his ear?"

Dad bent down, took a close look at his face, paused then said,

"We're in the wrong room! That's not Tully! Oh shit!"

The entire time we were in the wrong room for hours mourning over some other dead guy, who looked a lot like Travis Tully, but just a bit better.

Dad and I did the right thing. We didn't let anyone know we had screwed up. We were respectful as we slowly left the room. We stopped and shook everyone's hand, hugged some folks, cried a little and finely got out of there.

We walked down the hall further and there was everyone we knew and Travis Tully in the room with an open casket.

By then, Dad and I just waved our hands and said, "Hi Tully!"

Then we mixed a drink and started partying with everyone. Dad and I were just glad to be at the right funeral. This was one hell of a wake just like Travis would have wanted. It was sad, but everyone was making the best of it.

271

After the funeral, it was back to the boat in Hampton.

Key Largo, Bayside Resort-Cay Club circa 2008

Chapter 27

Rose

Just like Travis Tully, all good things must come to an end. One door closes and another one opens. I began to feel that my time on the docks of Hampton was coming to conclusion. It was here I had relived my youth in a very adult way and never regretted a minute of it.

Many new nightspots had opened up in other areas of Hampton and neighboring cities started having competitive concerts that drew the crowds away from our downtown docks. We as a country had also begun a terrible recession that would play havoc on everyone, including *Jim Baugh Outdoors TV*. It was a period we would survive but not without a lot of prayer, huge sacrifice, and Xanax.

Everything has a silver lining and the recession is no different. The economy meant unreal deals on housing and I always wanted to live in a waterfront condo. I decided to sell the boat I was living on and make an offer on a nice waterfront condo on the Chesapeake Bay. I made the seller a very low offer, that if he took it... well, there was no way I could lose on this deal. I was wrong. Like some other people, I had know idea just how bad things economically were going to get in the near future.

Marching forward and before I knew it the boat was gone and I was living in a small condo on the Chesapeake Bay. My dream had come true. I renovated the condo so it looked like something in Key West and even put in an art gallery. I had one wall in the gallery dedicated to P.D. Cooper original pirate drawings. I also have my Wyland hanging on its own dedicated wall. Each piece of art in the gallery has its own custom spot light, with dimmer switch illuminating the artwork. I am home.

To help with the Key West feel I started to breed parakeets. I let them fly around the condo and they roost in my Sago palm trees at night. Really cool, and always freaks guests out when they come over.

After my condo was renovated things had settled down a bit and I was busy producing and editing *Jim Baugh Outdoors*. Figuring that I am not really a loner, maybe it was time to try the online dating thing one more time. So I signed up for the shortest period I could and tried the internet dating scene once more.

This time it was horrible. 1000 women online and I were not interested in any of them. Must have been a slow week or something, just did not seem to be much to pick from. I mean nothing that would even generate sending a wink.

Then on the last page, there was a picture of this very pretty lady with red hair. I read her profile and figured, heck she is a bute! She had a nice profile and seemed like a fun gal, plus her kids were grown and gone. Maybe I will get lucky here and she will reply….. She did not.

No problem. If the only attractive woman online does not respond to me then that is just fine. The holidays were coming up and if I was not dating anyone that would save some bucks on the Christmas gifts. My experiences dating around the holidays were never that great anyway.

A month goes by and my time was up for the online dating. I only went out with one lady during that month and it was a disaster. Her name was May and she was a beautiful girl, however it only took a couple of dates to figure out she was an alcoholic who also was on meds for depression. The woman drank all the time. On our first date I had two iced teas and she had six beers. I was not happy with how my online date was going.

I took one more look before signing off of computer dating for good. Once again I saw nothing that interested me. Then there she was.

Ahhhh, what the hell. There is that red head again, it is not going to cost me anything to try one more time. So I sent her a brief email. That was it. Done!

This time I got a reply.

We sent several e-mails back and fourth before eventually she gave me her phone number and we started talking on the phone. We talked up a storm about anything and everything. One night, we spoke on the phone for eight hours. That is correct, a GUY talking on the phone for eight hours. What can I say. I was very interested in this lady and I haven't even met her yet.

You know when you talk to a woman on the phone for eight hours while drinking wine, there are some issues that come up. For instance, how do I go to the bathroom and talk at the same time? My excuse was this.

"Ahhhh Rose, that's just the water running, I am doing a little cleaning in the kitchen while we are chatting." Then I would flush the toilet and cough at the same time, while running quickly out of the bathroom. Later I found out that she was doing the same thing.

It was time for our first meeting and date. I am always apprehensive about a first date, because I never know if I will live up to any expectations. Even worse, what if she just has no physical chemistry with me and only wants to be friends? These things happen of course, and you never know until you actually meet.

Considering the issues I had with some of the women I had dated, my plan was to put everything out there on our first date and see how she handles it. Here is what was going to happen:

A friend of mine was hosting a Lady Kay party and wanted me to be there to help support and talk up the Mr. Kay line. In return, I would receive some cologne or

276

something. P.D. Cooper and a host of pirates were going to be there including the cook from the local Chinese restaurant, who was a professional knife thrower and some female dancers from the Crystal Cock Cafe.

The phone call went like this. "Rose dahlin, would you like to have our first date this Sunday afternoon?"

"…..Yes Jim, that would be wonderful, what do you want to do?"

"Well Rose, I would like to take you to a Mr. Kay, Lady Kay, pirate party complete with Crystal Cock dancing girls, Chinese knife throwers and I am bringing smoked rockfish."

" OK Jim, sounds like a party to me!!"

When Rose came to my condo door I was a little worried at first glance. This woman was just too pretty. Surely she would not go for an old bald fisherman like me. She truly was beautiful. Flowing long red hair, awesome figure, perfect skin and crystal blue eyes that looked like the Caribbean Sea. Let me tell you that combination of red hair and blue eyes just killed me! I really thought she was a knockout.

She was very nice, but gave no signs to me she was very interested. We just talked up a storm, had some wine, and left for the Mr. Kay, Lady Kay, pirate party.

Lots of my friends were there at the party and everyone gave Rose the big look over. She did look stunning and I got the thumbs up from all the guys. Hell at this point, I didn't even know if she liked me. We had only just met. To be honest I thought she was just being nice to me and really was not that interested. She was being the lady that she was and being sociable to everyone. Rose was enjoying herself, turns out she has a very funny personality and can crack a lot of jokes. This lady was a lot of fun to be around.

The party continued for several hours and I was standing near her. She lightly grabbed my arm and pulled me close to her, then grabbed my hand and placed it on her leg, holding hands. I felt like I could feel her entire soul, just by touching her fingers. Some people are like this, you feel their passion and heart simply by the touch of the hand. Rose was one of those people.

It was not until that moment that I realized that maybe the mustard test had been passed. She liked me and maybe she did not find my looks too offensive.

Afterwards back at the condo, there was no way I was going to be pushy and try anything. A kiss on the cheek was all that I had planned. She left and then I called her to see if she would like to get together the following weekend.

On our next date, we talked for hours and sat on the balcony by the water drinking wine really enjoying ourselves. She told me about what she recently had been through with her business.

Rose had worked in the interior design business for years, before she decided to open up her own design and kitchen cabinet business. Things took off quickly, however then everything came to a screeching halt. The economy took a massive dive and we were heading into the big recession that would also affect my buiz greatly, much more than I ever dreamed possible.

Home construction and building stopped. All custom cabinet business just slowed to nothing, and she had to close up shop. Rose ran the company by herself and it was a hard blow. During the last year of running the shop, she had been dating a guy who really took advantage of her and even took a lot of her income. He was a cheating, three timing bastard, who left a scar on Ms. Rose in a bad way.

Sometimes I noticed her hands would shake some. Also, she said she liked to take a lot of naps sometimes sleeping most of the day. I thought these were signs of possibly some sort of depression considering what she had been through, I understood. Rose acknowledged that

278

closing the buiz had affected her a lot and was going to get some help to even her out some. In a way, she was a very fragmented person. This was easy to see why, considering her recent life changing turn of events.

One thing is for sure, I can relate to tough economic times. This recession was getting worse and the economy was like a giant toilet being flushed with many people including me, being caught in the whirlwind downward spiral.

Rose was a good person of Christian faith. I felt she was worth the effort and I would stand by her while she was adjusting. Also, I wanted her to be able to trust a man again. This was not the time for me to be pushy with her at all. She was a good lady and I was going to be patient.

I wanted to clear the air.

"Rose, I find you to be a very attractive person in many ways and there is something I would like to run by you. I have had some rather interesting experiences over the last few years regarding women and I would like to take this slow. I don't want to do anything to ruin what could possibly be a great relationship. Maybe it would be a good thing if we took our time to get to know one another, before any real sexual relations. If things continue to work out down the road, then that is a different story. But for now I don't want to pressure you at all to do anything. I just want to get to know you very well first."

She said, "I respect and feel most comfortable with that as well. I have been through the grist mill with the last guy I dated, so taking time is good for me."

We continued to have a wonderful evening on our second date. After her kiss goodnight, I began to wonder if this was going to be the extent of the kiss. It lacked a lot. But I did not push, was going slow and taking my time.

Every week we talked on the phone and continued to date every weekend. I was amazed just what a hilarious personality Rose had. She could crack me up at any moment and her sense of humor was a bit twisted. To give you an example she thought the movie, *Silence of the Lambs* was a comedy. Now that is funny! She kept calling out to me, "Precious, here Precious." I got her back though. Figured out there was a *Silence of the Lambs* voice for my GPS in my car. I loaded it up and just knew she would not be able to stop laughing when she got in the car and the GPS would say, "Benjamin Rothbow... a head, take a left."

I saved this until I got to know her better for a special occasion.

Every week it started to bother me more that the good night kiss just SUCKED! Come on. I really liked this woman a lot but if she was going to be such a bad kisser, how is this going to work out in the long run? Other than her horrible good night kisses, everything else about this woman I just loved.

We had been dating around three months and we were getting to know each other quite well. The thought seriously crossed my mind about talking to her or possibly just remaining friends, because I could not see me being with someone who was such a bad kisser. The next time I saw her I was going to confront her about this. At least that was my plan anyway.

Rose came over the next weekend and I cooked her a nice dinner and we sat and talked on the sofa having a nice evening. It was then that I thought maybe we could have some friends over and have a themed dinner party. I suggested we throw a *Silence of the Lambs* dinner party and serve rare lamb and fava beans. She insisted we do it, so we did plan on a movie dinner party with some of our friends.

It was getting late and we enjoyed each others company so much, I just let the bad kiss topic slide for now. I was tired and was not up for bringing it up anyway. I walked Rose to the door and before I could lean over for a peck on the lips, she had nailed me with a kiss from a foot away.

I have never seen a tongue that long in my life. She gave me a kiss that would send me through the roof. Frankly, I was paralyzed from the neck down. I have never been kissed like that in my life. Now, I know what is like to be kissed by a giant octopus. It was 20 thousand leagues under the sea. ...she was the pus, and I was the submarine.

I said, "Rose, what the hell was that! You have been holding back on me big time, girl! Geeezzzzzz where did you get that thing! Do you have to roll it back in or what? Is there a spring attached?"

Rose said, "I only roll it out for someone if I think I am going to be in a relationship with him. I waited until I knew you better, wanted to make sure you wanted me for me, not my talents."

I said, "Now Rose, I am not sure just how talented you are, maybe we better try this one more time so I can make sure?"

She laughed and after one more brief 45-minute kiss, she left and started to go home. Before she left I decided to nickname my new friend. Rose's tongue, *Anaconda.*

Anaconda would be my new pet friend that would come out and play with me, then retire to its cage.

Wow! Now old Jim is getting really excited! A beautiful woman with red hair, ocean blue eyes, awesome body and a tongue named *Anaconda* that would make Gene Simmons cry for mercy. I sure am glad I met this lady. Things are looking up!

After several more weeks of seeing Rose, I was ready to ask her if she would like to go down to Miami and the Florida Keys to film some shows and also feature the Miami Boat Show.

"Jim, I could really get away. Last year was a very hard year, and I really have gotten close to you. This could be a lot of fun for us. I'm in, let's go!!"

Fortunately, I had just gotten my final sponsorship signed off with my marine sponsor after five revisions. We were heading into the BAD recession and advertising budgets were being cut all over the place, ours included. The sponsor funds would not come in before the Miami Show in February however would arrive shortly after our return. I had my mortgage money in the bank just enough for the upcoming payment. That money is all I had left and is what I used for expenses to travel to Miami with. No big deal. I would have a check waiting for me when I got back.

Going to the Miami Show is important for our program because we get good concentrated face time with our sponsors. The segments we film down there have also always made for great stories on our show.

I told Rose to plan on being gone a week or two. It was good timing for her as well; she had not yet started a job and was looking forward to getting away. She met me at the condo with tight white shorts, white pumps, and a tight knit blue v-neck, with pearls around her neck. Her red hair was flowing down her back. She looked me in the eyes and said,

"Take me….. to Key West."

…Then she laid a big one on me. What a way to start the morning!

The automatic hidden lights on the red Corvette popped up the second I inserted the key in the ignition. The leather upholstery was soft, shiny, and her smooth legs looked so good sitting there in the passenger's seat.

VRRRROOOOOOOOOOOMMMMMMMM!!!!

We were hauling ass at 4 am in the C5 Mag Red Corvette heading to Miami leaving nothing behind but 100 mph road dust. The Corvette is a great ride, but really starts hugging the ground at 110 mph. Rose never realized it because the car rode so smooth and low to the ground.

She said, "Jim you really seem to be a good driver and enjoy it. I like that. You would never know we were doing 70 in this thing, the ride is just so incredible!"

I said, "It is smooth because we are doing 145 mph."

"...WHAAAAAT!"

We left Hampton Virginia and got to Florida in 5. 5 hours.

Corvette... there is no substitute!

Before we knew it the temperature has raised enough to take the top off the Vette. We were enjoying the warm wind surrounding us and the tall palms passing us by overhead.

Pulling into West Palm Beach Florida Rose and I were going to be staying with my old friend cameraman Wayne Baker. Wayne and his lovely wife Susan had a gorgeous condo on the water in West Palm that was one of the nicest places I had seen. It was beautiful.

Wayne and Susan asked, "Hey guys, wadda ya say we take ya to the Rum Bar for dinner."

My eyes got real big, 'Rum Bar? They have a restaurant dedicated to rum?'

I was really starting to like West Palm Beach Florida.

The four of us got there and this was one of the coolest places I have seen. Nothing but a bunch of tiki bars all out on the sand by the water with little huts that were actually kitchens! The tables were made out of rum barrels and we drank out of coconut rum buckets. We are talking an actual bucket of rum was the average-size house drink.

We ordered up some conk fritters, shrimp, and a clam bucket with a couple of lobster tails. We had a ball! I fired up a cigar afterwards and was loving life with my hot red head and bucket of rum punch.

Rose and I had such a good time we purchased a couple of those coconut rum buckets to go as souvenirs.

Thought they would look good back at my Mid Atlantic Key West Condo.

The four of us ended up in the hot tub and pool back at Wayne and Susan's place. Rose and I were having the time of our lives and were very much looking forward to the greatest boat show in the world that was all happening the next day. Exciting! Life is good!

Breakfast on Wayne and Susan's balcony overlooking Singer Island, the Atlantic Ocean, and the Inland Waterway was an awesome way to start our morning. The view from the front of their condo is just amazing. One of the best I had seen. We were having coffee and fresh mango grapefruit salad watching the boats travel up and down the Inland Waterway, while also watching the wind surfers surfing off of the beach at Singer Island.

There was also a conk boat that was pulling up at the marina to unload their catch. The ship's store there was having a special on fresh lobsters that sounded like to me would be a good thing to do for dinner sometime. I have caught live Florida lobsters while diving and thought they tasted a lot like a big New Orleans crawfish. In other words, I liked them a lot. The warm water lobster is quite different than the deep cold water creatures off of Maine. They are not the same tail although both delicious.

After Wayne had worked for me for years back in Virginia, he was offered a full time job as chief 3D animation artist for a large company in West Palm. The money was great and he had a good opportunity to invest in this fantastic property. The days of living in the soon to be condemned Mexican trailer in Ashland Virginia were long gone. I was very happy for Wayne and Susan to be living in such paradise as West Palm Beach.

The old Magnolia Tree had looked out for Wayne after all. Good prayers answered. They were truly blessed.

We said goodbye to our friends in West Palm and I had the Vette keys in my hand.

I inserted the key in the ignition, the LS1 engine roared and the RPM meter pegged the panel… and that was just leaving the parking lot. The mag red Corvette with the red head and my pet anaconda were flying once again, first class with trail dust blowing north behind us.

Heading south arriving in Miami didn't take long. We briskly pulled into the hotel at Biscayne Bay for the in-water portion of the Miami International Boat Show. Rose and I parked the Vette and walked down to the docks, where our sponsor's boats were in the water. Rose looked fabulous and heads were turning. She wore a white v-neck with blue shorts and white dock shoes. She was going to assist me in filming an interview with a factory rep that in the past would never give me the time of day.

I learned something. You get a lot further with a hot red head than you do a bald fishing show host. I saw the rep that I wanted to interview, walked up to him and said, "Hi there, let me introduce you to Rose, was hoping you would give us a few minutes on camera and talk about your new boats?"

"Why sure, Jim, that would be great! Is Rose going to be with me on camera?"

"Sure man, right after I get finished with you."

The guy gave me like an hour on camera and then took us out on his boat for some filming offshore. I filmed all the "B" roll I needed for the entire Miami Boat Show and we had only been there for about two hours. I was feeling very good about how well things were going. Once we got back to the dock I saw the man who signs my contracts, and he approved our deal just before we left for Miami. Good thing too because money was getting very tight. His name was Gene and he was head of advertising for our marine sponsor.

"Hi, Gene, great to see ya man! We just got some awesome footage of your new boat crashing through some nice waves in Miami. It is going to look great on film!"

Gene looked very depressed and said, "Ahhh, that is real nice…. Jim." Then he looked very somber and cleared his throat.

"Ahhhh Jim…… I have something to tell you."

"….. Sure Gene, what's up??"

"Ahhh ahhh ahh ….. You know that agreement we made before you drove down here?"

"…..Yeah man, what about it?"

"Ahhh …. We just heard from headquarters across the big pond and we have to lay off 25% of all our work force globally even maybe close a division, and I doubt I will even have a job when I get back to the office. All advertising is put on hold we can not honor the agreement we just made with you and I am terribly sorry."

Talk about one sinking twenty pound ball of depression traveling down my throat right down to my stomach. Sadness, shock, anxiety, worry, depression all hit me in a second with the weight of a fright train. The chills going down my spine could have made ice cubes. An imploding submarine is what my insides felt like.

I could also tell by talking to Gene that this seriously upset him and he was also worried what the future was going to hold for him. This was a period of time early in 2009 after the presidential elections, and our country was really diving deep into a massive recession. The marine industry was suffering in a bad way and they had to make drastic measures to stay in business.

My second thought was that there would be no check waiting for me when I got back and I used my mortgage money to go on this business trip. We already had shoots lined up in the Keys and I was in Miami. I looked at Gene very politely and said, "Gene, I understand, and you will not have any problems from us. We have appreciated your support for the last 15 years and hopefully we will work something out after the Miami Show. Let things settle down a bit and I will revise our last proposal. We will see if we can come up with something in a couple months."

I could tell he was relieved that I played the cool card because he explained to me that they had to cancel all advertising and some companies were threatening law suits etc. I shook his hand and thanked him again. Then he was called away for a meeting with his boss.

Gene did not look happy when he left. Our marine sponsor had been good to us for 15 years and I was so upset that the economy had gotten so bad for everyone. I did not know how we would all pull through these hard economic times. I decided to put my faith in the Magnolia Tree and try to figure out what to do next.

So there Rose and I were standing on the dock in Miami and I was without my major Marine sponsor. No contract, no checks waiting for me when I got back, no money in the bank, just the balance of my next mortgage payment in my left pocket.

What the hell was I going to do now?

Rose was standing there looking at me with a little sadness in her face.

I thought silently to myself. I had a pause moment so I could think clearly what to do. Geeezzzze. After about a minute, I looked at Rose and yelled out in a loud voice,

"...Key Largo or Bust! Baby, we will be there within the hour! Let's get the hell outa here now!"

We quickly took the top off the Corvette, jumped in and hauled ass to Key Largo as fast as we could.

VVVVRRRRROOOOOOOOOOOOOOOOOMMMM!

We had little traffic and the Vette was sucking down the road hauling ass. We got there in a little over an hour.

We arrived under the sun drenched palms and white sandy beaches wind blown, mentally ragged, economically challenged and tiredly sober. Miami and the rest of the world were now behind us. In front of us were the Florida Keys and first stop was the liquor store.

Rose said, "You know honey, we have those coconut rum buckets. I bet we can make up some of that rum punch for the afternoon, what do you think?"

I said, "Your genius will be rewarded and your talents will not go unrecognized."

Loading up the Corvette from our liquor store run was quite a sight. The hatchback area of the Vette was square full and we had literally two boxes of rum and mixers that all had to be placed nowhere else but in Rose's lap. Fortunately, it was only a short drive to the Cay Club where we would be staying in Key Largo.

The coral colored paint of the Cay Club offset by the green palm tress and blue waters of the Gulf Coast was a perfect setting to land our C5 Corvette and stay for a while. I had planned on staying five days, however when I go to the Keys I seriously don't want to ever head back North again.

There is just something about the Keys that calls me like a Labrador to a Frisbee Factory.

Key Largo has always been my favorite Key and as soon as we checked in, we unloaded the bar. For that moment I tried to put Miami behind me. Loosing a major sponsor contract and living the recession was extremely upsetting, so I did my best to once again get refocused quickly.

The only thing on my mind now was taking a break and partying with the redhead, swimming in the Gulf, and drinking rum. This, at least for the next few days was a good plan. There was nothing I could do about our marine sponsor for the moment, so we might as well enjoy ourselves over the weekend while we could!

The Cay Club is my favorite, a quaint nice little resort and beach right on the Gulf of Mexico. I love the swimming pool, inside and outside beach dining, and the sushi bar. This place had it all and it was small. Hell, I did not need anything else. Rose loved the place and she reminded me that this day was not only the first day of our stay in the Keys, but it was Valentines Day! I got on the phone in the room and made reservations for the outside restaurant that was having a special Valentines dinner party complete with all night fireworks and a Caribbean dance band.

After I made the reservations Rose had already mixed us a bucket of Rum, and then she brought out the pet Anaconda. I couldn't believe what awesome tricks this pet could do. WOW, after four hours, we put the pet back in its cage and mixed up some more fresh buckets of rum and headed to the pool.

By now we had been drinking rum since we arrived late in the morning and we were not feeling much pain. There were several people at the pool who got *Woke UP* once Rose and I got there. We were ready to party and got the crowd rolling big time.

The crowd mostly consisted of elderly couples who were snowbirds, older retired people from up north who like to winter in the Keys. These were some relaxed people who were ready for some lively entertainment and Rose and I happened to fit the bill.

Rose started telling all the women in the pool some age defying secrets about how she keeps her facial skin so smooth and wrinkle free. I can't divulge the secret, all I will say is that when we left the pool, some of the old husbands came up to me and thanked me.

"Jim, we just love Rose, and thank you! My wife would never consider that before and we have been married for 40 years, now she wants to stay an extra night! And I booked it!"

By that time I had enough rum in me and I wasn't that concerned about what type of facials the snowbird wives by the pool would be getting. But I was happy for them. It all was just a blur anyway. Rose's rum bucket was empty and I was heading back to the room to re-stock our Coconut Rum Punch supply.

Entering the room I saw a plastic trash can with a liner that soon would make for a great ice bucket. I put together more rum and mixers to take back to the pool. Everything was just about ready when my cell phone rang in the room. I was going to see who it was, but not answer it. Hell I was in Key Largo and not going to take calls for the next several days.

It was Gene, my marine sponsor who I just left earlier that morning. Considering how much I had to drink I was not sure if It was wise for me to pick up the phone or not. I had sort of a,

"What da hell" attitude…..I answered the call.

"Hello, JB here."

"Jim, its Gene. Hey dude, we are just getting ready to jump on this new boat that has triple 300's rigged on it, would make for a great shoot! Why don't you come over from the Convention Center and jump on the boat? Dude…you'll get some killer footage!"

"Ahhh, Gene? Ahhh……I am not in Miami."

"What? I just saw you this morning. What are you talking about Dude?"

"Well Gene, I shot the interview for the show and filmed all the in-water boat footage. Then my contract was cancelled, so there was no need for me to stick around. When I left you, the redhead, myself, and the Corvette were in Key Largo in less than an hour."

"You're kidding me, right?"

"No Gene, not at all. There was no need for me to stay in Miami, sorry man."

Then I said, and I will never, never forget this,

"Gene…… look man, I can't really talk now. I have to get back to the pool. I am packing the rest of the bar and have to get back to my sexy, good looking, fairly dunk redhead with her Anaconda tongue and purple bikini."

There was silence on the phone. Then I said, "Gene, why don't you skip Miami and come down and join us, you may not have a job anyway when you get back."

He laughed his ass off and said,

"Anaconda what??? Jim, you don't know how much I would like to take you up on your offer. Go have fun and I won't bother you anymore. Just call me after the Miami Show and we will definitely do our best to work something out."

"Sure Gene! Have a great show and I am off to the pool."

I am not sure, but I got the feeling that Gene had a new respect for me and how I did business. He probably never thought that I would have hauled ass out of Miami, more like I would still stick around, kiss butt, shoot for free without a contract, etc. Not that they were trying to take advantage of me, but I was there with the camera so they figured I would stick out the show.

Not a chance. I could not for several reasons.

My ass was in Key Largo before you could say rum bucket. Had our contract not been cancelled… then that would be a different story. Filming for a company when you're not under contract could bring up liability issues should something happen. So I was out, gone to Key Largo partying by the Gulf Coast of Mexico drinking rum in the swimming pool playing with the red head.

It was getting late in the afternoon. Rose and I went back to the room to play with our pets and get ready for dinner. Rose looked fabulous. The woman knows how to dress and has the nicest legs I ever saw. I was ready for our special Valentine's dinner on the beach.

On the way to the beach dining area Rose and I detoured to go see the sun set in the west over the Gulf of Mexico. This was a good plan. We found a white, sandy point of the beach with this huge palm tree that was bent over towards the Gulf. The palm leaves were lovingly touching the sand. The *Sandy Palm Hotel* is what I called it.

The sunset was majestically beautiful and it was one very special heart felt moment.

Pause. Catch our breath………. Knock all the sand off us….

Ok…We returned.

Out on the beach were a bunch of dining tables set up in and around a tiki bar area, where this Caribbean dance band was set up. This was going to be a long dinner party with fireworks going off every 15 minutes. The Gulf Coast was glistening, the stars were out, and fireworks were blazing through the palm trees right over our heads. This was Valentine's in Key Largo… Wow what a ride, nothing like it!

Certainly, the most romantic Valentine's I had ever experienced and my sadness about losing our contract, for the moment was washed down with the first rum bucket.

I was on a roll! Rose and I were dancing the night away and everyone was having a very good time. The only area where we made a mistake was the rum. We started early in the day and never stopped. Now it was nearing one in the morning. I certainly was feeling no pain at all, none.

Rose is a small-framed woman with a perfect body…. but she is a tiny little thing. Very sweet and petite would be a good description. It really didn't dawn on me that she was not going to handle as much rum as me, someone who is twice her size. Pretty amazing that she held up as well as she did.

The waitress came by to clear our tab that we had incurred during the previous seven hours. The bill was not that bad, it was a mortgage payment, but not that bad. While pulling the little cash I had left in my pocket I remembered that Rose and I had spent some quality time around sunset, lying out in the sand by the Gulf under a low lying palm tree.

Rose said, "Honey Bun…Precious Cargo. While you take care of that I am going to the ladies room."

Off Rose went. She seemed fine when she left, however rum has a way of hitting you all at once. Rose would soon find this out.

My tab was taking forever to clear. Must have been all that sand and lint they had to pick out of the bills.

Once I had everything settled, I went to the ladies room to find Rose. No Rose. I went back to our table, no Rose. I looked all around the bar and restaurant, no Rose. I went up to the room, no Rose. I went to the sushi bar, no Rose. I even checked the Corvette, no Rose. I went back up to the room to check again, no Rose. I searched the pool, no Rose. I walked the entire property, no Rose. Called her cell phone 10 times, no Rose.

I walked back down to the parking lot, no Rose. I said out loud in the parking lot, quite loudly to myself, "Shit! I have lost Rose in Key Largo! FUUUUCK! What do I do next?"

I walked the perimeter of the Cay Club again very upset, and eventually went back to the room and opened the door. There standing in the hallway looking straight at me, shaking and quivering like a fish out of water, was Rose. Tears were pouring out of her eyes and she tried to speak, but couldn't. The woman was in shock. I grabbed her and hugged her. She had lost it. I tried to settle her down to no avail. She was unbelievably upset, like she had seen a ghost or something. I gave her a glass of water to drink and asked her to please tell me what was wrong. This is what she got out,

293

"Flahahahashing lights, loooooost, Treeeeeeeeees, caaaarrrrrrrrra, Pohoholice, Waaaaahhhhh hhhhhhhhhhh!!!!

Crying her eyes out, shaking.

I said, "What?? I got some of that but, did you say - Police?"

She nodded her head yes and started crying more and more and more. I could not settle her down, so I took her in the bathroom and sat her on the edge of the tub. She liked that, but then fell backwards in the tub hitting her head. Not hard, but a nice little tap.

I said, "Stay there and don't move. This is a good place for you right now, I don't think you can injure yourself sitting inside the tub, I will be right back."

I went and got her a Xanax and a shot of rum. This I knew, would settle her down and it did. She then told me what had happened.

Rose came out of the bathroom, not remembering where she was and took a wrong turn. She ended up walking through the woods of palm trees and reached a crime scene in process.

Four police officers had guns drawn on the liquor store where a robbery was taking place. All the police cars had their flashing lights on and spotlights flooding the building.

Rose came out of the darkness and walked right between the robbery and the police cars. She had a million watts of light pointed at her and she was staring down the barrel of four guns. In her hysteric drunken state she asked crying, "Excuse me Mr. Police officer, could you please tell me how to get back to my hotel, I am looosssst."

"Ma'm, you are in a crime scene in progress - get out of the way NOW!!"

"Buuuttt Iiii am looossssssttt! Please, would you help me???"

By now one of the officers drew down his weapon and went over and pulled her over behind a police car. He

294

knew she was a tourist, drunk, and probably staying at the hotel behind them. He said, 'Lady, can you see that sign right there about 20 yards away??'

"Yeeeesssssssss."

"Can you walk??"

"Iiii thhhinnnkk soooo."

"Go to the sign and take a left. That is your hotel. Go there and stay there. You should not be walking around this late at night in your state."

Rose walked away, swerving, and the policeman redrew his gun on the robbery.

She made it back to the room and that is where I found her. The police officer was very nice not to have arrested her for drunk in public.

Of course we were in the Keys. If they arrested everyone for drunk in public in the Florida Keys they would need an exit strategy the size of Texas. I was grateful she got back unharmed.

The Xanax kicked in and she went to sleep. She didn't wake until 10am. When we woke, up she was fine. She was very glad to have that behind her and she was ready for our day in the Florida Keys.

It was a beautiful morning the sun was shining through the white wood shutters of our window and the shadows of the palms where dancing by the screen door.

It only took a moment to pack the cooler...Today's destination.... Key West.

Cruising with the top down in the red Corvette heading South on US 1 passing Islamorada, Marathon, Duck Key, Big Pine Key and eventually reaching Key West is without a doubt the most scenic and fun ride in the United States.

The sparkling clear blue waters of the Gulf Coast were on our right and the Atlantic Ocean to our left. It doesn't get any better than this. Rose was sipping on a beer enjoying the wind blown salty air ride cruising through the

Keys. We couldn't turn our heads north if our lives depended on it. Once I am in the Keys, I never want to leave.

We arrived in Key West and soon hooked up with a friend of ours named Al Dente. Al was an Italian fellow who we knew from Virginia Beach and he owned a chain of about 80 Italian restaurants. Al had just built a mansion in Key West and he wanted us to stop by for some cocktails. Al is a great guy and was at home with his Swedish girlfriend, Havesom Beaver.

We had a few banana daiquiris and Al said, "Guys, lets jump on my boat and circumnavigate Key West. We will have a great view of the sunset and I'll take the blender with us."

Great idea! We packed up a cooler and cruised out of his waterfront home boating down to the front of Duval Street in Key West. There were thousands of people all lined up to watch the sun set.

This was a sight I will never forget. God, I love Key West! The Magnolia Tree is in full bloom now. One enormous orange ball inch-by-inch, dipping westward into the sea illuminating every ripple in the water.

We were blessed with a beautiful mango infused daiquiri sunset.

Rose loved the boat ride and after we returned to Al's home we stayed in Key West and enjoyed all the sights and entertainment. After a couple of days of the Bull and Whistle, Captain Tony's and Sloppy Joes, we stopped by Wylands Gallery then pointed the Corvette back to Key Largo.

We stayed for two more days in search of the perfect rum bucket and enjoyed more glorious sunsets on the beaches of Key Largo. The sand never left our feet.

It soon would be time to head north.

Cruising with the top down on a beautiful February day heading towards Miami, a feeling of sadness started to creep in. Neither Rose nor I wanted to go back. We together fell in love with the Florida Keys. As much as I love the Chesapeake Bay, the Blue Water of Key Largo really touched my heart. We were passing Miami at a little after twelve noon.

I said, "Rose Dahlin, do you have to be back tomorrow, or can we cheat and stay another couple of days down here. Look…we are here, the weather is perfect, and hell it is snowing back in Virginia. Whadda ya dink Rosey?"

"Honey, I don't even have a job yet! Let's stay a while longer."

I picked up the phone, "Hey Wayne, JB here! Rose and I were thinking of coming and staying a couple of days in West Palm with you guys on the way back. Are you guys up for some rum and pool time? I will fix dinner!"

So before Rose and I got back to Virginia, we stayed another couple of days and did nothing but cook seafood, swim in the pool and hot tub, snorkel in the ocean, drink rum and play with the pet Anaconda. We both felt better about making the most of our trip and Rose finally was exhausted.

While I was driving the Corvette back to Virginia, Rose slept the entire time. This gave me time to think about all that had happened on this Florida Keys trip.

What stood out in my mind more than anything else was that never in my lifetime have I laughed so hard and enjoyed myself so much. I did it with Rose and what was left of a mortgage payment, a red corvette, cancelled contract, rum, sand, the Florida Keys and a pet Anaconda.

When I was approaching southern North Carolina we were already getting some snow flurries. My head began to focus about what I could do to save our marine sponsorship that I had lost in Miami. While driving, I came up with the idea to promote Go Green fishing and boating.

The economy sucked and gas prices where on the rise big time.

Once back home there was six inches of snow in Hampton, Virginia and I thought I would immediately put together a small package for our marine sponsor that would enable us to promote the economy of recreational boating and fishing.

Our marine sponsor liked the idea and did end up signing a new contract with us a month later. Thus was born our new showboat the *Go Green Fishing Machine.*

The next couple of years would prove very tough economical challenges for *Jim Baugh Outdoors* as well as my sweetheart Rose. No one had any money, especially us. But with a lot of prayer, sacrifice and the grace of God, we made it through.

Rose was offered a management position with a design company where she could also do interior designs again and work on a good salary, commissions, and received good benefits as well. Things had begun to turn around for her. Meanwhile I had learned what not only the value of a dollar was, but the value of a penny as well.

As far as the show is concerned, *Jim Baugh Outdoors TV* had been broadcasting for 22 years and already started filming for its 23d season. After our Miami trip that year our budget was cut over eighty percent. Certainly, we had to make a lot of adjustments in order to make it through. The following year's things economically worsened tragically and then very slowly began to build back up.

One thing is for sure whatever the future is for *Jim Baugh Outdoors* will be directed by the hand of the good Lord. I put my faith in Him, because he always has better ideas for me than I do.

That is where I put my trust.

.... Five years later, I drove Rose to Sara's Creek and walked her around the marina where I caught crabs as a young boy.

I showed her where we had our Owens boat tied up on "A" dock, when I was only five years old. Then I walked her to the bathroom where I busted out the window with an ashtray when I was locked in as a kid. I showed her where we used to swim in the river and play on the beach by the inlet. I showed her where we would go to listen to music and I even showed her where I got my first kiss. I showed her a lot of things from my childhood that day.

Then I walked Rose down past the garden by the pool and there stood in front of her in all the glory of creation, the Old Magnolia Tree. Rose cried. She knew what this Magnolia had meant to me throughout my life. It is here under a full white bloom in May, where I proposed.

We flew down to Key Largo and arrived at the Cay Club where our children and a few close friends were waiting for us. Rose was wearing a purple sundress with a low cut V neck, diamond stud ear rings, a white pearl necklace, a diamond left ankle bracelet and violet high heel pumps. We all walked down to the beach on the Gulf of Mexico and there as the sun set, we said our vows and got married.

Our family and friends celebrated under a clear, starry sky, with the warm ocean breeze blowing off the Gulf. It was a very special moment in all our lives.

The next day Rose and I went to Key West and stayed for four days and visited the Dry Tortugas by boat. Later, we caught a plane and honeymooned in the Lesser Antilles. Beautiful Barbados is where I finally was able to visit the Mount Gay Rum Factory. Once again, Rose and I were drinking Rum Buckets playing in the pool by the crystal blue waters of the Caribbean Sea.

In the years to come, Rose and I would later reside in the towering palm tree paradise of Key Largo.

Chapter 28 \ In Closing

It Takes a Little Faith

"Dear Heaven, I give thanks to thee
For things I did not know before,
For the wisdom of maturity,
For bread, and a roof, and for one thing more...
Thanks because I still can see
The bloom on the white magnolia tree!"

~Helen Deutsch

Those times long ago as a child, standing by the old Magnolia Tree at the marina during church service helped give me the faith it took to make it through some tough times. Especially as a kid, raising kids, and later building a business then trying to survive a bad recession, miracles happen everyday and pretty much every moment of the day. Life itself is a miracle, every breath.

We all like to ask the Lord for our own blessings and miracles to help solve the problems in our lives. Some people don't believe in God, Jesus, or anything really. Other people believe in just about anything. I cannot speak for other people or other religions.

However I can speak to my own experiences that have over and over proven without a doubt that the Lord does answer prayers. Sometimes the answer is no, he usually has a better plan than what we ask for in prayer.

I prayed as a young child for the Judge not to die of a heart attack and live at least past 40. Being married to the bitch from hell was enough to kill anyone and only prayed that one day the Judge would marry an angel. I prayed for the Lord to dictate my path in life regardless of whatever obstructions. I prayed for the health, happiness and future blessing of my two kids. I have prayed for many, many, things throughout my life everyday. All prayers have been answered and in a better way than I could have ever thought of.

Doubt and fear are the work of the Devil. Not the Lord. This is something I have to remind myself everyday.

You know sometimes when you ask for something from the man above, you don't expect to get an immediate answer. One day, I was super stressed at the parking lot at my bank because while I was parking my car, it died. I was on the phone trying to pay a mortgage payment, but something was wrong with the bank system and they were not able to process my payment.

I will never forget I looked up to the sky over the open hood to my car and prayed, "Dear Lord, all I want to do is make my payment and get my car running, this is just starting off to be a horrible day and I need some help please! Thank you, and Amen!"

Literally as I said Amen arrives a tow truck and pulls up exactly right next to me in the parking lot.

The lady jumps out and I ask, "Have you got a jump, my car died?"

She grabs her portable battery and jumpstarts my car in less than a minute. As the tow truck is pulling away the bank calls with their fixed computer system and processes my payment.

Now it was not until I was driving away, I realized what happened. Remember about prayer; be careful what you ask for you might just get it. In this case, I did need it and I got it.

To the atheist or naysayer the thought would be that this was just a coincidence, and that is fine. But, I did ask myself, "When was the last time a tow truck ever pulled and parked next to me?" …. Never. The Lord works in mysterious ways most of the time. My glass is always half full and never half empty.

The only time my glass is half empty, is when I am having a cocktail.

Looking back when I was a senior in high school playing defensive tackle in the Friday night game all was about lost. We were on our goal line and the offense had less than an inch to go before they scored on us, causing us to lose the game. There were only seconds left on the clock and not winning this football game was becoming depressing reality.

As I got down in my stance, I felt 100% that these guys were coming right over our middle and score. Then our team would be called SHIT for the entire next week. I was not happy because I did not have the faith that we could stop this team from moving ahead only an inch or so.

All I figured was that I was going to give it everything I had and let the chips fall where they may.

The ball was hiked on three and the quarterback jumped up behind his guards and was ready for the win. I just exploded forward and pushed up, only to be pushed back down by about six guys on top of me.

Everyone was screaming and yelling and starting to jump all around. I could hear stomping, because the ground was vibrating and my face was buried in the dirt. This was it. Once I could get up from all the football players on top of me, I would have to listen to the coach stick his ugly face in front of my mask, call me an idiot, weak, and a real great guy for causing us to loose the game. This, I was not looking forward to. Right then I really wished I was hiding in the auditorium practicing the piano.

Finally! I got up from the ground and started walking to the sidelines and this reporter grabbed me from behind, spun me around and asked how close was it. I held up my J R Tucker High School Tiger Paw and held up my fingers with a span of only about three inches. I thought this guy has some nerve making fun at me like this, loosing over a couple of inches.

I seriously at that point, did not even know we won the game. I did not. Then a couple of my close buddies started hugging in full football gear jumping up and down happy as hell, that not only did I not give them two inches, but pushed the guards and quarterback three feet backwards.

We had won.

I did not let them pass, and I had no faith at all I could do this.

Many times, I have thought back to that moment. Even when you are facing sure loss, you can still win. Just giving it you're all 100%, and having a little faith can really move mountains. Very true.

In closing is my favorite glorious hymn written by a sea faring English clergyman who once was a prominent supporter of the abolition of slavery. By the docks of Sara's Creek we used to sing this in the salty air and wind swept parking lot. Proudly and reverently under the luminescent, white blooms of the old, towering Magnolia Tree, voices would reign high. Never more true words have been scrolled…

At least for me.

The first two verses are below. Do yourself a favor, Google the rest and sing along.

Amazing Grace, how sweet the sound
That saved a wretch, Like Me.
I was once lost,
But now I am Found.
Was blind, but now
I see.
T'was Grace that taught
my heart to fear.
And Grace, my fears relieved.
How precious did that Grace appear,
The hour I first believed.
~John Henry Newton

The End.

Picture of the Magnolia Tree still standing at York River Yacht Haven on Sara's Creek, Yorktown Virginia.

Acknowledgements

I would like to thank New York City playwright David Johnstone and author Joe Jackson for their kind advice and direction. Special thanks to Melissa Miller, Nik Morton, & Kate Collins at Solstice Publishing and to Donna Bozza for her excellent editing assistance. Lastly, to the many characters who have inspired me to write this novel. Many have passed, however they will never be forgotten.

Photo Credits: Captain Don Malkowski, *Sunset at St. Barts* and Jim Baugh, *Corvette at Pea Island* Hatteras North Carolina.
Original Charcoal art drawing, *My Daughter Jennifer* by piratical artist, Captain Pirate Pete Devlieg
Cover jacket design by Jim Baugh.

HOOKED

"The steady stream of hilarious stories in Hooked will keep the reader turning pages in anticipation of the next adventure. As I read this book I felt more like I was sitting in a crab shack overlooking the Chesapeake, picking crabs and drinking beer while an old friend across the brown papered table regaled me with stories a salty as the rim around a Margarita glass and as lyrical as a well sung as a sea shanty."

~ Award Winning Author and Playwright, Mark Covington

"It's good when anyone can take a humorous look at their own life. Jim Baugh pens a memoir full of quirky characters and life lessons learned. I was touched by the way he cares for others and how he never forgot what he learned under the old Magnolia tree."

~ Best Selling Author, Ed Robinson

"The people throughout Jim Baugh's life are many and EXTREMELY colorful – to call them characters is putting it mildly. Non-stop hilarious stories, with bits of heartbreak peppered in, keeps the reader turning those pages."

~ Author Penny Estelle

"Hooked" by Jim Baugh is a rip roaring, sometimes raunchy, often time's poetic and powerful read. You'll have a blast between these covers.

~ Writer, Donna Rich

"TV personality Jim Baugh cranks up the engine of the story and runs it full throttle from start to finish."

~ Author, Frank Allen Rogers.

Jim's sequel to HOOKED, "AFTERMATH" Available in paperback and ebook.

HOOKED 2
By Jim Baugh

Aftermath
Triennial Memoir 2011-14
NEW
Jim Baugh

AFTERMATH

Triennial
Memoir
2011-14

Jim Baugh

"Aftermath"

A triennial memoir post HOOKED
By Jim Baugh

And

Interview with the Author

By Lizzy Stevens

AFTERWORD

By Jim Baugh

The following three years after my first novel *HOOKED* was published in early August of 2011 remains among the most amazing, challenging, miraculous three years of my life. I chronicled this triennial memoir in "AFTERMATH" and found it so difficult to believe that all of this has happened........ And I have survived to write about it. Without a doubt almost to the day the book was released, for a lot of reasons my life changed in a rather dramatic way. Remember the old saying be careful what you pray for because you might just get it. Well I got it all right, with the force of a tsunami.

There are two life changing events that happened as a direct result of my first novel *HOOKED* being released.

One: *Jim's BBQ restaurant* located at *The Big Pink*.

Two: I met my soon to be wife Donna. The following pages will reveal this difficult to believe story of both.

But first…

I have received a LOT of questions over the last three years about the book. Many people did not understand that it was indeed a true life autobiography and everything in the book happened. There was very little exaggeration or embellishments, although there were some, mostly necessary to aid in compositing and fictionalizing of characters. Bottom line, it was all true…except just one thing.

I never remarried. At the time "Rose" was living with me when I finished writing *HOOKED* and I knew that we were not going to end up united in matrimony for many reasons. It was towards the end of our relationship which

311

put me in a quandary about how to end my autobiographical book. I believed positively in the sanctity of marriage and wanted to end the novel on a positive note. Through a LOT of prayer I believe I was going to remarry, however it would be forthcoming and to someone who would be new to my life, someone I had never met before. The complication was I had not met this lady yet and I was finishing the book.

I remember clearly not knowing what to do. I prayed harder about it one day while cycling around the lower Chesapeake Bay and like a flash it came to me. Yes! I would have to write the first "real fiction" in *HOOKED*. I would celebrate wedlock at the end of the book and live happily ever after in Key Largo. Sounds good to me!

Believe it or not, this is pretty much what happened but on a different Key and a later time. However, it took three years and a rollercoaster ride no amusement park could ever match. This was one scary, turbulent, and miraculous journey that only could be possible by the white bloom of the Magnolia Tree.

It may be difficult to understand at first glance how massive loss of income, foreclosure, and even death can all be positive things. Sometimes paving the right path in life requires hard sacrifices. The following pages will show just how true that statement is.

Today is July 4th 2014, Independence Day. Peering off an old creaky wooden front porch just visible through the windmill palms, I see a tangerine orange sun dipping below the horizontal calm reflective waters in the Gulf of Mexico. The salted driftwood doors are open in our little summer island casa rental allowing the soft Gulf breeze to cool our quaint rustic island quarters. I am writing these words while being berthed by an open window under a myriad of cascading tropical palms drenched with luminous hanging Spanish Moss in the historic palm shade island of Cedar Key, Florida.

Here in Cedar Key I have finished editing our 25th anniversary *Jim Baugh Outdoors TV* programs that will broadcast in early autumn, and I am also writing the second edition of *HOOKED* and my triennial memoir, "AFTERMATH" as well as a screenplay.

One thing is for sure. If success is an achievement forged by the fertile garden of failure, then I have been very well versed.

Godspeed,
Jim Baugh

"All who call on God in true faith, earnestly from the heart, will certainly be heard, and will receive what they have asked and desired."

~Martin Luther

"AFTERMATH"

An A to Z Triennial Memoir That Packs a Punch

- One crock pot
- Yes officer I have a flashlight
- Foreclosure dating
- Wow! You really do keep a clean car
- DUMP HIM TONIGHT!
- Excuse me dahlin, could you run that past me one more time?
- Church + Legal Pad = Homeless
- Yard sale
- So you don't believe in Miracles?
- Welcome Home
- One more Judge in Heaven
- On the Road Again
- Cedar Key
- Message from Earl

One Crock Pot

Winter can be a cold, desolate ugly beast, especially during the time of the great recession of which I was in deep like a boat anchor in quicksand. I was writing *HOOKED* during early February 2011 and the entire country was in serious financial despair. Remember the automobile bailouts by our government? Boy, now there is an indication of how bad things had gotten. The housing market also crashed worse than anyone could have imagined. A lot of us who purchased homes prior to the crash now know what an upside down cake feels like that was baked at a 1000 degrees. Things were tough! The real estate crash meant housing values plummeted affecting many economic aspects of our country and…my world.

Numerous people did not have money for their mortgage, much less discretionary income to travel, fish, purchase boats, outboard engines, cars, etc. Across the board the depth of the failing economic times were felt everywhere and businesses were having extremely difficult times. Trying to sell sponsorship advertising during this recession period for *Jim Baugh Outdoors TV* was like asking Jimmy Hendrix to play country music on a washboard. It just was not going to happen.

To make things worse my father the Judge was in declining health. Congestive heart failure was killing him and my dad was the worst patient in the world. He was just too proud of a man to be sick and hated being confined to a hospital room for any duration. One morning helping my dad get dressed at his home he said in a low serious voice with great determination:

316

"Son, I really wish I had died in the hospital."

The stubbornly proud southern Judge did not want to live if his disability was continuing to worsen. This was a very hard thing for a son to hear, all I could do was encourage him that things would get better. He was in an emotionally and physically difficult time and his angel put every ounce of energy she had in taking care of the Judge. He would have never lived as long without her by his side.

During this ordeal I would travel to Richmond to help dad and commute back and forth to Hampton. While I was at my condo trying to figure out how to pay bills without a penny to my name, I was also faced with having to put my best friend, our old arthritic chocolate Labrador Retriever, Tina Turner Baugh to rest. Adding to the numerous colossal stresses was the fact that I also was attempting to dissolve my relationship and remove my live-in unhinged girlfriend Rose from my home and my life.

I knew things with Rose were heading downhill fast. The vodka decanter was always on low tide regardless of how often I filled it. One day I walked into my home and there she was drinking her vodka and milk watching *Say Yes To The Dress* on cable TV.

"Ah, Rose, what is this you are watching?"

"Oh Jim, its *Say Yes To The Dress*! This and *Hoarders,* I just can't watch enough of."

"Ok Rose, its Friday night 6:15pm I am and glad this will be over at the bottom of the hour. It's time to put on some music and enjoy the weekend, maybe even catch a few minutes of the national news."

"No Jim, you don't understand. It's a *Say Yes To The Dress* **MARATHON** and they are having shown one right after another 24 hours a day until Monday! There's plenty of milk in the fridge and I just filled the decanter, it's going to be a great weekend!"

...No freakin way.

317

I had to figure out how this would not happen again in the future. Cancelling my cable service did in fact help out on my bills, and it for sure got rid of *Say Yes To The Dress.* In fact the show I really wanted Rose to be a fan of was *Say Yes To The Door.*

Things were bad and I tried everything to make extra income. I kept working on selling sponsorships while also applying for sales positions with television affiliates, radio stations, production companies, and even car stereo stores. Not one offer came in from anywhere.

I happened to talk with an old friend Denny Barber on the phone and asked him if he knew of anyplace I could find some extra work. Denny with great enthusiasm said,

"Jim...You won't believe how much money I was making selling boats at the new Trout Pro Shops! I was making six figures easy; the only reason why I left was because I went back to West Virginia to help take care of my dad. Jim you would be great selling those boats, nothing to it and the money is great!"

"Thanks Denny, great idea. I will head over there soon and speak to the manager, with any luck I will be selling boats by the weekend!"

So I drive to the new Trout Pro Shops looking for the manager I talked to on the phone, only to find out that the company had just the day before downsized, laying off all mid -level managers and half the staff. I asked an employee named Johnny who was one of the few remaining people I could find who still worked there about a possible sales position in the marine department.

"Say Johnny, I am here to try and apply for a position selling boats, my old friend Denny who used to work here said this is the place to be and I would sell a ton of product. Who should I talk to?" Johnny said,

"Yeah Jim, I remember Denny, he was a great salesman and did very well here along with our other marine sales associates…But, I don't think it is possible that you can work here."

"Why Johnny? I am very experienced around boats and even have my own, but currently cash deficient fishing travel show on TV. I think I could sell the hell out of boats here!"

"Well Jim, here is the deal. Corporate just had massive layoffs and even closed several boat factories. The economy has hit the marine industry very hard, and we had to let go of almost all of our salespeople. For the few marine salesmen we have the commission structure has changed…There IS NO commission anymore and salespeople are now on minimum wage only. Plus if you look at the near vacant sales floor, they are inexperienced college kids working part time only. Sorry."

After my conversation with Johnny I realized I had "Missed the Boat" so to speak. High commissions and lots of boat sales were now a thing of the past. A day late and a dollar short was soon to be my mantra.

I was 49 years old and had no idea what to do next, and the bills kept coming. My emergency savings secure and untouched for years, were now all gone. There was nothing left. This old camel was looking for water in a sea of sand with not even a mirage in sight.

The good news in all of my despair was that I had one thing. The one thing that had carried me through my entire life and had never failed me once.

My faith.

I had one other thing that also was on the horizon, my soon to be released uproarious autobiographical novel, *HOOKED*. My book was going to be released and available by August 2nd which was also my 50th birthday.

I remember sitting on a nearby beach thinking I had no idea what was going to happen with my life. I was in fear of losing everything. I said a lot of prayers that day. I prayed that I would not lose my home and things would get better. However, whatever was going to happen was going to happen for the best and I would maintain my faith and steadfast course.

Immediately when *HOOKED* was released reviews started coming in from newspapers, other media, authors, and readers. They were all five stars. The reviews to me were stunning and I was glad to know that readers "Got it". This was an unrestrained rip-roaring, boisterous secular book about the power of faith, all based on a true story, a story that was my life. This was the idea from the beginning and I prayed about it wholeheartedly before I ever wrote the book. Here was a way to plant seeds of faith to a huge audience who could relate to the story. I was in fear of losing everything, but at least my novel was well received as soon as it was launched. Now, things get REALLY interesting!

As a part of our contract with our publisher we would agree to do certain things to promote our books. One popular promotion authors were doing was author interviews and posting them on various online blogs. I thought it was a good idea, however the few I read were boring and unimaginative. So, I came up with a way to promote my book and other authors as well in a virtual online bar called, "Jim's Bar". This virtual bar would be set in the Florida Keys similar to Captain Tony's in Key West.

I created the look of the bar by photoshoping all sorts of pictures I had of my ventures filming down in the Florida Keys. I also would put all sorts of crazy artifacts in the bar including a jukebox where inside lizards mated regularly on the hour. Because of all the cooking we have done on *Jim Baugh Outdoors TV* I had plenty of food pictures, so I used those as well and ended up creating this amusing, authentic-looking virtual bar that only existed online.

What I did was actually announce on the internet a grand opening for Jim's Bar. I would write dialog, tell stories, and have regular updates as to what was happening at Jim's Bar. All of this was entertaining to do, a great writing exercise, and was immensely humorous. Then a strange thing happened.

Jim's virtual online bar in the Florida Keys. Is it real?

I got a call from my publisher,

"Hey Jim! I wanted to contact you and get something straight. Jim's Bar is not real, correct?"

"That's correct; it is virtual and available only online. It is just a fun way to feature our book and other authors, why?"

"Well, Jim...We are getting inquiries from people who want to know where this bar is because they want to go. They think it's real!"

While I am talking to my publisher on the phone, I had previously paid just enough money to the electric company to allow my doorbell to ring. I hang up the phone and opened my *hopefully not soon to be foreclosed* door, and there stands one of my good friends Jake and his brother Eddy.

"Jake! Eddy! Hey guys, great to see y'all! Come on in and have a bloody mary. Just got off the phone with my publisher and you won't believe what's happening! Too funny!"

"Jim, had to stop by and tell you I just read *HOOKED* over the weekend and could not put it down. It was great, laughed my butt off. But hey, hold the bloody mary, we just stopped by to congratulate you on the book and the new bar, we saw the pictures online of the Mexican Brunch. I know you opened it up here in Hampton, where is it? We are starving. Let's go!"

I said, "Umm. Jake…Jake, what did you just say?"

"Eddy and I just stopped by to let you know we are heading over to your new restaurant and we may call some friends to meet us there, is Jim's Bar downtown?"

"Umm. Well… Jake, I think you better sit down. I need to make something clear. There is no Jim's Bar. It is a virtual online blog where we promote our books and feature guest authors in a very entertaining and creative way. It is NOT real."

"Jim, you just love to pull pranks. Dude I just saw your Mexican brunch special online and quit messin' with me cause Eddy and I are hungry man!"

"Well Jake, I don't know how else to tell you this but it only exist on the internet. As a matter of fact my publisher just called before you arrived informing me that people are contacting them to find out how to get to Jim's Bar because they want to go there. I am shocked that this has happened. Did you really think this place was real?"

Now Jake with a very blank stare on his face just sat motionless and was looking a little depressed because he had been looking forward to this Mexican Brunch at Jim's Bar. He started to laugh, and laugh pretty hard. He looked at me and said and I will never forget, "Jim, guess what. We are going to make Jim's Bar a reality!"

Now, I am the one with the dumfounded look on my face. I sat silent and just looked at him not having any idea what he was taking about. Jake said,

"Now Jim, you know we own the restaurant, tea room, music venue called *The Big Pink* in Phoebus. I have the upstairs bar that is only used for storage. Let's turn that into Jim's Bar! It would be great! You could tell fishing stories, have your show on a big screen, tell jokes, do card tricks, and we even have two pianos you could play. What do you think, let's do it!

I was laughing and not sure Jake was serious at all. It turns out he was very serious and thought it was a terrific idea. I did not. I told Jake,

"Man that is sweet of you but, the last time I was in the restaurant business I was 24 years old running Jim Dini's Magic Bar and I don't want to repeat that HELL again. The restaurant business is too tough! Thanks Jake, but I will have to pass on this one."

Jake, Eddy and I had a lot of laughs about this and after about an hour of visiting they left.

The next day I was at home trying how to figure out how to save my economically malnourished derriere from financial ruin. I kept trying to get sponsorships going for the show, and making more calls trying to find whatever jobs I could. At the end of the day I was left with a big fat "0".

Realizing that I had to do something, the thought of Jim's Bar crossed my mind because there simply were no other possible opportunities out there. I called Jake and said,

"Jake, JB here. Say, what exactly did you have in mind with this Jim's Bar thing? Do you seriously want to discuss it?"

He did. We met and decided that I go take a look at *The Big Pink* and see if it was possible to do something like the virtual Jim's Bar.

The Big Pink was a beautiful, old historic Victorian house that had a large addition built on to the side of the building. Also known as *"The Pink"* because they had painted the aging Victorian a vibrant pink color much to the tone and shade of Pepto Bismol. *The Big Pink* was located in the center of town and was considered the epicenter of Phoebus, Virginia. The Veterans Administration Hospital was only blocks away and homeless people were regularly walking around our sidewalks. My first visit to *The Big Pink* I was fortunate enough to meet the most famous of all the local homeless, his name was "Charlie Tuna". Charlie in his continuous intoxicated state would introduce himself like this, "Hi I am Charlie Tuna, the Otis of Phoebus."

The Big Pink home of JBBQ. Standing out front Tortuga the Pirate.

Needless to say my first real visit to the Pink was quite an eye opener. The interior of the Pink was eclectic and beautiful. Charming, romantic, cozy, and rustic are all good ways to describe the comfortable atmosphere.

When Jake showed me the commercial kitchen I was surprised to see how small it was. Although it was a tiny space, it did have a sham that is an excellent slow cooker. These machines are fantastic for cooking prime rib, BBQ, just about anything that needs to be cooked low and slow. Fortunately, outside of the building there was a large (not being used) smoker that was totally covered with overgrown weeds. Behind the smoker was a very old abandoned carriage house dating back to the 18th century that in its day was a shot house. That's correct, liquor by the shot! This old carriage house would later be named by Jake as, *The Pit Shack*. A dim light bulb went off in my head; I looked at Jake and said,

Foreground JBBQ Smoker. The Pit Shack can be seen behind the wood delivery.

"Jake, your idea of me telling fishing stories and doing card tricks behind the bar upstairs is not going to cut it. BUT! Believe it or not, you already have everything here

326

to make gourmet BBQ without purchasing any equipment, no additional capital investment at all.

"Really Jim? Let's talk about it."

"Well Jake, you already have the slow cooker in the kitchen and the smoker outback. If we can get Eddy your brother the master carpenter to build some sort of kitchen sink area in the Pit Shack, we would have all we need to get into the BBQ business. The thing is, there aren't any good BBQ restaurants in the area, and we might actually be on to something."

Jake is a very creative person who loves ideas, a talented musician and a successful business man. He loved this idea and along with his sweet wife Bennie Ann, we immediately put together a rather simple business plan. I felt comfortable with Jake and Bennie Ann because they were dear friends of mine and I knew they were pillars of the community. I had known Miss Bennie Ann going way back when I was in my twenties managing cable TV. The three of us would be 50\50 partners in the BBQ buiz, it would require no capital investment on my part however…I would have to do all the cooking for the entire BBQ restaurant, shop, co-manage in the evenings, and do most of the advertising to get the word out.

I would take on this responsibility while still selling sponsorships and producing *Jim Baugh Outdoors TV.* This would be a massive and very physical undertaking on my part. My thoughts were in the beginning I probably would not make enough money doing this venture to pull me out of debt; however it would be a good opportunity to co-brand *Jim Baugh Outdoors TV* with our own restaurant and recipes. This also would be great experience for the second novel I was writing, *Cooked.* So, I agreed to partner in this venture and prayed that some TV sponsorship would soon be on the horizon.

There was no money for capital improvements or redecorating for the new *"Big Pink featuring Jim's BBQ"* restaurant. So I called in all my friends that could help us out with anything they could. The biggest donation was probably from my good friend Pirate Captain P.D Cooper. He agreed to showcase a lot of his nautical original pirate art in Jim's Bar. So since it cost us nothing, we put up P.D. Coopers art everywhere. These nautical pirate drawings lined the walls and captured the hearts, minds, and imagination of everyone that would come to the bar. It was great!

Some samples of the Piratical Art from P.D. Cooper on display JBBQ.

"My Daughter Jennifer" original drawing by P.D. Cooper also on display at JBBQ. This is the piece of art we used for the "Eyes" on the jacket cover of HOOKED. This drawing also was hung in my home as a part of my art collection for many months. It is one of my favorite drawings.

    I will never forget for the rest of my life that first day we opened JBBQ. Here I am trying to refinance my home in order to save it, bills were stacked up on the counter, my dad was in the hospital with congestive heart failure, my old severely arthritic dog Tina needed to be euthanized, and a I had a girlfriend that did not know what an exit sign was. All these tumultuous, taxing things were on my mind as I carried down the stairs of *The Big Pink* and rested on a buffet table…

One crock pot.

That was it. One crock pot filled with my own version of slow cooked pulled pork that me and Captain Earl had perfected for years. There simply was none better. Not before or since has there ever been BBQ this good, and no one else has ever tried our technique. It takes a lot of hard work and time to produce this kind of pulled pork and most restaurants could never afford the extent of love and care it takes to produce such smoked BBQ Butts. As good as it is, I still remember looking at that one crock pot sitting on the buffet table thinking there is no freakin' way this one butt is going to save my financial butt. Howbeit there was a glimmer of hope!

I talked to my mortgage company and they assured me I would qualify for a new refinance program they just started and that if approved, that would take care of a lot of my problems. So I started the paperwork process with the bank, kept trying to sell TV Sponsorships, and also began my Jim's BBQ Restaurant venture. Just aggressively plowing forward with faith and persistent prayer was all I could do.

I started with one lonely, black ceramic crock pot. Very, very quickly the word got out and within a few weeks I was behind the upstairs bar with 10 crock pots plus chafing dishes full to the brim with BBQ. I would be behind the bar with a packed crowd and literally served dinner from behind the bar similar to that of a Japanese steak house. This was not that foreign of an idea to me because it reminded me of when I would play multiple keyboards in my progressive rock band, or entertaining performing close up magic at Vegas tables in Atlantic City.

The difference here was that instead of keyboards or cards, I was dealing with BBQ ribs, pulled pork, jerk chicken and jalapeno corn bread. These full dinner entrees were all cooked and served up by me, behind Jim's Bar at *The Big Pink*.

One night Jake came to the packed bar and saw the one man JBBQ chaos that was going on and could not believe it. He met with me afterwards and said we had to expand things. We would move the dinner food items into the kitchen and free me up from behind the bar so I could manage more, entertain, oversee the kitchen, and make sure things go smoothly. Great idea! Bennie Ann ask if my daughter Casey would like to work some and I knew she was looking for employment, so Casey soon became the nighttime kitchen manager and sometimes would also run the downstairs bar. The entire place pretty much was a family affair, and everyone loved it!

There was a lot of joy working with my new friends and family at *The Big Pink*. I met some great people and working with Bennie Ann was just a hoot. She was sort of like my sister but from another mother. We really had a great time working together and Bennie Ann was an extremely hard worker and the ultimate hostess. She continued to run part of *The Big Pink* as a successful tea room and it was known as the best anywhere in the area. In a way we all together had come up with a very Southern, eclectic restaurant venue.

Burlesque show at JBBQ hosted and produced by Pirate P.D. Cooper

The Big Pink had morphed itself into a picturesque Southern tea room, gourmet smoked BBQ restaurant with a scratch kitchen, historic bar, and live acoustic music entertainment complex that at times featured dinner theatre style burlesque shows. Plus, upstairs in the loft bar was the best nautical original pirate art gallery you will ever see. We even had a life size one armed fiberglass pirate standing at the entrance of *The Big Pink* we named Tortuga. People loved it! Customers were always getting their pictures taken outside with the pirate and sometimes cars would pull off the streets just to have their photograph taken with Tortuga. Sometimes people looking from a distance actually thought he was a real live pirate. The overall atmosphere of *The Big Pink* was incredible and unlike anything else in the country.

Tea anyone? Tea room at the Big Pink, the ladies loved JBBQ.

Adding to the fun was usually my old chocolate Lab Tina Turner Baugh. Tina loved hanging around the restaurant trying her best to terrorize the feral fat cat community consisting of ten not so tamed cats. These were the cats that ate up most of my JBBQ scraps of pork bone, meat and fat. They were some healthy pussies that you did not want to mess with. Tina got her nose scratched way more than she cared to. These cats got so huge eating my pork fat that eventually a lady stopped by the Pink and dropped off dry diet cat food in a bag.

Celebrating Veterans Day with some free JBBQ
for our patrons from the V.A. Hospital.

I have to always keep reminding myself that the Good Lord sure works in mysterious ways sometimes. During this period I realized one of the greatest gifts of this restaurant venture was NOT the possibility of saving my home, it was the fact that my daughter Casey and I got very close. We worked together almost every day, and she lived with me at the condo for a while until she got settled in Phoebus. The nights working with Casey were extremely special. Customers loved the father daughter team and everyone just really loved Casey Baby.

Almost every late night when things slowed down upstairs we would close off the bar, then Casey and I always had a nightcap together while we listened to the band playing downstairs. As tired as I was at the end of the day hauling and cooking up hundreds of pounds of BBQ working all day and night, I still wanted to stay with Casey enjoying the company, cocktail and music.

There was never any amount of money in Fort Knox that was worth this precious time with my daughter. I began to realize the blessings and the path that I was on, even if it meant losing my home. There are things more important than material assets. A lesson I would continue to learn.

The little money I would make at the restaurant was almost enough money to cover groceries and a few bills. Casey needed a car and I was riding my bike everywhere so I was happy Casey ended up with my car. I love biking and have done it most of my life. Excellent exercise, although I did get into a bit of trouble one night on my bicycle. Never thought it was imaginable that such a fuss would occur by simply riding my bike home after a very long day of work.

I doubt those police officers stopped anymore cyclists after they stopped me!

My JBBQ Partners.
Far left: Bennie Ann. Far Right: Jake. Center: Casey Baugh.

The Big Pink JBBQ Feral Fat Cats.

Opera singer and waitress Rebecca serving up Tex Mex at JBBQ.

Music guest Rickety Shack from Murfreesboro Tennessee preformed at JBBQ.

Friday night Bluegrass, BBQ, and Beer show with the Wampler Brothers Bluegrass Jam.

Advertisement promoting one of two piano concerts Jim Baugh preformed at JBBQ. Guest guitarist none other than legendary thumb picking champion Matt Thomas.

Jim's Bar B-Q
Victorian Station, Hampton Virginia

Yes officer I have a flashlight

A woman without a man is like a fish without a bicycle.

~Gloria Steinem

Late at night after closing I was leaving Jim's BBQ riding my bike to go home minding my own business and here out of nowhere comes a police car flying at me. Slams on the brakes, lights flashing, an officer jumps out of his car and yells "HAULT!" Next another police car comes flying up behind him and corners me on the sidewalk. I am stunned and can't figure out what I must have done.

Both officers approach me with their hands by their holsters and I am thinking what the hell did I do? Officer says,

"Do you have a driver's license?" I said,

"Yes, but do I need it? I am on my un-motorized bicycle officer, but will gladly give it to you."

"Sure, thank you Mr. Baugh ...Ok Jim we are going to run a check on you but please tell me do you have a light?" I said,

"You want a smoke? I don't have a lighter, sorry officer."

"No Mr. Baugh, a flashlight!"

"Aaaah, I don't... think... But why officer? Don't you have one?"

"I do… but Jim, it doesn't look like you do."

"You see Mr. Baugh, since last summer we have had a high incidence of people getting hit by cars at night so our department is making a new initiative to inform patrons of the importance of having a flashlight on your bike at night, and we WILL issue tickets for it. Soooo, do you have one?"

Now remember I am dirt poor, with no car just trying to get home after a long day at the restaurant. The last thing I needed was a ticket for riding my bike, a ticket that I had no money to pay for. So I thought about it and said,

"Aaahh, officer I sure wish I did, and I am sorry, certainly understand why I need one now and will do ASAP.

… WAIT... WAIT… WAIT!!!! I DOOO Have a flashlight!"

"Mr. Baugh may I see it?"

"Sure, it is in my… Man Purse."

Both policemen look at each other with this very, "Oh Boy" stare as I dive down into the bottom of my man purse and there it is! I yell out loudly,

"Here it is, my pink key chain mini flashlight vibrator!"

"Mr Baugh excuse me, what in the world is that and may I see it?"

"Look, just turn the knob and the flashlight turns on. And so then does the vibrator."

"What the hell Jim!"

"Officer sir, I have carried this in my man bag because I wrote a funny story about it in my novel *HOOKED*. Once in a while when I run into someone who has read the book, I will ask them about the DC Nympho flashlight story and they bust out with laughter. Then I reach down and pull it out to show them it is real. Always gets a big laugh." The officer says,

"DC...What?"

"Sir, the DC Nympho, this is her flashlight vibrator."

"That is funny Jim, but I am afraid it is not big enough."

I looked at him and said, "That's what she said."

The three of us had a huge laugh and they let me go with only a warning. When it comes to key chain flashlight vibrators, I guess bigger is better.

Now, the next day, I am searching on the web to see if any new reviews have come out on *HOOKED*. The book has gone viral and is all over the place online. I came across one site that was a marriage counseling website that sold products, (books and adult toys) to better marriages and relationships.

Sitting right there was a picture of my book *HOOKED* under flashlight vibrator for $15.95. I laughed for hours.

Whoever would have thought so much humor would come out of a $5 key chain mini flashlight vibrator that was purchased as a gag gift eight years ago and ended up on a marriage counseling website to help relationships.

Continuing with the flashlight humor, when Bennie Ann heard about my police car vibrator incident she went out and purchased a big flashlight and presented it to me. Hopefully keeping me out of trouble while peddling home at night.

Soon, some things in my life slightly started to change for the better. They had too! I believed that I had a strong future ahead and would still accomplish many things however I knew it was necessary to clear personal obstructions in my path that were holding me down.

Fortunately "Rose" and I finally parted friends and I truly wished her well. She had gotten quite evangelical and was getting in some areas a bit much to handle. Rose had gone to a mental health doctor and was prescribed meds to help her with some issues she had. It was difficult to tell if they really helped her but I was glad she at least made the effort at least once, and she did it on her own calling. Rose had some sweet qualities but I was not the answer to her problems and she would be better suited with someone else respectfully.

The last time I saw her I told her politely to go marry a minister, and that is exactly what she did. No kidding, she almost immediately went on a Christian dating site and hooked up with a minister that lived half way across the country. On their first phone call these two decided they would get married, and about six months later they happily did. Today she is successfully traveling and living with her clergy husband in an RV ministering to the race car industry. No doubt, I think she found her evangelical calling on wheels and the race car industry has now been saved.....and so have I.

God bless them both.

On Jim's "Smoke" breaks, he regularly biked to Buckroe Beach

Foreclosure dating

I've been on so many blind dates, I should get a free dog.

- Wendy Liebman

My first spring at Jim's BBQ and the bellowing smoke of
Hickory, Cherry, and Apple wood all blazing out of our
BBQ smoker must have been good for business because we
did have a pretty good season. Everyone was working their
tails off and we were regularly setting new sales records at
the restaurant about every week or so. It was exciting, but
honestly more work than anyone wanted or planned. The
business was a good way to pay for some of the much
needed upkeep and repairs to the threadbare Victorian
building and by this time we had a fairly decent set of
regular customers.

  One of our regulars was a friend of mine called,
"BC". BC I think was the first to invent the motto, *Come
Back Strong.* When he would talk about his dating life, BC
would always smile and say he has been dumped by
women more times than a contestant on the Donald Trump
show. He was an older fellow whose hair style featured a
three directional layered comb-over. I once asked him if he
thought a new contemporary hair style would be more
appealing to the ladies and his reply was this,

  "Look Jim, just think. When the comb-over comes
back in style I will be the first in line!"

  BC was a great friend and customer who always
made me laugh no matter how tough a day I had. I was
certainly appreciative.

  Casey and I sort of had an entire new family at *The
Big Pink.* Jake, Bennie Ann, Eddy, other employees and
our customers all felt like a family. It was very nice
however, I must say that the restaurant business dollar for
dollar is among the hardest work in the world. There just is

not a lot of profit after the very narrow margin at the end of the day. Considering we also did not sell liquor and we were only able to be open four days a week, things were always tight. I thought it would be a good idea to really try and beef up business on our slowest night, Wednesdays.

I also considered that "Rose" was finally clearly and happily out of the picture and enjoying her wheels of faith biblical motorhome journey. Now it was time for me to get back in the game. I was hoping and praying that the old Magnolia Tree would shed some grace on me and help in finding my partner to spend the rest of my life with. But how was this going to happen?

Sitting at my computer going through old contacts in tourism trying to drum up some TV sponsorship business, I came across the name and information of the tourism director on the Eastern Shore. Her name was Donna and I had spoken with her briefly in the past on the phone about featuring her area on our show but it went nowhere. However, I thought I would follow through again while I was thinking about it and happened to visit her page on a social networking site. She had her bio posted and it really caught my eye. She had been a writer most of her life, college degreed, and was the tourism director for the Eastern Shore. I thought now this person is someone I would really like to meet! So, I sent her an email asking her for a little date to Jim's BBQ and I would love to meet her and buy her a sandwich. She sent me a nice reply, "Well, I am dating someone however if sometime I am in the area, I do love good BBQ!" That was about it, a simple and pleasant reply to my request that let me know she was not available. I really did not hear much from her again.

But the BBQ sandwich offer I made to Donna started to give me an idea. Could this be another dim lightbulb resonating in my mind? Let's see now, how in the world can I date when my home is in pre-foreclosure, there was no money at all for anything, and now I did not even own a car. Well, I came up with a successful game plan that was quite hard to believe. Even broke, nearly homeless and no automobile, I got more dates than Geico has insurance salesmen. You would have thought I was the last man on earth. Hell, I had them standing in line.

Here is how I did it.

My game plan originated from the fact that I wanted to build business at Jim's BBQ on our slowest night, Wednesday. Since no one had any idea on how to do it, and basically any idea was better than nothing, I combined two problems with one solution.

Problem one, Jim needs to meet women but has no money or car to do so.

Problem two, Jim's BBQ wanted to build business on Wednesday nights.

Solution for both:

"LADIES NIGHT at….. JIM'S BBQ!"
Every Wednesday

Yes, that is what I did. This horse was not able to go to the water for a drink so I made the water come to the horse. I started advertising like crazy Ladies Night at Jim's BBQ all over the internet and we offered food and drink specials plus live acoustic music by a strolling blues guitar player. Once I posted the advertisements everywhere I could for free, I then honed in on my target market that was sure to bring the ladies in, the online dating sites!

I had no money to go to the paid sites so I checked out the free ones. Sure enough, packed full to the brim with profile after profile of beautiful ladies who I felt for certain deserved a Wednesday night on the town at Jim's BBQ! I spent some time and wrote up a great introduction asking a lady for a date that would accomplish my two objectives. Find a possible love for the rest of my life, and to increase business on our off night. Online I would find attractive ladies I would want to meet, I then copy and pasted this same message on all their profiles.

"Hi, my name is Lance Manyon and I liked your profile. Please ponder at mine because I feel certain we have enough in common to warrant at least a meeting. Without being too forward, I am inviting you to my gourmet BBQ smoke house called Jim's BBQ. I am sure you would love the food and atmosphere. But I must warn you I am a very, very shy person and don't feel comfortable or at ease on first meetings.

I would prefer you simply come on out as a customer and have a glass of wine, maybe a sandwich or dinner if you like. This way there is no pressure at all. You would not feel obligated to be nice to me if you were not attracted to me. As a matter of fact, it may even suit you better by calling eight or ten of your girlfriends and all of you come out for our Ladies Night. This way, you are just out with the gals and there would be no pressure at all. You still would get to meet me, talk with me, but it would all be as a manager- customer relationship. After you and your friends leave for the evening if you would like to meet me again for coffee, just shoot me an email. No problem and no pressure. What do you say?"

Almost every time I would get emails back saying,

"Thank you Mr. Manyon, that sounds like a wonderful idea and I love good BBQ! Would it be too much to ask to hold reservations for let's say about seven of my friends for next Wednesday night?"

Ok, I was on a roll. This was working like a champ. It was as easy as cutting warm butter with a hot knife. I was meeting a lot of new ladies every week and we actually had some business on a Wednesday night. One evening Bennie Ann walked up to the bar and was a little stunned at all these pretty ladies filling up the upstairs bar. They all looked like they were from out of town, because they were. Most of them I had coming from the Virginia Beach zip code area. Bennie Ann would look around the room then look at me and start laughing. She knew I was up to something. I happily told her how I was getting all these women in here and she thought it was the funniest thing she ever heard. This was a very successful way to meet the ladies, a little like shooting fish out of a barrel. However, once I met the Southern blue eyed pageant beauty from Tennessee, I had to slow down on the online summer dating invites because this honey was worth trying to really date.

Her name was Savanna. Much like the Southern Georgia town, she was truly beautiful and a real estate mogul. I think at the time she was one of the most successful realtors in Virginia Beach. She came out on a Ladies Night invite and we hit it off pretty well. She was attractive and very Southern with a charming polite warm personality. After she had come out to the restaurant several nights she stayed until closing and things were getting a little "hot." After she laid a big kiss on me I was in fear of what would happen next. My genius in figuring out how to meet ladies while broke with no car did not yet include what to do with them after I caught one.

Savanna looked at me with those big blues and said, "Let's get out of here baby and go for a drink. Then maybe head over to my side of town."

Now remember she drove to the restaurant in her Mercedes, I rode to work on my bicycle. This was not someone who would understand or probably want to hear about my trials and tribulations so I had to act quickly and think of a way out of this without giving too much away. Here is what blurted out of my quivering, cash-starved hickory smoked lips,

"Savanna, I would love to. But although the restaurant is closed, my work here continues to go on for hours. I have to close out, clean, and then prep the BBQ and get out on the smoker before I leave at 2am. Is it possible to get together, maybe on my day off like a Monday?"

Certainly she understood and had no problems with that. I figured I came up with a way to buy me a little time until I figured out this automobile obstacle. We both walked out of Jim's BBQ and there was her new white gleaming Mercedes Benz already running because of her handy remote control ignition switch. I opened her car door, gave her a kiss goodnight and off the Mercedes went out of Phoebus heading towards Virginia Beach.

Once I could no longer see her car visible in any direction I quickly locked up the restaurant, jumped on my bike and peddled my home.

"I'll take the black one."

Wow! You really do keep a clean car.

In less enlightened times, the best way to impress women was to own a hot car. But women wised up and realized it was better to buy their own hot cars so they wouldn't have to ride around with jerks.

~Scott Adams

You can only make the water come to the horse so many times before things start to dry up. I was running out of excuses with Savanna as to why I could not travel to her side of town to see her. Figuring if I was going to really date then solving this four wheeled gas powered, inspection sticker required, insured moving vehicle situation is going to be a necessity.

Here was my dilemma. I really was getting close to re-landing a marine sponsorship. Things would be getting better very soon, I thought. When our marine sponsorship was up and running again I would go out and simply purchase another tow vehicle just like I had always done. However, I was doing fine biking back and forth to work and really enjoyed it. Plus I did not have the money to expense the car out yet anyway until the sponsorship came through. So none of this was really a problem except for one thing... Dating. It does make it tough when you don't have wheels to get to the other side of town. So, without any solution to the situation and wanting to spend a little time with the blue eyed belle from Tennessee I did the one thing that made sense.

I called pirate P.D. Cooper for advice.

Once in a while, some good pirate advice can be just the ticket to save the day. I called P.D. and explained the situation and he immediately cured my dilemma and did it in about two seconds. He said,

"Now Jimmy! Don't you be frettin' no more! You don't think I actually go pick up my ready wenches in my old inspection sticker-less non-insured beat up no AC 1961 rusted pickup truck with an exhaust leak, do ya'? I pirated a deal with my buddies at Harry Cox Car Rental and reserve one several times a month. It's the cheapest best solution for transportation and you always drive a new car! The ladies LOVE IT!"

Now that was some good pirate advice, what a great idea! This car rental was only five blocks away from Jim's BBQ and first thing I did was go check out Cox Rental. Turns out half the employees there had previously partied on my boat downtown and also had their share of free bilge water rum on P.D. Coopers pirate boat. They also had ordered Jim's BBQ for lunch several times and could smell the hickory in my shirt as I walked through the door. The girl sitting in the back that I did not recognize lifted her nose in the air, took a deep breath then looked at me and said, "I want to eat you!"

Laughing, I started talking to my friend there named Tran and ask him just how cheap I could rent a car. He said if I did not go over 300 miles and did the weekend special I could have a midsize car for only $19 bucks a day. The fee would only be for Friday and Saturday, no charge for Sunday and I would return the car on Monday. Then I ask Tran,

"Hey bud, is it ok if I can keep the car on Monday maybe up until 5pm?"

"Sure Jim, as long as we are not sold out and need to rent it. Rarely would that happen so the odds are with you."

353

Right then his phone rings and the person is talking to him on the phone. Tran then concludes the call by saying,

"Yes Mam. If you pick the car up by five the previous day, there is no fee for that day and you can keep the car overnight leading into your next day rental." Then he hangs up the phone and we continue our conversation. I said,

"Tran old friend, you mean that if I come the day before the rental by 5pm, I get to keep the car for that overnight without any fee?"

"Correct Jim. We don't really promote that too much but if a customer ask..."

I said, "Ok, so let me get this straight. I rent the car for only $19 per day for two days. But I can pick the car up on Thursday afternoon and return it Monday afternoon?"

"Yes Jim, by the way if you are busy over at the restaurant we can send a driver over to pick you up no problem. Our drivers are always looking for something to do and they love JBBQ."

WOW! Now I got a car for five days for $40 bucks? That does not seem possible but that was the deal we pirated. I could not go wrong. This I could do on a somewhat regular basis until soon our sponsorship would come through and I go by a tow vehicle. Heck back at the restaurant I always pushed hard for tips up until I reached the $40 buck mark, after that I knew I was in the clear for weekend dating with gas powered four wheel mobility. While I was at Harry Cox I only ask one thing to Tran,

"Tran, say what color do the cars come in?"

"Color? Jim do you mean make of car?"

"No Tran, I mean the color. This is crucial and very, very, important. What colors do they come in and

MOST importantly, what same color car do you have the most of?"

"Jim we do have a lot of black midsize cars in a variety of makes both foreign and domestic. Lots of black ones."

"Great Tran! Gimmie a black one... to go!"

So Tran does the paperwork and minutes later the chauffeur comes out with a black midsize something or other make of car. I did not care as long as it was black. Tran did not understand why the color was so important. He would later figure it out about five rentals later.

Now I am off on my date with Savanna in my all new shiny black super clean car ready for a great night. I drive and pick up Savanna and she is really impressed. Now I never lied about not having a car, had she ask I would have told her it was a rental and I was waiting to buy a tow vehicle soon when our sponsorship came through.

Savanna riding comfortably in my super nice black car then said, "Jim I must say you keep a really clean car."

I answered, "No not really, someone else does the cleaning."

She laughed, thought I was joking, and then she says, "You weren't kidding about being allergic to cigarette smoke. I don't think I have ever seen no smoking stickers on a car's dash before."

"Well Savanna, truth is I use to put them on my boat on the flybridge and on the stern, people still would bring their cigarettes and smoke on board. I hated it. I just don't allow cigarette smoke; I am highly allergic to it."

Then the conversation changed to dinner and we had a nice comfortable evening. A couple of weeks later we went out again, and here I go calling Tran to deliver my five day car rental for $40 bucks. The only thing I told Tran was the car had to be black. But, this time there was a problem. The car was black but this rental had a sunroof.

Savanna and I are out on another date and it was pouring down rain. I knew the sunroof was going to blow my little car rental scheme however, I guess the gray interior and the grey sky through the sunroof just called no attention. She never noticed it. On this car the license plate was from Michigan. Rental cars come from all over the states. She never noticed and I did not say a thing. Another weekend gone by with a great car! I loved this.

I did one time have an issue when I met her back at her Mercedes and we found out her car battery had died. I told her no problem we had a set of jumper cables so I pull open her hood and connect the cables. Then I go over to my car, the black rental and pop the hood to connect to the battery. BIG PROBLEM!

There just was one cover over everything in the engine compartment. I could not even find the battery or terminals. This was a new black car whose under the hood mechanics were totally foreign to me. I quickly said, "Hey Savanna, while I am doing this would you mind walking over to that store and getting me a cup of coffee for the long ride back."

As soon as she was out of listening distance I got my good friend Captain Earl on the cell phone.

"Captain Earl, help me man, I am on a date, her car died and I don't know how to even connect the battery terminal on the rental. This is some new car, black, and the entire engine compartment is covered!"

Earl quickly asked me the make and model of the car at first I just said, "It's black!" Then I had to actually look in the glove compartment to see what kind of car this was. Fortunately Earl knew the car and walked me through how to remove the compartment cover and locate the negative post which I would have NEVER found. Then he described where the positive terminal would probably be and I found it.

By the time Savanna got back to the car with my coffee I was off the phone, the cables were connected and all I said was start her up!

Vrooom Vrooom! All ok! And off she went.

So I rented black cars whenever I needed them that summer. One time there were several bills I had to pay and it wiped me out for the week. I had a date coming up for the weekend and not knowing what to do because my wallet was vacant of the $40 bucks necessary to pay for the black car rental.

So, it was time to really put my old DD Tip jar in action. I set the jar on the bar and had Casey write several signs that said, *"Jim and Casey weekend donation fund."* For a couple of nights I told all our customers who came to the bar to please donate so I could have enough money to rent a car for my date and Casey would also have some pizza, beer, and extra grocery money for Saturday night. My daughter and I would split all the tips when we closed and we hoped for the best.

This is the actual DD Tip Jar that was written about in
HOOKED.
DD Tip jar was also used as the JBBQ tip jar in the main
upstairs bar.
All items were authentic.

Fortunately our customers were very gracious to the
DD Tip jar. In one night Casey and I raised enough tip
money for all of her weekend expenses and I had
enough to rent a car and buy dinner for my date. That is
how we made it through that weekend. Never in my life
did I think I could have been in such a position that I
found myself in economically, but we just did what was

necessary to get through each day. The DD Tip Jar did end up helping us out on more than one occasion.

One of my customers owned a car dealership and I told him how cheap I was renting cars and for how long. I asked him for advice and he said,

"As long as you are renting that cheap, just keep doing it until you have to buy your tow vehicle. It is the best and most affordable route to go, even better than leasing."

It was good advice and that is what I did. As long as I kept showing up in a black midsize car, no one ever knew that I owned a car or not. To my dates, it always looked like the same car. Again, had anyone asked I would have told them. But no one did, they really had no reason to do so.

Savanna was a very sweet intelligent successful lady, however I realized as nice as she was; this probably was not going to be the woman I would be settling down with. We were just very different people. She was very much into the golf thing, socials, fancy parties, etc. I just am not the type of person that can hang around a golf course all day. Traveling, fishing, boating, cooking, music, and writing are really my interest.

The frame of mind I had was to try to meet someone that I was really going to connect with and partner with for life. Someone that would have similar interests and that could even maybe work together with me on various projects. This lady I was looking for, praying for, and wanted was someone I clearly had not met yet. But at least I was out there trying.

Remember what I keep saying about prayer; be careful what you ask for because you might just get it.

Well it was the end of summer; ladies night had run its course and I decided to park the black cars for a while. I was working hard at getting TV sponsorships signed and working my fingers to the bone at Jim's BBQ. My thought was to kick off September with a bang just working as hard as I could in every area of my life including continuing to get my home refinanced and saved. I had a lot on my plate.

Next thing I know it is late August getting ready to close out the month, and to my great surprise I get a call. One I did not expect at all.

Last ladies night at JBBQ, a nice farewell.

Bay-Leigh and Donna.

DUMP HIM TONIGHT!

When you know, you just know.

~Jim Baugh

Donna. That was a word I had not heard of for a while. I had received a message that said,

"Hi there Jim! Going to be coming through and want to take you up on that BBQ sandwich you offered back in the spring."

Really? Ok... WOW! Looks like I may get to meet this person after all. I was surprised but looking forward to it. I invited her to stop by on Bluegrass Friday for some JBBQ and I would show her *The Big Pink*.

What a sight! Friday night Donna glided through the upstairs of Jim's BBQ while I was behind the bar and it felt like the wind had been knocked out of me. Here was this beautiful, gracious woman with a magnificent aura, phenomenal legs and the prettiest big smile I had ever seen. She was wearing a gorgeous white summer dress that seemed to light up and glow just like her flowing blond hair. I introduced myself and she sat right down beside me and I was just trying to catch my breath. I don't even remember whatever stupid words came out of my mouth but whatever it was fortunately did not offend her too much because she stayed.

We laughed and talked for hours, the chemistry between us was just fantastic. There was an immediate and overwhelming attraction at least for me, and I was incredibly excited. We are both writers and worked in and around the tourism industry so we had an awful lot in common. This first meeting with Donna may be the best first date I ever had. Especially on an initial encounter there are always insecurities and you wonder if the person you are so infatuated with has any inkling of feeling the same way about you. This crossed my mind; however things were going so well I thought I would let her know just how happy I was to finally meet her, and certainly wanted to start really dating her. So at the end of the evening I had planned the "BIG MOVE", yes walking her to her car I gave her a kiss goodnight.

WOW! Now that was a KISS! I thought I would fall to me knees, she had so much passion it blew me away. This half Italian, half German lady gave me a kiss that for me was like the shot heard around the world. What was going through my mind was that I sure hoped this lady gives us a chance to date, because I am already pretty crazy about her.

After this totally awesome kiss I open her car door, she gets in, starts her car and puts her little VW convertible bug in reverse. As soon as the car moves not even two inches she rolls down her window. My male ego starts to kick in like a gallon sized Red Bull, I am thinking that maybe that kiss I gave her was really something special and she was rolling down her window to tell me how much she likes me and I am surely the man candy hunk for her.

Donnas' window creaks down about three inches, she looks at me and says this, and I will never forget,

"Jim, hey just a reminder…I am dating somebody."

It felt like someone had just shot me with a musket or maybe a cannon. I was not sure if my brain was allowing me to fully comprehend what she had just said to me. I had no idea what to do or say. The vision in my mind was of the Hindenburg exploding. Hell, her car was in reverse and she rolled down the window to tell me she is still dating someone. What the hell? This may be one of those few times in my life I was at a loss for words. Without thinking, and being somewhat in a mild state of shock I simply said,

"DUMP HIM TONIGHT! Pick up your little cell phone and dump him **NOW!** Yes you heard me; you must get rid of him now! The reason is every minute you spend with him you are taking away time from us and that is just totally wrong!"

She looked at me like I must have been crazy. I am sure she thought who am I to have the audacity to say something like that. She sort of laughed it off as she was driving away. I called her while she was driving home to thank her for coming, drive home safe, and to please dump her boyfriend. For the most part that was about it.

We had sparse communication after that. I had other things that were creeping into my daily life that I had to deal with like finally putting our family dog Tina Turner Baugh down.

About a month or so had passed; I still could not do it. Finally Casey called me to remind me that on Monday we had planned to take Tina to the Vet for the last time. We did. Casey and I were crying our eyes out. We will never forget as they walked Tina out of the Veterinarians office and took her in the back. Tears are on my typewriter as I write this; it is still a very difficult memory. Never did I think it would have been SO hard.

Just before we put Tina down Casey and I took her to Buckroe Beach for her last run in the sand to chase seagulls. She was so arthritic she could not run or hardly walk, but she tried. On the way to the Vet's we stopped off and got Tina her final meal, a cheeseburger which was always her favorite treat. It was a Monday and it was raining. Casey and I will forever remember just how hard that day was.

JBO TV show mascot and family dog, Tina Turner Baugh at Buckroe Beach for her last walk on the beach.. This picture was taken only an hour before we had to put her down.

The three days following were terrible, I could not get over how bad I felt. I just put Tina down, my dad's health was deteriorating, I had no money and would lose my home if it was not refinanced by the mortgage company. I was on my bike riding getting exercise and rode the remainder of the day.

The next day Thursday I got up and rode again. I was peddling hard and praying, peddling and praying,

"Dear Lord, I ask you... is this it? Why all this at the same time, cant things get better? Please help me to turn things around and let's get this train moving forward. Please! Amen!"

Literally at that exact moment when I said Amen my cell phone rings! I am sure it was a bill collector. They just loved to call me night and day back then. I looked at my phone and it is,

Donna!

A text message displays these words, "Jim I hope you are well, just wanted you to know I bought your book *HOOKED* and am going to read it over the weekend."

I thought, gee, this is a surprise. How nice. I answered her and told her thanks and enjoy the read.

Two days later on Saturday I start getting these messages on my phone from Donna.

Did you really do that?
Was she a real person?
I can't stop laughing at your book!
Ha! Ha! Ha! Ha!

Sunday she finished my novel and messaged me.
I finished HOOKED and absolutely LOVED it!

I finally called her and said, "Thank you Donna, glad you liked the book. But let me be clear, I don't want to communicate and get involved with someone I am attracted to who is in a relationship with someone else. It would be too hard for me."

She replied, "I am not dating anyone right now. And I very much would like to get to know the person who wrote this book. Can you come over to my house for dinner tomorrow?"

It was like asking a fish if it likes seafood. Gee, let's see, how fast can I say YES!!!

Clams are popular on the Eastern Shore and Donna and I had a delicious clam's casino dinner at her house on the Shore. We talked for hours and I was so glad and happy that she thought enough of the book to have me over for dinner. Probably that night was our first official date and we continued to see each other falling in love more and more every time we were together.

Donna and I are two people that can talk non-stop for hours on end. For whatever reason, our chemistry is such that we just complemented each other very well. I enjoyed being with her so much I had no interest in dating any other women. I was taking myself off the market, fully concentrating only on our relationship.

We were approaching Christmas time and I knew we had not known each other long enough to get engaged, however I did want to give her something to signify that I was committed to her and to her only. Thanks to my good friend who is one of the owners of Goodman's Jewelry Store, I was able to purchase with literally the last penny to my name a small, yet very pretty pre-engagement ring. I gave this to Donna for Christmas and explained to her I wanted us to give this relationship a real shot. I loved her and always wanted to be with her. She agreed, accepted the ring and was very happy about it.

Now one thing about Donna, she is a VERY passionate person. She is half Italian and the other half is first generation German American which is a rather incredible combination. At times I did not know whether to make her pasta or just salute. In all areas of our relationship things were going fantastic. Intimacy between us was super magnificent and I could not have been happier. With Donna in my life, my home hopefully being refinanced, and a soon to be sponsorship on its way, the future was looking increasingly better!

Yes! Things are looking up!

Donna standing with our friends, two of the best Blues men around who regularly played at The Big Pink Jim's BBQ. To the left Bobby Blackhat Walters. On the right, Herbie Desseyn.

Casey Baugh and Donna at JBBQ enjoying the best ribs in the world!

RESTRICTED
AREA

Excuse me dahlin…
Could you run that past me one more time?

Dry spells are for wells, not me.

~Jim Baugh

Finding your partner you have been looking for IS a big deal. This brought a lot of happiness in my life and I did not doubt that Donna was going to be the one. We continued after the holidays in loving bliss, the restaurant was doing good business during the winter and I was still working hard at saving my home, getting sponsorships sold and closed for *Jim Baugh Outdoors TV*.

Then it happened! Dammit!

I was sitting on the sofa relaxing with a cocktail in my hand and I get… "THE CALL!" This is a phone call that probably most men would never, never, never, ever, ever, ever want to get! But I got it. Oh boy, this one came out of left field and I was not prepared for it at all.

"Jim…Donna here. I love you too, are you sitting down? I have something I want to talk with you about."

I could already feel the alligator-size softball heading down my throat right down to the pit of my stomach. I had no idea what I would hear next but I did not think it was going to be good. She continues,

"Jim, I just came back from my prayer group and something has been bothering me for a while now and I want to talk with you about it. I have made the decision and feel it is the right one to strengthen my faith and try to lead a better Christian life. There are things that I am doing that I should not be and I am going to make some changes. In an effort to do the right thing, I have decided to abstain from any intimacy until I am in a union blessed by God. There will not be any more sex until the day I marry. This has always bothered me and now I am going to do something about it."

Silence...

....

"Jim are you there?

....................Hello?.......Helllllooo???"

I said, "Excuse me dahlin, could you run that past me one more time?"

She repeats what she just said and out of my soon to be sex-starved lips angrily comes these vile words,

"NO FUCKIN WAY! You have GOT to be kidding me. Are you.... SERIOUS?"

I could not believe the words I was hearing. Believe me this is the last thing I wanted to hear and the fact is I did not believe the same way she did. BIG problem! I was mad, angry, and whining like a child that lost his ice cream cone. I was so mad I even started to dislike her prayer group. After all, anybody that is going to talk my partner into celibacy is NO friend of mine! I tried to talk her out of it to no avail. I came up with everything I could think of to convince her she was looking at this totally wrong. To my dismay, I had no luck trying to alter her mind. I was pissed off but tried my best to maintain composure.

I quickly tried the quick save and spit out these much less than honorable words, "Donna, you can't go by what your prayer group or the bible says about this because everyone has a different interpretation of what the bible says is right and wrong, and by the way, I don't believe there is any such thing as a **Born Again Virgin**!" Geeze, gimmie a break!"

Donna got mad at me because of the "Born Again Virgin" comment. She really was getting hot under the collar but I wanted her to get hot somewhere else, no luck.

371

The conversation was battled out several times before she made clear to me that her decision was not based on a prayer group. Her decision was clearly a personal decision between her and the good Lord.

Well, that one stumped me. I could not argue with that at all. If she was spouting out bible verses that has been interpreted differently by 50 different denominations and religions, I would have continued to argue the point with her. However. once she said this was between her and God, and she knew it was the right thing to do, I could no longer argue with that. She was correct in her decision. I hated it, but really could not argue it.

So I thought to myself, my gut is telling me to end it now because I just don't feel the same way. I understood her position, but it was not for me. Being the poster child for celibacy was not in my game plan. Hell, I was the past award-winning sex machine so proudly acclaimed by the DC Nympho! I have my pride dammit!

But my heart and brain were telling me differently. I loved her, and I simply asked myself would I be happy if I could not be with her. The answer was no, I enjoyed our time together too much. I was not going to find another Donna. So I called her on the phone and decided I would tell her this,

"Donna, here is what I will do. I do not agree with you at all and I am not saying I will be able to be abstinent in our relationship, especially since we have already been intimate for quite a few months. But what I will say is that I will try my best to honor your request. If you accept that, then we can move forward."

She accepted it. The one thing I had going for me about all of this was that I was not sure she or I could hold out. My brain was thinking just give it some time and see what happens. As I found out in the near future Donna was committed to her new strengthened faith, and she was not budging an inch. A small hug or kiss on the cheek was all that old JB would be getting from now on and I HATED IT!! I hung in there and did the best I could. She appreciated that and maybe was surprised I was going along with it because this was a subject we did not agree on to any degree.

The fact is I was trying to honor her request because I loved her, and hopefully that meant something.

I did not have too much free time to worry about the fantastic times we were NOT having between the sheets, the future was not looking bright for my home that I loved. I still was trying to get my Condo refinanced and move forward.

The stressful delay was killing me.

And so was this....

Church + Legal Pad = Homeless

You cannot spend your way out of recession or borrow your way out of debt.

~Daniel Hannan

Sometimes people can really shock you. I had biked to the beach for a much needed rest and I happened to bump into a friend of mine. This fellow I had known for quite a few years and he and his wife Susan were always super nice to me. His name was Dan and he had retired from some military missile construction company and had more money than Bill Gates. He never could talk much about exactly what he did but I got the idea there are some countries that have used his product with great success. Dan called me over on the beach for a talk and I could not believe what I was about to hear. In a low serious voice he said,

"Jim I want you to know that Susan and I are aware of the situation you are in with your home and we feel terrible about it. She and I talked it over and we are very happy to help you out. You just give me the amount, and I will write the check to your mortgage company. It does not matter how much it is and it is not a loan, it's a gift. We have more millions in the bank than we know what to do with and we like to help people out whenever we can, we just don't want you to advertise it. So, what do you need and I will send the check out tomorrow."

There is no way to describe the grace I felt by what Dan had just told me. I was shocked and never thought I would hear anyone say those words to me. My first thought was that maybe tonight for the first night in a long time I would be able to sleep. Some stress about losing my home would be subsided. My second thought was not to immediately except his gracious offer. I told Dan,

"That may be one of the most gracious things anyone has ever attempted to do for me and I cannot thank you enough. You and Susan are real angels and have come at a time of need for me and I did not even ask for it. I thank you both, but will not except your offer until I hear from my mortgage company. If they finally approve my refinancing then things will be ok and I would not need any gifts are loans from anyone. I will stay in touch and thank you again." Dan went on to say,

"If it does not work out let me know ASAP and we will take care of it."

I thanked him again and also was a little shocked that anyone would ever be this nice. I happily rode my bike home with relief in my soul. I told Donna about this and she said that Dan's offer was incredible and she was happy for me. Dan and Susan are one of those rare couples who are Christians with more money than the Federal Reserve. They take it on themselves to find people who need help that can't seem to get it anywhere else. They are very good people and I was so appreciative I did not have the words big enough to express my gratitude. The situation now was regardless of what the bank did, I was going to be able to keep my home.

Then something else happened that changed things. I went to church. Yes, I asked Donna to go to this church that I liked in Chesapeake called Western Branch Community Church. The founding pastor was Dr. Jim Wall. I always thought he had a great talent for communicating messages of faith in our current societal times. So we went that Sunday and guess what the service was about.

DEBT!

This was a great service and message about financial responsibility and debt. The bottom-line of the message was to try your best not to be in debt or owe anybody anything. This is an AWESOME lesson to learn and an wonderful way to live your life. One thing this did was encourage me to do something I should have done long ago and that was to get out a legal pad, calculator and start to really figure out this mortgage problem I was facing in detail.

Now these are not the exact figures but an example of how crazy the situation was. I got out my yellow legal pad and started to do the numbers. Don't forget we were in the great recession and housing values had plummeted worse than quality television during the writers' strike. Here is what I realized.

The recession hits big and real estate bottoms out. Condos like mine were rarely selling at any price regardless of their value. My home took somewhere between a 50% to 70% loss in value meanwhile the mortgage of course was based on my purchase price. This means that homeowners like me were so upside down on their real estate investment there really was no way out. Throwing more money into the pot would only mean throwing good money after bad.

It's like trying to save a sinking ship, you bail as hard as you can and do everything possible in order to save your vessel. However, once the ship has sunk and is on the bottom of the ocean floor there really is no need to keep bailing water.

There was an additional problem with my home equation and that was the property had continuing raising association fees that became the highest in the entire area. On top of which the association had additional mounting assessments to homeowners fairly regularly and in the five figure range. Just this factor alone is enough to kill a real estate sale. Again, the horrific economy and massive fees and assessments meant nothing was moving or selling. I was stuck like a 13 foot Steinway in an elevator.

So my legal pad clearly showed me that if I took another loan or gift, I would never be able to get out from under the condo, never. Also considering my horizon hopefully included getting married and possibly changing residence somewhere way south; it did not make sense to be stuck buried under a condo I could never sell. So once I would finally hear from the bank as to what they were going to do regarding my refinancing, I would then have to make a decision as to what I was going to do. After all the mortgage company did not know I had been to church, listened to the "debt" sermon and started to really crunch numbers on the legal pad. Only about a couple months had passed when I finally heard from the mortgage company.

Declined. No refinancing. They would not re-qualify me. No help at all was going to come from the bank.

That's ok, because if I wanted to keep my home I had the ace in the hole! My rich friend who is eager to send that check to the mortgage company and save me from my despair was only a phone call away. But was that really the right thing to do? Take money; get more and more in debt with a home that would never surface to see air again?

Everything had to go, even the pets. Left to right: Blue, Rude, Allie, and Tweety.

Yard Sale

Giving debt relief to people that really need it, that's what foreclosure is.

~ Jamie Dimon

Certainly one of the hardest decisions I ever made was not taking any gifts or loans, and losing my home. This was my residence that I loved and worked hard for. It was tough, nothing like this I ever thought would happen to me and it hurt SO bad! I thanked Dan for his generous offer and how much it meant to me that he would bail me out, but it was not the right thing to do.

I was losing my home but did have something left, and that was a clear path. I had prayed in the past that I would be able to keep my home, however if losing it was the right thing in order to move forward, then so be it. I put my trust and faith in the good Lord regardless of the difficulty I was going through.

I then lost every material asset in my possession.

My home and all of its contents... Gone.

I also mutually agreed to close Jim's BBQ. To continue with the restaurant meant a serious capital investment, larger staff, and full time commitments from everyone. No one wanted this, me included. The endless hours at Jim's BBQ would be better spent in producing television so we all happily agreed to move on. I lost my home, closed my restaurant, and soon would sell off whatever piece of personal items I had left in an estate sale. I had to. It was the wisest decision and there was no way I was going to keep my art gallery in a storage bin. I would sell it all and hopefully raise enough money to buy maybe an $1800.00 old used car and have a little grocery money left over for food.

This is exactly what happened. I had an estate sale. A lot of my friends came over and bought up everything I had. Let me tell you what a wreck I was the morning of the *lets make a deal* estate sale. My stomach felt like one giant knot the size of an aircraft carrier. Here is something you should know about just how good people can be. Most of my friends all came out to help by buying my personal belongings. That day and every day up until today while I am writing this not one person, NOT ONE of my friends ever mentioned to me foreclosure. No one ever mentioned it. All they did was show their support and love by buying stuff so I could finally get out of there. Curt, Jan, Chris, Karen, Mike & Donna, Kevin, Joel, Elliott, Eva, James and others are truly some quality friends. I thank them all and everyone else that bought something at my yard sale. People showed a lot of grace that day.

Still, even though you know you are doing the right thing selling off your possessions is a very strange feeling. I remember worrying most about my parakeets and palm trees. Where would I find a home for them? Fortunately I did, thanks to Eva and lots of other great friends. I had taken great care of my Sago Palm tree that sat in my condo. This plant was a source of pride for me and everyone loved this palm, it truly was beautiful. This huge palm helped give my home that Florida Keys atmosphere that I had strived for in decorating my condo.

It was difficult for me personally to lose everything including my plants that I had taken such good care of. Sacrifice and loss **IS** difficult for sure, but I never thought it would get so bad I would even lose my sago palm. I kept my faith but did not know where I would be going and figured it would be a while, if ever, that I would see another palm tree.

Believe it or not my biggest fear was not losing my home, it was losing Donna. I did not think she was going to stick with a guy who just lost everything he had worked for his entire life. I was just sick about this and Donna knew I felt that way. She cleared the air.

"Jim, I know you are upset about losing your home, but I love you more today than I ever have. You lost everything but you never lost your faith. You handled this with grace and dignity plus on top of which you have continued to honor my request. I love you."

I was amazed. I also really for the first time began to think there might be something to this entire celibacy before marriage thing. I began to think gee, respect, honor, dignity, aren't these the things we all want in a committed relationship? Here standing before me was exactly that! I felt good about it and as I grabbed Donna's hand and walked out of my home for the last time, I felt that the tide must be turning soon.

Luckily by the grace of God I did find an old fourteen year old car for $1800 that Donna affectionately called "Mitzy" short for Mitsubishi. I pulled out of the parking lot of my foreclosed condo with only a small suitcase of clothes, my piano, and Donna.

I never looked back.

So you don't believe in Miracles?

Nobody sees the obvious, nobody observes the ordinary. There are more miracles in a square yard of earth than in all the fables of the Church.

~Robert Anton Wilson

I had made the decision to lose my home based on prayer, faith, and a yellow legal pad. I trusted that the Lord would not steer me in the wrong direction but being human, I did wonder sometimes if I had made the correct decision. At the time the numbers made sense to lose the home and not put one more penny in it. I prayed and prayed and prayed for the Lord to show me clearly what to do, and I did it.

But...was my home really a barricade that was keeping me from moving forward? How would I ever know for sure? The answer that would come could not be any more direct than if a lightning bolt struck me in the head.

Only TWO months after Donna and I walked out of my foreclosed condo I get a call from my old friend Terry, a friend of mine who had been a neighbor while I was living at the condo.

"Hey Jim! How is it going old friend! Hope you are well and I wanted to pass on some news to you."

"Hi Terry, awesome to hear from you, whats up?"

"Jim you're not gonna' believe this. You're going to be soooo glad you got out of the condo when you did. They were doing some small maintenance work on the condos' the city got involved and were going to

382

condemn the building. Turns out most of the structure was rotten and fear of collapse!"

"You have got to be joking!"

"Not at all Jim. And get this. The association did their proper due diligence and found a good construction company to do all the repairs so the city would not condemn the building. However to pay for it each condo has a new additional assessment of $20,000 each. That 20 grand each condo owner has to pay is due in full in only a matter of months."

Chills went down my spine. What I thought was the hardest thing I had to deal with, losing my home turned out to be a HUGE blessing. Had I stayed there I would have taken the loan, then in only 60 days would be faced with coming up with an addition $20,000 bucks! That would be on top of the ridiculous increased per month condo fee and my monthly mortgage! I would have had to file bankruptcy.

The good Lord plucked me out of that condo in the nick of time, a little like jumping off the stern of the Titanic and landing in a life raft. WOW did he answer my prayers! This also helped the community because my foreclosed condo sold to a real estate flipper in days. This meant that the new owner would be current on the monthly condo fees, and of course have to come up with the additional $20,000 in assessments. My fear of not being able to sell the condo during those recessionary times were confirmed by the reality than even after a year from my departure that beautiful gorgeously renovated heavily discounted condo has never sold. Tough market for sure.

This could not be any more of a clear example of how when something in your life you think hurts so bad, but yet the good Lord knows better and is actually looking after your best interest. I was so sad to lose my home, and yet relieved to find that through faith in my darkest hour, is where maybe I found my true character and peace.

My thoughts and prayers have been with the people that still live in that community. Many of them are my friends and I only wish them the best. Staying there was just not meant to be for me. AMEN!

*Donna's cat Sailor on Mermaid Bay Beach watching the
Sunset westward over the Chesapeake Bay.*

Welcome Home

For the two of us, home isn't a place. It is a person. And we are finally home.

~ Stephanie Perkins

I was homeless with only some grocery money that would carry me for a few weeks. Since I had nowhere to go I did what I thought was a good idea and called up my favorite hotel Hatteras Landing in Hatteras Village North Carolina and ask them if I could stay there for a week if I did a story on the Outer Banks. They had always worked with me in the past so I thought it was worth a shot.

Donna and I arrived in romantic Hatteras the week after I lost my home and I did write one fun article featuring the Outer Banks. I had asked Donna to help me write it and she did, our writing chemistry was unbelievable. It gave me the idea that we should be working together with *Jim Baugh Outdoors TV*. Donna was an excellent professional writer, had good on-camera experience and knew the tourism industry. She was not only beautiful and a great gal but extremely talented as well.

I was just taking everything one day at a time. However, what I had just been through and considering how romantic Hatteras Island was I was hoping to ...you know, "get a little". I tried and this was a mistake.

"Jim darn it keep off of me! I have my limits too you know and I don't need this temptation. Your hands are like an octopus! Keep back!!

"Donna, that's not my hand."

I tried to soften my attempt with humor, but it did not go over well. Donna was upset at me and I was a bit furious that even after losing my home, there was not even a little *"Amore!"* Of course I was disappointed and angry.

But heck, what can I say I was missing intimacy a lot and we were even sleeping in the same bed! I finally settled down and we both moved forward. I also learned that it would be best if I began sleeping on the sofa. I would in the future reign in a new nick name, *Sofa Jim.*

When we left Hatteras I returned Donna to her home on the Eastern Shore and I went to my ex-brother-in-law's home in the mountains and stayed there for a week. I was homeless and nowhere to go. While I was there I was working everyday on sponsorships for the show doing anything trying to get some business going. I was also talking to Donna every day and she wanted me to come by her home when I left the mountains.

Mitzy and I arrived on the Eastern Shore and it was great to see Donna. I also saw something else. One of only two oil paintings that survived my estate sale was hanging in her living room. My Wyland was also hanging in the dining room. She gave me a big hug and said she wanted to talk with me.

"Jim, I love you and I want to tell you something. I would like you to consider this our home. We can live and work here together. If you really like it after we are married we can just keep this beach house. It would be a great place to have our kids, grandkids, entertain, work and live our lives."

Well, now I am a bit stunned because Donna had never mentioned this before. I really did not know where I was going and had actually started looking at places to live. Then she says,

"Now Jim, I know you must have spent your last penny on groceries while we were in the Outer Banks. I am positive you don't have ANY money left."

"Yes Donna that would be correct."

"Well, I have same money in savings and I am going to cover all expenses for a while until you get your feet on the ground. My money is our money and this is our home now. I will give you a debit card for your gas and groceries, all you have to do is cook."

I could not believe that Donna was doing all this. Talk about 'walking the walk.' This lady hands down was showing her love and proving it beyond anything I have ever experienced. I was blown away. To this day I can hardly believe the love and grace that Donna showed for our relationship. It was amazing!

There was just this one thing… The no intimacy deal was still in full force. I slept in the guest room. She slept in the master. I was grateful for all she did for me and us, but I was still having a difficult time with this zero intimacy policy. I did NOT like it and angered me often. I also had problems with my male ego, you know, if the boys found out I was in a celibate relationship I would be the laugh of the town. Fortunately this private issue was just between me and Donna, and her prayer group. Oh boy, lucky me!

I walked out on the porch one day and Donna was just laughing up a storm, she looked at me with this beet red face and says,

"Jim you will not believe what I just did. I sent my prayer group leader a message telling her that although you and I are living under the same roof, we are totally celibate and obeying the Lord's word." I said,

"Well, that would be best if that was just between us, but I understand she is your good friend and you did not want her to have the wrong idea about what you were doing. I understand. So, why are you laughing so hard Donna?"

"Because... I did not send it just to her. I accidently sent it out on our mass mailer via text on my cell phone! I am sorry!"

Ok, whatever male ego I had left now has vanished like disco at a Lynyrd Skynyrd concert. Donna thought it was hilarious, I on the other hand saw NO humor in this at all. Now, everywhere in town I go people are going to point fingers at me and say instead of the Elephant Man, "It's the Celibate Man! It's the Celibate Man!" Believe me I much preferred the award-winning sex machine title. I left Donna on the porch, went inside and made a stiff cocktail hoping this mass text mailer was just a bad dream.

The next couple of weeks passed and I noticed two things surprisingly happened. First, everyone at church, friends and neighbors were especially nice to me. It was enough to where I really did notice it. Second, when Donnas' daughter came to visit us and for the first time she came and gave me a really big hug. She was being exceptionally sweet to me.

I noticed both these things and it pondered the question as to why. So I ask, "Donna, I have noticed that your friends were atypically sweet to me over the last couple of weeks, and your daughter was so kind to me, I was just wondering what I have done to deserve such reward."

"Jim, I think the cat is sort of out of the bag. Most all of my friends and the church know that you are honoring my request and trying to do the right thing. My daughter knows this as well. They all know that I have been through hell in the past with two marriages. They like the fact that you are honoring me. It shows great respect and dignity, my friends and family care about that."

Ok, so here is another little light bulb going off in my head. I am not for this no intimacy policy however if it gains the respect of her family, friends, and the good Lord to boot, than these are all very positive benefits. I began to feel better about things, I was learning.

One day in my sexual frustration I asked her this, "Why zero tolerance? Can't we fool around just a little bit, come on it has been like eight months now?"

Donna said clearly, "For me it is all or nothing. I know this is a sacrifice Jim. It is for me too! That is what you keep forgetting; it's not ALL about YOU! I enjoy intimacy very much and miss it as well. But I just don't gripe and complain every time the thought comes to my mind, like someone else I know!"

Well, that was a good answer. Donna had already proved her passion and I also reminded myself that she had done more for me than anyone else in many years. She also stuck by me when I thought she would bail. Her words to me helped me understand that it is a sacrifice. I remember what my football coach used to say, "No pain no gain." The philosophy of sacrifice is necessary in order to achieve goodness or greatness. This is usually true in every area of life.

Nothing is easy. I can relate to this. That is when Donna spoke of sacrifice it rang true to me. I understood.

Donna and I had to watch the pocketbook carefully because no money was coming in. We were able to meet friends for a dinner party at their home one evening. Guess what the main topic was. *Sexually transmitted diseases at 50 + years old.* This was an interesting conversation and made me think of a lot of things. First how lucky Donna and I are to have never had this issue, and of course the situation we were in it would not be possible to contract anything. Hey, no sex means no STD's. I thought how would I like to be 50 years old and catch something that would stick with me for the remainder of my life. NO THANKS!!

That night I began to think that although I did not really agree with Donna's mandate of no intimacy until marriage, I did truly start to see some benefits not just for us, but for society. Something I never thought of before ever in my life.

Physical needs regarding intimacy can get a little squirrely. You are denied something you want desperately. One night I had this futuristic dream that was WAY out there. It shook me up so much when I woke up I wrote it down. Writing about this dream I then realized what the dream was about. It was about the want and desire of something you can't have and the sacrifices one makes to achieve goals. The story actually was pretty good and a wild futuristic read. This turned out to be my first published Si-Fi short story called *ROXSWELL.*

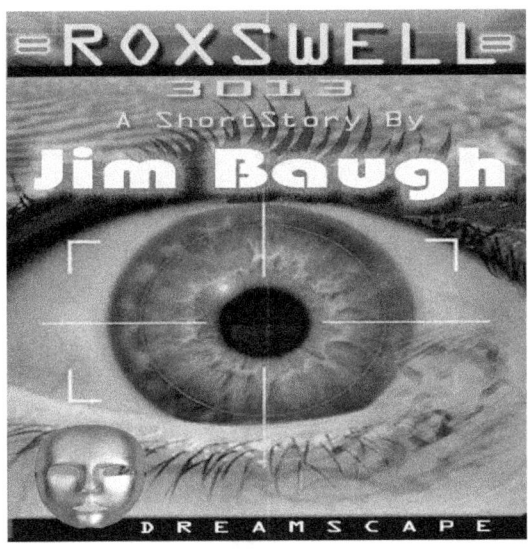

New Year's day came and went, along with Valentine's Day. Boy now there was a fun one. It is snowing outside on Valentine's Day and your beautiful sexy lady is snuggled up in her big master bed with two cats. I on the other hand am stuck in the guest room. Alone, miserable, a bit pissed off because of the 100% zero intimacy policy on what is supposed to be a day glorifying romance. I certainly considered this to be the worst Valentine's Day ever.

It's a lot like wanting to ride the awesome thrilling fun roller coaster that you love at the state fair but you can't, because you don't have a ticket. All you can do is… standby.

I think I took three cold showers that night.

Things began to happen. I went to work immediately and did not stop for six months. Our 25th anniversary for the show was the next year and I was hell bent on signing on some tourist locations and featuring them. The fall is a bad time to be selling sponsorships, budgets are already spoken for in most cases, but I did not give up. I would work all day, exercise, then cook Donna dinner, take cold showers, then retire to the guest room.

Arthur Matthews "Pete" Baugh. Aka, "The Judge"

One more Judge in Heaven

I am not ashamed to say that no man I ever met was my father's equal, and I never loved any other man as much.

~Hedy Lamarr

Donna and I had been working tirelessly all fall and winter producing *Jim Baugh Outdoors TV*. We had signed the areas we were going to feature and our production schedule was full. This would be the first time Donna and I would be traveling together to produce programming for the show and we were both very excited. We are also anxious to get out and see some new places and meet new people. The sales part of producing television is pretty much a desk job. This was a hard winter and we were so ready for a road trip.

The week we were to leave to go on the road filming we were all excited about traveling to see family and my dad the Judge for his 80th birthday. Donna and I got up early that Saturday and already ordered his birthday balloons; we were walking out the door to pick them up when I got the call.

My dad the Judge had passed away in his sleep only moments before we were getting ready to leave to see him. He was at the river awake that morning and seemed fine, then laid back down for a nap and never awoke. He passed away in his sleep.

Only days later after my father's passing, Donna and I would leave to film the New River Valley and Smith Mountain Lake. Below is the tribute I wrote about my father. The only dad I know that on a hot August day would hike hauling in an ice cream cake for his son's birthday at Boy Scout Camp. Best dad in the world. We all miss him greatly.

In loving memory April 12-1934 - April 12th 2014

Pete Baugh –"The Judge"

Was both mother and father to me. What a huge challenge to raise two young sons while in the midst of building his law practice and dealing with numerous personal trials. My dad managed to pull it all off in his own inimitable style.

Yet even as a young boy I recognized the heavy burden of stress my dad carried. I started praying back then and never stopped that the man I loved more than anything else in the world would be blessed with a long life and a great marriage to a beautiful lady.

I am always grateful that my prayers and then some –were so awesomely answered. I especially ponder these miracles today.

For this Saturday, on his 80th birthday my father passed. Dad lived a very full life and had the love of many. In my eyes and theirs, he was a great man.

Even though in declining health these last few years, he still wanted to contribute and remained an active judge. Much of the credit for this goes to his dedicated wife of thirty years, Clarice Baugh, an angel on earth.

Clarice took wonderful care of a proud Southern Judge who did not take a hankering to having to depend on anyone. Hell hath no furor like the Judge having to give up one iota of independence. I thank Clarice with all my heart, though there are not enough thanks worthy for what she did for my dad. She literally kept him going and the beauty of it all, even as difficult as my father could be –he appreciated it. He loved her very much.

Dad blessed me with endless wonderful and profound memories, first out starting as a young boy listening to him preaching to our Methodist congregation, to my teen years sitting in on one of his hearings first as an attorney, then later as Judge.

My passion for boating and fishing comes from Dad. That it turned into a lifelong profession I love is in large part due to him. He was there at the beginning as co-founder and CEO of Jim Baugh Outdoors TV. We traveled together, spending great times on the water filming and fishing. I am forever grateful for his guidance, leadership, and advice. Without his support, our fledging program would not have survived and I would not be celebrating its 25th year.

My dad always told me, "Jimmy, you can grow up and be anything you want to be, anything, even a ditch digger. But just make sure of one thing –you are the best dam ditch digger to ever be!"

It stuck with me. Whether with my music, producing, writing, raising kids, cooking, whatever, I remembered his words to give it your all. A simple but profound lesson, it helped me through tough times.

Compassion for others was something the Judge also taught me and in quite an amazing way. As a young boy, my dad took my brother and I Christmas shopping to pick out things that we liked. He then loaded all the toys in the car and we hit the grocery store. When we got home, we wrapped all the presents. I was thinking this was all a little weird, now we knew what we are getting for Christmas!

After baking the Christmas turkey, Dad told us to get all the presents and help load the car with the food too. I did not understand what the heck was going on but you don't question the Judge. We arrived at a tiny, dismal house. The three of us walked up and rang the doorbell. A woman with five kids hovering around her waist answered the door. She was shocked to see us. Dad instructed us to get all the food and presents out of the car and bring them inside.

The presents and turkey were not for us but for a destitute family who had no food, and no Christmas, until Judge Baugh showed up. What a lesson in helping others. What a GREAT father!

Dad was also an Eagle Scout so he recognized the important lessons scouting taught boys. Pete was proud of all his grandchildren and especially happy when my son Ben Baugh achieved Eagle Scout. His funeral instructions asked that instead of flowers folks might consider donating to the Boy Scouts of America.

I want to give a special thanks to Ms. Donna. Saturday we were getting ready to leave the Eastern Shore and head over to see Dad and Clarice for his birthday when we got the call I always dreaded. Donna has been a Godsend in helping me through this difficult time.

During my six-hour walk on the beach Saturday, I realized that the good Lord took my father on one of the most beautiful of days. In true Judge-style, Dad made a notable departure on the morning of his 80th. It was a graceful exit from his beloved home on "The River" and his dear Clarice with him. Instead of mounting health problems, pain and suffering, my dad now knows only peace and joy.

He dearly missed the many friends and family that passed before him. Now, he is joined by his father (my grandfather) also a Southern Judge –Emerson Daniel

Baugh, my grandmother Maggie Lee, Uncle Tom, Pierce, and "The Crew" that I grew up with on the docks of Sara's Creek. Surely, they're all in heaven causing quite a ruckus.

Shout out to Pete:

Dad, you, and "The Crew" try to stay out of trouble up there! When it is my turn to come see you, I promise I will bring that sailor sandwich from Chiocca's. Sorry, you left before we had a chance to go back. It will be the ultimate "To Go" box.

Thanks for being the best Dad a son could ever pray for in this world. Your family and friends, we already miss you terribly. No one can ever replace you.

With great love and affection –your son always,

~Jimmy
For Donations Boy Scouts, Heart of Virginia Council (Formally Robert E. Lee Council)

Left: Little Pete and Hambone. Dad loved Hambone and spoke about him often.
Right: Dad served in the Army, 101st Airborne Infantry Regiment during the Korean War. He was stationed in Alaska.

Donna and Jim filming at the Bull and Bones BBQ
Restaurant while on location
featuring the New River Valley of Virginia.

On the Road Again

It is a rough road that leads to the heights of greatness.

~Lucius Annaeus Seneca

After the death of my father and seven months of hard work producing finally we were packing up to go on the road filming. I ended up signing eight travel destinations to be featured in our 25th anniversary specials. Plus our marine sponsorship I had been working on for close to two years finally came through. In our exhilaration Donna and I set the date for our wedding in May.

Only a few days afterwards Donna approached me with the realization that even after we announced our wedding, we would have to postpone it. I had not looked at the calendar carefully enough. All of the production had to be scheduled in a very short time during the spring. We would be gone almost the entire time filming and producing. In addition whatever little money that was starting to come in would not be here in time for a wedding in early May. Business had to come first, so we postponed the wedding, regretfully.

Then I immediately realized something else. We had promised to have a small ceremony that only our kids would attend; this was a small family affair that our children were looking forward to. Here is the fly in the ointment. Our kids had scheduling conflicts for quite some time including leaving to go out of the country for at least two months. It was not until late July that all our kids would be able to attend our wedding.

Ok, I can do the math. That means that if we wait until early August to get married and continue this celibacy path, it will be around a year and a half since we would have had ANY intimacy! OUCH! This is really stinging

401

and I am NOT a happy camper! Here I go with my mouth again,

"Donna! There is no way! This is nuts and I can't do it. Something has to give, this is just not fair and we have to figure out something. I will NOT wait until August and continue this zero intimacy path, enough is enough!"

I then went to bed in the guest room by myself, pissed off not knowing what to do next.

The next morning I was calm, and I apologized. I figured my concentration would be best spent on work and I would continue to take a lot of cold showers, pray a lot, and fortunately the amount of work I had to do would not allow me to focus on much else.

So Donna and I hit the road producing our 25th anniversary specials traveling to the New River Valley, the Outer Banks, Tighlman Island and St Michaels. These are all beautiful places and very romantic... More cold showers would be required by me.

On the road filming Donna and I made a great team. We worked nonstop on the road and had some 15 hour work days. One night I came back to our accommodations around 11pm after a LONG day of filming and hardly had enough energy to open the door...but I still was thinking about how great it would be to make a little *Amore*! As I found out again, that was not going to happen; I was a bit angered. She knew I was not happy about waiting until August to get married. I could not hide my disappointment and frustration.

We were filming at Smith Mountain Lake when Donna said she wanted to talk with me. So here it goes, whenever a woman says she wants to talk with me I always get a little chill going down my spine. She says, "Jim, no intimacy for over a year has been tough on us and I am aware you have found it difficult at times, we both have. You have honored my request and I think we need to wed before this celibacy path becomes more destructive than positive. If it is ok with you I have decided our happiness is most important, if you would like we can get married as soon as we arrive in Florida in June in only a few weeks. We will be there all summer while our beach house is rented in Virginia. Our kids won't be there because as you know some are out of the country. But I think this is for the best, it is time."

"THANK YOU! YES, I AGREE!"

I was very happy and now saw the light at the end of the tunnel. However thanks to my conscience, that light began to dim.

After about a week of thinking about this I did what I did not think I would ever do. Postponed our wedding again. I said, "Donna, you aren't going to believe I am going to say this, but here it goes. I feel bad that we are cutting the kids out of our wedding. I don't feel right about it. I will agree to wait and postpone our small wedding until August 2nd, my 53rd birthday. The kids will be back and have plenty of time to get down to Florida. My only stipulation is this, no more postponements and no more celibacy after August 2nd under any circumstances. If I am dead, I am still showing up for that wedding!"

I know as I am writing this there will be people that will not believe that Donna and I went for one and a half years most of the time living under the same roof with total celibacy before marriage. It was one heck of a journey that taught me a lot of life lessons. I even wrote an essay about it and it was published in Church For Men Magazine.

So here in a nutshell is what I learned from my experience. If you are out there, single and you were like me and would never consider a celibate relationship before marriage, ask yourself these questions.

- By taking sex out of the equation is it possible to find out quicker if someone is more compatible with your mind, heart and soul?

- Are respect, honor, trust and dignity important to your relationship?
- Was God joking when he penned the 10 commandments?
- How willing am I to contract S.T.D.'s that will stick with me a lifetime and that I may pass on to my future partner?

It is really pretty simple. If you are on a first date and you tell your suitor you are taking sex out of the equation until marriage, do you think your date is going to stick around? If they don't, then you know you made the right decision in telling them.

Sometimes I wish I knew back in my early days of being single what I know now. The fact is during my ten years of dating during my forties, had I taken intimacy out of certain relationships I would of figured out real quick than not only should I **NOT** be sleeping with such a person, I should not even be in the same room with them…Or the same planet for that matter! This would have saved me tons of time, stress, money, and heartache.

Anytime you are dating and you ignore red flags because you are physically attracted to the person, that is the time to exit the relationship. Don't wait either, run like a Tarpon on a Florida flat and don't stop.

Lastly, I am not a Bible thumper by any stretch of the means. People love to throw the Good Book up in the air and use various verses and their own interpretations to support their opinions about whatever their issue or agenda is. This is easy to do, ministers do it sometimes Sunday mornings, politicians do it when the opportunity makes them look good, and we the common people at times will do it as well. This is the atheist biggest target against Christianity is that Christians can never agree on the various interpretations of the Bible. This is the reason we have so many denominations, people can't agree so they go off and have their own version of what the Bible teaches.

All of this I can generally understand. But let's cut straight to the chase.

Talk about a blue print for a wonderful life and a peaceful society. If the entire world took heed abiding by the ten commandments we would have no wars, nor murder or crime, probably no hunger, children born into loving whole families, and it also means that my bicycle would not have been stolen twice in Phoebus Virginia.

"Thou shalt not steal."

It had been a long year and a half. The three years since early August 2011 when *HOOKED* was released has been full of blessings of which I am eternally grateful. The good Lord answers prayers, and sometimes in ways that are far greater than we can imagine at the time.

One would have thought that putting your dog down, closing a business, losing my home, the death of my father were all tragic things. In actuality these were blessings.

Thank you Lord!

I was successfully removed from the worst most horrendous real estate investment one could ever make!

Thank you Lord!

I prayed my entire life for the Judge to live past forty, he made it to 80!

Thank you Lord!

That beautiful woman that I had prayed about and had not yet met in my life, the one that would show her love in every way possible... Donna.

Thank you Lord!

In addition by late spring Donna and I had produced our 25th anniversary specials for Jim Baugh Outdoors TV, secured our marine sponsorship and by June 1st and were heading to Cedar Key for the summer. All of our kids were doing fantastic with good jobs, doing well in school, and leading great lives. There was a lot to be thankful for as we headed to the sunshine state.

*Donna and Jim, Cedar Key Florida on Jim's 53d Birthday,
August 2, 2014.*

Cedar Key

Everyone wants to live on top of the mountain, but all the happiness and growth occurs while you're climbing it.

~ Andy Rooney

With Donna successfully renting out her beach house to summer vacationers and the completion of our field production work filmed for the TV show, we headed down to Cedar Key Florida for the summer. Donna had been researching this quaint historic little Island for a couple of years and she really wanted to spend some time there. So she found a small house for us to rent and auspiciously off we went.

We both fell in love with Cedar Key right off the bat. No doubt, we had an immediate connection to the place. Very remote, quiet, no traffic, endless Sago Palm trees, a place that probably was like Key West in the late 1890's way before it was commercialized. Donna and I felt at home the second we arrived.

We brought our work with us, both of us had a lot of writing to do and I immediately started editing our 25th anniversary programs that would air during the fall. I could not think of a prettier place to work. Each day for exercise I would ride my bike all over the island enjoying every single palm tree that I passed.

Donna and I went to several different local churches to meet some folks. All the services were wonderful and this place is for sure true old-fashioned Americana. I called Doris the music director at the Methodist Church and asked if I could practice on their piano while I was staying here for the summer. She agreed to meet and ask me to play for her and the church pianist. So I did, they were the sweetest ladies. When I finished she said she was happily getting a key made for me so I could come in and play anytime I wanted. Sure enough the next Sunday she presented me with a new key to the Cedar Key United Methodist Church. Over the summer they asked if I would play some selections during Sunday service and I was more than happy to! The congregation was very appreciative and seemed to like a little Jazz thrown into the service. They all made Donna and I feel very welcome.

A lot has happened over the last three years with the tide bringing in change with almost every cresting wave. I certainly have learned a lot during this time. I can never thank enough my kids Ben and Casey, my friends and extended family for their support during the past years. It has been quite a journey. Throughout it all I am blessed to have a partner in Donna who stood by me during the worst of times with grace, beauty, understanding, love, and faith.

August 2014, a remarkable time!

This is a special month. I had proposed to Donna earlier under an Eastern Shore Magnolia Tree and now our wedding day soon approaches with endless palm trees on the horizon. This Leo began the approaching sturgeon moon with a fun and joyous commemoration on August 2nd my 53rd birthday. It was a beautiful palm shade day enjoying Cedar Key and Donna treated us to a wonderful dinner at Florida's historic Island Hotel. It was one of those birthdays you always remember and cherish for a lifetime. Dessert... Key lime pie with an illuminated candle and a big kiss!

Donna and Jim birthday dinner August 2, 2014

This week in August is also the three year anniversary of the release of *HOOKED*. Had that not occurred, I would not be in Cedar Key with Donna getting married. August is also the official anniversary month celebrating Jim Baugh Outdoors 25th year in production. Also this August is the one year anniversary of closing Jim's BBQ and during this time, I had lost my home. Certainly this is clear evidence that a lot can happen in a span of only one year, however the best is yet to come…

Jim & Donna, August 22, 2014 married on Cedar Key Island

On August 22nd as the westward twilight vanished below the violet blue aqua horizon, Donna and I exchanged vows by the warm Gulf Coast waters on Cedar Key Island. We toasted our marriage dockside at the Low-Key Hideaway under the most beautiful transcending sky that only God could have created. We had a Christian ceremony, both of us read to each other words that we had written about our love, and read aloud together for the first time. It was truly a beautiful and heartfelt ceremony. We honeymooned in Florida for the remainder of the summer and early autumn. I could not be more blessed.

If anyone ever needed any more proof, including me that the good Lord does answer prayers, and usually in a much bigger way than we ever can imagine, than this triennial memoir is it.

...and I am so grateful, I lived to tell about it.

"I sacrificed a palm tree, and then was blessed with a rainforest."

~Jim Baugh

Message from Earl

I was planning on my future as a homeless person. I had a really good spot picked out.

~Larry David

It is true that one of my favorite writers comedian Larry David was financially broke doing stand-up comedy with no home spotting out places he could sleep on the streets of New York City. Being homeless and sleeping on the sidewalks was the future he was facing. I to could have been in the same situation, homeless,

Today, Larry David is one of the wealthiest and most successful people in the entertainment business. This kind of turnaround does happen to people, but does not happen to everybody.

While on the Eastern Shore Donna and I fairly regularly attended the local Baptist church and certainly found it a welcoming place. Reverend Russell would end up being our minister for our second wedding ceremony for our family who could not attend in Cedar Key.

Several times while sitting in the church pew during service this little short older fellow would holler out, "Amen! Amen!" He was an enthusiastic man that enjoyed Reverend Russell's services a lot. I never officially met this man but I knew his name was Earl. I had also seen him hanging out at the local liquor store just standing by the door. It was just a guess but I thought like he looked like a homeless alcoholic who was probably the town drunk. I also heard someone once mention that the church helped to look after Earl and helped him with many things including food and housing.

There were times I thought Earl was inebriated while sitting in church. This was not my business and I did not know the man at all. On occasion during the greeting I would shake his hand, say hi, and that was about it. I did think it was cool that this man was very excited about his faith. He wore a big cross around his neck and obviously was very appreciative of the help the church was giving him. Earl was very proud of his Christian faith and had no problem letting folks know it.

One thing is for sure, everyone in town seemed to know Earl. Evidently he was born and raised right there on the Shore but unfortunately had led a pretty hard life. I did not know the details and only was around him during church service a few times. I knew him by name and sight. That was it.

One day I was thinking about Earl and how he reminded me of Charlie Tuna who I had met in Phoebus back in the days of Jim's BBQ. My friend Jake always tried to help Charlie by giving him food and even shelter in the old Pit Shack. I had witnessed both a friend of mine Jake, and now a church show their grace and humanity towards people who were homeless drunkards. However they helped these poor people without any judgment what so ever. All they did was show grace and compassion.

It was around 11pm on a Friday night when Earl was pronounced dead on the side of the highway after being struck by a tractor trailer. He died instantly. The hard life that he had lived was behind him now and he had gone to meet his maker. He was wearing that big cross around his neck even at the time of the accident.

The next few days the town sort of went silent. There was a lot of sadness in the air. I walked into the local hardware store and the clerk was talking on the phone about the passing of Earl. Customers were

413

walking in the store with sadness in there face and discussing with the owner about the tragic accident that took Earl's life.

Before I left I ask the clerk about Earl and that I only knew him as someone I would see once in a while in the church pew on Sunday Mornings. The clerk said,

"I knew Earl all my life. He had a hard row to hoe and could never really catch a break but we all liked him."

That day I continued to realize how important grace is, it's amazing. And amazing grace is something we all need so much more of.

I don't think when Earl left this earth he realized how many lives he touched. To an outsider a quick glace one would say, Earl was just a homeless drunk. Or, Charlie Tuna was just a homeless panhandler always looking for a hand out and a bottle of anything.

...But not so.

These are people whose paths are not for us to judge. And that is one of the biggest areas of my life that I am continuing to work on. Not being judgmental.

I think Earl's life and the compassionate community that helped him left us a good message and that is this,

Simply by showing grace to people, you in turn are blessed by it.
RIP Earl Wade.

INTERVIEW WITH THE AUTHOR
(First published July 2011)

Jim Baugh Host of Jim Baugh Outdoors TV and Author of HOOKED
By Lizzy Stevens
*International Best Selling Author &
Solstcie Publishing founder, CEO*

LS: Tell me a little about why you wrote *"Hooked"* and what initially was the inspiration for such a funny book.

JB: It probably initially started when I was around five or six years old. I grew up on the docks of Gloucester Virginia and the characters on the boats and docks were just larger than life, always doing practical jokes, fishing, just having a ball. Growing up I always thought those times were very special and wanted the memory to live forever.

Then, during my forties I was single again after a great marriage of 25 years. When I was thrust upon the online computer dating world, things changed real fast. The people I would meet and the stories were just WAY to funny.

I was dating the woman in *HOOKED*, the DC Nympho, and we were in the swimming pool laughing how funny online dating was. We swapped war stories, then I began to get an idea. Produce a game show called, *"Meet My Match Game"*. Well, the idea turned into a screenplay, then finally a book. However it took me a few years to figure out how to combine the story. I wanted to also include in the story line my memories of growing up on the docks in Gloucester, and also the hilarious behind the scenes antics of producing a southern outdoor show.

LS: Sounds like a great idea! Then you started to write?

JB: I tried, but could not. I started with a screenplay and kept wanting to direct and block shots as opposed to just writing. That slowed me to a halt.

LS: What did you do??

JB: I called a high school friend of mine who had been a successful playwright in New York City and ask for advice. He simply said it did not matter if it was a book or screenplay; just get it down on paper. So, since I had been a columnist for 20 years, I figured I would try the manuscript approach.

LS: Did that work?

JB: Yes, I wrote the book in 12 days.

LS: That is pretty much impossible, no one writes close to 400 pages in 12 days.

JB: Well, I was actually also editing *Jim Baugh Outdoors TV* as well at the time. This is hard to explain, but once I figured out how to write the book, it was like turning on a garden hose at full power. I usually write in my head anyway beforehand. When I sit to physically write it is more like just a constant stream of dictation coming from my mind. I write music much the same way.

The manuscript just flowed at full speed. Afterwards it did take over four months to edit and polish, that was where the real work was, because for sure I had to do a lot of fictionalizing and compositing of some characters.

I was so truthful in my writing, I would have gotten in BIG trouble with certain people had I not fictionalized the book. That took some careful writing because although

416

fictionalized, I did not want the essence and truth of the story to be changed, and it was not.

LS: What were the hardest and the most enjoyable part of the editing process for you?

JB: The hardest would be continuity- that can be a real bear. Especially when you're fictionalizing, changing names and places, etc.

The most fun was the humor. Once mostly edited I would read through the manuscript and look for ANY place that I could expand on to bring out the true humor of the actual true life situation.

The characters in *HOOKED* are so larger than life, simply by writing true to their character was funny enough. That was key, getting the character down so that the reader could feel like the person was sitting right in their living room. This, I believe worked very well in the book. You don't feel removed from the characters at all, you feel like they are sitting next to you. That, is one of the things that makes *HOOKED* so special.

LS: Was there any stumbling block in the story? No mental block at all?

JB: Yes, the ending. In the screenplay outline I had the ending down, however for the book, different story. I was stuck. So, I left it as is, Rose and I would come back from the Keys, and then simply go into the final Chapter that was a very short chapter. Sort of my wrap up about faith and how it pulled me out of many difficult times throughout my lifetime.

To be honest, the last chapter, chapter 28, I did not write. The man upstairs wrote it, I just took dictation.

Very true, this happened one night at around 3 am, I woke up from a perfect sleep. Wide awake and it just came to me, this vision of how to perfectly end the book, and I was only a third of the way through writing it at that time.

The vision was of this football game when I was in high school, and we had won a game by only inches. I sat down and starting writing this final chapter, not making any sense at all to me, again, I felt like I was taking dictation, not writing. Once done, I read it and thought, gee, I don't know how this is going to work at all, but will leave as is. Then I wrote the rest of the book.

Sure enough, chapter 27 flowed into chapter 28 like it was destined to be. Like I said, I owe the credit to someone else, not me. It is a very inspiration ending and has effected just about everyone that has read it. Wish I could take credit.

LS: That is quite an incredible story, sound like you have a very important co-writer?

JB: Yes, you could say that. I only wrote that Rose and I got married during the last week of editing. That was not in the first draft of the manuscript. I did get stuck on that one as well. But with some guidance from you know who, the "Big Guy", I was clearly directed to end it getting re married on the beach in Key Largo. This is the only thing in *HOOKED* that actually had not happened, but hope to one day.

Getting remarried in the book was a big deal, here is why. It enabled me to wrap up all the messages in the book, all the themes came together, and it was about the most positive reflection on a relationship one could have.

In *HOOKED*, there was quite a bit of trouble with woman. Two or three mental cases, bizarre dating stories, etc, etc, so ending *HOOKED* on such a positive note helped smooth out the message. I could not have figured a better way to wrap things up.

LS: What are some other books that you have been reading lately?

JB: I just finished Bill Bruford's autobiography and loved it. Also recently read Kitchen Confidential and Jaco. Next I am reading Joe Jacksons How I left the state of TN and am a better man for it.

LS: Sounds good Jim! Thank you so much for being our guest today and look forward to your next novel.

JB: Thank you and appreciate the time. This has been a lot of fun, thank you, Godspeed!

About The Author:

Jim Baugh has been producing television shows since 1987. Programs include: Award winning Jim Baugh Outdoors TV (220+ episodes), Ski East, Classic Fishing with the Bassmasters, Fishing Virginia and RV Times. Broadcast include: The Family Channel, The Outdoor Channel, The Sportsman Channel, Fox Sports, America One and NBC Universal The Comcast Network. Jim also holds a Bachelor's Degree in Electronic Music and a minor in Piano from Virginia Commonwealth University. He writes, performs, and engineers all the soundtracks for his television productions and regularly performs solo live Jazz piano concerts.

Jim Baugh has written over 300 columns for numerous magazines since 1989 including: Motor boating Magazine, Fishing Smart, The Chesapeake Angler, The Sportsman Magazine, Woods and Waters, Colonial Outdoors, The Nor' Easter, Virginia Beach Sports Fishing, Church for Men, and Travel Virginia Magazine.

His first published book, "HOOKED" was released by Solstice Publishing early August of 2011. The book instantly won critical acclaim earning all five star ratings and was featured book of the month by the publisher during the first month's release. Jim's first short story ROXSWELL was published in February 2014 and "A F T E R M A T H" Triennial Memoir in September 2014, also by Solstice Publishing.

Jim's fourth book, "COOKED" stories behind the recipes will be released after the HOOKED screenplay has been completed in late 2016.

In Memory
"CC Emerson" Cedar Key Florida
August 31st, 2014

This was one cool Cat. RIP

Other Solstice Titles
By
Jim Baugh

Roxswell

This short story is an almost exact account of a dream I had one early Sunday morning in January 2014. This dream was a subconscious representation of the desire in my real life of wanting something very badly, but not able to have without a lot of patience and sacrifice.

This period in my life, around two years saw many life changes. Homes lost and found, financial ruin and gain, loss of dear friends, and gaining new ones. Very hard sacrifices only to be rewarded by gain of biblical proportions, at least to me. So, in our sleep sometimes our mind can create an adjacent world that is only a fragmented reflection of our real one. What this rather bizarre dreamscape really represents to me is to walk by faith and not by sight.